UNWELCOME TO BLiMPO. ZiLLiONS AND ZiLLiONS SERVED.

BLIMPO

THE THIRD CIRCLE OF
~ HECK ~

DALE E. BASYE

ILLUSTRATIONS BY BOB DOB

A YEARLING BOOK

THIS BOOK IS DEDICATED TO MY DAD, DALE, WHO—DESPITE HIS COMPLETE
LACK OF ORIGINALITY IN NAMING CHILDREN—TAUGHT ME THAT
A WRITER'S GREATEST TOOL IS STICK-TO-IT-IVENESS, UNLESS, OF COURSE, YOU
HAPPEN TO BE A FLY WRITING YOUR MEMOIRS ON FLYPAPER.

Text copyright © 2010 by Dale E. Basye
Cover art and interior illustrations copyright © 2010 by Bob Dob

All rights reserved. Published in the United States by Yearling, an imprint of Random House Children's
Books, a division of Random House, Inc., New York. Originally published in hardcover in the United
States by Random House Children's Books, a division of Random House, Inc., New York, in 2010.

Yearling and the jumping horse design are registered trademarks of Random House, Inc.

Visit us on the Web! www.randomhouse.com/kids

Educators and librarians, for a variety of teaching tools, visit us at www.randomhouse.com/teachers

The Library of Congress has cataloged the hardcover edition of this work as follows:
Basye, Dale E.
Blimpo : the third circle of Heck / by Dale E. Basye ; illustrations by Bob Dob. — 1st ed.
p.   cm.
Summary: Eleven-year-old Milton Fauster puts aside his own escape plans to help his sister,
Marlo, who is in training to be an underworld secretary, and best friend, Virgil,
who is stuck in the circle of Heck reserved for overweight children.
ISBN 978-0-375-85676-1 (trade) — ISBN 978-0-375-95676-8 (lib. bdg.) — ISBN 978-0-375-89304-9 (ebook)
[1. Future life—Fiction. 2. Overweight persons—Fiction. 3. Brothers and sisters—Fiction.
4. Reformatories—Fiction. 5. Schools—Fiction. 6. Humorous stories.] I. Dob, Bob, ill. II. Title.
PZ7.B2938Bli 2010   [Fic]—dc22   2009015801

ISBN 978-0-375-85677-8 (pbk.)

Printed in the United States of America

10 9 8 7 6 5

First Yearling Edition 2011

Random House Children's Books supports the First Amendment and celebrates the right to read.

 CONTENTS

FOREWORD

As many believe, there is a place above and a place below. But there are also places in between. Some not quite awfully perfect and others not quite perfectly awful.

One of these places may seem to some, from the outside, like a big fat joke. But, I assure you, none of the unfortunates trapped within are laughing (unless one of their generous thighs happens to shift in an unfortunately farty way in their chairs).

This place—located at the bulging midsection of Heck—is, like so many realms in the underworld (and many above), completely full of it. Yet, almost immediately upon arriving, you feel as if you've stuffed yourself full of dozens and dozens of empty doughnut holes. That is to say, you're left with only a sugar-scented vacuum, leaving you hungry for more.

And, down in this place of ample curves that—ironically—doesn't grade on a curve, more is in short supply (unless you mean more humiliation, more insecurity, and more exploitation—they've got loads of that!). Even more of a good thing, you'll find—on the off chance that you actually stumble upon one down here—isn't necessarily a good thing. Take dimples, for instance. A couple are cute on the cheek, but when they start appearing all over your body, suddenly no one is lining up to pinch you.

With that in mind, this place called Blimpo is, in and of itself, a recipe for disaster. An insufferable, unstuffable soufflé so full of itself that it's only a matter of time before the whole thing collapses.

The mysterious Powers That Be have stitched this and countless other subjective realities together into a sprawling quilt of space and time.

Some of these quantum patches may not even seem like places. But they are all around you and go by many names. Some feel like eternity. And some of them actually are eternity, at least for a little while.

1 · SCAMMING THE FAT

VIRGIL'S STOMACH RUMBLED like a gastric earthquake, registering somewhere between a 6.7 and 9.4 on the digestive Richter scale. He was starving, but that was only half of it. His belly was also waging a protest against Blimpo's aptly named Gymnauseum.

No matter where Virgil looked across the strobe-lit gym, the checkered pattern of the walls—painted in Pepto-Bismol pink and vomit-green hues—wobbled in sickening throbs. Between the hunger and the nausea, Virgil's stomach was currently more active than the rest of his body had ever been.

Like Virgil, the other boys in the bleachers were hunched over with hunger at the sight of their seldom-seen-yet-surprisingly-*appetizing* vice principals on the raised platform below. It was, apparently, the first time in years that the vice principals had descended from the floating castle that bobbed above Blimpo, tethered to the Circle's inner courtyard. Virgil could instantly see why. Even the girthy girls perched across the auditorium—normally separated from the boys in Girls' Blimpo but brought together for this special assembly—were rubbing their distended bellies with want.

The Burgermeister sat imperiously on an over-stuffed, wheat-colored throne. His face was a pinkish-brown gray, as plump and shiny as a roasted frankfurter, with a lattice of crisscrossed marks that made him seem flame broiled. Grease stains darkened his plush, ketchup-colored armrests; his round, pickle-colored head cushion; and the lettuce-green blanket he kept on his lap.

Next to him, melted in a conical chair, was Lady Lactose, a vision of creamy arrogance, patting the vanilla hair scooped high atop her head in soft spirals.

Virgil wiped his drool-slick lips. Teachers, principals, and most every flavor of authority figure usually filled him with dread. But now, as he stared down at the Burgermeister and Lady Lactose, he was filled with the barely controlled urge to tie a bib around his neck and tuck into his vice principals with a fork and a spoon. It was as if he were at the Gobble 'n' Hobble back home in Dallas, that all-you-can-eat (and more) place that made you sign a waiver before it granted access to its legendary Bonanza Buffet.

The potent aroma of just-grilled hamburger and just-churned ice cream wafted from the stage. Considering the inedible slop the kids were served in the Cafeterium—or, as the boys had dubbed it, the Lose-Your-Lunchroom—the smell made Virgil ravenous. And, judging from the bellyaching he heard gurgling from his fellow students, he was not alone.

The Burgermeister slicked back his greasy, poppy-seed-flecked hair until it looked like a rearing tidal wave. He leaned into the microphone set before him.

"*Guten morgen,* students of Blimpo," the Burgermeister said as he wiped his oily meat hooks on his checkered lederhosen. "How *geht es* you all? You *wundern vermutlich* why you're here?"

"More like wondering what you just said," muttered Hugo DeWitt, a boy with a dark crew cut and massive cheeks that nearly swallowed his nose and mouth, seated next to Virgil.

Lady Lactose scowled at the wave of confusion that spread slowly throughout the crowd like a spill soaked up by a paper towel. She tilted the microphone toward her. The pained squeak of the metal reverberated throughout the Gymnauseum.

"May I?" Lady Lactose asked the meaty monarch.

The Burgermeister nodded.

"Of course, my sweet."

Lady Lactose glared at the baffled boys and girls.

"The Burgermeister and I are very busy pseudo-people, and we didn't call this assembly to simply chew the fat. If we had, we'd be here all day, by the looks of it."

A small drip of milk leaked down Lady Lactose's forehead. The Burgermeister took her hand.

"Try not to lose your cool," he cautioned.

Lady Lactose sighed and blotted her forehead with a lace napkin.

"What I meant to say . . . *children* . . . is that the Burgermeister and I have a very special announcement that involves all of you . . . every bit of you, actually."

She motioned for Dr. Kellogg, a short man just over five feet tall seated nearby, to approach the stage.

Clad completely in white, from his galoshes to his tie, Dr. Kellogg took each step in spry little jumps. Even his hair and goatee gleamed as white and shiny as vanilla Frostee-Freeze. He hopped up onto the stage.

"Children, your beloved health education teacher," Lady Lactose announced.

Dr. Kellogg raised a megaphone to his whiskery chin. "Good day, students," he said with elfish vigor. "You are about to become part of a great experiment, a new chapter not only for Blimpo, but also for Heck—perhaps, even, for all of the underworld!"

He clapped his white-gloved hands. The double doors on either side of the Gymnauseum burst open. A team of demons in white laboratory smocks heaved nine massive objects covered in gray tarps toward the stage.

"Thank you, diligent yet forsaken creatures!" the doctor declared as the demons grumbled and skulked away.

Dr. Kellogg beamed.

"In an attempt to liberate ourselves from the Transdimensional Power Grid and from our dependence on fickle paranormal energy sources, we—the vice principals and I—have uncovered a *new* source of power."

A skinny man in white greasepaint and a black-and-white striped shirt crept from behind the thrones of the Burgermeister and Lady Lactose.

"That must be the vice principals' flunky, the French Fried Fool," Hugo muttered to Virgil, licking his lips.

The French Fried Fool smiled, accentuating his expression by framing his face with open, wriggling hands. Golden, deep-fried dreadlocks peeked out from beneath his harlequin cap.

"Yes, Fool," Lady Lactose said loudly and slowly, as if the man's silence was a medical condition that affected his ability to hear and discern. "You may have the honor—"

The French Fried Fool hopped into the air like a flea on a hot plate. Lady Lactose raised her fudge-tinted eyebrows as he put his gloved fingers in his mouth, drew in a deep exaggerated breath, and then pretended to whistle.

Eight men dressed just like the French Fried Fool flounced into the Gymnauseum. Each stopped in front of one of the mysterious concealed objects and walked in place. The French Fried Fool dove off the stage and took his place beside the ninth tarp-covered thingamajig. Dr. Kellogg raised the megaphone to his mouth.

"And this new energy source is . . . ," he declared with a grand, sweeping gesture as the group of fools yanked off the tarps.

"*. . . you.*"

Virgil leaned closer, hoping that a few inches might help him make out what the odd contraptions were. They didn't.

The gray metal machines resembled human-sized hamster wheels set within huge circular cast-iron enclosures. They opened slowly on either side, their walls like big pie tins, until the sides rested on the Gymnauseum floor. The machines reminded Virgil of the tire-shaped carrying case he used to tote his Hot Wheels around in when he was a little kid, back when he was alive.

"Behold, the DREADmills," Dr. Kellogg said as one end of his thin mouth curled up with secret amusement. "Dynamic Regenerative Energy Accumulation Devices. The focus of Blimpo's new *Fatness to Fitness Center!*"

A large dark girl with a kinky orange-brown halo of hair shot her hand up.

"You said that the energy was *you*."

"*You*, actually, not me," Dr. Kellogg clarified. "And, yes, you may ask a question."

"Whatever." The girl shrugged. "But what do you mean by you . . . or *us*?"

Dr. Kellogg smiled and raised himself up on the balls of his feet, growing from short to merely submoderate in height.

"An excellent, if disrespectfully posed, question. You, the student body of Blimpo, will supply our circle with its own energy source."

A demon with a hammerlike head stood up awkwardly from its seat in the bleachers, reading a question from a note card.

"What a brilliant idea," the demon said stiffly. "Can you tell us about all the fun we'll have as . . . um, *students* . . . in the DREADmills, doing our part to make Heck a better place?"

On the bleacher below Virgil, Thaddeus Papadopoulos, a Greek boy who looked like an overinflated parade float, shook his head.

"That is *so* not a student," he said. "How lame."

The demon sat down quickly while Dr. Kellogg pulled out a note card from his vest pocket.

"Wow, I wasn't prepared for so many great questions!" he replied, looking down his sharp, beaklike nose at the card. "Well, off the top of my head, each DREADmill is like a self-contained mini movie theater, where you simply take a leisurely stroll on the conveyer belt while delighting in, um, shall we say *customized* entertainment. And, as an advantageous outcome, you're generating precious electricity in the process. It's a win-win!"

The girl with the frizzy sunrise for hair raised her hand again. Dr. Kellogg swallowed nervously as he looked out at the boys and girls. He prodded the hammerhead demon with his eyes.

"Are there any more questions?"

The demon stood up suddenly, fumbling for its note card.

"Yes, *you*," the doctor said.

"Finally, we students can actually *contribute* to the afterlife, instead of just whining and sucking it dry," the demon said. "So, not that there needs to be any more benefits to the DREADmill program, but if there were, what would they be?"

Dr. Kellogg laughed, which made his bright white whiskers dance the hula.

"Another unexpectedly thoughtful question!" he shouted through his megaphone. "Since the answer is of an administrational nature, I relinquish the floor to our vice principals."

The doctor bounced off the stage as Lady Lactose nodded demurely. She tapped her dainty ladyfinger on the microphone, not so much to test the microphone's functionality, but rather to create a thunderous boom that exploded inside each student's skull.

"Thank you, Dr. Kellogg, and thank *you*, courteous, engaged-but-not-overly-so student."

The hammerhead demon bowed stiffly, as if pounding an imaginary nail, and took its seat.

"In addition to the joy of participating in this great experiment," Lady Lactose continued, "you will also be developing a healthier, less repellent spiritual body. As further incentive, each session spent inside the DREADmills will act as a Metaphysical Fitness credit applied directly toward your Soul Aptitude Tests. Meaning, the more weight you lose watching movies and making energy, the higher your grade and the greater the likelihood of you spending your adult afterlives lazing on clouds and plucking harps, rather than suffering the unspeakable atrocities . . . *down there.*"

A wave of "oohs" spilled out across the auditorium. Virgil frowned as he studied the dozens of children sitting hopefully on the bleachers. The wooden seats sagged beneath them, as if the students were fat birds perched atop power lines.

Fat chance of us kids ever ascending anywhere, he thought sadly to himself.

The Burgermeister smiled slyly at the children's subtle shift in attitude. It was time to seal the deal. He grabbed the microphone with his greasy hands.

"Before we say *auf wiedersehen*," he declared in an oily gush, "zere iz just *eine more thing!*"

The double doors swung open, accompanied by a puff of fragrant smoke. The children gasped.

It was the most succulent smell that had ever passed through Virgil's nostrils. A bright red shack on wheels parted the gate of rich smoke, bringing with it the folksy, tinny strains of "Turkey in the Straw." It weaved slowly through the maze of DREADmills, then pulled up to the front of the stage. Welded above the mobile cart's windshield was a barbecue-sauce-colored sign with HAMBONE HANK'S HEART ATTACK SHACK spelled out in ribs.

An enormous red-faced man wearing a white, sagging chef's hat emerged from the cart.

"Chef Boyareyookrazee," Virgil muttered with contempt. The chef lorded over the Cafeterium with wicked glee. He treated it like his own personal chamber of culinary horrors. He knew that his captive diners would grudgingly consume whatever he made—no matter how disgusting. That morning's meal of booger-frosted scornflakes, eggs Benedict Arnold, and guinea pork sausage, for example, was still debating how to best escape Virgil's belly.

Chef Boyareyookrazee can't possibly have anything to do with that delicious smell, Virgil reflected, just as another figure stepped out of the cart.

Behind the chef emerged his exact opposite: while

Chef Boyareyookrazee was stubby, round, and dressed completely in white, this figure was tall and lean and wore a black hooded cloak that completely obscured its face. The sleek, imposing creature regarded the crowd with eyes submerged in shadow. It had a collar around its neck that it rubbed with irritation. The only features that Virgil could discern were an occasional flash of moist, black snout and the glint of fangs.

The French Fried Fool hopped up and down, rubbing his belly with his hand. His posse of mute performance artists did likewise.

The Gymnauseum was suffused with sweet, tantalizing smoke. The intoxicating fog was so strong that Virgil wasn't sure if he was smelling it, tasting it, or dreaming it.

"*Danke*, Chef Boyareyookrazee and Hambone Hank," the Burgermeister said with a nod.

"Hambone Hank?" muttered Thaddeus. "That creepy guy in the robe must be some sort of gourmet ghoul."

The Burgermeister held out his beefy arms majestically.

"To zelebrate diz great day," he announced, "*wir haben eine* delicious *mahlzeit* for you all!"

The children, who could barely grasp the fact that they were in a gymnasium in the afterlife lorded over by a talking burger and milk shake, much less understand *German,* whispered to one another in puzzlement.

Lady Lactose sighed and tilted the microphone toward her pursed, cherry-red lips.

"What the Burgermeister means to say is . . . *come and get it.*"

The sound of a dinner bell rang through the speakers in the corners of the Gymnauseum. Although Virgil had been raised in Texas, it was only in this moment that he fully understood the meaning of the word "stampede." The boys and girls rushed down the bleachers like a cascading waterfall of ravenous want. The scrape of tight corduroy Capri pants and miniskirts (part of the mandatory and fiercely unflattering Blimpo school uniform) was deafening.

Virgil was momentarily stunned by the sudden pandemonium around him before his stomach complained, in its unique language of spasms and slurps, "Giddyup if you want some grub!"

So Virgil listened to his gut, pulled up his neon-green suspenders, and tromped down the bleachers. Pitchspork-wielding demons attempted vainly to shape the chaos into something resembling an orderly line. Chef Boyareyookrazee doled out baskets overflowing with meat slathered with rich, red-brown sauce.

A pale, dark-haired girl with stringy pigtails gasped rapturously as she, the first in line, sampled Hambone Hank's barbecue.

"*Oh my gawd!!*" she exclaimed between her first and

second bites. "Even though I'm in Heck, my mouth just went straight to Heaven!"

The Burgermeister, Lady Lactose, and Chef Boy-areyookrazee shared sly, conspiratorial smirks. The cream of the realm leaned into her charbroiled king.

"See them line up like pigs at a trough, chowing down on every lie we've fed them."

Virgil, on the outside of the meat-fueled melee, could *just* hear the vice principals' voices over the speakers.

The Burgermeister chortled.

"Our plan eez, much like our vaistlines, expanding immensely!"

Virgil caught Lady Lactose's icy gaze. She rose and smoothed her silky, buttercream gown, scowling.

"Let's blow this Popsicle stand," she muttered, glaring at the mob of barbecue-sauce-smeared children with disgust.

The French Fried Fool pretended to whistle. The other mimes clapped their hands over their ears, as if *this* pretend whistle was much louder than the *previous* pretend whistle. After shaking their chalk-white heads and straightening their berets, the mimes formed two lines in front of the wide folding metal door behind the stage. They crouched down low and made as if they were tugging at two great ropes in order to raise the door. Surprisingly, the door clattered open, the mimes heaving as the slatted metal door rolled up into the ceiling on twin rails.

"Goodbye, children," Lady Lactose declared into the microphone without a trace of fondness or regret. "Congratulations on your good fortune. We look forward to exploiting . . . *to working with you* . . . on this momentous project that will serve as a model of innovation for the entire underworld. Now we must return to our rightful thrones above to work out the details. But don't think that we are looking down on you from our floating castle. Instead, we hope it is an opportunity for all of you to look *up* to us."

Virgil, his empty stomach jumping up and down with excitement as he neared the front of the line, watched as the Burgermeister, Lady Lactose, and the French Fried Fool strutted through the doors and out to the open commons beyond. In the roofless inner courtyard at the center of Blimpo rested an inflatable, forty-foot-tall, canvas-skinned castle. Fastened to the roofs of the castle's three cylindrical towers were three hot-air balloons, girdled with brass lattice and cables.

"Here you go, kid," Chef Boyareyookrazee said as he thrust a basket brimming with delectable meat and sauce into Virgil's hands. "Now eat and run." The red-faced man snickered. "I have a feeling you'll *all* be doing a lot of that from now on. *NEXT!*"

Virgil shambled away, transfixed by the vice principals as they entered their inflated castle.

It's like one of those Grub-a-Dub-Dub fast-food places you see in the middle of nowhere when you're on a long trip with your family, Virgil thought as he stood in the open, wide-mouthed doorway. *After a few dozen billboards, you're counting down the miles, like it's Christmas on a bun with a side of birthdays. But after you've stuffed your face and driven away, you feel kinda sick and sad inside.*

A dozen sandbags were tossed out of the castle's windows. The blimp kingdom wobbled and gently lifted off the ground, floating up for about a hundred feet until the six slender cables tethering it to the ground grew taut.

"Up, up, and away," Virgil mumbled as his mind journeyed back to his time in Limbo, when he, his best friend, Milton, and Milton's sister, Marlo—the thought of whom made Virgil blush—had attempted to escape using piles of confiscated clothing and jars of buoyant Lost Souls to create a big balloon that would, theoretically, take them back to the Surface, aka the Land of the Living. But their escape had proven only one-third successful. Marlo had been captured by Bea "Elsa" Bubb, Heck's Principal of Darkness, and Virgil, realizing that the soul balloon had only so much lift, let his skinnier, lighter friend Milton float to freedom—or at least a better place, Virgil hoped.

Dragged back to the present by the heady scent of barbecued meat, Virgil stuffed a handful of Hambone Hank's succulent food into his mouth. The flavor assailed Virgil's senses like a quarry full of Pop Rocks splashed by a tidal wave of ginger ale. The taste was complex, mysterious—haunting, even—and Virgil's tongue tried valiantly to explore every delicious nuance. It was the most lip-smackingly, finger-lickingly wonderful thing he had ever eaten.

Maybe his selfless act in Limbo came with some reward, Virgil thought as he wolfed down the basket of meat and fresh hush puppies. The only thing that could make this moment any better would be if his friend were here by his side to enjoy it with. *Milton's probably thousands of miles away,* Virgil thought with a wistful grin, *just chilling somewhere, living the good life. And after his time in Heck, most any life would seem good in comparison.*

2 · LOST SHEEP ON THE LAM

MILTON THREW HIS weight against his customized, tricked-out shopping cart and plummeted down a steep ridge toward a barbed cyclone fence. His stomach felt like it had sprouted wings and was trying to flutter frantically out of his gaping mouth.

"Pick up the tempo, Popsicle!" yelled Jack Kerouac, the lanky, dark-haired leader of the Phantoms of the Dispossessed—or PODs—from his speeding cart below. "Us cats gotta scat and make a mad conga line out of *Squaresville*. To the ultimate scene."

Jack and dozens of his PODs—Milton's adopted family—hurtled behind their fortified shopping carts toward the heavily guarded barrier . . . and their potential undoing.

Milton, still running, felt for his glasses, hidden in the filthy POD disguise he wore to avoid detection by

Bea "Elsa" Bubb's team of demon spies. He squinted at the guards teeming on both sides of the eighteen-foot-tall fence, oblivious to the oncoming assault due to a thick, clinging mist.

The fence's gleaming, corkscrew razor wire grinned maliciously back at Milton, like the product of an especially evil orthodontist. The sight shot a wave of electric panic through Milton as he leaned into another switchback on the sloping bank. He joined the phantoms as they drove their shopping cart chariots, sporting corrugated metal shields and barbed spikes, in a line down the bluff, forming a vicious, winding dragon of metal. Milton clutched the handle of his cart so tightly that his pale white knuckles became almost translucent.

For the last few weeks, eleven-year-old Milton had been detained in a refugee camp in some bleak, forgotten badlands on the outskirts of Heck, lying low, waiting for the right opportunity for escape. And, with the last shopping cart fortified and the blanket of mysterious mist tucking itself in around the fence, the time was nigh. *Now*, even.

"It's just like I wrote in *The Dead Beat Scrolls*!" Jack shouted as Milton caught up with him on the plunging slope. "'The mad ones are made to move. But even these dispossessed souls, uneasy and noble, will find their day of rest, in a place beyond.'"

Jack had apparently been a big-shot writer years ago up on the Surface. And all the PODs were buzzing about his latest book, *The Dead Beat Scrolls*—his first since his death—one that had come to him in some kind of wild dream.

"Right, the Margins," Milton replied dubiously. "'Where nomads and know-mads make their rightful home at the very edge of wrong, and puzzling jigsaw spirits become one glorious whole.'"

Jack, a lunatic grin smeared across his face, let out a bloodcurdling whoop. The demon guards patrolling the fence stopped their drill. They looked up, shocked, as the dragon of carts hurtled toward them, slicing through the mist, unstoppable.

Beyond the fence, the mist thinned, revealing glimpses of the wasteland beyond. Milton saw strange, woolly blobs cantering in the distance. They brayed freakishly in a way that made the flock of goose pimples on Milton's arms migrate across his whole body.

But Milton couldn't abandon the PODs now, especially after all they had done for him: harboring a known fugitive and—when they had been captured and put in this awful, barren place—engineering a bold escape before Milton could be processed and identified.

Milton pushed back with his foot, propelling his speeding cart faster, and peered ahead to see an ancient POD named Moondog at the front of the line. Dressed as a shabby Viking with the wind whipping his long white hair about like an angry ghost, Moondog seemed infinitely brave. Perhaps the fact that he was completely blind had something to do with it. Though unable to see, Moondog was far from sightless. He was endowed with—if not quite a sixth sense—something slightly more than the standard-issue five.

"I hope we didn't miss our checkout time!" Moondog howled as his shopping cart rammed into the fence.

The twisted chain link screamed as it was torn apart by the carts' jagged sawtooth fenders. Clouds of thick, sickly yellow grit were upturned into the air as the speeding locomotive of PODs barreled through the fence.

"Brace yourself!" Jack barked against the din of squealing, scraping metal, his dark cowlick dancing above his wild eyes.

Milton hunkered down as he shot through the gaping wound in the fence. Behind him lay gnarled sections of chain link, like a swathe of scar tissue left after a robot's appendectomy.

He grinned, accidentally getting a mouthful of mist that stank like hard-boiled eggs. Milton swallowed down the sickening, sour taste.

"What a gas!" Jack roared. "Those guards were totally caught *off* guard!"

But, as Milton made out a guard in a nearby tower cradling a bulky walkie-talkie, he realized that soon all of the Netherworld would know of their escape, including Bea "Elsa" Bubb, Heck's self-serving, evildoing, stomach-churning, and—worst of all—Milton-hating Principal of Darkness.

Jack stood atop his still-speeding cart, extended his arms, and embraced the stale wind rushing past him with abandon.

"Now let's take this wigged-out riff straight to the Margins!" he shouted to the dozens of ragtag PODs as they charged onward through the stark tundra.

The fierce, fathomless eyes of the phantoms blazed with triumph. They whooped and waved their arms in the air like they just didn't care, though they did—very much so—perhaps for the first time in their afterlives.

"So you seriously think that the Margins is a real place?" asked Milton, who—even as a wandering soul in an afterlife crowded with phantoms, demons, and assorted dead historical figures—was ever the pragmatist.

Jack caressed a pendant of glittering, silvery liquid that hung from his neck. It burbled faintly at his touch.

"I don't think," he said. "*I know.* Some truths hang out in your heart, because your brain won't let 'em crash, dig?"

Milton shrugged as Jack broke from the line, kicking his way ahead. Milton, wary of being the caboose in this grim, colorless land, scooted alongside the nervously energetic POD.

"But what if . . . the Margins is just . . . a dream you had?" Milton panted.

Jack rubbed the back of his grimy neck with his hand.

"The only diff between our dreams and our lives is, like, the position of our eyelids," Jack replied with a shrug. "See, all our crazy lives are just stories written on sheets of binder paper, and we PODs are the scribbles in the margins. It's where those who don't belong *belong*. It doesn't matter if it's real or not. If you think you belong somewhere, then you do."

Milton and Jack reached the front of the barreling parade of souped-up shopping carts. Moondog pondered the horizon with vacant eyes.

"Something wicked that way we go," Moondog howled, his arm pointing ahead into nothing.

Milton turned to Jack.

"What does he mean?" Milton asked.

The PODs' leader reached for his pendant, gently squeezing it in his hand for comfort.

"Moondog is, like, way ahead of us in many ways," he said gravely. "He is experiencing something that we have yet to. Something . . . *wrong*."

Milton looked ahead. He could just make out the indistinct creatures he had seen earlier in the distance. The mist distorted their unnerving brays so that they sounded both eerily far away and frighteningly close. Milton hoped for the former but knew in his gut that something wicked was coming closer than anyone could have imagined. But wherever he and his adopted family of phantoms belonged, it wasn't here, in this stinky, dispiriting patch of nothing in the armpit of the afterlife.

3 · CREATURE DISCOMFORTS

BEA "ELSA" BUBB straightened a stack of papers on her desk that she had only just straightened. To the untrained eye, they were now as straight as they would ever be. The principal had spent the last hour organizing the top of her massive mahogany desk until everything was as functionally drab as inhumanly possible so that the desk conveyed professionalism, an unwavering sense of duty, and the keen precision of today's ambitious, career-driven demoness.

But the truth of the matter was that she was procrastinating, avoiding the two official, unopened Pentagrams that lay in her sinbox like two grenades with misplaced pins.

She sipped her piping-hot HostiliTea and summoned

the courage to open the first of the two envelopes, the one delivered just five minutes before the second. She ripped it open with her index talon.

BEASTERN UNION PENTA-GRAM

To: Bea "Elsa" Blob, Principal of
Darkness, Heck

The principal gritted her fangs. They *always* got her name wrong.

From: The Big Guy Downstairs

Her pulse raced at the name: The Big Guy Downstairs. Lucifer. Satan. Mephistopheles. A hunk by any other name, she thought, is just as . . . *hunky*.

Defective immediately, you are to be
given a promotion for your negligible
involvement in thwarting the
Grabbit's attempt to destroy Rapacia
and its surrounding realms using the
Hopeless Diamonds to create a black
hole. Stop. Your official title,
Principal of Darkness, will now be,
from this moment of eternity onward,
The Principal of Darkness. Stop. This

promotion will not, in any way,
result in an increase in salary,
status, or medical benefits. Stop.
You will, however, enjoy the
privilege of added responsibilities,
increased workload, and intensified
accountability. Stop.

Yours, etc., the Big Guy Downstairs

Bea "Elsa" Bubb allowed herself a grin.

It was a promotion in only the loosest interpretation of the word. Actually, the word—not to mention the definite article "the"—was the only thing about her promotion that was, in fact, an actual promotion. But still she held on to this shred of power tightly in her claws, literally: the Penta-gram was crumpled, and the palms of her claws had five white half-moons pressed into them. Every demon had her day, and today was the first day of the rest of her afterlife: a chance to make everybody pay, and pay dearly. Up front. In cash.

The Principal of Darkness snickered. Cerberus, the three-headed hound of Heck nestled in her hideous lap, stirred awake. His mistress's breath was like a delectable blend of anchovies and two-day-old garbage. Cerberus considered his owner with his left head, by far the most inquisitive. Bea "Elsa" Bubb patted the red silk bow stapled onto its sleek, vicious skull.

"It's okay, my pwetty whiddle puffkin," she cooed. "Mummy's not hurt; she's just laughing at everyone else's expense!"

Cerberus, after discerning that none of this had anything to do with either rat liver pâté or pony giblets, resumed the nap that two-thirds of him was already taking.

Principal Bubb puffed out her chest with pride, stretching her bile-green muumuu past the point of its manufacturer's suggested level of strain. She felt as if she could take on the whole underworld. The principal eyed the second Penta-gram. She snatched it up and ripped it open with playful vigor, like a feisty cat abruptly ending its playdate with a baby bluebird.

BEASTERN UNION PENTA-GRAM

```
To: Bea "Elsa" Blob, ~~The~~ Principal of
Darkness, Heck

From: The Big Guy Downstairs

Defective immediately, you are to be
stripped of your promotion in that
one Milton Fauster has—for the second
time—eluded your capacity to contain
his eternal soul, blah, blah, blah.
Stop. His having escaped Limbo using
```

the buoyancy of Lost Souls only to
return undetected, then escape again
with the help of itinerant phantoms
is inexcusable in its nonability to
be condoned. In addition to your
immediate unpromotion, a copy of this
Penta-gram will be added to your
permanent file. Stop. We would also
appreciate it if you returned your
added promotionary "the" in the
return envelope provided. Stop.

Yours, etc., the Big Guy Downstairs

A drop of salty water fell onto the Penta-gram, smudging the postscript somewhat.

"Darned sweaty eyes," Bea "Elsa" Bubb cursed as someone hammered on the door of her not-so-secret lair.

"'Scuse me, Principal, ma'am," apologized a birdish demon as it poked its beaked, sparsely feathered head into her chamber. "You asked me to tell you if anything was amiss, miss."

Bea "Elsa" Bubb glared at the twitchy demon through red-rimmed eyes. Her acid reflux, that great prognosticator of impending bad news, lapped against the back of her throat like toxic waste.

"Please tell me that this has nothing to do with the PODs," she said wearily.

The demon's down fluffed up.

"Oh no, nothing to do with PODs," he chirped in reply.

"Good," the principal sighed.

"It's the Phantoms of the Dispossessed."

Bea "Elsa" Bubb was suddenly stricken with a case of full-body heartburn.

"PODs *are* phantoms," she seethed.

The bird demon shrugged.

"I suppose that's one way of looking at it," he clucked.

"IT'S THE ONLY WAY OF LOOKING AT IT!" the principal shrieked. "I was supposed to personally inspect the captured herd . . . flock—whatever you call a grubby group of nomadic phantoms—*today* to see if that pernicious pip-squeak Milton Fauster was still traveling with them!"

"And there's nothing to stop you from doing that, ma'am."

"Really?"

"Other than the fact that they just now escaped."

"*Escaped?*"

"Yes. Flew the coop."

While the Disdainment Camp and the Wastelands surrounding it were technically not under her jurisdiction—the Big Guy Downstairs had subcontracted dominion of this worthless surreal estate to one of his underachieving nephews—there was an aspect of this situation that could very well be her problem.

It was short. It was infuriating. It nagged at her, mocked her, following her close like a piece of toilet paper on her hoof. Two words containing countless irritation. *Milton Fauster.*

She had to nab that little twerp, and the PODs were the only lead she had. The problem was that the Wastelands were, to put it mildly, off-putting. To put it the opposite of mildly, *appallingly treacherous.* Even Bea "Elsa" Bubb had her limits, and trudging across the dismal, dangerous, and deranging Wastelands on her own two hooves was it. Luckily, for an administrator, it was not only possible to pawn off dirty deeds to someone—or something—else, but it was also expected. And so Bea "Elsa" Bubb rose from her chair (sending the lapdog-suddenly-without-a-lap Cerberus to the floor) and decided to delegate this duty to something else. Something even more treacherous than she.

Principal Bubb clacked down the concrete hall of the Unstables, a secret facility just a whip's crack away from Limbo's Demonitor Hall (where today's sniveling demon simps become tomorrow's only slightly more impressive demon guards).

Bea "Elsa" Bubb had called ahead to make sure that her unannounced appearance didn't go unnoticed. Still, the only thing that met her at the Unstables' swinging double doors was the stench of ammonia and fresh "beast patties." Finally, a stocky demon with a pierced bull's nose and clad in filthy overalls trotted over to her.

"Principal Bubb!" the creature snorted. "Might I say that this is indeed an honor?"

"I didn't come here to shoot the bull," the principal said. The demon beast master winced. "Sorry . . . nothing personal."

"Anyway," Principal Bubb continued as she clasped her claws behind her back and surveyed the stalls with a slow, steady gaze. "I've come here because I have a little problem . . . and I need him solved."

Her goat eyes settled on an enormous, dark green wolf with a long braided tail.

"What is this?" she asked.

"It's a Cusith, ma'am."

"What does it do?"

"Bays, mostly."

"Hmmm," she murmured. "What I need is more of a . . . bloodhound. Something hardy, made to thrive in hostile conditions—the Wastelands, specifically—that can track someone for me."

Just then, a tremendous series of *thunks* erupted from the last stall, followed by fits of skittish scrabbling. The principal looked over with interest.

"What was that?" she asked as she strutted toward the stall, the only one walled off with double-ply chicken wire.

"Flicks," the demon answered with disgust.

The stall reeked of over-roasted coffee beans. The suspended lights of the stall swung as if they had recently been disturbed. Crowded in the stall among broken coffee bean hulls and soiled clumps of straw were five bloated . . . *flicks*. Massive. Like swollen, waterlogged boars. Their harpoonlike proboscises trembled as they greedily sucked up thick, tarlike coffee grounds from a trough. One of them hopped, startled, hitting the roof with a reverberating *thunk*.

"Half flea, half tick, and *totally* unpredictable," the beast master clarified.

Principal Bubb was fascinated, both put off and drawn in by the quivering, impossibly large parasites.

"How come they seem so . . . jumpy?" she inquired.

"That's because they're *nervous* flicks," the demon replied, moving the ring in his nose so that he could better pick his moist snout. "Flicks, as I'm sure you can imagine, suck blood. Well, we don't really have enough in supply—even the ectoplasmic 'shadow blood' we all have pumping through our veins down here—to satisfy their appetites. So, instead, we just feed them a lot of really bad coffee . . . and there's no shortage of that down here! It seems to satisfy them, just makes 'em terribly edgy."

The principal rubbed the hairs on her chinny chin chin.

"So they probably can't wait to get their snouts on the real thing, then, eh?" Bea "Elsa" Bubb said as she fished out a roll of parchment from her genuine kitten kit bag.

The bull demon nodded.

"Boy howdy! They'd probably travel across Heck and back for a taste!"

She handed him the roll of paper.

"Have them get a whiff of this," she said with a cruel grin.

The beast master nodded and carefully pushed the scroll through the chicken wire. The flicks held their long, quivering noses up to the parchment before hopping madly, knocking into the hanging lamps above and shattering the bulbs.

"Good golly," the hulking beast master yelped, pulling the roll back through the wire. "What's on this thing?"

The principal smirked as she unrolled the parchment.

This Indenture,

by and between Heck, a branch of the Galactic Order Department, itself an independent offshoot of the Cosmic Omnipotence and Regulation Entity, hereinafter,

whether singular or plural, masculine, feminine, terres-
trial, extraterrestrial, and/or interdimensional, desig-
nated as "Soul Holder," which expression shall include
Soul Holder's executors, administrators, assigns, and
successors in interest, and Milton Fauster . . .

"Ah," the demon observed, "a legally binding covenant—"

He scanned the contract down to the bottom, where the name "Milton Fauster" was scrawled in rusty-brown cursive letters.

"—signed in blood. Now they've got a nibble, and they'll be wanting the main course."

The principal crossed her pudgy, varicose-veined arms.

"As much as it pains me to say so," she grunted, "I need the boy in one piece. I need irrefutable *proof* that I captured him."

"Not a problem." The demon nodded, winking one of his beady black eyes. "I can rig them with trackers so that when they're extra agitated, like they get when they've cornered something, you'll know that you've got your man . . . or boy, in this case."

The demon leaned in close to the principal.

"I can't guarantee that he'll be, you know, completely intact," the beast master whispered. "Due to the unnatural size of the proboscis, I doubt if they'd be able to draw blood from a boy, depending on his size. But that doesn't mean they won't try. It'll probably hurt like the dickens, and he might wish that they would just finish the job. Of course, considering the Wastelands, something might have already beat them to it."

The principal stared at the high-strung flicks through the chicken wire. They considered her with their dull, red, hungry eyes.

"Oh, I don't mind if the little simp is knocked around a bit," Bea "Elsa" Bubb said as the vertical slits at the center of her curdled-yellow eyes tightened with purpose.

"Or a little pale from, shall we say, *an impromptu blood donation.*"

4 · SCRAMBLED EXiLE

MILTON CLUTCHED HIS threadbare coat as another salty gust of wind high-fived his face. The phantoms, just under a hundred of them, pushed onward through the gray, gritty realm.

Moondog had referred to this bleak tract of despair as the Wastelands. It was like the land that time—and *everything*—forgot.

"It's a place where addled, abandoned memories, hopes, and wishes go," said Moondog, responding to Milton's thoughts in that eerie way of his, not so much reading his mind as flipping through it like a magazine in a doctor's waiting room. "Ripped away from the people who originally had them, never to find their way back again, then ground into dust and wind."

Another blast of briny, stale wind hit Milton in the face. It was like inhaling the steam from a pot of boiled tears and old-lady perfume. He shuddered at the thought of being struck in the face by someone's stray remembrance. Jack pushed his shopping cart alongside Milton and Moondog.

"'These rootless souls lean forward into the confusion, prowling the dreaming darkness to find their rightful place,'" Jack said, the words flying out of his mouth like a saxophone solo. "'Yet past the raggedy madness of the senseless nightmare road is a place on the edge of sight, where every sigh goes to die.'"

Milton wiped the salt—or abandoned memory—from his stinging eyes.

"Cheery, like a burned-down toy store," Milton deadpanned. "Let me guess, another inspiring quote from *The Dead Beat Scrolls*."

Jack smiled his nervous, impish grin.

"Everything belongs somewhere, Popsicle," he said. "We've all got our fit, dig? You just have to keep on trying on the clothes that fate gives you."

The caster wheels of a hundred shopping carts sliced through the coarse gravel and dust.

"We didn't belong up there, and we don't seem to belong down here either," Moondog said, his blind eyes coated with a white film that made it look like he had tiny onions in his sockets. "It's like when you take apart a car engine and put it back together again. You always seem to have some stray parts. Society is the engine and we PODs are the leftover bits that no one can find a place for. With our unique balance of faults and virtues, the Powers That Be and the Powers That Be Evil just couldn't place us in their tidy little hereafter. So we roam."

The front caster wheel of Milton's cart became stuck in a glob of yolky sludge.

Here I am, in the middle of nowhere, stuck in someone's gross, abandoned memory, Milton groused to himself. He gave it a kick with his sneaker.

"Memories are just energy, Milton," Moondog said after casually leafing through Milton's thoughts. "See, everything has got to go somewhere, whether it's a person, a memory. . . . It's just a question of charge. When it's all juiced up, it's on the Surface, alive, making mischief. When it's spent, it goes . . . well, down here."

Jack stopped his cart and studied the horizon while playing nervously with his cowlick. He turned to his tribe of sullen phantoms.

"Divining Rod," he called out over the crowd.

Rod, a steely-eyed man with a braided beard, stepped forward. He held a Y-shaped branch lightly in his palms.

"Lay some divine magic upon us," Jack asked. "A righteous, so-help-me path. Like *solid*."

Rod pointed to Jack's pendant. "That'll throw off the reading," he said in a voice like crumpled butcher's paper.

Jack pulled the pendant over his head—something

Milton had never seen him do before—then tucked it in the back of his khaki pants.

Rod held the forked branch in his outstretched hands, sweeping the point slowly across the Wastelands.

"What's he doing?" Milton whispered to Moondog. "Trying to find water?"

Moondog scratched at the unruly beard that coiled out of his face like the branches of a hardy white bush.

"Nope, even better: Liquid Silver," Moondog replied as he set down his walking stick. "It always leads us to fortune, especially since the deposit for the stuff is so dern good."

The point of Divining Rod's branch began to wobble. His sweeps became tighter, more focused.

"Deposit, like with bottles and cans?" Milton replied. "So you're telling me that there's *recycling* in the afterlife?"

Moondog laughed and nodded. His Norse-style robe, which made him look like a bedraggled Thor, rustled in the wind.

"Are you kidding me? The whole *place* is recycled," he replied. "The same old song only played in a minor key. We'll come across a deposit station every so often. We pour in the Liquid Silver and get food and supplies from these odd lockboxes. We don't know why, how, or where the stuff comes from—not even my fifth-and-a-halfth sense can crack it—but beggars can't be choosers. Even professional beggars like us PODs."

Divining Rod's branch trembled furiously. He set it down and pointed beyond the Wastelands.

"There," he declared.

Milton noticed something shimmering in the distance where Divining Rod had instructed the phantoms to go. Warped, hazy structures materialized. If he squinted through his glasses, Milton could just make out rusted trailers overrun by thickets of brambles. The structures winked in and out of existence like weak, dying lightbulbs. Then, in one great flash of clarity, Milton saw the unmistakable outline of a circus tent. The largest that he had ever seen, like the Matterhorn upholstered in striped orange and green canvas.

"*Please* tell me you see what I see," Milton told the phantoms at his side.

"Well, I don't exactly *see* it," Moondog replied. "But I *do* sense it. . . . It flickers in my thoughts, like the reception on an old TV. It's like this place is caught in between two frequencies and can't quite get a fix on either one."

The phantoms trudged onward across terrain as flat, dull, and appealing as old pudding skin. After a grueling twenty-minute slog, the PODs moved past a small, partially enclosed arena littered with bumped-off bumper cars, their once-cheerful colors pockmarked and blistered, and their electrical poles bent forever at half-mast. Weeds grew through the cracks in the concrete.

The final structure was the towering big top—the

biggest, toppiest big top ever—with several great gashes in its striped orange and green canopy.

The PODs stood before the tent, which was surrounded by thatches of dead, reddish brown briars.

"What is this place?" Milton asked no one in particular.

"Savage Bumble's . . . Tragical . . . Confusement Park and Midway," a stocky phantom named Cody replied simply.

Jack, Milton, and Moondog stared at the round, red-faced man. Cody blew a strand of dirty-blond hair from his face and pointed to a collection of large dull-bronze letters strewn about the overgrowth nearby. The letters were clustered in mangled groups, as if the once-intact marquee had been ripped apart by a cyclone.

"Let's check it out!" Milton said, his inner toddler hopping with excitement.

Jack rocked back and forth on the balls of his feet.

"I don't know," he murmured uneasily, staring at the direction Divining Rod had divined. "Demon guards are bound to be tailing us. Plus we're low on provisions and can't, like, afford to gas and groove at the circus for some freak show kicks, dig?"

A chorus of distressing brays reverberated throughout the grim, gray valley.

"Wherever we go, we'd better get there in a hurry," Moondog said, looking yet not looking around him. "We're disturbing the locals."

"*We're* disturbing *them*?" Milton asked with a full-body shiver.

"Bewilderbeasts," Jack said in a hoarse whisper. "We're, like, solid as long as we don't lamp directly at them."

Milton's unease ratcheted up a notch.

"You mean not look at them?! That's like trying not to think of . . . a banana cream pie."

A chorus of "mmm"s rumbled from the famished phantoms.

A trio of creatures emerged from a bank of mist. The cluster of dark, restless shadows stalked the ground, heads hung low, eyes burning red, then blue with an insistent, dumbfounding pulse. Moondog locked eyes with the creatures, though—since he was blind—that lock was rusty.

"Bewilderbeasts mean that we must be near the Disorient, by the dried-up At Sea," he murmured. "A fitting place for a confusement park."

Without warning, the herd charged toward the phantoms.

"They're attacking!" Milton yelped. "We've got to run!"

"No, Popsicle, *chill*," Jack said calmly as he put his hand on Milton's shoulder. "That's what they want: for us to wig out. That's how they grease . . . *how they feed*. First they capture your attention and then they capture everything else."

The bewilderbeasts galloped closer, their hoofbeats a syncopated rhythm that lulled Milton into a stupor. The fur of the shaggy creatures twisted and contorted the light into something hypnotic and impossible to describe—and impossible to take your eyes off of. The herd leader leveled its mesmerizing gaze at Milton. Milton, like the proverbial deer in headlights, was caught.

"Don't look at it!" Jack barked. Milton tried to look away but, transfixed by the creature's shimmering fur—swaying back and forth, oozing like fronds of jelly light—he couldn't. Soon, all Milton could see was the alternating red-blue-red-blue of the creature's eyes that seemed to lock in time with Milton's slowing pulse.

Suddenly, a scream pealed from the mist-shrouded herd of bewilderbeasts. In the blink of an eye, a swooping shape had attached itself to the creature charging toward Milton. The bewilderbeast screeched, the unmistakable shriek of something about to be killed. Nothing was as frightening, Milton thought in the abrupt silence after the creature's scream, than some terrible creature terrified by something even *more* terrible.

"We've got some nasty party crashers here," Moondog said solemnly. "Some big, bad bugs that make bewilderbeasts look like My Little Ponies."

Milton gasped as a bewilderbeast broke from the herd, wrapped in a tendril of vapor, before something sprang onto the squealing creature's back, then dragged it back into the cloud.

Worry crept into Jack's rugged face.

"I suggest we make like bananas and split," he said, stepping up to a large flap in the canvas tent and widening it for his followers. "In here, dig? Do the circus thing, like Popsicle here suggested. And wait out this bad scene."

The PODs pushed their carts into the tent in a single-file line.

Milton looked nervously over his shoulder. From the mist, he saw a bristly, reddish brown creature bound into the air with a swift jerk and land by one of the outlying trailers. In its front legs, it clutched the body of a bewilderbeast that it appeared to be . . . *sucking the life out of* with its long, tubelike mouth. It was some kind of gargantuan, leaping . . . *flea* or . . . *tick.*

The creature was quickly joined by another. And then another. The mottled creatures quivered and scanned the confusement park with their dull red eyes.

Moondog grabbed Milton by the shoulders and heaved him into the tent.

"Incoming," he croaked as he closed the tent flap behind the last phantom. "And they're hopping mad!"

5 · STARK, RAVING MADAME

"SHE W–WILL S–SEE you n-n-now," said Farzana Daffney, a willowy, impeccably dressed girl.

Standing next to her, thirteen-year-old Marlo Fauster felt like Farzana's photo negative. Farzana's hair was red and effortlessly sleek while Marlo's blue mop had taken an hour to become perfectly unkempt. Farzana was dressed in a creamy designer outfit so crisp and form-fitting that it was hard to distinguish whether Farzana was wearing *it* or it was wearing *her.* Marlo, on the other hand, was going on day three of her fave black velvet vintage top and bulky, knee-length tulle skirt.

Even the two girls' manners were in stark contrast. Farzana seemed so rushed and on edge, like she was strapped to a perpetually teetering chair in a room covered with explosive eggshells. Marlo, however, was the poster girl for calm: a kleptomaniac presently content to take nothing but her own sweet time.

Marlo traced the scrupulously crisscrossed stitching of the black leather door with the tip of her finger. Both Farzana and Marlo eyed the imposing door in silence, only Farzana did so with hyperventilating fear while Marlo viewed it as the portal leading to a whole new afterlife: a backstage pass to privilege and power ripe for abuse.

After preventing the Grabbit—Rapacia's greedier-than-all-get-out vice principal—from sucking the entire underworld into a black hole using two priceless diamonds and an atom smasher, Marlo had been rewarded with an Infernship, serving the Big Guy Downstairs in this place wedged between Heck and h-e-double-hockey-sticks. It was a reward that was both welcome and a little bit unsettling: like drinking from the water fountain after gym, only to have the water pressure change when someone flushes the toilet.

"M-Marlo," Farzana pressed. "Madame Pompadour d-doesn't like to b-be kept waiting." The girl rubbed the goose pimples on her slender forearms. "B-believe me . . . I kn-know."

Marlo glanced down at her scuffed shoes. She quickly rubbed them together, partly to look more presentable for her new teacher or boss or whatever, but also as a subconscious shout-out to fellow Kansan

Dorothy from *The Wizard of Oz*. Only, after clicking her own heels together, Marlo was still here, outside the hide-upholstered door of Madame Pompadour, the woman who ran Heck's Girl Friday the Thirteenth program.

"Okay, fine, I'm ready," Marlo said.

Farzana rapped her bony knuckles on the leather door, hard enough to strike wood beneath the plush padding.

A voice—slow and deadly—hissed like a gas leak in an orphanage from inside the office.

"Yessssss? I don't recall asking to be disturbed."

"Um . . . right, m-madame," Farzana replied. "But y-you said you w-wanted to meet the n-new—"

"Eternity is too short to spend it waiting for you to f-f-finish a sentence, *Miss Daffney*," Madame Pompadour replied. "Have you had your Beauty Cream today?"

Farzana cowered as she pressed open the door. "Y-yes, m-madame. I mean, no."

"Please have a glass at once. Your stuttering is most unladylike. It makes you sound like a scuffed CD."

Marlo stood mutely in the doorway. Farzana attempted to nudge her inside the office with sweeps of her wide, uneasy brown eyes, but Marlo was having none of that. She'd go in when she was good and ready, on her *own* terms.

Farzana shoved Marlo inside, then closed the door

behind her. The leather squished inside the door frame as it shut, making Marlo feel as if she was being sealed inside someone else's tomb.

The room was thick with the smell of leather and an intoxicating musk. Faint light leaked from above through ten red, recessed lights that formed the shape of a pentagram. Pressed against the far wall of the office was an imposing desk built from mahogany coffin lids, by the looks of it. A sleek figure was bent over a calendar on the desk. On the wall behind her was a large octagonal mirror and next to it a velvet scratching post.

"If people are going to barge into my office simply to stare, I should charge admission," Madame Pompadour said in a clipped voice with just a whiff of snooty French.

The woman suddenly looked up. She had large cat eyes that glowed red for just a split second before cooling to a brilliant green. She wore a gorgeous purple snakeskin bodysuit with a little cowl that fit over her head and came to a point in a shiny widow's peak on her forehead.

Marlo's eyes traveled away from the woman, whose affectations reminded Marlo of some freakish Reese's Peanut Butter Cup dreamed up in a mad doctor's lab: "Hey, you've got a cat in my snake!" "Hey, you've got a snake in my cat!" "Mmmm . . . tastes like the snobby, psychopathic headmistress of an underworld charm school!"—to the octagonal mirror behind her.

"Do you possess the ability to speak?" Madame Pompadour spat through a small, pursed mouth. "Why is it that all my girls lately arrive with some kind of crippling speech disorder?"

Marlo smirked. If this supremely stuck-up woman wanted a battle of wits, Marlo thought as she wiggled her tongue for a prebout stretch, then the swords were drawn.

"Of course I can talk," Marlo replied. "I was simply waiting for you to tell me what I'm supposed to be doing here—"

"I don't recall granting you permission to speak," the woman said dismissively. "I simply wanted to know if you *could* speak."

Madame Pompadour made a few quick notes in her red leather Vilofax.

"That doesn't even make sense," Marlo replied with a shrug. "But I was always taught to respect my elders, *ma'am.*" She stretched the last word as if she were pulling back the loaded pocket of a slingshot.

Madame Pompadour rose—*reared*, actually: her back arched, her arms pressed onto the desk, and her head jutted out in front of her.

"*Madame,*" she said slowly, with a great deal of restraint. "You will address me as madame. Always. Never *ma'am*. Ma'am is for . . ."

She twitched.

". . . more *mature* women."

Madame Pompadour sat down like a Jill-in-the-box recoiling back inside its tin cube of a home.

She scrutinized Marlo up and down, as if she were removing each of her organs in a mental game of Operation.

"'Pretty' isn't the most *apt* description of you, is it?" she asked in a way that wasn't anywhere *near* being a question.

Marlo, much to her exasperation, flushed red, completely ruining her hard-earned china-doll complexion and undermining her position as "plucky challenger" in this war of words.

"Well, *madame,*" Marlo replied, squeezing out a delicate glob of sarcasm, "pretty is boring. Saying that someone is 'pretty' is like saying that something is 'fine.' It's not really saying anything. I'd take 'interesting' over 'pretty' any day."

Madame Pompadour's lips curled into a slight smile, a curved dish full of sour milk.

"I suppose you are somewhat *interesting,*" she replied coolly while propping her chin up with a paw-like hand. "Like a peculiar bug smashed on the windshield of one's Maserati. That's a type of *car,* by the way."

Madame Pompadour slid a manila envelope marked MARLO FAUSTER from across the desk and brought it near her chest. She pulled out a letter opener from her top drawer, a dagger with a bejeweled hilt glittering with emeralds.

"Let's cut to the chase," she said as she sliced open the envelope. "You've been entered into a very prestigious program—Heck's *Infernship* program, to be precise. To be even *more* precise, the Girl Friday the Thirteenth Finishing School, where today's young ladies become tomorrow's deceptionists, heckutaries, and badministrative assistants."

Marlo swayed as her mind caught up to her present situation. When Chairman Mammon of the Netherworld Soul Exchange had offered Marlo an opportunity to make a difference from *inside* the system—rather than from her usual vantage point way *outside*—she thought it could be just the ticket, if not out of Heck, at least out of the kiddie pool and into the VIP Jacuzzi with all the other "playahs."

If her first five minutes in Madame Pompadour's finishing school were any indication, Marlo was in the same old game only with a new name: like how soccer is considered "football" to the rest of the world.

"And let me clarify for you, since I can tell from your bone structure, your dull expression, and your overall lack of refinement that you are not the smartest outfit on the rack," Madame Pompadour relayed, "this is by no means a guarantee of you becoming an Infern for the Big Guy Downstairs. Do I make myself clear?"

"Crystal Light," Marlo replied.

Marlo wanted to sit down. Having a bad attitude was draining. Her feet hurt. And everything in between wasn't feeling so hot either. But there was no place to sit. Girls were forced to, Marlo assumed, simply stand before Madame Pompadour as she tore them apart from the inside while they slowly crumbled on the outside from physical exhaustion. But not this girl. Marlo was unbreakable. Impenetrable. Like an armadillo wearing Tuffskins. Like a steel-plated Twinkie. Like an algebra equation.

"I take only the truly exceptional," the cold, composed woman explained. "But I am making an exception in your case, out of coercion—*respect*—for certain influential personages that have taken a shine to your dull little self. You are being forced upon me . . . but I like a challenge. Even if I don't like *you*."

Marlo's thieving eyes were drawn to something dangling from Madame Pompadour's slender wrist. It was a gorgeous charm bracelet laden with elegant vintage hearts. Each heart had a tiny face and name etched into it, too small for Marlo to read. They tinkled in the hush of the office.

"I begin my training with simple, repetitive tasks that help mold my girls into young ladies worthy of the opportunity that they have been given," Madame Pompadour continued. "Otherwise, it's like handing a monkey a razor and shaving cream, turning your back, and *not* expecting them to end up all . . . stubbly."

Madame Pompadour's perfect pink mouth curled into a sneer.

"Judging from your upper lip, it looks like you could benefit from 'monkeying around' with a razor."

Marlo's hand shot to her upper lip. It felt as if a woolly caterpillar had decided to take up residence just south of her nose.

"You'll begin by answering phones, mostly. And running errands for . . . *him*. The Big Guy Downstairs. Actually, the Big Guy Just Down the Hall. He has an office here for when he needs to get the *you-know-what* out of *you-know-where*."

Marlo stared past Madame Pompadour's shoulder into the mirror. Nothing in it was distinct, just dark smudges and swirling blobs. Suddenly, the blobs clotted together to form Marlo's reflection.

Marlo gasped at the drab, dumpy girl in the octagonal mirror. Her hair appeared to be a rat's nest, and not in a cool-and-expertly-crafted-to-look-punky-yet-casual kind of way, but as if it actually harbored vermin. Marlo's face looked hideously swollen, as if she had drunk an aquarium's worth of salt water and slept upside down for a year. And what had happened to her chin? Had it been blown free of her immortal self in the marshmallow bear explosion that had taken her life?

Madame Pompadour slapped closed her red leather Vilofax.

"Are you even listening to me?" the woman hissed through pointy white teeth. "Do I need to repeat myself and reenact my words in a closed-captioned puppet show so that you can *follow along*?"

"No, ma'am . . . *madame*," she replied thickly, as if her head were stuffed full of overcooked oatmeal. "I'm . . . *listening*."

Madame Pompadour sighed and took a dainty lap of catnip tea from a small porcelain cup. Meanwhile, Marlo fought the pull of the woman's mirror. It was as if her eyes were fastened to it with Silly Putty, and the more she struggled to free her gaze, the more the putty stretched and contorted her reflection.

Farzana peeked into the room. The sound of the door opening—a slurping, backward belch—coaxed Marlo from her stupor.

"Excuse me, madame, but it's time for your two o'clock with Sheila Shylock and Lady Lily Lassiter," Farzana said in one fluid, perfectly enunciated breath. She wiped away her milk mustache with a quick sweep of her tongue. Madame Pompadour cocked her eyebrow.

"I thought my two o'clock was at four?"

"No, madame. At four you're meeting with the lab about your latest line of lovely lemon liniment for learned ladies."

Madame Pompadour nodded.

"Fine, then," she said as she jotted down a note in her Vilofax. "And I believe that Miss Fauster here could use a glass of Beauty Cream."

Marlo pried her eyes from her homely image. "No . . . madame," she managed. "I'm lactose intolerant. *Severely.* It does things to my plumbing that I wouldn't wish on, well . . . *you,* even. Once I went on an aerosol cheese binge and woke up the next day in the hospital."

Madame Pompadour glared at Marlo.

"That's . . . *unfortunate,*" she grumbled while tinkling her bracelet with her fingers. "My Beauty Cream is a unique blend of ingredients designed to create a foundation of poise and refinement. I will have to think of other . . . *means* . . . of drawing out your charm."

The haughty woman opened her top drawer and plucked out a small red velveteen pouch. She pushed it across her desk.

"It's a welcoming gift," Madame Pompadour explained. "It also doubles as a cell phone. So I can keep my girls close—no matter where they are."

Marlo's curiosity got the best of her (hopefully it would kill the cat that got her tongue), and she turned to receive her gift.

She picked up the pouch, loosened its drawstring, and pulled out a gorgeous, tortoiseshell compact case. Marlo marveled at its ornate, filigree embellishments.

She flipped it open with her thumb. Tiny blue lights surrounding the mirror inside the compact's lid strobed in a mesmerizing pulse. Marlo stared at her reflection, overly magnified so that her face looked like the surface of the moon.

"You're welcome," Madame Pompadour said wearily. "My, we have a lot of work to do, don't we, Miss Fauster? But that is all for now. You may leave."

Marlo cradled the compact in her palm. It radiated peculiar swells of electricity that throbbed in time to her own heartbeat. She couldn't take her eyes off herself, though—horrified by what she saw—that's exactly what she wanted to do, more than anything. She trembled as she scanned the ravaged, cratered surface of her face in the mirror.

"Marlo," Farzana whispered with urgency, waving Marlo to her as if trying to coax a duck across a busy highway.

"It's really quite simple," Madame Pompadour explained with passive disgust. "You do exactly what you did to get *into* my office, only in reverse."

Madame Pompadour returned to her Vilofax. To her, it was as if Marlo suddenly ceased to exist. The problem was, Marlo was beginning to feel the same way.

6 · iN THE FLiCK OF iT

INSIDE THE MASSIVE tent was—somehow—an even *more* massive carnival. It was crowded with lurid signs (BE-HOLD: EL HOPPO THE MEXICAN FROG BOY! for instance), sideshow exhibits, and baffling rides. *A carnival on the edge of time,* Milton thought.

He looked above him at the swaying wooden sign, daubed in bright yellow and blue: STEP RIGHT UP . . .

And so Milton did, passing beneath the sign to the frozen, painted metal automaton standing between the hundred or so fearful phantoms and the midway. The figure wore a black top hat and a pin-striped vest, waist-coat, and pants. It held a varnished wooden cane with what looked like a mummified monkey head on top. As Milton scrutinized the figure, it twitched to me-chanical life.

"From the instant you are born to the moment you

expire, the clock is your executioner," the automaton relayed in a deeper-than-expected voice. "There's no escape from the great finale of life where each of you is destined to play your farewell performance."

More PODs huddled together around the robotic curiosity.

"Or *is* there? Can one actually delay that final moment when the bony hand of death scrawls one's name in his crowded diary?"

The automaton's mouth squeezed and scraped into a smile.

"Of course there is, ladies and gentlemen, and that is why I am here. . . ."

The figure waved its arm toward the midway in a grandiose gesture.

"I am Savage Bumble, and this is my Tragical Confusement Park!"

Suddenly, three very large *somethings* landed on the roof of the tent. The fabric puckered dangerously inward. The creatures' legs scrabbled for purchase, tearing into the canvas.

Through the shredded canvas roof, one of the creatures dropped the lifeless body of a bewilderbeast onto Swami River's Fortune-Telling Booth, smashing it to splinters.

The phantoms around Milton screamed and slammed their shopping carts into one another in desperation. He gaped, stunned, at the roof above his head as it was slowly yet purposefully scratched to ribbons. Jack pushed his cart to the head of the line and waved his arms for attention.

"Hey, cats, cool it," Jack said calmly. "We've got to scatter. Take to these crazy tents and caravans and force those crazy bugs to hunt alone. Hurry. *Like now!*"

The edgy phantoms frantically broke off into clusters. Jack led a group of older, slower phantoms to a tent marked AMAZING CURATIVES AND SUPERNATURAL SALVES! just past an empty platform marked HUMONGOUS HEXED RABBOT. Milton felt like he often had back on the Surface during gym class after all the teams had been picked: shunned and awkwardly alone.

"C'mon, boy," Moondog said as he tugged him toward a pink and green caravan, "you're my good-luck charm."

Milton grinned, and the two hastily wheeled their carts into the mouth of the horseshoe-shaped midway. They scrambled past a Loop-Die-Loop—a mechanical contraption composed of three eggbeater-like blades with coffin-shaped passenger carriages attached—and into a booth, identified by a sign as the MAUSOLEUM OF MAKE-BELIEVE PLAY-FELLOWS.

Inside the garishly painted booth were rows and rows of jars—*soul* jars, by the looks of it—like the ones Milton had stolen from Limbo's Assessment Chamber. These jars were smaller than the Lost Souls Milton had used to escape from Heck, yet the souls themselves were similar, only thinner and far less substantial, like watered-down ectoplasmic broth. They were also strangely cheery.

One jar held what looked like wisps of dull-pink cotton candy while another held glittery globs and speckled, purple-gray goop.

Moondog was right: Everything *is energy,* Milton reflected. *So why not imaginary friends? A child makes them as real as anything. And just because a kid stops believing in them doesn't mean that energy just disappears. It moves on . . . ultimately settling here . . .*

A female phantom's scream ripped through the air. Milton spun around toward the woman as a monstrous flea-tick sawed through the canvas roof above her with its harpoon nose. The creature fell on top of the Bury-Go-Round—a small roller coaster with an abrupt end at a mound of dirt—fifty feet away from Milton and Moondog. The pair dashed through the mouth of a spacious tunnel with hinged wooden doors at the far end of the carnival. Lurid orange letters declared it the KILLING TIME ZONE.

The bloated, speckled flea-tick skittered toward the tent. Its amber eyes glowed weakly, like twin laser sights in the darkness. Its proboscis quivered until pointing directly at Milton. The jittery creature's eyes flared.

"Let's go!" Moondog shouted as he grabbed Milton

and heaved him and his cart into the tunnel. He quickly upended the cart and spilled out dozens of metal scraps, forming an impromptu barricade behind them.

"What about *your* cart?" Milton asked.

"Blast the cart!" Moondog barked. "I can always spend another eternity collecting more junk!"

The swollen creature scuttled up to the mound of metal and stabbed through the shopping cart's carriage with its snout.

"Why does everything always want *me*?" Milton mumbled, backing away with fear and disgust.

Moondog, with surprising strength, hoisted Milton up, set him into his shopping cart, and pushed him farther into the tunnel.

Inside, movie projectors cast glimmering, dull 3-D images onto the walls of the tunnel. As Milton raced past them—a passenger in his own cart—he saw a man shaving, a teenage girl waiting by a phone, a fidgety toddler in the backseat of a car, a businessman at the airport, boys loitering outside a convenience store, and dozens of other less-than-memorable memories.

"The *Killing Time* Zone," Milton observed. "A place full of moments that were killed . . . *wasted*."

The flea-tick flailed its front legs with frustration at the scrap metal and shopping cart barrier. Sweat trickled down Moondog's face as he pushed onward.

"You're really gettin' the hang of bein' dead, kid!"

he puffed. "This place feels like a collage of time con-
tinuums. Boring little scraps of reality left on the cutting-
room floor of life."

A crash thundered through the tunnel, followed by
a dozen or so scrabbling feet. Milton and Moondog
charged down the tunnel as the creature, now joined by
another, skittered ever closer.

"Stop!" Milton shrieked. Moondog screeched the
cart to a halt. Its front caster wheels dangled off the
edge of a precipice.

"I didn't see *that* coming!" Moondog gasped.

Beneath them was a steep drop into what looked
like a roller coaster of spooled time-space laid on a
shimmering "track" of moments. All of the segments
of track had one thing in common: hundreds of people
staring at hundreds of television sets.

Milton turned. His mouth went slack with fear as
three flea-ticks forced their bloated, disgusting bodies
down the tunnel, taking peevish swipes at one another
with their long snouts. The trio of overgrown parasites
stopped and judged Milton and Moondog with their
emotionless red eyes before rearing back.

"Get us out of here!" Milton shrieked.

The three plus-sized parasites sprang forward.
Moondog hopped on top of the shopping cart, crowding in next to Milton, then kicked both of them off the
edge of the tunnel with his workboot. They plunged
down the track of residual, barely solid energy. Milton

gripped the side of the cart as his stomach pitched into a somersault.

The shopping cart plunged down through countless living rooms, dens, and basements—a chain of people lounging on couches staring blankly at flickering screens. The "ride" began with clean-cut families sitting, enrapt, before large boxes broadcasting warped black-and-white images of cowboys and Indians. The shopping cart sped through the shimmering vignettes, each one fading behind Milton and Moondog just as it was experienced. The tracks leveled out, and the shopping cart whizzed past shaggy-haired people mesmerized by colorful images of spaceships and war.

"Brace yourself," Moondog cautioned. Up ahead was a series of loop-the-loops. The cart jerked as they entered the tight coils of time. The g-force bent Milton's neck so that his chin was jammed into the top of his chest. Around him was a repetitive blur of cop shows and sitcoms.

"Must . . . be . . . reruns," Moondog muttered.

They shot past the loop-the-loops and ascended steadily along the track, entering each bit of wasted time as if flipping through a stack of moving postcards. Milton looked behind him, past Moondog's whizzing white mane. The flea-ticks stumbled down the track, their barbed, spindly legs slipping on the insubstantial clusters of time energy. They tried sucking, in vain, the vaporous wraiths of moments around them.

Milton and Moondog climbed upward, streaking through images of teenagers lying on their stomachs, feverishly playing a variety of video games—first Pong, then Pac-Man, then Legend of Zelda, Final Fantasy, and Halo in ever-quickening succession.

"Uh-oh," Milton murmured as he saw the track abruptly end up ahead. "I think we're running out of time."

7 · DROP-DEAD GORGE-OUS

"HOLD ON!" MILTON yelled as he and Moondog, hunkering down tight, sailed off the track. The airborne cart shot through the end of the tunnel, spinning like a corkscrew for a few dozen feet, until it burst through the canvas of the confusement park tent. Milton's stomach felt like he had swallowed a child's wind-up toy.

A shred of the coarse, sturdy cloth snagged on the cart's sawtooth bumper. The gash in the side of the tent widened as Milton and Moondog hurtled back into the Wastelands.

"Grab the canvas!" Moondog ordered as they plummeted outward and, unfortunately, downward. Milton hugged the fabric while Moondog clutched the rough cloth with his long, yellow nails. The shopping cart tore free and plummeted forty feet to the ground, where it smashed to its original, prewelded state of castaway parts.

Milton winced as he and Moondog, their arms wrapped tightly around the stiff canvas, swung down and slapped into the side of the tent. The impact knocked the wind out of Milton, and the fabric cut into his palms, but he held on for all he was worth. They hung suspended in the air as a crowd of PODs gathered beneath them, their carts laden with newly acquired curiosities.

The confusement park tent creaked and buckled as the disintegrating canvas pulled itself apart.

"Let go!" Moondog bellowed. Milton and Moondog tumbled down the steady slope of the tent and fell to the ground.

Jack was a hundred yards away with a mass of PODs—nearly all of them—staring gravely at the tent. He waved Milton and Moondog forward with his lanky arms.

"Beat it out, Popsicle!" he yelled. "The sky is falling!"

Milton turned around to see the towering tent crumple behind him. Moondog grabbed Milton's hand, and the two ran briskly as Savage Bumble's Tragical Confusement Park collapsed in a fluttering heap of shredded canvas skin and splintered wooden bone.

Panting, Milton surveyed the PODs' shopping carts.

They were bulging with exotic new wares—a bewilder-beast pelt and a creepy ventriloquist dummy, for instance. This motley group of wandering phantoms was many things—eccentric, spooky, touchy—but one thing it wasn't was wasteful.

"Where did those big sucker bugs go?" Milton asked Jack.

The lively POD leader—pushing a cart stacked with jars of Make-Believe Play-fellow souls—looked toward the rumpled mess of tents.

"Just after we, like, scattered, they left us alone and pulled an Amelia Earhart . . . a total disappearing act."

"Well, they sure didn't leave *us* alone," Milton said.

A horrid popping sound came from the crumpled mass of canvas. Milton noticed great lumps pushing up from inside the tent, like five kernels of testy, oversized, parasitic popcorn.

"Sounds like they're trying to feed on those lo-cal locals . . . the wraiths," Moondog said. "That won't keep them occupied for long."

Cody licked beads of sweat away from his upper lip.

"Where should we go?" he asked.

A gust of wind thinned away the clots of mist clinging to the horizon. Milton could see a plump, swollen hill in the distance. Atop the mound was a walled fortress, with what appeared to be a castle hovering above, gently wobbling in the breeze. Greasy smoke billowed out from the fortress's parapets. The tendrils—dense bacony plumes—beckoned with their delicious scent.

Madge, a POD with skin like chapped animal hide, sniffed the air with relish.

"You can't go wrong following the smell of bacon," she remarked as she adjusted the tight denim cutoffs that were a few generations too young for her.

Milton took off his glasses, fogged them with his breath, and gave them a quick swipe with his sleeve.

He squinted through a thinning patch of mist until an arched gate came into focus. The gate was, for all appearances, a gaping golden mouth. Two bulging brass tubes, like long, shiny sausages, were welded into lips, while the inside of the wide portal was lined with sharp, polished spades resembling teeth. Milton could just make out words written on the golden arch above: UNWELCOME TO BLIMPO. ZILLIONS AND ZILLIONS SERVED.

"Blimpo!" Milton exclaimed. Blimpo was the circle of Heck reserved for *well-upholstered* children. It was undoubtedly where Milton's best friend, Virgil, had been sent after Milton's escape from Limbo. This was the friend who had sacrificed any chance he had of leaving Heck so that Milton *could*. Ever since, Milton's memories of his big-hearted friend had been tainted with guilt.

And, just as wiping a smudge from his glasses had

brought Blimpo into focus, suddenly all of the shape-less thoughts and feelings crowding Milton's head and heart came together with crisp, clear urgency.

"I need to get in there," Milton said.

Moondog laughed.

"You want to break *into* Blimpo? What are you, a glutton for punishment?"

Milton, his eyes bright, smiled.

"Maybe," he replied. "I just know that I have a big friend in there who I left behind, and I owe him a big favor. I also know that I'm not doing anyone any good out here."

Jack put his hand on Milton's shoulder.

"You're either very brave or you just flipped your wig, Popsicle. Maybe that's what bravery is all about: just not knowing any better."

The air seemed to split with the sound of tearing canvas. Milton spun around to see the flea-ticks lashing out at the fallen big top with their barbed legs.

"Those suckers are done with the diet platter," Moondog said. "And they want some *serious* food."

Jack nodded and turned to the mob of PODs look-ing to him for direction.

"We're cutting out!" he yelled.

The PODs surged away from the remains of Savage Bumble's Tragical Confusement Park in a single-file line, slogging up the swell along a path outlined by dead briars. A sign nestled in a gap of the hedge read

The smell of bacon grew headier with every step. Milton could see something surrounding the bulging mound of Blimpo up ahead: a moat of some kind. From his vantage point, it appeared to be filled with a shimmering pink, undulating liquid. However, with every step, the liquid looked more like . . . *meat*. And, as the group of vagabonds neared, Milton could hear lapping rumbles and moans, like a million empty, protesting stomachs.

Moondog surveyed the moat with his sightless eyes. "Someone's been sneaking a peek at my nightmare journal," he muttered.

Milton neared the moat and gasped. Filling the chasm surrounding Blimpo were hundreds of glistening pink zombielike creatures. Their gaping, toothless mouths were in constant motion—like newly hatched chicks at the sight of a mother bird returning to the nest—and their round, bulky bodies were covered with glistening bumps. The creatures climbed over one another, trying to free themselves from the moat, but kept sliding back into the pit, giving the chasm the look of a lava lamp bubbling with mewling meat.

A POD toward the end of the procession screamed. Milton whipped his head around. Behind them in the distance, he could see several fat, dark blobs hopping in the mist above the flattened confusement park.

"Well," Moondog sighed, "it looks like we are royally—"

"*Food*," interrupted Jack, who had been staring at the moat, deep in thought.

"What was that?" Milton asked.

"We're food . . . or at least *you* are," he explained. "But food can either be a meal or . . . *bait*."

"Oh, I get it," Moondog said, rubbing his beard and nodding.

"Can someone fill me in, then?" Milton said.

"You'll lead the stampede," Moondog said. "Get those hopping nasties snapping at your heels, right to the edge of the moat, then . . ."

"*Then?*" Milton asked.

"Then you either turn on a dime or get drawn and quartered."

Jack hopped up on top of his cart and yelled through his cupped hands.

"PODs!" he shouted. "I suggest we make like a tree and leave!"

Jack leaped down and pushed his cart off toward the chasm, his loyal phantoms close behind, kicking up clouds of dust that whorled across the horizon in little twisters. Milton, startled by the sudden burst of speed, raced to join Jack, who whooped with excitement, sounding as exhilarated as Milton was frightened.

Dark shadows flashed before them. Milton looked above at the uniform haze that served as "sky" in this realm: a murky, perpetual twilight, or dawn, depending on your outlook. The flea-ticks were hopping in great leaping strides alongside a few terrified phantoms at the back of the line. They did indeed only have eyes—and red, creepy ones at that—for Milton.

The roiling chasm was now only a dozen yards away.

"You gotta make like an egg and . . . scramble," Jack said as he sprinted onward. "But, before you go, here . . ."

Jack held out his pendant to Milton.

"Just a way of getting in touch with me," Jack continued. "If you ever need us . . . just rub the pendant. That seems to activate it. Then Divining Rod can lead us straight to you."

"Thanks," Milton said as he took the pendant and held it tightly in his hand.

"Now it's time to . . . fall back, Popsicle," Jack explained. "One cart at a time . . . until you're the last. Take my cart and then, when you're right at the lip staring down at the big pink uglies, push it over and make yourself scarce . . . ball yourself up and hide in the dust."

"You make it sound . . . so easy," Milton replied, panting.

"Hey, life and death are easy," Jack replied. "It's us crazy cats who do the living and dying that make it all complicated. Now, don't lose my pendant, see? It's a *borrow.* I'll see you soon, and you can lay it back on me, got it?"

Milton nodded while he quickly slipped the necklace over his head, never breaking stride. He took Jack's shopping cart and fell back. Cart by cart, the shiny gray snake of PODs coiled along the chasm's edge. The flea-ticks hopped closer, becoming more erratic, confused by the clouds of dust and bacon smoke. Milton leaned into the cart and ran for all he was worth.

Milton's pendant dangled into the barbed-metal mesh around the lip of Jack's cart. He tried to raise his head for one last glance at the colossal parasites pursuing him, but the pendant caught on a gnarled tangle of spikes. The shopping carts ahead began veering abruptly to the left, one by one, until Milton was only a few yards away from the moat's edge. Sweat trickled into his eyes as he struggled to tug himself free. Finally, the chain broke. Milton shot a frantic look over his shoulder. The flea-ticks were crowded together, a dozen yards away, in one nasty, bristly lump, fighting over which would be the one to take Milton as its prize. Their red eyes smoldered, crazed with bloodlust. Milton could see, from his unfortunate vantage point, that each of the creatures had a collar around its neck with the inscription THIS FLICK PROPERTY OF HECK. IF LOST CALL 1-976-666-BUBB.

"Bubb!" Milton shouted as he shoved Jack's cart into the pit of globby, glistening pink creatures. He dug his sneakers into the dirt and fell down to the ground in a great cloud of dust.

Coiled up in a ball with his borrowed navy peacoat pulled up over his head, Milton peeked above. The five fat, monstrous parasites sailed overhead, as if in slow motion, and plunged into the pit. Milton crawled to the edge of the chasm and peered with horror at the gruesome scene.

The flicks' harpoon mouths stuck into the sides of the ravenous, roly-poly creatures in the moat. They swelled as they fed, stretching to capacity until their skin became translucent. The flicks tried to flee, but the slimy creatures in the pit held on to them—trying to eat what was eating *them*—until the flicks popped like balloons.

A wave of stink gushed out of the chasm, like someone had put moldy cauliflower and skunk blood in a big blender and set it to *pew*-ree.

"Whoa!" Moondog exclaimed as he helped Milton to his feet. "If that's the smell of victory, I'd hate to get a whiff of defeat!"

8 · TAKEN TO THE CLEANERS

MARLO ANXIOUSLY SCANNED the rows of dinner jackets hanging in Kloven Kleen Do-or-Dry Cleaners. Hundreds of jackets hung on the coiling mechanical rack, all of them—to Marlo's eyes—exactly the same: snazzy and modern, yet with a squared-off, vintage 1950s silhouette.

The demon "helping" her—a jaundiced woman with cobweb hair pulled tightly in a bun—tapped her long, French-manicured talons impatiently on the glass counter.

"Do you have a ticket?" the squat demon asked in a huffy tone, as if Marlo were a particularly stubborn stain that would simply *not* come out. "As you can clearly see, I have more dinner jackets than you've had hot dinners. And the dinners are *always* hot down here. Even if it's cold cuts and vichyssoise."

"Ticket?" Marlo repeated.

"Yes, a *ticket*," the demon grumbled. "A small card with a number printed upon it that matches with a corresponding tag affixed to a particular piece of clothing, giving the holder the legal right to pick up said article of—"

"Yeah, yeah, yeah," Marlo spat back. "I'm taller than you, lady, so don't try talking down to me—you might hurt yourself. I'm just new to this whole dry-cleaning thing, okay? It's always seemed like a big scam to me."

"Maybe that's why there are more dry cleaners per capita down here than anywhere else in the universe," the dry-cleaning demon replied dryly. "Be that as it may, I still need a ticket."

"That's not all you need," muttered Marlo as she opened the modified bowling bag she used as a purse.

Marlo had been sent on her first errand for the Big Guy Downstairs so quickly that she had barely enough time to fill her bag with the junk Farzana handed her and her head with Farzana's stuttered orders. Marlo *did* seem to remember something about a tick-tick-ticket.

"Here," she said, handing the irritating demon garment worker the stub she had found from the bottom of her—in Madame Pompadour's words—*gauche* bag.

The demon scrutinized it.

"It's torn," she replied, holding the ticket in front of Marlo's face. "Every ticket is supposed to have three numbers. This only has two. Number six-six . . ."

Marlo sighed. "Can't you just check everything between six-six-zero and six-six-nine?" she replied. "Wouldn't that be something covered by, oh, I don't know . . . *your job?*"

The demon growled—not a grumble from someone being grouchy, but a deep guttural rumble.

"And did I mention that this was for . . . *the Big Guy Downstairs?*"

The demon gasped, then tried to hide her shock with a halfhearted chuckle, which was all the woman could manage, having only half a heart. Marlo could slowly feel her confidence coming back, now that she was away from Madame Pompadour's icy *haute* clutches.

"If I had a penny for every time someone tried that one on me," the demon replied, shaking her puffy head like a wasp's nest in a storm. "I'd have . . . a lot of cents."

"Well, if you have any *sense* left, then I suggest you bring me ten coats . . . *now,*" Marlo said defiantly. She wasn't going to let anything, especially not some dried-up dry cleaner, blow her very first errand as the devil's Infern-in-training.

The demon stalked back to the racks and jabbed a red button several times with her talon. She yanked ten dinner jackets from the mechanized rack, stormed back to Marlo, and threw the jackets down on the counter. The demon glared at Marlo through wicked slits.

"Okay, *little girl,*" she hissed. "Which is yours?"

The jackets—fine wool sharkskin in nightmare-black yet still strangely iridescent—were *exactly* the same.

"Can't I just take them all and return—"

"Do you have ten tickets?" the demon spat back.

"Well . . . no. Not exactly."

"Then you, well . . . *can't,*" the demon mocked. "*Exactly* . . . unless . . ."

"Unless what?"

The demon leaned her waxy yellow face close to Marlo.

"Unless you'd like to play Let's Fake a Deal!" the demon squealed, clapping her talons together with excitement. "Where I put a receipt in one of the jackets and, if you guess correctly, you win!"

Marlo's face crinkled with skepticism.

"Win what?"

"All of the jackets!"

Marlo rubbed her chin in contemplation. "And what if I lose?" she asked dubiously.

The demon smiled, her fangs as yellow as her face. "You *still* win!"

"Win what?"

The demon laundress extended her flabby arms grandly.

"You get to run your very own dry cleaners for all eternity!" she cooed.

Marlo snorted. If she had drunk chocolate milk within the last twenty-four hours, it surely would have shot out of her nose.

"What idiot would play a game like *that*?!" she replied.

The demon deflated with an unfortunate, audible hiss. "It seemed like a good idea at the time," she replied sadly.

Marlo had no idea what to do, not that that had ever stopped her before. Suddenly, she was struck by a flash of less-than-divine inspiration.

"Isn't six-six-six the sign of the beast or something?" Marlo commented. "Like, the devil's special number? I had an album called *Smack Your Apocalypse* by a band called Six-six-six that was always singing about that kind of creepy stuff."

The demon sighed. Her breath smelled like a bowl full of corn nuts and ranch dressing forgotten under the seat of an old car.

"Number six-six-six is here to remove a dark red stain that I am hoping is wine."

"And the rest?"

The demon glanced at the tags. "The same."

Marlo blew a strand of blue hair out of her face. Normally she'd just go with her instincts. But she didn't want to screw this up.

"I'd like to use a lifeline," Marlo said as she fished out her new compact phone.

The demon laundress shook her head.

"No cell phones . . . and that's my final answer."

Marlo nervously chewed an already-nibbled nail as she eyed the clock on the wall.

"Fine, I'll take this one," she said, grabbing number six-six-six.

"Not so fast," the demon said, snatching back the jacket.

"Oh, right," Marlo replied, handing her the credit card.

The demon ran the card but continued to clutch the devil's dry cleaning.

"Well?" Marlo said. "Can I take it now or what?"

The demon looked behind her at a sign by the clock that read EXCELLENT QUALITY ONE-HOUR SERVICE.

"As the sign says, we offer excellent quality one-hour service," the demon explained, "and you've only been here ten minutes, so I'll have to continue serving you for another fifty minutes."

Marlo's dark eyes bulged.

"You did *not* just say I had to wait another fifty minutes!"

The demon smirked a mouthful of crooked fangs.

"Oh, I most certainly did. I can't breach Kloven Kleen policy. That wouldn't be fair to our customers."

Marlo let out a deep, supremely irked shriek and went to sulk in the waiting area, her arms and brows crossed with a lot of outrage and not a little anxiety.

Marlo bolted into Madame Pompadour's Deception Area, the dinner jacket—enveloped in clear plastic with the words KLOVEN KLEEN ♥S ITS KUSTOMERS written on it—draped across her shoulder. She stopped in front of Farzana's desk, panting.

"I know . . . I'm late . . . but that . . . stuck-up witch . . . doesn't need to know."

Farzana's quivering eyes nearly popped out of her skull. Her pupils gestured to something over Marlo's shoulder.

"She's probably too busy eating live puppies for lunch—"

"Puppies, while delicious, are far too hard to come by down here," Madame Pompadour said from behind Marlo. Marlo jumped. She turned slowly, her head as thick and fuzzy as the lint trap on a Laundromat dryer.

"I—I—I," Marlo stammered.

"Aye-yi-yi?" Madame Pompadour jeered. "What are you, some kind of *bandito*? Is Cinco de Mayo early this year?"

Farzana laughed nervously.

"H-h-ha h-h-ha."

Wow, Marlo thought, *she even* laughs *with a stutter.*

"Miss Daffney," Madame Pompadour hissed, "please refrain from talking until you've had your Beauty Cream!"

"Yes, m-madame," Farzana replied. "It's just that the c-cart hasn't g-gotten here y-yet."

Madame Pompadour grabbed the dinner jacket from Marlo. She ripped off the plastic, wadded it up in her pawlike hand, and tossed it onto Farzana's desk.

"Recycle this. Send it to one of Heck's preschools for a toy."

Farzana nodded. "Yes, m-m-m—"

Madame Pompadour sniffed at the garment with her tiny pink nose. She arched her eyebrows, or would have if she had any, and glared at Marlo with glowing green cobra-cat eyes.

"What is this, Miss Fauster?"

It's a flippin' fudge-covered Christmas tree, Marlo thought to herself. *What does she* think *it is?*

"Um, I'm going to go for *dinner jacket,* madame—"

"Is this some kind of joke?"

"Believe me, I know funnier jokes than this," Marlo answered, trying desperately to keep from trembling. "Like the one played on *you,* having to spend eternity with girls like *me.*"

"This is the wrong jacket," Madame Pompadour replied.

Of course it is, Marlo moaned to herself before replying with exasperation, "But the ticket was torn!"

The edges of Madame Pompadour's lips curled with a sly, nearly imperceptible smile. The imposing, impossibly skinny woman with her perfect skin stretched across her perfect cheekbones gave the jacket another dainty sniff.

"Even if it *was* the right jacket," she continued, "it hasn't had *nearly* enough pungent sulfurous smoke infused into the fabric."

"Infused?" Marlo asked, confused. "Don't you mean *removed*?"

"No. *Infused,*" Madame Pompadour clarified. "And where are the pants?"

Marlo's dead heart stopped.

"P-pants?"

Madame Pompadour tapped her baby-alligator-skin shoes in time with her own impatience.

"I had no idea that stuttering was a contagious condition!" she hissed. "The matching pants. Where are they?!"

Marlo had, unbeknownst to her, backed into Farzana's desk.

"Do *not* tell me that you lost Satan's pants!"

Farzana surreptitiously dialed a number on her compact. The phone on her desk rang.

"H-hello, M-madame Pompadour's office," she answered. Farzana's large, quivering eyes rolled from Marlo to the madame. "Oh . . . yes . . . I'll tell her."

She hung up.

"That was the d-d-dry cleaner," Farzana said. "He said that there was a mix-up and that he was very s-sorry."

Madame Pompadour couldn't decide which of her Inferns to fix her glare fully upon. She sighed, ferociously, so that you could practically smell the potato chips she had licked for dinner the night before. Dragging the coat behind her, she strutted across the room and pulled open a huge closet: bigger than a walk-in, it was more like a *run-in* closet. Inside were dozens of the *exact* same dinner jacket. Madame Pompadour threw the latest one onto the floor.

"Just be sure you don't make another mistake, Miss Fauster," she scolded as she swept past Marlo on the way to her office. "Even if it isn't yours."

Madame Pompadour slammed the leather door behind her—as much as one can slam a plushly upholstered door—leaving, in her wake, a frozen Slurpee of silence.

Marlo turned to Farzana.

"First off, the dry cleaner was a *she* . . . just barely," Marlo said. "Second, there was no way she would have called, and lastly, even if she did, she is physically incapable of uttering the word 'sorry.'"

Farzana chewed her lower lip and reviewed a blank page on her Vilofax.

"So that leaves me with . . . *why*?" Marlo inquired suspiciously.

Farzana's hands thrashed about like freshly caught flounder on the deck of a fishing trawl.

"Well, the m-more I help you out, the sooner I g-get . . ." Farzana faltered, not meeting Marlo's eyes. "Get a new friend."

Marlo wasn't quite buying it; however—as someone whose hobby was stealing—she didn't tend to buy much.

"Hello, young ladies," a stooped, ancient demon interrupted as he pushed a cart of mail and beverages into the Deception Area. "I'm here to deliver the goods . . . or the bads. Mostly the bads."

The hairless creature, his spine like a croquet hoop, trundled over to Farzana's desk. His cart was spilling over with bills, catalogues, hate mail, and pitchers of Beauty Cream. He handed Farzana a glass full of the luminous milk.

"Milk?" he offered, holding a glass out to Marlo.

"Not unless you want me getting sick all over you." Marlo grimaced.

The demon grinned, his face crinkling like a dead leaf in autumn.

"Who's the new girl?" the ancient creature asked Farzana in a leathery croak.

"The name is Nunivyer," Marlo replied. "Nunivyer Bizness."

The demon shrugged.

"Not much use rememberin' their names," he said

as he deposited a small stack of mail onto Farzana's desk. "She goes through them so fast. Still, if this one works out, then you'll be able to—"

Farzana set down her glass of Beauty Cream suddenly and picked up her phone.

"Hello, Madame Pompadour's office," she said loudly, wiping her mouth. "How may I deflect your call?"

Marlo hadn't even heard the phone ring. *Something smells fishy,* she thought.

The old demon farted, munching on a sardine he had fished out of his pocket as he wheeled his cart away from Marlo's desk.

"I'll stop givin' you gals the business and leave you to yours," the demon said over his shoulder. "Always a pleasure meetin' Madame Pompadour's new toys . . . before she breaks them."

"Whatever," Marlo muttered. "Go postal somewhere else."

The decrepit demon lurched his squeaky cart away down the long, winding hall. The plush hallway was carpeted with a wool and brimstone blend that sparked and smoked if you scuffed it just right. It, apparently, led toward the offices of the Powers That Be Evil.

Marlo eyed the mail on Farzana's desk. She loved mail. Especially when it wasn't hers. It was like a mini Christmas. One bundle, in particular, caught her eye.

"What's this?" she asked as she walked over to

Farzana. The package was a long glossy cylinder. It seemed like some kind of magazine, only with a large hollow tube for a spine.

"It's the new issue of *Statusphere* magazine," Farzana explained with a smooth lilt as she sipped her Beauty Cream. "Madame Pompadour is the publisher. It started out as a hobby, a way to relieve stress from running the Infernship program. But now it's been taking up more and more of her time."

"Wow," Marlo said as she picked up the magazine. "I'd hate to see her when she's *stressed*."

Marlo tugged free the gleaming gold ribbon that bound the peculiar magazine together. The pages were shiny blank plastic, and the whole thing was nearly impossible to hold. It was more like a large, space-age roll of paper towels than something you could read.

"I don't get it," Marlo said. "How does it work?"

Farzana sighed as she set down her pen, leaving unfinished her doodle of a two-faced girl with wings flying above a sea of flames.

"First, you put your arm into the spine. The cylinder."

Marlo, her face scrunched up in confusion, slipped her arm through the magazine's tube. The magazine began to hum. Marlo could feel a faint tingle on her forearm and a freaky . . . *tightening*.

"Now, you just sort of clear your mind, and it turns on."

Marlo closed her eyes and thought of her interest in

Girl Scouts, which was the closest thing to absolute nothing she could think of. The magazine sprang to life, like a startled, electric porcupine with pages for quills. Marlo opened her eyes.

Each page of *Statusphere* was a thin, flexible LCD screen displaying a series of gorgeous, glamorous, moving images. It wasn't just a magazine; it was like wearing a carousel of constantly updated fashion movies. *It's creepy,* Marlo thought as the tube constricted around her arm. *It's like* I'm *the battery that powers it.*

"But why?" Marlo asked. "It's really cool and all, but why not just a regular magazine?"

Farzana eyed the magazine on Marlo's forearm with unease.

"Madame Pompadour says that a fashion magazine is *out* of fashion as soon as it hits the stands. *Statusphere* actually keeps up with every fad and trend in *real time.*"

"Hmm," Marlo murmured as she walked back to her desk, transfixed by the constant parade of bored, skinny women in size-triple-zero dresses, with the occasional hot, sullen guy in the latest suit thrown in for good measure.

"The format," Farzana continued as she slipped on a pair of surgical gloves and carefully sliced open a smoking letter, "also allows for some . . . *interactive* elements."

Farzana shot Marlo a quick, nervous look before returning to her duties.

"She probably won't need you until lunch," she continued. "You should check it out."

Marlo flipped the pages and stopped at one with the flashing headline: IS MARLO FAUSTER A HIDEOUS TROLL? A STATUSPHERE QUIZ!

The page was divided in two, with the quiz on one side and—to Marlo's surprise—a picture of Marlo on the other.

"But how?" she mumbled before her mind grew fuzzy, and, suddenly, all she could think about was how she'd give anything to be like the girls in the magazine: conventionally yet impossibly pretty.

9 · A DISGUSTING DISGUISE

"THEY'RE PURE APPETITE," Moondog said as he faced the pit of creatures, taking them in with his mind. "I'm not registering any intelligence whatsoever. We're talking sack-of-hammers, box-of-hair, twelve-shy-of-a-dozen-scale ignorance. They're basically just animated suits of skin, looking for something to eat."

Milton, still quaking from his brush with being a flea-tick's snack, stared into the chasm as the creatures blindly crawled and slipped over one another, flailing for food.

"How come they don't just eat each other?" he wondered aloud.

"Well," Moondog said, trying to wave the air clear, "apparently there's nothing in those blubbering beasties but a whole lot of bad, bad gas. Guess that keeps them from going all cannibalistic, you know: not wanting to have a fart-to-fart nosh on one another."

Jack walked over to Milton and bundled him up with a bewilderbeast skin.

"Here's some primitive drape for you, Popsicle," he said. "To keep the shivers from delivering."

Milton gawked at the strange, shimmering pelt. He stroked the peculiar fur of the rugged bewilderbeast hide.

"Hmmm," Milton pondered, gazing into the pit. "Those things are empty on the inside but hungry all over. Maybe I could use them as some kind of . . . disguise."

He studied the golden gate near the cluster of edgy PODs. It was separated from Blimpo by the moat of creatures.

"A way to walk into Blimpo undetected."

Milton, filled with the energy that arrives with a dangerous new idea, bounded toward Cody's shopping cart. Inside, tucked among vintage comic books and camping supplies, were bungee cords and coat hangers.

"Do you mind?" Milton asked as he rifled through the cart.

Cody shrugged his shoulders. *"Mi junko es tu junko."*

Milton twisted the coat hanger into a hook.

Jack clapped his hands together.

"Looks like our little Popsicle is going fishing!"

Milton scooted to the edge of the chasm on his belly, holding a rope of knotted bungee cords, one end tied to Cody's shopping cart, the other hooked to the bewilderbeast hide. Milton slowly cast the balled pelt into the chasm, twitching the bait to make it seem alive. Within seconds, several of the round pink creatures were clamoring over one another to get closer, staring at the bewildering ball stupidly. Suddenly, one stretched its mouth wide and galumphed toward the bait, swallowing it in one great gulp.

"Now!" Milton yelled.

Cody yanked his cart backward, hoisting the hungry beast up and over the lip of the chasm.

The bungee cord snaked out of the creature's great mouth. Milton gazed into its eyes. *It's like peering into a hollow jack-o'-lantern with the candle snuffed out*, he thought.

Jack stepped toward it and drew a bowie knife tucked beneath his belt.

"I'm guessing you won't have the stomach for this," he said to Milton.

"You guess right," Milton replied, turning away.

Jack knelt down beside the creature and went at it with a series of precise sweeps of his blade.

"I was on the road a lot . . . up there," Jack explained in between grunts. "You pick up a lot of odd skills living off the land. It wasn't always pretty . . . but it sure was beautiful."

Seconds later, there was a great gush of gas.

"Whoa," said Cody, pinching his nose, "that fart has more personality than most people I know!"

Jack scowled at Cody while Milton tread hesitantly toward the deflated-yet-still-quivering creature. He gawked at the shuddering suit of skin.

"Is it dead?" Milton asked.

Jack shrugged his shoulders. "I'm not even sure if this thing was ever, like, *alive*."

He poked it with the hilt of his knife. It recoiled, vaguely, like a worm. Jack leveled his deep dark eyes at Milton.

"You sure you want to do this, kiddo?"

Milton shivered and frowned.

"'Want' isn't exactly the right word," he replied. "But I know I should at least try. I have to."

Moondog sidled up to Milton to gawk at the meaty rug wriggling on the ground.

"A great philosopher named Plato once said, *'Do or do not. There is no try.'*"

"I'm pretty sure that was Yoda," Milton replied.

"Who's Yoda?" Jack asked.

"A little green puppet wizard," Milton replied. "He made sense by *not* making sense. You guys would love him."

With more than a trace of disgust, Milton knelt

down beside the skin. He slipped it on slowly like a bologna jumpsuit.

"Eww!" he exclaimed as he pulled it up over his pants and, finally, over his head. "It's even worse than trying on suits with my mom."

The creature's flesh slurped around Milton until he was snugly inside.

Madge stepped up to Milton with a box chock-full of Duck and Cover Girl cosmetics. She scrutinized him.

"Well, I like a challenge," she said in a husky smoker's voice as she opened the box. "You'll be my Sistine Chapel. C'mon."

She led Milton, who staggered like Frankenstein's monster, to her shopping cart. It was a thrift store on wheels, overflowing with mismatched clothes and accessories.

Madge sifted through the clothing with deft authority. A thousand possible clothing combinations flashed in her head until she finally settled on a baggy navy-blue terry jogging suit, black socks, sandals, and a red World Wrestling Entertainment cap.

"So this is your artistic statement?" Milton said as he ogled the ugly collection of clothes.

Madge folded her overly tanned arms and scowled.

"I wasn't given much to work with," she grumbled. "Actually, I was given *too* much to work with, which is why I went for coverage."

Madge rifled through her makeup case and handed

Milton a large tube of Maximum Factor Industrial-Strength beige cover-up.

"Put this all over your . . . um . . . *body*. I hope I have enough."

After fifteen minutes of painting, tweezing, prodding, shaping, and—above all—camouflaging Milton's lumpy suit of borrowed flesh, Madge held a hand mirror up to his face.

"I should have had you sign a waiver first, but I've done all I can."

Milton examined his face. He grimaced, and about two seconds later, the face in the mirror grimaced back. Milton looked like a mummy wrapped in lasagna instead of bandages. But, he did have to admit, he at least looked human. Gruesome, like a few hundred miles of bad, unpaved road, but like a boy. His face felt, though, as if it had been injected with a dentist's office full of Novocain.

"Smile!" Moondog said as he trained an old Polaroid camera at Milton and flashed his picture.

With several quick, artistic scissor-snips, Moondog cut the photograph into a small square.

"This should do nicely," he mumbled as he set the square expertly on a document, blew on it, and then clipped it onto a folder.

"Here you go," Moondog said as he handed Milton the folder. *"Jonah."*

"Jonah?" Milton replied through thick, flapping lips.

He examined the folder through the clear gelatin of the creature's eyes. Beneath his hideous picture was a professional-looking dossier, of sorts.

JONAH GRUMBY
Age: 12
Cause of death: necrotizing fasciitis
(flesh-eating disease) and edema (swelling)
Soul reading: obvious propensity toward
gluttony; lack of willpower
Assessment: Blimpo

Yours with Barely Contained Civility,
Bea "Elsa" Bubb
Principal of Darkness

"Nice," Milton said, impressed—though his face had trouble conveying that. "Right down to . . . *her* . . . signature. How it tries so hard to be dainty and professional, but her vile, despicable personality oozes out like—"

"Not a fan, I see," Moondog interjected. "Anyway, if you *do* manage to get in, these should help grease the wheels of bureaucracy. So, what's the plan, Stan? I mean, *Jonah?*"

Milton stood up, feeling as if he were in a space suit made of hamburger. What creeped him out most of all was the creature's tendency to constrict around his midsection in slow spasms, like he was a caribou inside a Winnebago-sized anaconda.

"My plan is cunning in its simplicity."

Jack and Moondog looked on with anticipation as Milton shambled toward the golden gates of Blimpo.

"I ring the bell," Milton explained, pointing to a small, clown-shaped speaker with a red button for a nose. A rustling in the pit caught their attention, and they all looked down.

Several creatures jostled Jack's upturned shopping cart at the bottom of the chasm. The creatures, not registering it as food, rumbled past it.

Milton glanced over at Jack, who eyed his heap of personal effects with a sad, faraway fondness. His pendant glittered like a distant star.

"I'm really, really sorry," Milton offered. Jack's normally happy-go-lucky features were crinkled and sad, like wadded-up gift wrapping. "Your pendant got caught."

Jack nodded solemnly.

"It's cool . . . it was all jelly and died for a noble cause," he said. "Besides, what would I do with a few dozen jars of Make-Believe Companions? I, like, have problems enough relating to my *real* companions as it is."

Milton stepped up to the gate. He studied the golden archway, then pressed the shiny red nose with his newly pudgy forefinger.

"Hello and unwelcome to Blimpo," squawked a bored voice through the small speaker just above the buzzer. "How may I waste your time today?"

Milton cleared his throat, no easy feat considering he now had two.

"I was just . . . dropped off by the stagecoach. I'm a new kid, here to endure unspeakable torment for all eternity, or until I turn eighteen, whichever comes first."

The voice sighed, which—due to the tinny speaker—sounded like a cold shower of static.

"I wasn't expecting a drop-off."

Milton looked anxiously over at Jack and Moondog.

"Well," Milton said, proceeding with caution, "I suppose we could impose upon the principal—who was particularly testy this morning, I might add—and have her send another stagecoach, at great personal expense, only to turn it right back around after my admission has been cleared—"

"Yes, well, oh, here it is," the voice lied. "I'll lower the bridge over the Gorge and have someone fetch you right away."

A section of the fortress slowly fell away, stretching toward the gate.

"You guys should scram," Milton said.

Jack gave a quick, frantic wave of his hand. The waiting phantoms moved their shopping carts into formation before wending away. Madge, Cody, and several other haggard phantoms flashed Milton quick smiles before staring intently at the road in front of them.

"Thank you," Milton said humbly, shaking Jack's hand. He moved over to Moondog and gave him a big hug.

"Whoa, little guy," Moondog exclaimed gently as a tear leaked from his sightless eye. "Please don't squeeze the shaman."

"We need to split, like the seams on a sumo wrestler's jeans," Jack said abruptly as the bridge, resembling a long tongue made of red planks, lowered, hitting the outside of the gate with a resounding thud.

Jack turned to Milton as he brushed the dust off his khakis. "Don't sweat the clown suit, kiddo," he said with a smirk. "All the best of us are laughed at in this nightmare land."

Jack and Moondog bustled away to meet their fellow PODs.

Soon, the phantasmic caravan was nothing but a long, silvery eel in the distance, slithering away until the sickly haze engulfed it.

The gates opened with a horrid metal-on-metal screech.

A demon in a slick, padded beige bio-suit and mirrored helmet strutted out to meet Milton. Dangling from its neck was what looked like a turkey leg with intricate notches cut into the bone. The demon stopped just outside the door and considered Milton.

"Youch," it said through its helmet. "You're so ugly, you could turn milk into yogurt just by looking at it."

"And hello to you," Milton replied as he and the demon crossed the bridge. The creatures below writhed and hopped with dumb excitement.

"What's with the necklace . . . and the suit?" Milton asked.

"You like my birdie bling?" the demon said as it played with the poultry hanging from its neck. "It's a Turnkey leg, the keys to the kingdom. And the suit is pure tofu: *just in case.*"

The demon looked down into the Gorge with a mix of disgust and fear. "Even the Pangs won't touch the stuff."

Pangs, Milton thought. *So that's what those hungry meat creatures are called.*

Milton crossed the tongue bridge into the open maw of a doorway and was swallowed up by Blimpo in one quick gulp.

10 · NOT JUST ANOTHER KITTY FACE

Is Marlo Fauster a Hideous Troll? A *Statusphere* Quiz!

Is Marlo as gross as everyone says she is? Does her body look like it was designed as a dare between Dr. Frankenstein and the seven dwarves? Is she so ugly that when she walks by a bathroom, all the toilets flush? Find out!

1. Marlo needs plastic surgery.
   A. True
   B. Modern science is not currently skilled
      enough to deal with the problem that is her.

2. Marlo avoids mirrors because:
   A. Her vision is 20/20 and her face is
      nasty/nasty.
   B. She can't afford to replace them all.

3. Marlo's butt is so big that:
   A. They still can't find the last chair she sat on.
   B. She's actually taller when she sits down.

4. No matter how much Marlo diets,
   exercises, or uses makeup:
   A. It just doesn't take.
   B. It's like putting whipped cream and
      chocolate jimmies on a pile of dog poop.

5. Marlo is to popular as:
   A. Fish are to skydiving.
   B. Egypt is to ice hockey.

Marlo's hands squeezed the LCD page until it crinkled in little puckers of refracted light. Next to the quiz in the magazine's video sidebar, Marlo's image stared back at her: contorted, blemished, puffy, and growing homelier with every question. But she couldn't take her eyes off herself. It was more like the magazine was reading *her* than the other way around.

What could anyone possibly see in me? she wondered.

Suddenly, like a life preserver thrown into a lake of self-pity, a name floated to the surface of her mind. Zane Covington! The cool, moody boy she had met in Rapacia who had not only helped Milton evade capture when the Grabbit's ceremony went south, but also saved him from becoming a solid-gold, Milton-shaped statue at the freaky gilding grip of King Midas. Marlo could almost see Zane's deep brown eyes now: admiring eyes that saw something in Marlo that she couldn't see in herself.

She felt around the pocket of her vintage waistcoat and slipped out the note that Zane had written her before she was sent down here to begin her Infernship program.

M, the note began. Marlo could feel a bubble of excitement float up from her toes to her chest, where it mingled with the strangely pleasant nausea that spilled out from the pit of her stomach.

U R 2 Kool.
Z

Sure, it wasn't exactly poetry—not like *I wish I had enough magic dust to sprinkle away your problems, all except the problem of me,* from "Dust2Dust" by the Funeral Petz—but to Marlo, this glorified text message was packed tight with sentiment. Just clutching the note helped to loosen the doubt that gripped Marlo's bones. It made her feel as if her heart were leaping through hoops of fire. As if—

"Hey, new girl, or whatever your name is."

Marlo's knees slammed into the underside of her desk. Standing above Marlo was a thin brunette with highlights, glowering down at her with a look that could freeze boiling salsa.

"I'm here to see *Madame Pompadour*," the girl said. Marlo noticed that, despite the girl's cozy-as-a-crutch-made-of-icicles demeanor, she was scared. Even her solid-gold grenade-pin earrings quivered.

"The name's Tara," Marlo replied. "Tara Yurfaceov."

"She's expecting you," Farzana interjected, having suddenly materialized by Marlo's side.

I'll have to tie a bell around that girl, Marlo thought as Farzana hurried the girl into Madame's office. Just before Madame Pompadour's imposing door closed behind the girl, one of her earrings fell to the carpet, holding the door slightly ajar.

Farzana returned to her desk and picked up the phone.

"Who was that?" Marlo asked.

"B-Beulah Heard," Farzana replied as she dialed a number. "She was the d-devil's latest Girl Friday the Thirteenth. You know . . . *what we're all training to b-be.* But he goes through them like p-potato chips. They're never quite right. And Madame P-Pompadour is going to have a hissy fit about it!"

Farzana swiveled her chair away from Marlo and began whispering into her phone.

"I'm c-calling about my application . . ."

A thought crossed Marlo's mind—crafty and fleeting like a possum darting across a freeway in the dead of night. The phrase "know thine enemy" popped into her head. And, even though she wasn't completely sure what "thine" meant, Marlo knew that if you wanted to get the best of someone—say, Madame Pompadour—then you had better do *your* best to know everything about them.

Marlo padded across the carpet, carefully, so as not to distract Farzana from one of her totally-not-work-related phone calls. She pressed her palms against Madame Pompadour's door and gently pushed it open, as close to "barely open" as possible. Marlo scrunched one eye shut and peered into the office with the other.

Beulah stood trembling before Madame Pompadour. Despite her expensive outfit—cropped leather jacket, empire-waist dress, and leather ankle booties—it was clear that the devil's former assistant was being dressed *down*.

"Explain that again to me, Miss Heard?" Madame Pompadour growled. "Perhaps *I'm* the one who *mis-heard*. It sounded as if you said that the Big Guy Downstairs relieved you of your duties after *just six days*?

Considering that I spent *six months* training you, that's hardly a worthwhile return on my investment, is it?"

Beulah's knees knocked together like two wood-peckers kissing.

"No, ma'am . . . *madame!*" Beulah sputtered. "It isn't. I mean, yes, he relieved me, and, no, it isn't a worthwhile return on your investment. I . . . I don't know what I did wrong. He was just so . . . so . . . ."

Beulah wept into her hands.

"Horrible!"

Madame Pompadour batted a small ball of pink yarn back and forth on her desk.

"That's pretty much his job. Being horrible. In fact, he holds the patent on 'horrible.' He just mixed 'horrid' with 'terrible' and *voila!* It's nothing to take personally. I, on the other hand, take *everything* personally. Especially my reputation as a cultivator of first-rate Inferns."

"But I did everything I was trained to do! He said that I lacked spunk and fire . . . that I was blank, unin-teresting, and dim. As if! Then he compared me to a couple of weird animals I'd never heard of—a toady and a sycophant!"

Madame Pompadour made a sound that was the exact opposite of a purr. More of a *rrup.* "Did he tell you what he *was* looking for?" she grumbled.

Beulah wiped away a streak of mascara running down her cheek. "He said he wanted an assistant with sass . . . with vim and vinegar."

"You mean 'vigor.'"

"No, he specifically said 'vinegar.' And that he wanted someone to take under his wing."

Madame Pompadour snorted. "That's ridiculous," she chided. "He hasn't had wings for thousands of years."

She leaned back in her chair and contemplated the tiny glass sparrows that hung from her chandelier.

"So the Big Guy Downstairs wants an assistant that reminds him of . . . *him*? Difficult . . . opinionated . . . exuding a distinct sense of style. But someone like *that* would be hard to mold, hard to control. It would be a delicate balancing act to get someone brash and bold enough for him to feel a connection with while *still* maintaining complete control so that I can pull the little poppet's strings. . . ."

Madame Pompadour looked down her delicate nose at Beulah.

"You still here? You're yesterday's catnip. Now hand me back your compact."

Beulah, blubbering, placed her tortoiseshell compact case on Madame Pompadour's desk. The madame snatched it up and flicked it open.

"You girls are my eyes down there," she muttered. "How can I keep tabbies on the Big Guy Downstairs if he keeps removing my moles?"

Madame Pompadour rubbed a beauty mark on her chin before jabbing a series of eye-shadow palettes in a particular sequence. The mirror flickered with images: a dreary marble lobby; a burnished bronze desk; and the occasional flash of a hulking, horned beast in a dapper, pin-striped suit. Mostly, though, the compact's mirror was filled with images of Beulah either crying, wringing her hands, or drinking Beauty Cream.

Madame Pompadour was distracted by a doleful sniff. Beulah hovered between the desk and the door like a forlorn fly caught in a draft. Madame Pompadour tossed the compact in her bottom drawer, where it joined a colony of similar tortoiseshell surveillance devices.

"Another shuttle bus should be leaving my office for the door in fifteen seconds," Madame Pompadour said crisply, as if each word had been starched and creased. "Make sure that you're on it, back to Lipptor or Precocia, or wherever I made the mistake of recruiting you from."

"SNIVEL!" Beulah sobbed as she ran for the door. "It was *Snivel!*"

Marlo bolted back to her desk just as Beulah fled the office.

The phone rang, a weird line that had never rung before—not on Marlo's shift, anyhow—a line labeled VTV. Marlo slipped on her headpiece and punched the line.

"Hello, Madame Pompadour's office. How may I deflect your . . . *of course.*"

"Screepy," Marlo mumbled as she put the call

through, some frostbitten biddy wanting to be transferred to Madame Pompadour's "vanity," of all places. Marlo glanced at Madame's door: still open just a smidge, thanks to Beulah's fallen grenade-pin earring.

I just hope her ear doesn't explode, Marlo pondered as she crept back to Madame Pompadour's door. *I know that something's going down in Kitty Town. It's just a matter of figuring out* what.

The spade-shaped mirror behind Madame Pompadour's desk had unfolded into a reflective confessional booth of sorts. The woman's perfect oval face was split into three—*just more to loathe,* Marlo thought to herself—before her reflection dissolved, joined by another, similarly self-absorbed face.

"Good afternoon, Lady Lactose," Madame Pompadour said with a wink as the reflection before her finished its preening. "Might I say that we both look *marvelous*?"

A woman with a milky complexion curled her cherry-red lips into a smile. *Who's the ice-cream cone?* Marlo thought.

"How sweet," cooed Lady Lactose, smoothing her creamy, soft serve–styled bouffant.

Marlo wasn't sure what the stuck-up lady's story was exactly, but she assumed it was a trashy read with a wicked ending. Marlo scratched her forearm. Even watching someone as milky as Lady Lactose gave Marlo an allergic reaction.

"Thanks to the miracle of VaniTV, we can discuss our little *endeavor:* perfect face to perfect face," Madame Pompadour purred. "Firstly, the latest issue of *Statusphere* has proved to be our biggest seller to date, and this success has put a long-cherished dream of mine on the fast track—that is, to turn *Statusphere* into its own VaniTV network."

Lady Lactose's smile was a banana split of delight. "You've outdone yourself!" she cooed. "But how, exactly, would this all work?"

Madame Pompadour's dainty paws worried apart the ball of yarn on her desk. She weaved the string into a cat's cradle.

"It's revolutionary, actually. Every second of our twenty-four-hour, seven-days-a-week programming will be piped through every mirror in the underworld."

Lady Lactose gasped. Madame Pompadour chuckled.

"Yes, everything from compacts to oversized wall mirrors. It's a way for everyone, everywhere, to get even . . . *closer* . . . to their favorite magazine."

"This sounds like it would require a lot of energy," Lady Lactose said coolly. "The whole point of the DREADmill experiment is to *stockpile* energy, not squander it. We need to hoard enough power so that when DREADmills are installed in every Circle of Heck, we can—when the time is right—wrest power away from the Big Guy Down—"

"Yes, yes," Madame Pompadour said nervously.

"No need to fret yourself into a froth. The Statusphere VaniTV network wouldn't take *away* from the DREAD-mills. Quite the opposite. See, much like the magazine version, VaniTV would feed off the longing, envy, and insecurity of its audience. And this power will not only make us rich, but will also keep us eternally beautiful, keeping that vexing demonization process forever at bay."

Madame Pompadour tinkled the charms on her bracelet.

"It's something I've been perfecting for quite some time," she added. "But now it's ready for *prime* time."

Lady Lactose stirred her tea with her little finger, causing it to lighten.

"Forgive me for losing my cool," she replied. "I'm just under a lot of pressure."

Madame Pompadour licked her thin pink lips.

"Like a can of condensed milk." She smiled. "Not to worry. It's all cream under the bridge. We'll both be having the last lap—I mean, *laugh*—when all this is over. At least I know *I* will . . ."

"What was that?"

"Nothing . . . just saying that I know I will be . . . *delighted* with how you spread VaniTV through your ever-expanding-and-in-want-of-an-elastic-waistband cir-cle. See, I think Blimpo would be the *perfect* test audience for VaniTV. A place where self-loathing runs rampant—literally, in this case—just waiting to be tapped and—"

"Marlo!" Farzana shouted. "What are you d-d-doing?"

Marlo jumped and shut the door reflexively, though the gold grenade-pin earring kept it open a crack.

The faintest of breezes ruffled the small stack of papers sticking out of Marlo's file, which was splayed open atop Madame Pompadour's desk. Madame Pompadour's faultless face clouded with suspicion. Her keen cat ears pricked at the sound of her Inferns squabbling just outside her door.

"You n-never interrupt one of M-Madame P-Pompadour's calls!" Farzana scolded as Marlo made her way back to her desk.

"I thought I heard her choking on a hair ball," Marlo said as she grabbed a pad of paper and a pen.

Madame Pompadour . . . Lady Lactose . . . Statusphere . . . VaniTV . . . DREADmills . . . Blimpo . . . Marlo jotted down.

What does that no-feeling feline have cooking in her Meow Mix? Marlo wondered. *Whatever it is, she's probably keeping the lowdown on the down low . . . as secret as a girl's specially pH-balanced antiperspirant.* In any case, Marlo felt that—for the first time since her Infernship began—she might have the upper hand. Marlo knew *something,* even if she wasn't exactly sure what it was she knew. And knowledge was power. Like electricity. She didn't have to understand how it worked, as long as it *did.*

Meanwhile, Madame Pompadour flicked a switch beneath her desk.

"I'll be in touch, Lady Lactose," she hissed softly as her mirror folded back to its original full, uptight position.

Nothing is going to short-circuit my little power play, she mused as she padded across her office for the door. *And power takes power. That's exactly what they'll all be begging me for after I pull the plug on the underworld.*

Madame Pompadour followed the crack between her door and the jamb until her eyes settled on a shiny gold earring. She knelt down—a surprisingly difficult task in her tight, snakeskin A-line skirt—and examined the grenade pin, then glared at Marlo, scribbling away, through the crack in the door. Marlo looked up and locked eyes with the madame.

Marlo gulped. Madame Pompadour held the pin in her hand, and, judging from her suspicious scowl, the grenade had just been lobbed.

11 · FRIENDS IN WIDE PLACES

MILTON SLID OPEN the curtain of the Blimpo boys' dressing room. Gaping at himself in the mirror, he realized that his appearance had been instantly upgraded from Merely Hideous to Thoroughly Ghastly with a Slight Chance of Projectile Vomit. From his plaid beret with safety orange pom-pom, black-and-white horizontally striped Lycra T-shirt, and neon-green suspenders (which suspended nothing, not even disbelief) down to his triple-corduroy Capri pants, Milton—now Jonah—was so ugly that circus folk would probably pay to see *him*.

The escort demon took off its helmet. Its eyes were dull and coppery, like an old penny at the bottom of the well that had failed to deliver on its promise. The demon regarded Milton with amusement.

"A face that only a blind mother wombat could love. But you're in luck," the demon said unconvincingly. "Just in time for afternoon tea. The Lose-Your-Lunchroom is down the hall."

"The what?"

"*The Blimpo Cafeterium,*" the demon clarified. "It has earned itself a little nickname. You'll soon learn why."

The demon walked away in its slick tofu suit down a fluorescent-lit hallway. Milton stepped out into the hall to follow it but was momentarily stunned as the floor wobbled and "sprang" beneath his newly immense feet. It was like walking across a long trampoline made of old creaking wood. As Milton stepped tentatively across the undulating floor, he was broadsided by his own reflection cast in the gleaming walls. His image was warped like a fun-house mirror: hold the fun. Milton's Jonah disguise—a barely recognizable blob—was distorted into a wider, lumpier, and now-completely-unrecognizable blob.

The demon looked back at Milton over its curdled soybean shoulder.

"Just follow the sound of bellyaching," it chortled wickedly. "There's plenty of that around here."

★ ★ ★

The Cafeterium, or Lose-Your-Lunchroom as the locals called it, was not what Milton expected. It actually looked kind of nice. The tastefully lit room was monopolized by a large oval waterway shuttling little buoyant plates of food. The plates, elegant boats upon closer inspection, were laden with delicious cargo—jumbo grilled hamburgers, towering ice-cream sundaes, apple pie, pizza slices with layers of succulent toppings—leaving port from the kitchen, visible through a small opening in the wall, before embarking on their circuit around the room.

Milton's Pang suit rippled with hunger. He strode toward one of the boats—the SS *BLBTB* (bacon, lettuce, bacon, tomato, and bacon sandwich)—and ham-handedly grabbed the plate before it floated away. Just before he cast the sandwich, boat and all, into his ever-widening mouth, he noticed the sandwich's dull shine, flat coloring, and faint smears of glue around the seams.

"A plastic model," Milton moaned with disappointment as he capsized the sandwich and flung it back into the faux-food regatta. He noticed a small grate in the ceiling, where tufts of flavorful smoke drifted out. Someone snickered from the kitchen.

"That never gets old," muttered an enormous man with a red face like a landslide and a white sagging chef's hat on his head.

Milton, irritable not only from being hungry but also from wearing an uncomfortable disguise that was, in itself, starving, stomped over to the kitchen window. The cramped kitchen was a mess of pots, pans, and large familiar-looking jars. He thought he could detect the faintest whiff of barbecue.

"*Ha-ha,*" Milton said sarcastically. "You're a riot. Is there any *real* food here?"

The cook looked Milton up and down. His chins jiggled like bowls of Mexican jumping bean Jell-O.

"You must be new," the cook replied. "I always remember a face. And if I had seen yours before, I would remember trying to forget it."

Milton was tempted to lob the classic "I'm rubber, you're glue" comeback at the rude, revolting man, but his Pang tongue was more interested in eating than in arguing. The cook grinned, his cheeks a pair of round, shiny, rotten apples.

"Of course there's food," he said. "Wouldn't be much of a Cafeterium without food, now, would it?"

"Great! What do you have?" Milton replied with a glee that surprised himself. "Something sure smells good. . . ."

"You have your choice," the cook replied, shoving a plate through the window. "Bacon and eczema . . ."

Milton gawked sadly at the plate piled high with unappetizing lumps and flakes.

"And my other choice?"

The cook held out a mound of deep-fried carbuncles atop a stale, moldy biscuit in his grimy hands.

Underneath his fingernails was enough dirt to support a small organic vegetable garden.

"Kentucky fried chicken pox on a biscuit."

"What's the biscuit?" Milton asked with trepidation.

"One of Dr. Kellogg's 'Off the Eaten Path Dusted Double Lentil Trail Mix Biscuits,'" the cook replied. "With all the mold, it also acts as its own penicillin, which would come in handy, considering where this biscuit's been—"

"I'm fine, thanks," Milton muttered with disgust.

"Suit yourself," the cook said as he pulled down the blinds of the kitchen window.

Milton turned and ran straight into a pudgy, freckle-faced boy.

"Excuse m—*Virgil!*" Milton exclaimed with joy as he gripped the boy's shoulders.

Milton's best friend backed away suddenly.

"Hey, I like hugs as much as the next guy, maybe more so," Virgil said as he regarded the beast of a boy in front of him, "but usually I reserve them for friends."

Milton recalled he was draped in another creature—one that had been liberally smeared with makeup. He leaned into Virgil and opened his mouth as wide as he could, which was far wider than expected. Virgil gulped and backed away.

"Look, I know we all have big appetites here," Virgil

said, stepping back with his palms facing out. "But let's not do anything we'll both regret. . . ."

"It's me," Milton said as he pressed his face between the Pang's gaping jaws. *"Milton."*

Virgil peered inside the creature's mouth. A grin of recognition spread across his face, until it was suddenly clouded with alarm.

"We got to get you out of there!" Virgil yelped. "I'll try to find some Ipecac or ex-lax—"

Milton put his hand across Virgil's mouth. The chef peered through the kitchen blinds suspiciously.

"I'm in disguise," Milton assured his friend. "The name is *Jonah.*"

Milton tried to wink but wasn't sure if his Pang face had the subtlety for sly gestures.

"I came back to rescue you," he added.

"And you thought you'd get a snack first?" Virgil replied. "Not that I'd blame you or anything. That's what I'd do. You know, to keep my strength up."

Milton's real face blushed, but his hungry Pang mask was unabashed.

"It's just that, I wanted to . . . you know, fit in."

"Well, no one eats here anymore," Virgil said. "Chef Boyareyookrazee was just messing with you. I only came for more napkins. The *real* meal deal is outside. In the hall."

A bell rang, like one of those old triangular dinner bells they used to use back in cowboy times.

"It's time for gym," Virgil said desperately. "If we're late, they'll force us to spend extra time on the DREAD-mill. . . ."

"Gym?" Milton whined. Gym was his least favorite class even when alive. "But I'm starving!"

Virgil wiped a smear of sauce from his cheek. He eyed the cook behind Milton warily.

"I'll set you up with something *dee*-licious after class," he said with a grin, his lips flecked with saliva and his pupils dilated. "Promise. Let's go!"

So Virgil and Milton tromped down the hallway, their footfalls exaggerated by the hollow, bouncing wood floor. They sounded like a thundering two-boy stampede.

I'm in, Milton reflected as he manipulated his abundant, barely controllable body down the hall. *Now it's just a matter of getting out.*

Milton watched their enormous reflections—stretched out, gruesome, and distorted—and felt both of his stomachs sink.

"As easy as smuggling two elephants out of a maximum-security circus," Milton mumbled, discouraged, as he and Virgil pushed open the double-wide doors leading to the boys' locker room.

12 · HEALTH CLUBBED

MILTON AND VIRGIL wrenched themselves into their burlap leggings, like two enormous sausages attempting to slip on their own casings. The marriage of coarse burlap and plump thighs gave birth to a wailing nursery of welts.

"Can you help me with this?" Virgil asked, holding out his black rubber tube top.

Milton nervously cased out the empty locker room. It was pretty much an unspoken rule that one never, *ever* helped another boy with his gym clothes. It was a sure-fire way to guarantee that one's school social calendar would be jam-packed with torment, derision, and—more than likely—wedgies. Milton sighed and grudgingly helped his friend pull on his skintight rubber tube top. Finally, Milton tugged and jerked the smelly piece of synthetic workout gear into place.

The bell rang. Gym class hadn't even begun and Milton was already exhausted. He shambled toward the door. Though he was getting better at operating his Pang, it still performed with a slight lag behind Milton's will, like an old arcade game with an unresponsive joystick. They passed a warped fun-house mirror strategically placed by the exit, with the obvious intention of getting in one last demoralizing dig before the portly boys underwent the full-body anguish of gym. But Virgil—his attitudinal glass perpetually at half full—took a look at himself and shrugged.

"It could be worse," he murmured at the grotesque, contorted image staring back at him. Milton, however, was unrecognizable to himself. The surreal sight of Jonah was like watching someone else's out-of-body experience. He tugged straight his tube top, his reflection doing the same a split second later. Milton was his own puppet—a grossly overweight marionette of meat that was slowly digesting its master. Milton sighed (with Jonah sighing shortly thereafter) as he and Virgil parted the curtain of hanging chains and hooks and stepped into the Gymnauseum.

Beyond the entryway of red-and-black-checkered foam mats was a huge two-story-high open warehouse space filled with rows of peculiar machines. The gray metal contraptions were splayed open, their twin doors like the petals of sinister brushed-steel flowers. Tucked inside each one was an industrial-sized metal hamster wheel.

Demons in white laboratory smocks paced a second-story walkway edging the wall above the Gymnauseum floor. They scrutinized the open area below and scribbled observations on their clipboards. A short man dressed completely in white bounded up a flight of stairs to the walkway. He gripped the banister and smiled down at the children forced to assemble before him.

"Well, well," he clucked as he took in the sheer mass of Blimpo's student body. "And we're all about getting well here, in my Fatness to Fitness Center!"

His eyes—twinkling with a merry madness—settled on Milton and Virgil, who were still lingering in the Gymnauseum entryway.

"Hurry, my boys," he said with crisp, manic exuberance. "This is the only place where haste *doesn't* make waist!"

Milton and Virgil trudged across the foam mats to be further savaged by bad puns and good cheer, no doubt. The mats hissed beneath their feet before slowly refilling the jumbo-sized indentations left by the two boys.

"Remember," Milton reminded his kind-yet-often-naive friend, "I'm Jonah. Got it?"

Virgil nodded. "Yep, I got it. Jonah, like the minor

Hebrew prophet who was called by God to preach in Nineveh but—after disobeying and attempting to escape by sea—was thrown overboard in a storm as a bringer of bad luck and then swallowed up by a giant fish."

Milton stared at his friend, his Pang mouth gaping like a mackerel on the deck of a fishing troller.

"Yeah," Milton replied. "Something like that."

"Gym dandy!" the man in white declared with a clap of his hands. "As many of you know, I am Dr. Kellogg, your health education teacher."

"Kellogg?" Milton whispered to Virgil. "As in cornflakes?"

"Yep." Virgil nodded. "And his cereal isn't the *only* flaky thing about him."

Several blubbery boys collected around Virgil and Milton. Milton now knew what a main course felt like.

"Hey, Virginia. Who's the new kid?" asked a boy with short prickly hair and cheeks so big that he looked like a butt with eyes.

"It's *Virgil*, Hugo," Virgil answered. "And *his* name is Mi . . . um . . . *my* friend. *Jonah*. Jonah, these are the guys. Hugo, Thaddeus, and Gene."

Thaddeus scrunched his scrunched-up face at Milton. His flabby arms stuck out limply at his sides, like a dinosaur frozen in mid jumping jack.

"He looks like something my cat would have

coughed up, only magnified a million times," Thaddeus said.

"Let us not squander our energy on words!" Dr. Kellogg barked, his elfish demeanor more akin to a troll after soaking in a tub of Hyper Viper energy drink. "We must conquer the mouth, the gateway to the body. It gapes open, weak, for far too long—like the doors of a convenience store. The mouth should, instead, open only for healthful foods, such as Hambone Hank's Soul Food—"

A collective "yum" echoed throughout the Gymnauseum.

"—and my Off the Eaten Path Dusted Double Lentil Trail Mix Biscuits."

The "yum" was quickly overtaken and subdued by a chorus of "yucks."

The teacher's eyes narrowed. He scowled at his large pupils through his tiny pupils.

"But they are almost *completely* nuts!" he explained.

"Like you," Hugo muttered.

A wave of poorly stifled giggles passed through the crowd.

"And I will not tolerate snickers!" Dr. Kellogg snapped.

A loud rumbling erupted to Milton's right. Gene rubbed his bulbous belly.

"Mmmm . . . *Snickers*," he muttered with longing.

Dr. Kellogg scanned the group of boys with visible distaste.

"Another outburst like that," the teacher scolded, "and the nurses will administer a round of hot jalapeño colonics. Do I make myself clear?"

Milton forced his Pang suit to nod.

"Yes, sir," the boys replied in terrified unison.

"But let us not waste our precious energy outside of the DREADmills. . . ."

The doctor looked at the white watch on his wrist.

"Speaking of which, demons, please forcibly escort the students to their exorcize session."

The demons eagerly obliged, prodding the boys into the large hamster wheels.

"It's not so bad," Virgil consoled unconvincingly as he was led to the contraption next to Milton, "once you get used to it, that is."

Milton stepped onto the mesh wheel. The sides closed around him as if he were a fly in a metallic Venus flytrap.

"Just, whatever you do, don't fight it!" yelped Virgil over the squeak of the DREADmill's hinged walls.

Milton swallowed, with his Pang suit gulping shortly in kind.

"Don't fight what?!" he yelled.

And with that, the sides of the DREADmill sealed shut, submerging Milton in complete darkness.

13 · WALLOW THE LEADER

WELCOME TO GRIZZLY MALL: FORMER HOME OF THE STATE'S SECOND-LARGEST BEAR-THEMED MARSHMALLOW STATUE! read a banner draped above a massive charred crater, the last place that Milton and Marlo Fauster had stood together on Earth as living, breathing human beings.

Next to the scorched bruin-shaped shadow was a small plaque: COMING SOON: CHRISTO'S SOFT PRETZEL GRIZZLY BEAR TRIBUTE TO THE MEMORY OF MILO AND MARGO FOSTER ~~AND DAMON RUFFINI~~.

Above the mall commons on the second floor, just outside of the Grizzly Mall Food Court, was one of those seasonal stores. Only, instead of switching out storefronts every Halloween, Thanksgiving, Christmas, New Year's, Valentine's Day, and so on, Mazel Top-to-Bottom—owned by Michael and Marcia Smilovitz—catered to a very targeted audience, namely the Chosen

People of Generica, Kansas (which, at last count, topped out at just over a dozen . . . slightly more if you include nonpracticing).

Mrs. Smilovitz took down the Rosh Hashanah decorations in the window to prepare for her big Yom Kippur display.

"This will *really* knock them on their *tuchases,*" she said with a Day-Glo Yahrzeit candle in her mouth. "Could you hand me that neon Star of David, Warder Chango?"

A tanned man with a scraggly goatee wearing a blue robe stood at the base of the ladder.

"What? Oh yeah . . . *totally,* Mrs. Smilovitz. Here you go." Warder Chango handed her the electric six-pointed star. "And, like, thanks so much for letting us rent the back of your store for our . . . *club,*" he added.

Mrs. Smilovitz secured the Star of David at the top of the display with some spirit gum.

"Well, you seem like a nice enough bunch of goyim," she said as she scrutinized the star's placement with a scowl. "Except for that big mean boy . . ."

"Yeah, well, Damian has been through a lot," Warder Chango replied cautiously. "You know, dying, coming back . . ."

Mrs. Smilovitz climbed down the ladder.

"That's still no excuse to be so rude. But at least he's

not as skinny as the rest of you. Skin and bones! I'll drop you off a plate of blintzes as soon as I'm through."

She plugged in the star, which radiated to vivid, crackling blue life. Mrs. Smilovitz clapped her hands.

"Joy *vey!*" she cried.

Warder Chango looked at the clock on the wall. The big dreidel pointed to five.

"Whoa, I gotta go, Mrs. Smilovitz," he said as he rustled to the back of the store. "You know, almost time for . . . *choir practice.*"

"You kids have fun," she called out as Warder Chango parted the thick curtains leading to the store's stockroom.

Inside the room was a congregation—if you could call six men, two women, one little girl, one big boy, and a ferret a congregation—all wearing blue hooded robes and somewhat lost looks upon their faces.

"How nice of you to join us, Warder Chango," said the Guiding Knight, a tall, rat-faced man positioned in the back of the room behind an altar. "Now, at last, we may begin."

"Sorry," Warder Chango muttered as he joined his fellow cult members. "I was just helping out our land-lady."

The Guiding Knight cleared his throat.

"O, Lord, we—the Knights of the Omniversalist Order Kinship—beseech thee, fuel our humble labors in the promotion of truth and power, unity and control. Enrich our hearts with that most excellent gift of entitlement so that our acts may be full of the spirit of smug, secret self-knowledge. Give us strength to overcome our setbacks. . . ."

He paused as he surveyed his shabby, makeshift church, crowded with boxes of Hanukkah candles and bar mitzvah favors.

"And at last," he continued with a sigh, "may we enjoy the blessedness of the eternal realm that you have tastefully furnished for us, and us alone. . . ."

A large cruel-looking boy lazing on a dark brown Barcalounger at the back of the altar burped loudly. The Guiding Knight gritted his teeth.

"So may it ever be."

"So may it ever be," replied the small group of spooky acolytes.

The Guiding Knight banged a gavel against the altar and nodded his head to a dotty old African American woman sitting before a pipe organ. The woman sent her arthritic fingers to work across the yellowed keys, filling the stockroom with oozing waves of warped, crooked music.

The boy on the Barcalounger clapped in a slow, sarcastic way. The old woman smiled in misinterpreted gratitude. The Guiding Knight stiffened, straightening his purple velvet scarf affectedly.

"I, your Guiding Knight—whose purpose is to

superintend all procession—will hereby commence this meeting of the subordinate chapter of the lower Midwest sect of the Knights of the Omniversalist Order Kinship!"

The enthusiastic gavel-banger banged his gavel enthusiastically.

"First item," he declared, "and last, not to mention everything in the middle."

He turned to address the boy on the altar behind him.

"O, Damian Ruffino, our most valued Bridge to the other side, the one—"

"Second one, actually," chimed in Necia Alvarado, a bony girl with gleaming black eyes who languidly stroked a sleeping white ferret. "If you count—"

"We don't," snapped the Guiding Knight.

Damian sighed as he finished his bag of sunflower seeds. For some reason, ever since he was brought back to life using the etheric energy of twenty-seven sacrificed chickens, he had developed an intense craving for seeds and Gummi worms.

"You mean Milton Fauster?" Damian said with a smirk. "Good ol' Milquetoast? It's okay. You can say his dweeby name. I know he was your first choice to . . . to . . ."

"'To better prepare for our imminent arrival in the Next Life and hasten the Last Days, which serve as our new beginning,'" concluded the Guiding Knight with the offhanded authority of something recited so many times that it had become second nature.

"Yeah, yeah," Damian said as he pecked at a seed in his hand. "The one who dies first to make sure everything is ready for you on the other side, then calls for you and the other 14,216 people who believe in your—*our*—Omniverse, or whatever."

The robed congregation bowed their hooded heads as one.

"The everlasting everyplace where everything is possible," they murmured reverently.

"Right," Damian said, sitting up and dusting off his hands. "But the big diff between Milquetoast and me is that he didn't want to be your Bridge and I *do*."

The Guiding Knight held his fist to his mouth and gave a fake cough.

"Which brings me to our next item in our spiritual itinerary," he continued tentatively. "And that is the question of when . . ."

"When?" Damian asked.

"Yes, O, Bridge. When will you, exactly . . . *be* our Bridge? To the other side."

Damian—the reigning bully of Generica who had devoted his life and brief death to the art of intimidation, thuggery, and malevolence—glared at the man.

"I'm sorry," he said unconvincingly. "I don't follow you."

"Yes," the Guiding Knight said as his forehead

beaded with sweat. "Right, that's the point: *we* follow *you*. I—we—would just like to know *when* you will be sacrificed so that we may all be saved?"

"Oh," Damian replied with a yawn. "*That*. Short answer: when I'm good and ready. Long answer: when I have more . . . *believers*."

The congregation murmured.

"The problem with you people," Damian said, pulling the lever on the side of the Barcalounger so that he catapulted forward, "well, *one* of your problems, is that there just ain't enough of you. If I'm going back to Heck—I mean, the Omniverse—then I want to arrive with a real *bang*. Lots of followers. Enough KOOKs—"

"We prefer 'Knights of the Omniversalist Order Kinship,'" the Guiding Knight interjected.

"Whatever. I just want to have my own built-in army of devout do-whatever-Damian-says-ers with me so that I can *really* shake things up down under."

The white ferret on Necia's lap stirred awake.

"Ooh, look who's back from his widdle nap," Necia cooed as she scritched the animal behind its tiny ears. "My Lucky."

Lucky looked up at the girl, his eyes glazed with sedatives, and hissed.

"Someone got up on the wrong side of the cage," she said.

Lucky—Milton's beloved pet who had been left in

Necia's twitchy hands ever since his master had been "popped" in a tub of popcorn in a funeral home furnace—sniffed the air groggily and trained his burgundy eyes on Damian. The hair on his back raised as stiff as a brush made of porcupine quills. Lucky hissed and spat.

"Junior Knight Necia," the Guiding Knight commanded, "please do something about that disagreeable creature."

Damian shuddered as he locked eyes with Lucky.

"I have a few suggestions," he said with disgust. "Like maybe a charitable donation to an animal testing lab . . ."

Necia scooped up the animal in her dark, spindly arms and walked toward a cage in the back of the stockroom.

"He's so sweet when he's not awake," she said. "Looks like my widdle fuzzy wuz needs more of his special sleepy snack."

Necia stooped before the cage, opened its squeaky door, and forced Lucky—who, even when sedated, could still put up a formidable squirm—inside. She took a small eyedropper from a vile next to the cage and gave a few squirts into a bowl full of scrambled eggs and liver. Necia put the bowl in the cage, and Lucky, ravenous with hunger, went at the bowl like, well, a starving weasel-like animal presented with its favorite food. After a few lusty bites, Lucky's gobbling grew sluggish. He valiantly snapped up one last morsel of liver before passing out cold.

The Guiding Knight grew impatient.

"Damian—"

The brutish boy waggled his finger at the wooden, self-important man. The Guiding Knight sighed.

"O, most revered Bridge," he corrected. "How do you propose adding to our flock? We've always preferred a low profile, for sanctity's sake, not to mention tax reasons."

"Well, all that's about to change," Damian said, looking at his watch. "I'm taking this second-rate cult to the top. We're talking *Damiantology*! You know, fame, fortune, celebrities, lots of dues, hardly any *don'ts*, using negative energy for the public bad—"

"I believe you mean—" interrupted the Guiding Knight.

"I *am* mean—and I want everyone to be able to harness that awesome nastiness and take it straight to the top. Well, not actually *the* top, because that's where I'll be. But right below."

Mrs. Smilovitz parted the curtains. The Guiding Knight shot the organist a look. The old woman nodded and began to play. The congregation joined in.

"Oh, Lord, Kum Bay Yah."

Mrs. Smilovitz grinned and clapped. "Such beautiful

voices! Though I never could understand that *mishegas* song. So sorry to interrupt, but you have a visitor . . ."

"Not the FBI!" exclaimed the Guiding Knight with alarm.

The middle-aged woman folded her arms and glared at the man suspiciously.

"Um . . . *no*. You should lay off the cop shows, Mr. Nervous."

A man with thinning ponytailed hair popped his head in through the curtains.

"Excuse me, but I only had fifty cents for the parking meter, so I really got to get this party started. . . ."

Damian rose.

"Fellow KOOKs, I'd like you to meet my lawyer, Algernon Cole."

The man swished past Mrs. Smilovitz, straightening his Hawaiian hula-girl tie.

"Mr. Ruffino," Algernon Cole said with a toothy grin, "always a pleasure to see you . . . especially when you're alive!"

Damian galumphed past the confused Guiding Knight and off the altar, crunching discarded sunflower seed husks underneath his boots.

"Thank you, Mrs. Smilovitz," Damian said as he shook his lawyer's hand. "You can go now."

The woman scowled as she turned to leave.

"That big *shmendrick* makes me want to *plotz*!" she groused as she left the room.

"What is the meaning of this?" the Guiding Knight asked with a tinge of outrage. "We don't need a lawyer—there is only one *true* law we adhere to . . . apart from those necessary to maintain our nonprofit status."

Algernon Cole studied the small flock of peculiar parishioners.

"Is this a social club for those excluded from *other* social clubs?" he remarked. "I kid. Nice place. Understated."

Damian turned and faced his followers.

"Mr. Cole here is in the process of getting me a righteous settlement—"

"Two, actually," Algernon Cole interjected. "One from Generica General Hospital for fatal negligence when you died after being in that coma from the exploding marshmallow bear incident, and the other from the Barry M. Deepe Funeral Parlor for egregious incompetence with intent to inter; that is, lay to rest someone who was—obviously because I am talking to him!—still restless. So we're getting 'em at both ends, so to speak: one for letting you die and the other for trying to kill you! Most lawyers—and I'm a real one now, thirteenth time's the charm as far as BAR exams go— have to start off with boring cases. Not me! Though I've always been cursed with an interesting life!"

The Guiding Knight stepped off the altar and glided toward Damian and Algernon Cole.

"I still don't understand why he's here! I run a lean operation, I mean, *congregation,* with things kept on the down low."

"And look where *that's* got you," Damian sneered, his beady black eyes shiny with malevolent glee. "In the back of some crappy store in a lame-o mall."

The Guiding Knight stiffened.

"We were fine in our basement church at the funeral home, until things got . . . *complicated.*"

Damian shook his blocky, freckled head.

"You're thinking about this all the wrong way," he said smugly. "My settlement is going to buy us a proper home someplace. Really big with lots of free parking. And publicity. Maybe even infomercials. If you want people to believe that *you're* the one who knows the 'answer,' then you've got to shout it the loudest."

The Guiding Knight rubbed his sharp chin, mulling over Damian's words like an old computer chewing on new code.

"Well . . . we *could* use some more room—"

"And new robes," Algernon Cole said with a grimace. "Polyester, by the smell of it. You need a natural fabric that can breathe. Organic cotton really uncorks your chakras."

The Guiding Knight smiled. "Perhaps good things really *do* come to those who wait," he said with a look as self-serving as an open vending machine. "Looks like the all-seeing, all-powerful keeper of the Omniverse was really looking after us when he took Milton Fauster away without a proper sacrificial ceremony and gave us *you*."

Algernon Cole cocked his eyebrow.

"Did you say Milton Fauster?" he asked.

Damian bobbed his head at the mention of Milton's name. "What about him?" he clucked.

Algernon Cole shrugged his shoulders. "Nothing, really. Just a case of the 'small worlds.' Synchronicity and all. I had a meeting with the poor boy, in between his first and last deaths."

The man snickered.

"It's like you two are joined at the spiritual hip or something. . . ."

Damian's eyes narrowed. His feathered hair seemed to stand on end.

"Anyway," Algernon Cole continued. "We met at the Paranor Mall—a place that makes your KOOK church here seem as exotic as an unfinished furniture shop!"

"What did you two talk about?" Damian asked.

Algernon Cole smoothed out the lapel of his second-hand suit.

"Well, I really shouldn't divulge the contents of a meeting between client and counsel. But considering the client has passed on and I wasn't licensed at the time, I'm sure it's no big whoop. He wanted to talk about a book idea of his—"

"A book?" Damian interrupted.

"Yes," Algernon Cole continued. "Called *Heck*."

Damian began to vibrate like a big living pager.

"You don't say," he said with fascination.

"I *do* say . . . and I did," Algernon Cole laughed. "Ridiculous, I know. Not like my book, *Chicken Pants,* about a boy—"

"So, about this *Heck* book," Damian interrupted again. "What more did he say about it?"

"Milton seemed quite interested in certain contractual loopholes . . . ways of rendering a contract with— who did he say?—oh yeah: the *Principal of Darkness,* null and void. Isn't that rich? Apparently this principal is a woman."

Damian shook his head and snickered.

"Barely," he said under his foul breath.

"It was the queerest thing," Algernon Cole went on, replaying the event in the second-run theater of his mind. "He insisted on meeting in this weird mirrored booth. It must have been some kind of television, because inside—after we started talking—it was filled with the most horrific images. Demons, mostly."

Damian's jaw dropped open. Several spit-slick sunflower seed husks fell from his gums to the floor.

"You need to take me there," he declared.

Algernon Cole gave Damian a crooked grin. "That's

funny . . . not as in ha-ha but as in strange. Milton, I re-call, wanted to come with me to see *you* after you had been, um, *unplugged* by that mysterious *Get Butter Soon* messenger."

Necia fidgeted in the back of the room.

"Damian," she called out meekly. "There's some-thing you need to know. . . ."

"Not now!" he spat. Damian placed his hand on Al-gernon Cole's shoulder, not in a warm sense of frater-nity, but tightly, as if he were trying to manipulate the man's will by toggling the joint connecting his arm and trunk.

"*I need to go . . . there!*" Damian stated forcefully, coil-ing the words slowly, then giving them a verbal tug as if tightening a leash.

Fear flashed in Algernon Cole's eyes.

"Sure," he said weakly. "Perhaps tomorrow after—"

Damian squeezed the man's shoulder.

"*Now.*"

Algernon Cole swallowed and carefully—as if deal-ing with a vicious, predatory animal that he had stum-bled upon while hiking—moved Damian's hand away.

"Of course," he muttered calmly. "I'm still on the clock. We can just take our meeting to go. But . . . why is it so important?"

Damian stared off into space, rubbing his cheek. His finger picked at a small white whisker growing out of his jawline. He plucked it out and examined it. It was a tiny feather. Damian blew it away with a puff of breath.

"It's time to let the feathers fly, like at a juvie pillow fight," he murmured spookily. He locked his birdlike eyes upon Algernon Cole. "Let's just say I want to look up an old *fiend*."

14 · SCOFF AND RUNNING

THE DREADMILL WAS a dark, silent crypt that smelled of sour sweat and the sharp tang of fear. Inside, Milton was instantly seized by suffocating claustrophobia, like when his sister, Marlo, had sent him on a special scientific mission to see if the refrigerator light *really* went out when the door closed.

Suddenly, the machine hummed to life. The wheel began to turn, gradually at first. Milton trotted tentatively to keep up.

This isn't so bad, thought Milton as the wheel rotated. *Just a little jog. I don't know what Virgil was talking—*

Milton's thoughts were shattered as, all around him, the DREADmill filled with light and noise. A computer-generated trainer appeared before him: a tanned, shirtless, heavily muscled man with a blond military crew cut, twelve-pack abs, and a whistle hanging from his brawny stump of a neck.

"Attention, maggot!" the pseudoman barked. "Major Bummer here, to get your pathetic self in shape—"

Major Bummer scrutinized Milton.

"—and that shape is currently oval! You're a disgrace! Look at yourself!"

Milton couldn't, currently, look at himself, but he knew that the shrieking, computer-generated madman wanted him to feel intense shame.

"A man's body is supposed to be a temple," Major Bummer hollered. "Yours is a community rec center after a drunken paintball party!"

The wheel began turning faster.

"But since you're a new recruit, I'm going to go a little easy on you," the trainer said with a shark's grin. "Fear Level One!"

Milton was now in a dark forest. Towering, imposing pine trees swayed with a wicked wind, causing Milton to release a wicked wind himself. A savage, beastly roar filled the DREADmill, exploding from behind. Milton instinctively burst into a run.

"Fear Level Two!" Major Bummer barked, floating ahead of him like an antagonizing specter.

Now Milton found himself in a lush, prehistoric landscape, full of monstrous, darting dragonflies and a herd of apatosaurus munching foliage in a lazy, bovine rhythm.

A pterodactyl swooped down, squawking at a stegosaurus trampling flat low-lying vegetation some hundred meters ahead.

Apatosaurus, pterodactyls, and stegosaurus, Milton mused. *Must be the Jurassic or Cretaceous period. The only thing missing is—*

A deep, rumbling roar rent the air around him. The DREADmill trembled with violent footfalls.

"A Tyrannosaurus rex!" Milton screamed as he galloped faster, the wheel becoming a shimmering blur in front of him.

This is ridiculous, Milton thought feverishly, his mind whirring as fast as the treadmill he was trapped upon. *This is just some kind of motion simulator, like at the Punyversal Studios Kiddy Freak 'n' Fun Park in Florida. But why does this seem so much more . . . real?*

Major Bummer, his nostrils flaring like a winded gorilla, reappeared.

"Well, well," he said, looking Milton up and down with his ice-blue eyes. "Looks like we'll have to come up with something less . . . *run-of-the-mill.* Get it? Sometimes I slay myself . . . though I'd much rather slay you, maggot. Fear Level Three!"

Milton was now, for all appearances, in the north hallway back at Generica Middle School, the one that led from the locker room out past Threat Row—where all the bullies hung out—to the buses. The DREADmill urged Milton onward as a yellow and black school bus pulled up at the back of the school. Milton's heart pounded with a familiar anxiety, and his limbs went numb with fear.

"If it isn't Milquetoast Fauster," a cruelly familiar voice taunted from behind. Milton's insides turned to marmalade. "Damian!" he gasped. The principal architect of Milton's panic disorder—the sadistic, pathological thug who had brought Milton to Heck in the first place (granted, Milton had accidentally returned the favor, but that was beside the point).

"I'll even give you a head start, just to make things interesting," Damian purred like a preteen panther. "Of course, it will end the same way—terrible for you and terribly fun for me. . . ."

This is impossible, Milton thought as he trotted to the DREADmill's nefarious rhythm. *Damian's not here . . . I'm not there. But, somehow, the machine is drawing the fear out of me . . . which means—*

Milton gulped.

The machine can read my thoughts. Or at least my feelings. Which means—if I let it—it can see who I really am! Which means I have to pretend to be afraid of things I'm not really afraid of, like . . .

Milton's mind skipped back in time to his eighth birthday when Marlo had given him *The Big Pop-up Book of Totally Scary Phobias that You Never Knew You Had but Really Do.* One page in particular came to mind: a big pop-up peanut-butter sandwich that sprang to life,

accompanying a brief description of arachibutyrophobia, otherwise known as the fear of peanut butter sticking to the roof of your mouth.

"C'mon, this is as challenging as slow-motion
Pong," Damian said as he tenderized his meaty palm
with his fist. "The *least* you could do is to r-r- . . ."

Suddenly, Damian began smacking his lips.

"Rumphghgrllmyack!"

Thick gooey strands held Damian's mouth tight. As
he gaped, goggled, and gasped, Milton could see a lattice of sticky, pale brown muck in his mouth, as if a spider had woven a web of peanut butter (which would
undoubtedly breed, Milton thought, a case of arachno-
arachibutyrophobia). Now all that was left was for Milton to react as if terrified.

Milton ran as fast as a boy encased in a suffocating
clown suit of living meat could. The wheel hummed
like the blades of a helicopter. Soon, the school hallway
dissolved into the cavernous mouth of a giant, with
Damian morphing into the creature's uvula—that little
punching bag in the back of your, and everyone's,
throat. Globs of peanut butter clung to the roof of the
creature's mouth, with ropes of ooze hanging down
like stalactites.

A stitch in Milton's side formed a seam of pain up
and down his body. Major Bummer's disappointed face
appeared.

"I didn't think you had it in you," he grumbled. "And

you have a *lot* in you, by the looks of it. But you are running faster than your body mass index would dictate, so I guess I have to—*sigh*—give you a little flavor furlough."

With that, the computer-generated tyrant disappeared and was replaced by what looked like a TV show.

"We now join *Lost on a Dessert Island,* already in progress. . . ."

A teenage boy with a mass of curly blond hair and a pretty, slender girl with wide, dark eyes climbed a massive hot-fudge sundae.

"We're almost at the summit," the boy called to the girl as he, after scooping up a handful of mint-chocolate-chip-brownie-dough ice cream to make his next toehold, held his sticky hand out to her. "Can you make it?"

She gave the boy a mischievous smile.

"The question is," she replied, popping a double-fudge-dipped peanut-butter cup in her mouth after using it as an ice-cream pick, "can *you* make it?"

The two teenagers briskly ascended the frosty, delectable peak. Meanwhile, Milton's Pang skin began to quake with hunger. It rippled in painful waves of want, becoming slick with full-body saliva. Its chubby legs sprinted toward the enticing yet unobtainable treats before it. Milton felt as if he were trapped inside a haunted tracksuit. He fought to keep up with the creature's frenetic pace.

It's . . . not . . . fair, Milton chewed over in his mind, so exhausted that even his thoughts panted with exertion. *I'm either running . . . away from something . . . out of fear . . . or running toward it . . . out of desire.*

The teenagers on the screen reached the summit. Giggling, they parted clumps of cotton candy to enter a luscious grotto of swaying taffydills. Milton could even smell the sweet breeze wafting from the scene, savoring it with the taste buds all over his borrowed body.

A chocolate-milk waterfall cascaded into a foaming lake full of bobbing Oreo lily pads. Chocolate frogs croaked, trying to catch skittering Skittles with their long licorice tongues.

Milton's Pang suit convulsed with craving. Just as Milton felt as if his heart were a beat away from bursting, the screen surrounding him went dark, the wheel slowed, and the sides of the DREADmill opened in pneumatic wheezes until they rested on the Gymnauseum floor.

Two decomposing lizard demons hoisted Milton out of the machine. His body was frothy with a thick mixture of sweat and drool. One of the demons threw Milton a large, stiff white towel and prodded him toward the other boys, who were gasping by an industrial-sized black iron scale.

"Hmm . . . simply terrible, Hugo," Dr. Kellogg pronounced, eyeing the two hands of the clocklike scale as they settled on 227 pounds, 3 ounces. "I don't understand it—none of you have lost any weight in the last three days."

Hugo stepped off the scale, shaking his head. "I don't know, Dr. Kellogg," the boy said, scratching his crew cut. "I just haven't felt like myself lately."

In a flash, Hugo's chubby face . . . *changed*. More than just a sudden shift in expression, it was as if his face had turned into a puzzle, shifting and rearranging to become a quick succession of other people—an old African American man, a Chinese warrior, a young Swedish woman—until his features finally settled back to their original configuration. No one else had seemed to notice, and it had all happened so quickly that Milton was unsure if he had actually seen the split-second metamorphosis or if it had been the lingering effects of extreme physical exhaustion.

"You," the doctor said, gesturing toward Milton. "*Jonah*. Step on up."

Milton complied. The scale whirled around like a roulette wheel spun by an angry croupier. Dr. Kellogg caressed the scale with his gloved hand.

"There, there, dear," he murmured to his machine. "It will be over soon."

The hands finally settled on an astounding 416 pounds.

"Incredible," the doctor said, stroking his white goatee. "Well, I'm always up for a challenge."

He clapped his hands together. "Now, boys, let us

retire to the promenade deck for the remainder of our class. I hope to feed your heads so that, before the lunch bell rings, you will feel sated and sanctified."

Dr. Kellogg walked energetically toward a pair of glass doors at the side of the Gymnauseum. He flung them open and motioned for the class to make themselves comfortable on the piles of foam mats within. The teacher kneeled upon a backless posture chair at the front of the small room.

"Firstly," the doctor said, *"hygiene."*

"Hi, Doctor!" Gene replied cheerfully.

The teacher groaned.

"The art of taking care of yourselves," Dr. Kellogg clarified. "Specifically, for today's purposes, how to clean your navel."

The boys looked at one another in confusion.

"Some say navel buildup is the result of clothing fibers gathering at the scar site of your severed umbilical cord, while others—myself included—think it has more to do with the impurity of our thoughts," the doctor continued as two skinny nurses—as cold, stiff, and unyielding as a pair of rectal thermometers— wheeled in dollies piled high with boxes of Q-tips and rubbing alcohol.

The doctor rose and performed—for some reason known only to him—a series of deep knee bends.

"Regardless," he went on, "a sullied belly button can have a devastating effect on one's self-image, so thorough cleansing is crucial. While regular swabbing is critical, I have been formulating a by far more effective method. . . ."

The nurses traded looks of concern. Dr. Kellogg went over to a small chalkboard that hung on the rosewood wall. He scrawled a "1" across the board with a quick slash.

"The first step is to invent a shrinking machine."

Milton scooched over to Virgil. "This guy is one enchilada short of a combo platter," Milton whispered.

Virgil's stomach rumbled.

"Please," he said, "go easy on the food metaphors. Seriously. They don't go down well here."

The doctor scratched a "2" on the board.

"Next, hire a Navel-Ops team," he relayed with a pixie grin. "A crack team of professional hygienists proficient in cutting-edge swabbing techniques and state-of-the-art disinfection procedures. Arm them with ten-foot-long swabs so that when they endure the shrinking process, the swabs are roughly as large as your traditional cotton swab—"

Thaddeus raised his hand. "Why don't they just use regular swabs?" he asked.

The doctor scowled. "Don't be ridiculous, son. They would be entirely too small after the shrinking process."

"No, but after—"

"*Three,*" declared the doctor after scratching the number on the board. "Each team member should also have an alcohol-propulsion device strapped to their—"

"Doctor," interrupted one of the nurses.

Dr. Kellogg dismissed the nurse with an irritated wave. "Not now, Nurse Rutlidge."

"But I think it's time for your . . . treatment."

The lunch bell rang. The boys got to their feet with amazing alacrity.

"Boys!" the agitated doctor shouted while a nurse, pressing her hand on his shoulder, prepared a shot. "Remember to swab!"

Nurse Rutlidge stood by the door with a large silver tray of cotton swabs. Her skin crinkled like a withered cornhusk as she sneered at the boys. Each boy took a swab, rolled up their tube tops, and fished out globs of iridescent, rainbow-hued gunk from their belly buttons—Hugo alone fished out several tablespoons—and deposited the soiled Q-tips into a large metal drum.

The boys went back into the locker room to change. Milton sat down with a tremendous creak and peeled off his sweaty burlap leggings. His already-mottled Pang skin was as red and raw as Martian sushi.

"Hey, and *thanks* for telling me about the DREAD-mills," Milton grunted sarcastically as Virgil sat beside him.

Virgil shrugged.

"Yeah, they're a *major bummer*," he said. "Get it?"

"Yeah, I got it," Milton grumbled as he put on his tight corduroy pants.

"But you learn to get through the fear levels real fast so you can spend more time stranded on Dessert Island."

Milton rubbed his aching Pang thighs.

"Same difference, really. Exertion-wise."

A few lockers over, Thaddeus pulled on his striped Lycra bodysuit. Milton saw the pudgy boy transform into an elderly Eskimo, an angry Samoan, a cowboy, and back again.

"Did you see that?" Milton whispered.

"See what?" Virgil replied, looking over at Thaddeus a second too late.

"I don't know," Milton mumbled, rubbing his Pang eyes. "I must be seeing—"

The freckles on Virgil's face multiplied until he was, briefly, a German girl, a bucktoothed Spanish boy, a bald muscleman, and then finally his usual self.

"—things," Milton said weakly. "Are you . . . okay?"

"Me?" Virgil said, slipping on his slippers. "Sure . . . just starving. C'mon, let's go before he's all out."

Milton and Virgil followed the other boys as they dashed out of the locker room into the hallway.

"All out of those awful lentil biscuits?" Milton grimaced.

Virgil wiped a trickle of drool off his chin.

"What? No . . . *yuck*. That junk puts the 'die' in 'diet.' I'm talking *real* food. Hambone Hank's Heart Attack Shack."

Virgil's small dark eyes twinkled with joy.

"He showed up three days ago, after an assembly. And we've been going there ever since. You won't believe your mouth."

Milton trotted after his friend, who, in the space of several steps, had been a circus clown, a caveman, and a Brazilian supermodel. As they ambled down the hallway, following a plume of unbearably delicious barbecue smoke, Milton wasn't concerned about believing his mouth. It was his eyes that were worrying him.

15 · SiSTERS ACT UP

MARLO LEAFED THROUGH the shimmering pages of *Statusphere* that were currently fanning from her forearm. It took her mind off the fact that the epitome of all-evil was somewhere down the hall and that Madame Pompadour was coiled up in her office, looking for any reason to pounce.

Most magazines, as Farzana had lectured to Marlo, were passé the second their perfume inserts were gutted. Not so with *Statusphere*. The fact that its pages were perpetually updated wirelessly to stay on top of the latest fads meant that it was always one step ahead of your look, leading you forever along, trend over trend.

Marlo found that her mind grew fuzzier with every flip of the page. It was like wading in a stream, losing yourself to the water and letting the current decide where to take you. Marlo arrived at what should have been the end of the magazine but was instead the beginning of a new one: *VaniTeen*. On the cover were five flawless cheerleaders forming a human pyramid of perfection.

Marlo gasped. "Give me a flippin' break," she groused.

At the top of the heap, as always, was Lyon Sheraton: a girl who had stuck to Marlo in the afterlife with the humiliating tenacity of toilet paper to a shoe. She had met Lyon and her vacuous friend Bordeaux Radisson—whose IQ, weight, and shoe size shared the same number—in Limbo; then they had all been transferred to Rapacia.

If you took every snooty, popular, effortlessly cruel, and faultless-and-she-knows-it girl up on the Surface and put them in a big pot simmering over a low flame for a few weeks . . . well, that would be pretty fun, Marlo thought. More to the point, though, the condensed result would be Lyon Sheraton. A girl who had been given everything and only wanted more, especially if that meant that everyone around her had *less* as a result.

Meet the Nyah Nyah Narcissisters . . . Coming to a Circle Near You!

Pictured (from top to bottom, left to right): Head Cheerlessleader Lyon Sheraton, Strasbourg Hyatt,

Marseille Ramada, Dijon Westin, and Bordeaux Radisson. Be sure to have your face rubbed in Lyon's awesome new VaniTeen *column, "Lyon's Den," on page 65!*

Marlo, despite herself, obliged, flipping to the page out of a weird mixture of curiosity, boredom, and the knowledge that she was about to be profoundly irritated. She wasn't disappointed.

LYON'S DEN
A Column Mostly Written
by Lyon Sheraton

Do you know someone who has it all? Someone confident, cool, perfect . . . someone who's got it going on, 24/7/365?

No? Well, now you do!

Some girls like yours truly have a drive, that extra-super-special quality that puts them behind the steering wheel (or in the back of a limo). They know what matters to them, and they don't swerve for anything, even squirrels. They radiate an inner power (the girls, not the squirrels). They—she— *me,* is always herself, her fabulous self, and if no one likes it, they get a big fat Lyon Sheraton "W." And this "W" causes girls to instantly dissolve into tears, boys to soil themselves with humiliation, and teachers to transfer to other school districts (even the scary ones across town).

Then there are those—the rest of you—who sit in the passenger seat, just along for the ride, pressing your blobby noses against the glass, watching it all rush by.

I suppose that, from a certain perspective, I could be viewed as rude or whatever. Give me a break, people—it's called self-esteem! Which is supposed to be good, right? I've just got a lot more than you, that's all. It's like how you can't be too rich or too skinny, ever.

That's why me and my BFFs of the Nyah Nyah Narcissisterhood fulfill such an important service. Our awesomeness gives you something to strive for, even though you'll never, ever come close. We let you know what's possible: for us, anyway!

To see where you fit in the Statusphere, take my totally fun quiz!

Marlo's phone rang. It was that weird VTV line again. Farzana was on her own phone planning . . . *something*. It was hard to follow. She hadn't had her Beauty Cream since this morning, so her sentences came out like a jumble of frazzled words riding a short-circuiting escalator. Marlo could make out something about a trip, which was ridiculous . . . where would she possibly—

"Are you going to g-get that?!" Farzana mouthed, stuttering while even *pretending* to talk. Marlo sighed, slipped her arm out of her copy of *Statusphere,* and punched the line. Perhaps she'd pick up some more dirt on Madame Sour Puss-in-Boots.

"Hello, Madame Sour . . . um, *Pompadour*'s office," Marlo said, her tone an unbalanced load of professionalism and facetiousness. "How may I deflect your call?"

"*Oh . . . my . . . gawd!*" said the all-too-familiar-yet-somehow-unsurprising-to-hear-on-the-other-end-of-the-line, considering, voice. "We must have misdialed and accidentally got the set of *Extreme Makeunder: Extra Fugly Edition!*"

Yes, currently drilling her peroxide wit into Marlo's left ear was Lyon herself.

"Is this, like, that Gothicky uggo Marlo Fauster?" said Bordeaux with a designer knockoff version of Lyon's attitude.

"That gross girl you're always talking about?" said another voice, dark and aloof. "The one who made a fool of you in Mallvana?"

Marlo snorted as Lyon's fuming silence blared in her ear.

Back in Mallvana, the Grabbit had used Lyon and Marlo to steal the Hopeless Diamonds. But Marlo had ended up not only duping the Grabbit, but also playing Lyon *big-time:* stealing the diamond that Lyon had thought she had stolen from Marlo, then turning the whole thing around at the end, emerging—with her brother Milton's help—as the hero, saving the day.

"That's old news, anyway, Strasbourg," Lyon replied after a pause packed as tight with explosive potential as a cannon. "Like your streaked, dimensional shag."

"Did you call for any particular reason, Lyon?" Marlo asked, keenly cutting into Lyon's gloat time. "Madame Pompadour is a very important woman . . . or cat . . . or snake. I'm still not completely sure. But one thing I *am* sure of is that she doesn't like anyone wasting her time."

Lyon seethed.

"While you may have gotten some dumb Infernship answering phones for all eternity, I . . . *we* . . . have a shot at something *really* big . . . even bigger than *Statusphere!* At least that's what Madame Pompadour—*your boss*—said when she asked we of the coolier-than-cool Nyah Nyah Narcissisterhood to call."

"Asked *you* to call?"

Suddenly, Madame Pompadour's voice exploded from the phone's speaker.

"Is there any reason, Miss Fauster, why I'm not having my 3:33 conference call?" she said, her words flicking like a towel snapped in a locker room.

The girls on the other end of the phone snickered. Marlo sighed. "I was just . . . *screening,* madame. You know . . . trying not to waste your time."

"Too late," Madame Pompadour hissed. "Put my call through immediately."

Lyon chuckled. "This is *so* not over, *Thriftstore*."

"You keep saying that," Marlo replied, recalling the last time she'd seen Lyon, storming away like the spoiled postmortem princess she was, back in Mallvana.

Marlo knew that Madame Pompadour was up to no good. But the fact that she had enlisted Lyon and Bordeaux as her pampered partners in crime made the whole thing *personal*. Farzana stared at Marlo suspiciously as she whispered into her phone.

Marlo gritted her teeth and transferred the call to Madame Pompadour's vanity. With Farzana's googly eyes scanning Marlo like shifty searchlights, scrutinizing her every move, how would she ever find out what Madame Pompadour and Lyon were up—?

As she reached over her issue of *Statusphere* to hang up the receiver, Marlo saw from the corner of her eye a weird flicker on one of the pages. She saw five young, privileged faces—untouched by need, want, or a moment's deprivation—staring back at her. Two of the faces belonged to Lyon and Bordeaux. Another snooty, older face joined the haughty fray. *Madame Pompadour.*

"Miss Fauster, is something . . ."

Madame Pompadour's image tapped the page before flickering out.

". . . wrong? My connection seems somehow . . . off."

"Umm, no, I think we're good. I'll be hanging up now. This is me hanging up."

Marlo quickly unscrewed the phone's mouthpiece, plopped out the little microphone, screwed it back, and placed it inside the cylindrical spine of her magazine. The magazine's pages glimmered and flashed, melting from a high-fashion exposé on the latest designer belly buttons, belly clasps, and belly zippers to a two-page spread of Madame Pompadour's conference call.

Marlo waved her hand in front of the page. None of the perfect faces seemed to see her. Madame Pompadour's expression, though, was furrowed with suspicion.

"One moment, girls," she said before pitching herself out of her chair. "I smell a rat." She padded swiftly across her office to the door. Madame Pompadour peered out of her office with one piercing cat's eye. Marlo was hunched over her desk, leafing through her magazine. She looked up.

"*What?* I'm just reading your dumb old *Statusphere* rag, trying to distinguish the difference between 'hot' and 'cool.'"

Madame Pompadour shot Marlo a skeptical look, turned sharply on her well-heeled heels, and sealed shut her office door. Marlo sighed with relief and smoothed out the pages of her magazine, just in time to see Madame Pompadour set herself primly in her chair and flatter her vanity.

"We look lovely, Narcissisters," Madame Pompadour said solemnly into the mirror as she hugged herself with unabashed self-affection. The girls in the mirror repeated the gesture.

"And now," Madame Pompadour continued, "as the longest-standing Narcissister—"

"You mean the oldest?" commented Lyon.

"*Ouch,*" Marlo snorted, still snooping through her glossy *Statusphere* magazine portal.

The Narcissisters looked at one another nervously as Madame Pompadour, flawless to a fault, gave her delicate hand a quick lick, smoothed out her gleaming blond coif, and collected herself (her favorite hobby).

"Forgive me, Lyon," Madame Pompadour said. "Did you say that you wanted to stay in Rapacia as a greedy little nobody?"

Lyon swallowed.

"Um, no, ma'am. *Madame!*"

"Good. Then without further ado, I officially welcome you girls to the Narcissisterhood."

She dangled her charm bracelet in front of the mirror.

"To commemorate your passages from Nowheresville to the Statusphere, I have each of you on my charm bracelet. Now you'll all be, if not quite next to my heart, at least always near my grasp. I trust you received your complimentary Narcissister Compacts?"

The girls nodded.

"They are, like, totally awesome!" Bordeaux replied, her cornflower-blue eyes nearly popping out of their sockets. "But, *wow*, I thought I had a flawless complexion until I looked into my compact. I think I actually saw . . . a *pore!*"

The girls cooed and clucked in commiseration and pretended to pat her reflected image consolingly on the back.

Madame Pompadour smiled. The charm labeled BORDEAUX glowed and tinkled. Simultaneously, a fine crow's foot along Madame Pompadour's right eye faded.

"Yes, beauty isn't always pretty," she explained. "But the more you face the facts of your face, the more you can do to keep the imperfections of nature at bay. After all, knowledge is powder . . . and foundation."

She flipped a page of her Vilofax.

"So, I assume you are preparing for the very first Nyah Nyah Narcissister Underworld *In Your Face* Tour?"

Lyon smiled the only way she knew how: smugly.

"I've choreographed a number of awesome routines—"

"*We've* choreographed," interrupted Marseille.

Lyon rolled her eyes, which were as fiercely, uncompromisingly blue as a desert sky at high noon.

"*Whatever.* The point is we are so ready to bring it on in a big bad way. Where's our first stop? Lost Vegas? The Hellywood Hole?"

Madame Pompadour twitched her whiskers.

"Blimpo, actually."

"*Blimpo?!*" Lyon whined. "The circle for loser fatties?! *That's* our big debut? I *so* don't think so."

The fine fur on the back of Madame Pompadour's neck rose.

"I can't think of a better place to begin spreading our perky, polished message of unattainable perfection than Blimpo. Besides, all of the big shows have off-Broadway rehearsal runs."

Lyon coiled her tanned, thin arms together in petulant defiance. "I'm not doing it," she said flatly. "It's beneath me."

The other girls glanced nervously between Lyon and Madame Pompadour, as if watching two gunfighters squaring off in the Old West and wondering who would draw first.

"Of course, I can't *make* you do anything," Madame Pompadour replied. "Just like I can't *make* you star in your own Statusphere television show, *Pippi Mississippi,* on the Dismay Channel."

"Okay, I'll do it!" Lyon cried.

Madame Pompadour smiled, the kind that forms when you get something that you never doubted for one second you would get.

"Excellent. In the meantime, I'll have my assistant—my competent one—draw up the standard papers for your temporary releases from your respective circles," Madame Pompadour said. "For your vice principals to sign. I'll position it as a Heck *Badwill* Tour furlough. But I want the specifics of our deal kept on the *DL,* if you catch my drift. No Principal Bubb, no Big Guy Downstairs. So keep those beautiful profiles low until the time is right. And I'll be seeing you in Blimpo. I've business there to attend to . . . so this way, I can kill two birds with one cliché."

Madame Pompadour looked down at her phone and saw that both of her Inferns' extensions were presently engaged: one of the madame's many procedural no-no's. Farzana knew better than to have her lines tied up—that is, unless she didn't *know* that one of the lines was . . .

Madame Pompadour's cat pupils tightened into sharp slits. She shoved back her leather roller chair into her vanity, causing Bordeaux to yelp, and stormed across her office, grabbing the doorknob.

"May I help you?" Marlo puffed, having nearly yanked Madame Pompadour's arm out of its socket pulling open the door.

The madame rubbed her shoulder.

"I . . . what are you doing?" Madame Pompadour sputtered.

"Anticipating your needs, ma'am," Marlo replied. "Isn't that what you are training me for?"

"I told you not to call me . . . What were . . . You're trying to fluster me!"

"Fluster you, ma'am? Isn't that a little paranoid? Farzana and I were actually just talking about how you think everyone is talking about you. . . ."

"Why were both of my direct lines busy?" Madame Pompadour spat. "Were you eavesdropping again?!"

Marlo widened her eyes in an approximation of irreproachable cartoon innocence, like Bambi only with more eyeliner.

"I'm sure I don't know what you're talking about," Marlo replied before adding for effect, *"ma'am."*

Madame Pompadour was so flushed with rage that her silky white fur appeared pink and bristly. She marched back to her desk, yanked open her top drawer, and grabbed a coiled parchment.

Marlo noted the perfect faces in the vanity behind Madame Pompadour.

"Eeww . . . is that her?" Dijon, a redheaded preppy girl with wide green eyes, gasped.

"Wow, you didn't do her injustice, Lyon," added Marseille, an African American girl with straight, honey-colored hair.

"All I want to know," interjected Strasbourg, an olive-skinned brunette, "is who let the dog *in?*"

"I did," Madame Pompadour snapped as she muted her VaniTV. The Narcissisters continued to diss, rebuff, and otherwise disparage Marlo silently from behind the

desk. "Miss Fauster, since you seem to have nothing better to do than to eavesdrop on my conversations—"

"I know you're getting old and forgetful, but like we just discussed, I never—"

"One more word and you're Principal Bubb's way-too-personal assistant, back in Limbo with a big fat F on your Soul Aptitude Test to match the big fat L that's on your forehead, the one that everyone sees but *you*."

She threw the rolled parchment at Marlo.

"The devil is due for his lunch," she hissed. "And he is *very* particular about what goes in his mouth and on his forked tongue."

Marlo bent down and retrieved the parchment. She unrolled it, staring at the words with slack-mouthed disbelief.

"You've *got* to be kidding," she murmured.

Madame Pompadour laced her dainty fingers together and leaned back against her desk.

"I don't kid," she explained as she extended her claws languidly. "Even when I play, someone always seems to get . . . *scratched.*"

16 · JAiLHOUSE RUCKUS

"THANK-YOU-VERY-MUCH," the chunky teacher in the studded white-leather jumpsuit slurred into the microphone as he flipped his calfskin cape over his shoulder.

The boys regarded one another for a moment before hesitantly rewarding their teacher for whatever he'd just done—a sort of seizure from the waist down—with faint applause.

There was no mistaking who their Beginning Opera teacher was: Elvis Presley. This had less to do with the boys' knowledge of the King's music—Milton had only recognized him due to his face being plastered on the Psychomanthium, otherwise known as the Elvis Abduction Chamber, back in Lester Lobe's Paranor Mall—than the towering backdrop of red lights behind him on the small stage that spelled *E-L-V-I-S*.

"The first time I appeared onstage, it scared me to

death," Mr. Presley said as he stalked back and forth across the small, creaky platform. "Now that I really *am* dead, it all seems so darned silly. When I was out there, I really didn't know what all the yelling was about. So I asked the manager backstage, 'What'd I do?' And he said, 'I don't know, but just go back and do it again!'"

"You still got it!" shouted a jowly African American man with a bowler hat as he swept his sausagelike fingers across a piano.

"Ladies and gentlemen, Mr. Fats Waller!" he said, punctuating his shout-out with a wobbly judo kick.

Hugo, seated on a tiny metal chair with bowed, quivering legs, looked across the room with his pufferfish face.

"Ladies?" he murmured.

The dapper pianist rose to his feet.

"Thank you, boys," Mr. Waller said as he wiped his forehead with a handkerchief. "As I can tell by lookin' at y'all, you're all here on account of followin' your appetites. Now, there's nothin' wrong with that, within reason. Me? I blame my parents. I mean, what did they expect, namin' their son *Fats*?!"

"Now, now, Fats," Mr. Presley chided. "You shouldn't be disrespecting your momma and poppa."

Mr. Waller sat himself back down on his bench. "Of course, you're right, Elvis," the man said contritely as he plunked out "Chopsticks" on the piano as penance. "I loved my momma. She couldn't help that she confused hugs 'n' kisses with chicken-fried steak 'n' buttermilk."

"Well, regardless of how we all got here—me, mostly through Momma's fried peanut-butter sandwiches," Mr. Presley said with his low, tremulous voice, "we're all here to learn the finer points of opera."

Mr. Presley adjusted his belt. His buckle, as big and shiny as a burnished serving platter, blazed in the boys' faces.

"Let's see what we've got to work with here," he said.

Mr. Presley nodded over to Mr. Waller, who cracked his knuckles and played a stunning classical piece, his fingers summoning deep emotion from the keys.

Mr. Presley scanned the room with his blue eyes. "Let's start with you, son," he said, pointing to Milton, whose knack for being called on first had continued, unabated, into the Netherworld.

Milton stomped onto the stage. Mr. Presley winced as he got a closer look at Milton's hideous suit of meat.

"Mercy," he murmured as he flipped the chalkboard around. On the back were the lyrics to a French aria, or in Milton's case, complete and utter gibberish. "It's from *Faust*," Mr. Presley explained, "which I thought was appropriate."

The boys stared at their teacher with a profound lack of understanding.

"You know, the whole pact-with-the-devil motif . . . never mind. Now, don't worry, son. I'll sing along with you. . . ."

Mr. Presley drew in a breath that, like most every breath the husky man took, was deep. Filling his lungs to capacity, the teacher began to sing.

Milton did his best to keep up, which is to say, he lagged behind, baying like a mortally wounded basset hound. The Fausters were to singing as Napoleon was to Extreme Frisbee. Milton's Pang gullet only made things worse, drawing out each tortured "note" until it whimpered for release.

Mr. Presley pulled the emergency brake on their duet.

"We've all got talent, son," he consoled. "Some folks just got to dig deeper than others to find it. Now, let's give someone else a chance. *You*"—he waved his diamond-ringed fingers lazily toward Virgil—"step on up and show us what you've got."

Virgil rose nervously, his metal chair sighing with relief, and trudged up to the stage as Milton shambled off. Ever the good friend, Virgil tried to high-five Milton after his disastrous debut, but due to Milton's Pang-suited delayed reaction, he just ended up slapping him in the head.

"Sorry," Virgil mumbled to his friend as he stood before the chalkboard.

"Just follow my lead, son, and relax," Mr. Presley slurred supportively.

Mr. Presley began to mournfully croon.

> *"Au signal du plaisir,*
> *Dans la chambre du drille,*
> *Tu peux bien entrer fille,*
> *Mais non fille en sortir . . ."*

Virgil pulled in a great breath and began to sing.

> *"Bonne nuit, hélas!*
> *Ma petite, bonne nuit.*
> *Près du moment fatal."*

In a word, Virgil's voice was stunning. In another word, he was a virtuoso. In four more words, Milton was very surprised. Virgil's thrilling spectacle of pitch and tone was like a vocal fireworks display, and his breath control left the rest of the class breathless.

> *"Fais grande résistance,*
> *S'il ne t'offre d'avance*
> *Un anneau conjugale."*

Riding the melody as if it were a racehorse, Virgil scaled the piece to its summit, hitting the peak with a clear, beautiful note that pierced the heart.

Mr. Presley donned a pair of mirrored sunglasses, simply so he could peer over them in surprise. Virgil heaved in breathless confusion as if a spirit had abruptly fled his body. Mr. Presley put his hand on Virgil's great slope of a shoulder.

"*Diva* Las Vegas!" the teacher exclaimed in an amazed rumble. "All you need is a flashy one-piece jumpsuit and a manager/mentor who takes complete control over every aspect of your life, and we may get you a gig at Carnagey Hall in Sadia . . . nice captive audience."

As Mr. Presley plotted the details of Virgil's burgeoning career, the bell rang. The boys stomped toward the door. Their heavy footfalls knocked a picture of Mr. Presley's mother off the wall.

"Whoa, whole lotta shakin' goin on there, boys," he said sadly as he stooped down to pick up the picture, bursting a seam on his jumpsuit. "Before we return to sender, I want to stamp your young minds with a li'l something. . . ."

Mr. Presley hopped off the stage and turned to give his microphone cord a tug. Milton noticed that Mr. Presley had one white wing, delicate and impossibly small, like that of a hummingbird, sprouting from just beneath his left shoulder blade.

"Songs are dreams that you dream with your ears. So no matter what happens, keep singing a song. It's how you keep dreaming in a world of nightmares. Good night."

The lights went out, and the boys, confused, staggered out into the hallway.

"You were amazing in there," Milton said to Virgil as they lingered in the doorway. "I didn't know you had it in you."

Virgil's freckled cheeks reddened.

"Neither did I," he replied meekly. "I mean, I know I have a lot in there, but I didn't know I had . . . *that*. I swear, when I was up there singing, I felt so light. Like that soul balloon in Limbo. Like I could float up, up, and away."

Milton could see a fluttering from the corner of his eyes. In the classroom, Mr. Presley was chatting with Mr. Waller. His teensy-weensy wing flapped weakly when he laughed.

It must be weird, Milton thought. *Not quite a demon, not quite an angel. A large man, gifted with some kind of flight but too heavy to actually take to the air. He keeps singing, so at least part of him can float up, up, and away.*

17 · COOKiNG UP TROUBLE

IN A DARK, restricted hallway behind the Lose-Your-Lunchroom, the boys congregated like starving acolytes at the feet of a savory savior. At the center of the feeding frenzy was Hambone Hank's Heart Attack Shack: a bright red and yellow corrugated tin shed on wheels. Through vents on all four sides of the mobile hut poured the sweet tang of barbecue, the most mouthwatering that Milton had ever had the pleasure of inhaling. No wonder Dr. Kellogg's Off the Eaten Path Dusted Double Lentil Trail Mix Biscuits were growing moldy and stale.

Virgil, Hugo, Thaddeus, and Gene had faces smeared with red-brown sauce. Clutched in their hands were baskets overflowing with tender, mouthwatering meat—though Milton couldn't discern what it was the meat *of*. It didn't exactly look like brisket, chops, or

179

links, but rather a composite of all of the above, a delectable dream team comprising only the best, most appetizing cuts. There was also a selection of hot hush puppies and steaming black-eyed peas, but they were mostly ignored by the boys, who went straight for the meat.

"Eat up, boys," Chef Boyareyookrazee said with a smile extruded upon his sneer-shaped mouth like old, dried-up Play-Doh. "It's on the house, courtesy of your kindhearted vice principals. But hurry: it's for a limited time only."

With the promise of free, delicious food compounded with the threat of it being taken away, the boys gulped down their meals like Super Mario munching Super Mushrooms.

"His secret," Virgil managed to utter to Milton between bites, "is that he deep-fries the meat after he barbecues it. It locks in the flavor and throws away the key. . . ."

Milton peered inside the cramped cart to get a look at Hambone Hank. All he could really make out from the billowing clouds of burning mesquite and fatty fried fumes was a dark, robed figure with a sauce-and-grease-splotched apron reading SOUL FOOD WITH REAL SOUL. Occasionally the smoke would clear, and Milton could see that the cook, standing next to several large upturned jars, wore a hairnet and a surgical mask over his long nose. His dark eyes flashed at Milton, holding him in their gaze for just a fleeting moment, but that time felt like an eternity. It was as if Hambone Hank were reading Milton, judging him, with one short-yet-infinitely-deep stare. The tall, slender man seemed so familiar.

The bell rang.

"That's weird," Hugo said as he quickly gnawed a bone clean of any evidence of meat, like wiping a crime scene of fingerprints. "We're not supposed to be in class for another half hour. . . ."

Several scaly demons brandishing pitchsporks appeared at the end of the hallway.

"Hey, wide-loads," the darker of the three similarly serpentlike demons called. "Get your butts to the Gym-nauseum. And though it will be difficult for you, try to get them there in one trip."

The demons snickered as they prodded the boys down the hallway.

"Figures," Milton mumbled as he felt his Pang suit contract with hunger. "I didn't even get a chance to eat."

"Here," Virgil said, offering Milton his last bite of mouthwatering meat with a heroic lack of hesitation.

Milton smiled and gobbled up the tender morsel.

"Thwanks," he replied with a full mouth.

The taste was so incredible that Milton was temporarily paralyzed. So complex, robust, intense, and oddly . . . *haunting.* The flavors seemed to somersault in his mouth, each entirely different. It was delicious but, at the same time, unsettling. Strange, unconnected images flashed into Milton's mind with each flavor: a plane crashing, a raft bobbing in the middle of a shark-infested ocean, a car spinning out of control. . . . Milton swallowed and the disturbing images melted away.

He looked back as Hambone Hank growled at a pair of demon guards begging for a sample of his insanely flavorful barbecue.

"That's weird," Milton said. "He won't give the guards any of the food."

Virgil shot a quick glance over his shoulder. The mysterious cook bared his long white teeth. The demons trotted away, suddenly remembering a pressing engagement.

Virgil shrugged.

"I guess it's just like Chef Boyareyookrazee said. The Burgermeister and Lady Lactose just want to do something nice for us."

Hmmm, Milton pondered as he entered the locker room. *"Nice" like a farmer and his wife filling the pigs' trough. Nice with some kind of wicked agenda.*

Virgil stepped onto the black iron scale.

"I'm baffled," Dr. Kellogg declared as the hands of the scale settled on 247 pounds, 6 ounces. "You've all actually *gained* weight. Step off the scale, son. No need to put the machine through any more trauma than it has already suffered."

Virgil sulked off the scale.

"My system is scientifically proven to thermogenically burn fat, raise metabolism, and cure a host of psychosomatic ills while eradicating disease proneness and resetting the subject to its original weight blueprint!" the teacher said, scratching his white hair.

The boys stared at their teacher glumly.

"I'm flabbergasted!" he said as he raised his skinny white arms in frustration. "If you don't lose weight, you don't graduate, and if you don't graduate, this place will fill up with big-boned boys faster than you can say 'the buffet is now open'!"

Dr. Kellogg paced across the foam-mat floor.

"Into the DREADmills with you, then," he exclaimed with a toss of his hand.

"The DREADmills?!" Milton cried with a mixture of disbelief and trepidation: heavy on the trepidation. *"Again?"*

Dr. Kellogg glared at Milton and the boys.

"Orders straight from the top, Mr. Grumby," the teacher said, pointing through the glass ceiling at the balloon kingdom hovering above. "The vice principals are worried about everyone pulling their own weight—in particular, the fact that there is so much of it. So, from now on, every other class will be gym."

Milton clutched his tightening Pang throat with panic.

Is it my imagination, Milton wondered with fearful curiosity, *or is the Pang getting tighter and tighter, pushing me down, as if it's slowly swallowing me?*

"Gym dandy!" the teacher exclaimed with a clap of his immaculate white gloves. With that, the demon guards herded the boys into the DREADmills.

Milton was sealed inside the DREADmill's suffocating blackness. The machine switched on and the wheel began to turn. After a few stumbles, the DREADmill was filled with the cruel, high-definition image of Major Bummer.

"Well, well!" he bellowed in his husky, shout-ravaged voice. "If it isn't the boy so big he gives the school bus stretch marks!"

The wheel turned faster.

"Now, where were we?" the trainer said as he thrummed his fingers on his chiseled chin. "Oh, that's right: *Fear Level Four!*"

Milton was now in Limbo. He paced the familiar halls, the ones that winded aimlessly but always seemed to lead straight to . . .

"Mr. Fauster," a familiar voice hissed behind him.

. . . *Principal Bubb.*

His heart raced, with his body instinctually chasing after it.

"Where are you going in such a rush?" Bea "Elsa"

Bubb mocked as the hallway echoed with her clacking hooves. "I thought we could have a little chat, just me and . . . *what's left of you!*"

A trio of vicious snarls pricked Milton's ears.

Cerberus, Milton gasped as he ran faster and faster, trying desperately to fill his mind with frightful things that didn't scare him.

"Who do you think you are, Mr. Fauster? The Gingerbread Man?" the principal mocked, her wicked rasp of a voice sounding as if it were right beside Milton's ear. "I assure you that, not only can I catch you, I intend to dunk you in milk and bite your head off!"

Cerberus began licking his three chops with his three tongues. Peanut butter clung to his fangs.

"Or, I've got a better idea," Principal Bubb growled as she plopped crackers dripping with peanut butter into her mouth. They turned down a white hallway, ending at a great door ornately carved with gods rowing children down a river.

"Fear Level Five!" Major Bummer shouted, his tree trunk of a neck bulging with angry veins.

Milton was now in Limbo's Assessment Chamber, a massive round room of gleaming white marble and gold. He was pulled down the nine descending rings leading to the stage of polished gold. Milton tried desperately to run backward, away from the elaborate scale on the platform. His Pang skin jiggled with exertion.

Principal Bubb's voice taunted him from behind.

"Now, now, Mr. Fauster," she heckled. "Don't be like this. We just want to rip out your everlasting soul and weigh it, maybe take a few samples. Standard procedure. I'm sure we could get it back to you by, say . . . how does *never* sound?"

As the principal cackled, Milton moved his legs as fast as was physically possible. Thick, droolish Pang sweat coursed off him. His throat burned with each hungry gulp of air. Thoughts of clinging peanut butter were simply no match for the pure adrenaline of fear. *Real* fear.

The worst feeling Milton had ever experienced in this life or the last was the numb agony of having his soul removed, even just for a moment, upon his initial "appraisal" in Limbo's Assessment Chamber. As Annubis, the slender dog god that had extracted Milton's soul, had gently cradled it in his paws, Milton's sense of self had completely drained away, leaving him with an unendurable emptiness.

As Milton literally jogged his memory, he saw at the corner of his sweat-stung eyes, rows and rows of jars, jars of . . .

"Lost souls!" Milton gasped, tripping over himself.

"So clumsy," Principal Bubb mocked. "I've heard of having butter *fingers,* but butter legs? Oh dear . . ."

Milton quickly got up and began to sprint anew. The wheel wobbled with every pounding footfall.

Those jars! Milton thought, his mind racing as fast as

his feet. *Just like the ones in the kitchen and in Hambone Hank's shack.*

Major Bummer's disembodied head pressed itself against Milton's face.

"You may have won the battle of the bulge, but not the war of the waddle!" he shouted. "You make me sick! Get out of my sight!"

Major Bummer and the Assessment Chamber disappeared, replaced by a delectable paradise for the palate.

"We now join *Lost on a Dessert Island,* already in progress. . . ."

The blond curly-haired boy and the willowy girl walked cautiously down a forest path. The girl fell to her knees and examined a huge moist Hershey's Kiss.

"We're close!" she chirped.

They ambled down the path, following a trail of gargantuan Kisses.

The boy stopped suddenly, holding his friend back with an outstretched arm.

"What?" the girl asked.

"Shhh . . . you'll scare it," the boy whispered.

"Jeepers," the girl murmured as she saw, ahead of them in a clearing, a majestic chocolate moose.

Milton trotted on. While his Pang suit slavishly pursued the virtual Candyland before it, Milton's mind was on more than his stomach.

Lost souls, he pondered. *Owners unknown. Souls that,*

throughout eternity, had somehow lost their way. Captured and jarred up tight to be stored for perpetuity in the Assessment Chamber.

Milton snickered.

That is, unless you steal a bunch of them to make a soul balloon and escape back to the Surface.

The teenagers on the screen circled the hulking, dark chocolate elk. Tiny Tootsie moles snuffled around its sumptuous hooves. It began to nuzzle them playfully, almost begging them to nibble on its brittle toffee antlers.

But why would Hambone Hank have all those jars?

And then it hit Milton like a ton of Twix.

Soul Food with Real Soul.

18 · DISEMBODY AND SOUL

"HAMBONE HANK'S SOUL Food is *people! It's people!*" Milton exclaimed to the boys in the locker room, pacing with galumphing outrage.

"How can you . . . know that, Jonah?" Hugo puffed while attempting to shed his burlap leggings. "I heard that Hambone . . . keeps his recipe a closely guarded secret. Locked away in a vault down in . . . h-e-double-hockey-sticks, in the circle where all the telemarketers are."

"Exactly!" Milton deduced. "That means he must be hiding something!"

Gene blanched.

"You don't really mean . . . *people,* do you? As in *human?*"

Thaddeus shrugged. "Maybe Jonah means *Hunan*

food," he said as he pried off his black rubber tube top. "That really spicy Chinese stuff."

Milton shook his Pang head so hard that it jiggled like a bulldog drying itself off in slow motion.

"I mean *souls. Lost* souls. Tell them, Virgil."

Virgil held his round head in his hands, rolling it back and forth, as if he were hoping he could physically help his tormented brain to make the right decision.

"But it's so *good*," he mumbled.

Virgil sighed and propped his sad, puffy face between his hands.

"They *do* look a lot like those jars," he said grudgingly. "Remember when you went into the Assessment Chamber?"

The boys shuddered.

"That was *awful*," Gene recalled with quiet horror. "It was like being hungry . . . *everywhere*. Ugh."

"But do you remember the *jars*?" Milton asked.

"Sort of . . . I guess."

Milton swept his eyes across the four boys. A cobra tattoo gradually appeared, then disappeared along the side of Gene's neck. Hugo's button nose unbuttoned into a full-blown schnoz. Virgil's hair receded and swelled like a tide of hair lapping a scalp shoreline. Thaddeus's pouty boy boobs became a touch *perkier*.

"And, in case you guys haven't noticed," Milton observed, "you all have a strange habit of . . . *shifting* . . .

like there's a roulette wheel of people spinning inside of you."

The boys glanced at one another guiltily through the corners of their eyes, as if they were silently acknowledging a secret they all shared yet hadn't dared utter.

"What about this: we aren't losing any weight," Milton continued. "Do you all want to be here for eternity if we don't graduate?"

"Who cares?" Thaddeus declared abruptly as he cinched up his corduroy pants. "We'll just burn it off in the DREADmills."

Milton stood still, his massive arms akimbo, glaring at the boys with disgust.

"You're eating human souls and you couldn't care less!" he spat.

Hugo screwed his plaid beret upon his head.

"Well, it's no worse than what that friend of Virgil's did. What was his name? Melvin?"

"*Milton*," Virgil mumbled, eyeing his disguised friend uneasily.

"Whatever," Hugo continued. "Using those lost souls to free himself and leave you behind."

"Yeah," Thaddeus joined in. "I heard two demons transferred from Limbo talking about it, that those souls tried to reunite with their totally dead bodies. Some had even been *cremated*. How terrible is that?"

"Horrible," Gene muttered.

"Yeah, what a creep," Hugo said, walking toward the sulfur water fountain with huge sweeps of corduroyed thighs.

Milton sat down as the wind was metaphorically taken out of his sails.

"But it's morally wrong," he sputtered weakly. "It's like . . . *spiritual cannibalism.*"

Gene and Thaddeus rose to join Hugo by the door.

"But, it's not really . . . *that,*" Gene replied nervously, "if you don't know it is, that is."

Hugo pressed the door open with his meaty palm.

"First, you're wrong," he said. "Second, if you aren't, there isn't anything better to eat. Nothing even comes close. And . . . and . . ."

"Third," Thaddeus offered.

"And third, I just don't care. One guy's morally wrong is another guy's unquestionably delicious. So keep your crackpot theories to your big ugly self."

The boys left the locker room, leaving Milton and Virgil to share an uncomfortable silence.

"I felt so supported in all that," Milton grumbled.

Virgil sighed and faced his friend. "I tried . . ."

"Do or do not. There is no try," Milton mumbled to himself.

"Look, we really don't know for certain," Virgil continued. "And it's clear that none of the boys care about the ingredients. They're just thinking with their stomachs. . . ."

Milton glared at Virgil. "And what do *you* think?"

Virgil picked at his beret's orange pom-pom.

"What I think is . . . is that you're probably right. But . . . you come here like . . . like a cowboy, ready to take something on when you don't even know for sure, you know, what's really happening."

Milton sighed wearily.

Maybe Virgil is right, he thought. *Who do I think I am, anyway? I abandon my friend and my sister, making things worse for them, then come charging back in trying to make things right, not for them, but for myself.*

"Maybe if we registered a complaint, or a concern, anyway," Virgil suggested as he walked over to the swab dispenser on the wall. "There's a box right outside, goes straight to the vice principals. . . ."

"Fat lot of good that would do," Milton groused.

Virgil took a cotton swab from the dispenser by the warped Seems-Only-Fitting mirror.

"Ugh," he said as he worked out a sizable irides-cent glob from his belly button. "For the past few days, the boys have all been making belly button wax like nobody's business. Ever since Hambone Hank—"

Virgil tossed the swab into an overflowing swab re-ceptacle. "Anyway, I just mean that registering a com-plaint couldn't hurt, though I suppose that most everything could hurt here. I don't know what else we could do, really, short of messing with Hambone

Hank's recipe, switching the souls with something else. . . ."

A small grin formed between Milton's gelatinous Pang chin and misshapen nub of a nose. Though Milton was currently four-hundred-something pounds and counting, he suddenly felt as light as nonfat, lo-cal, no-carb air.

Milton rose, beaming, ambling toward Virgil with his clumsy borrowed body. Virgil gulped.

"What? You're scaring me."

Milton wrapped his massive arms around his friend, enveloping him. The Pang skin reflexively tightened around Virgil, thinking it was suddenly gripping warm, struggling prey.

"*Oww,*" Virgil squealed. "Too . . . tight."

"Sorry," Milton offered. "Still trying to get a handle on these arms."

Milton stepped away from Virgil, his bespectacled eyes glittering with perilous notions beneath his Pang sockets.

"I'm worried about you," Virgil said.

"You gave me a great idea!" Milton exclaimed through numb, oversized lips.

Virgil swallowed.

"Now I'm worried about *both* of us," he whimpered.

★   ★   ★

"Okay, we'll try it your way," Milton whispered as they walked down the hall. "We'll register a *concern*," he said, emphasizing the last word with sarcastic finger quotes.

They arrived at a speaker box in the middle of the hallway connecting the Lose-Your-Lunchroom to the boys' bunks. It was a smiling clown whose grin was stretched so wide it became a mocking leer.

"Hello and welcome to Blimpo's suggestion box," said the recorded voice, cracking in adolescent squeaks. "Your feedback is important to us. Please state your name and the quality of service you received. And don't worry: special orders don't upset us! Thank you for being sentenced to Blimpo."

The clown beeped.

Virgil looked nervously at Milton.

"Um, yes . . . ," Virgil mumbled.

"Please speak clearly into my jolly mouth," the voice added.

Virgil cleared his throat.

"Yes, I . . . this is Virgil Farrow and . . ."

Milton shook his head fiercely from side to side, his Pang jowls slapping his freakishly small ears.

". . . just me. I wanted to register a *concern*. About Hambone Hank's Heart Attack Shack. The food is awesome! And the service is really first-rate, efficient without a lot of meaningless chitchat—"

Milton smacked Virgil on the shoulder, gesticulating for him to hurry up.

"The problem is, or might be, anyway . . . We—I mean *I*—can't be sure."

Virgil wiped the sweat pouring down his face like a windshield wiper on a rainy drive.

"But we—I—think he may be using . . . *souls* in his soul food. Lost souls. Stolen from—"

"Thank you for your comments," the clown chirped from the cruel crescent of its mouth. "They help make Blimpo a bigger, *better* place to be punished. Have a *blimptastic* day!"

Virgil gazed expectantly at the pasty white clown face. Milton patted him on the back, restraining the Pang hand that wanted to clutch on to Virgil as if he were the ultimate entree.

"We did it your way," he said cheerily. "Now we'll do it mine."

Virgil turned to Milton with alarm. "What do you mean? I thought—"

Milton folded his arms together until they looked like a huge, swollen pretzel.

"Complaining was a great idea," he said earnestly. "That way, if the vice principals don't do anything, then we know they're in on it. Meanwhile, though, we have to take action. Just in case."

Virgil sagged sadly, like an empty carton of chocolate milk.

"C'mon," Milton said. "It'll be like old times. You and me, messing with the system. At least, this time, I promise: no wading in sewers, hip-deep in poop."

Milton's smile faded, like an old picture of a smile.

"Though we may find ourselves wading in something *far* worse."

19 · CALLING THE BIG SHOTS

"WHOA, PARLEZ-VOUS *déjà vu?"* Lester Lobe, a wild-eyed man with gray hair spilling out from beneath a tattered red fez, quipped as Algernon Cole and Damian stepped into his metaphysical museum, the Paranor Mall. A pensive cloud crossed the otherwise sunny, manic sky of Lester Lobe's face.

"I didn't expect to see you again after Milton's . . . *accident.*"

Lester Lobe gave Damian the once-over, then smirked at Algernon Cole, exposing a mouth full of nicotine-stained teeth.

"What are you, some kind of kinderlawyer now?" he said. "As if exploiting adults wasn't bad enough. But," he added, arms outstretched, spinning in a slow circle among his crowded cathedral of curiosities, "we all have our niches in life, don't we?"

Algernon Cole extended his arm from his beige suit cuff. He glanced at his Mickey Mouse watch.

"I don't have time to trip down memory lane with you right now, Mr. Lobe," he replied. "My client has a very specific request that I, as his counsel, am bound to execute."

Damian gazed, dumbfounded, at a life-size fiberglass alien statue. It grinned—glittering yet cold and aloof, like a faraway sun.

"This place is every shade of crazy," he said, wiping his rough-hewn nose.

Lester Lobe smirked. His bloodshot eyes quivered from his morning liter of Pace Breaker soda with a triple shot of espresso.

"The Paranor Mall is just a mirror held up to society, to see if it's still breathing," he explained. "UFOs . . . ESP . . . MTV . . . all of life's hard-to-explain phenomena have a place here, unlike in those snooty, big-city museums where they're only interested in leading you to the gift shop, not a new conclusion. *They* curate boredom. I, on the other hand, *cure* boredom."

Lester blew the tassel of his fez out of his eyes.

"Wow, you're that *other* kid who came back from the dead," he said with a spooky whisper that reeked of coffee and ashtrays. Lester looked over at Algernon Cole. "You really do run a specialized business: Central Kansas's go-to lawyer for once-dead minors. *Heavy.* If you get another client, I might have to dedicate a new wing."

Damian spat out a sunflower seed husk onto the floor.

"Just show us the way to the mirror booth, freak show," he sneered. "The one that Milquetoast used."

Lester puffed up with indignation. "His name was *Milton,*" he said, stepping closer to Damian. "And I don't have to show you nothing."

Algernon Cole stepped between them.

"Double negatives notwithstanding," he said to Lester, "this boy is about to come into some serious *moola* . . . so we'll be willing to pay a rather hefty admission price. That money could buy you a whole *fleet* of flying saucers with all the extras thrown in: air-conditioning, leather interior, universal positioning satellite . . . *the works.* So please take us to your chrysanthemum."

Lester Lobe rubbed the stubble on his chin as he eyed Damian.

"It's *Psychomanthium,*" he clarified. "And why is he so gung ho about getting in it?"

Algernon Cole glanced sideways at Damian.

"To tell you the truth, I'm not sure myself."

Damian widened the cruel, dark slits he used to glower at the world into something masquerading as sincerity.

"Well, speaking of . . . Milton—Milquetoast was my nickname for the poor little guy," he said. "It was what he ate for lunch every day. It was all he could afford. Anyway, I thought that I might try to use the psycho-whatever to contact him."

Lester folded his arms together. "Weren't you the kid responsible for killing him the first time?" he posed dubiously.

Damian wiped a dry eye.

"Yeah, and I'm all torn up about it," he replied. "I tell you, there's nothing like death to make you see life. It's like looking in the rearview mirror of a stolen car . . . you see everything race away behind you, except without all the sirens. And when I was toast—you know, dead—I saw Milquetoast, *Milton,* and it made me wish I could have a second chance to make things right."

He snickered and shook his head.

"In fact, I guess that a *lot* of what I did in the past could be—if you looked at it in a certain way—viewed as less than honorable."

Damian scratched himself indelicately just south of the belt border.

"Anyway, I just want to give a shout-out to my old friend and tell him, 'Hey, I hope there aren't any hard feelings.' Life's too short, you know? Especially when you're dead."

Lester Lobe sighed, not quite buying what Damian

was selling but—considering the sorry state of his finances—willing to try it out on a trial basis.

"It's over there," he said, waving a yellow fingernail toward the Psychomanthium, otherwise known as the Elvis Abduction Chamber. In the corner, beyond a mannequin draped in a ratty fake fur coat wearing combat boots and a tiara with a sign hanging around its neck reading MRS. BIGFOOT, was what looked like a photo booth covered with rhinestones and tabloid newspaper clippings.

Algernon Cole nodded to Lester as he and Damian walked through a maze of very odds and freaky ends to the back of the Paranor Mall.

Damian put his hand on the chamber's brass doorknob. A strange tingle ran through his extremities—an excitement, a sense of cruel possibility—like when he'd noticed a foreign-exchange student with a speech impediment on the first day of school. He opened the door and peered inside the six-sided box of mirrors.

As Damian stared at a half dozen of himself, that tingle became a full-body wooziness. He scratched the ground with his boots, a movement he found strangely comforting, and clucked softly under his breath. Lester Lobe eyed the boy with interest.

"Are you feeling a little not like yourself?" he asked as a Styrofoam flying saucer suspended above his head blinked and flashed. "Like your energy's a bit off?

That's what Milton kept talking about. Coming back with a little lacking in the spiritual juice department and needing etheric glue to keep himself together."

Damian ran his fingers through his hair as he stared down at his boots. A downy feather fluttered to the floor. Lester Lobe raised his graying eyebrow.

"How exactly *did* you get back to the land of the living, anyhow?"

Algernon Cole cut in between them, like an eager boy at his first school dance.

"He doesn't have to answer anything without a lawyer present."

Lester Lobe smirked and shrugged his shoulders.

"Well, when I see a *real* one, I'll let you know," he said as he walked away. "You two have fifteen minutes, got it?"

Algernon Cole grumbled under his breath and stepped into the dark booth. Damian shot a brief quizzical look at the pictures of Michael Jackson and a chimpanzee with a cowboy hat lacquered to the Psychomanthium's side before entering the chamber.

Algernon Cole fell back into a Fat Elvis beanbag chair while Damian, his head bobbing with nervous energy, paced in tight circles. The boy yanked a cord dangling above his head, and the booth filled with soft, red light.

"So," Algernon Cole said as he twiddled his

manicured thumbs, "are you satisfied? We're in a dreary box in the middle of some hippie's paranoid carnival. . . ."

Damian squatted over the beanbag chair, more hovering than sitting, as if he were hatching a large, heavily cushioned egg.

"What happened?" he asked. "When you were here with Milton?"

"Well," Algernon Cole reflected, "we both sat across from each other and—"

Outside, Lester Lobe flipped on a classic-rock radio station. A wave of heavy guitar music pushed by a rhythmic team of drums and pulled by a man with a singing voice so high that, if the world were made of crystal glass, he'd be Public Enemy Number One, shook the Psychomanthium.

"It's the principle of love,
  When push comes to shove,
  To overcome the darkness,
  And make light your heart's quest."

"And that burned-out *non compos mentis* was blaring his awful oldies. Other than that, we just talked about his book idea, *Heck*."

Damian shifted restlessly from foot to foot.

"What did he say about it?"

"Mostly how his protagonist was consigned to Heck

by mistake. A good kid sent away for a crime he didn't commit. The character signed a contract with the Principal of Darkness—can you believe that?—and Milton wanted my help in figuring out ways that such a contract could be rendered nonbinding."

"Like how?"

"Well, there are a number of options, though deciphering modern-day contract law is hard enough, much less factoring in a theoretical nether-realm dredged from some traumatized boy's imagination. But, firstly, the protagonist is a minor without a *guardian ad litem,* so it would be hard to uphold such a contract. Secondly, he was forced to sign this document under duress. And, lastly, there's the notion of fraudulent claims—a contract based on false promises— hardly a novel circumstance these days. I mean, just watch those terrible TV judge shows."

The music throbbed through the chamber.

> *"Why be anything else?*
> *A heart when it melts.*
> *Join the hubbub, hit the deck.*
> *After all: what the heck?"*

"So that's about it," Algernon Cole sighed, slapping his thighs. "Now, can we get out of here? This music is so awful they could use it on prisoners of war."

Damian looked at the six mirrors surrounding him.

They seemed to shimmer and ripple, like the surface of a still pond ruffled by a faint wind.

"There has to be more," he murmured.

"Nope, not really," Algernon Cole said, rising to his Birkenstocked feet. "Other than mumbling some supernatural mumbo jumbo right before the TV screens came on."

Damian's beady eyes bugged out.

"What did he say?!"

Algernon Cole sighed. "I don't know," he replied. "I forgot my ginkgo this morning. But it was something about guardians of the spirit realm hearing his cry and summoning those spirits from the other side. . . ."

A blast of cold wind blew through the chamber. Damian shivered as if a frigid gust blown off an Arctic ice floe had somehow made its way to Kansas.

> *"It's the principle . . . the darkness . . . be*
> *. . . elsa . . . a . . . hubbub . . .*
> *what the heck?"*

"That's just what happened before!" Algernon Cole cried as his and Damian's reflections warped into a blurry creature that bobbed to the surface of the mirror like a drowned, bloated clown dredged from the Cirque de So Lake. The freakish beast seemed to be, for lack of a better word, singing.

"I could get a *serious* pledge drive going up here, make this freaky church the biggest thing to hit religion since the Bible."

Principal Bubb shivered.

"Please . . . don't mention that insufferable, holy-ghost-written book."

Algernon Cole stirred.

"Book . . . Milton," he mumbled as he slowly came to.

Cerberus hopped up on the principal's lap. Two of his three heads growled.

"Who is that ridiculous man in the corner?" Bea "Elsa" Bubb asked as she soothed her demon lapdog. "And did he say what I *think* he said?"

Algernon Cole's eyes grew wide at the sight of Heck's Principal of Darkness.

"Criminy sakes alive!" he began to scream before Damian clapped his hand over the man's mouth.

"This," Damian explained, "is my lawyer. Apparently, he was also *Milton's* lawyer."

"That little creep had a lawyer?" she shot back as Algernon Cole's eyes trembled back and forth over her hideous image.

Damian nodded. "In between deaths," he clarified. "Asked a lot of questions about contracts." Damian took his hand away from Algernon Cole's mouth.

"Tell her," he said.

"Her?" Algernon Cole spluttered. "She's a . . . *she*?"

The principal scowled as she plucked a tube of

lipstick—Deep Bruise Kissy Fit—off her dressing table, gave it a twist, and smeared it around her gash of a mouth.

"Every inch a woman, little man," she smacked. "More than you could handle."

Algernon Cole turned beseechingly to Damian. "Whatever this is, make it stop," he begged.

"And you haven't even *smelled* her," Damian added.

"Mr. Ruffino," the principal said reproachfully, "I love a reunion as much as the next demoness—which isn't much—but if I wanted to be verbally abused, I would have stayed in middle management."

Damian nudged his lawyer in the ribs. "Tell her about Milton and his book."

Algernon Cole wiped away a fleck of foam from his lips.

"And just who . . . who am I speaking to . . . at . . . *with*?"

Principal Bubb exhaled a dusty, disgruntled wheeze.

"Bea 'Elsa' Bubb," she stated haughtily. "Principal of Darkness."

Algernon Cole shook and swallowed.

"Is this some kind of j-joke?"

Damian slapped him on the back.

"Just play along," he whispered into his ear. "I think Lester Lobe's got us on one of those practical joke shows, like *Suckah Punk'd*."

Algernon Cole nodded his head in slow realization.

"Aah . . . *I* get it," he replied. "I knew that had to be some animatronic device, like the Tunnel of Trepidation ride at Six Flags Wichita."

Algernon Cole tightened his gray ponytail.

"Well, *Principal Bubb*," he said with a wink. "As you know, being in *Heck,* you force children to sign a lot of contracts."

Bea "Elsa" Bubb folded her arms together in disapproval. "Yes, that is a significant part of my duties here. What of it?"

Algernon Cole pulled up his mismatched socks and smirked.

"It's just that, my good . . . *lady* . . . considering contract law as it stands up here, your indentures lack legal bite."

"What under Earth are you talking about?!" the principal hissed with a flick of her bile-green tongue. Damian slapped his hand over Algernon Cole's mouth.

"All this and more when I see you next time, if you give me everything I want."

Bea "Elsa" Bubb rolled her baby yellows.

"Of course you want something," she grumbled. "What is it?"

Damian bit his lip in contemplation.

"Hmm, that's a toughie," he said. "I guess what I want most is for everyone else to be miserable. But, in lieu of that, I suppose I would be satisfied with my own circle of Heck to run as I please."

Principal Bubb snorted.

"Is *that* all?!" she laughed. "How about I throw in the key to h-e-double-hockey-sticks while we're at it?"

Damian's eyes sparkled. "Yeah, that would be awe—"

"Here's how it'll go down, Mr. Ruffino," Bea "Elsa" Bubb declared. "You stay up there as my operative, feed me any information I need to capture Milton Fauster and/or otherwise undermine his exceedingly tiresome efforts, and when you're all through, bring me back loads of corrupted, easily manipulated souls for my sagging war chest. *Then* I will make you vice principal of any circle you wish upon your return."

Damian grinned malevolently.

"And you can't just wish for them all . . . like that wish for unlimited wishes. We're on to that irritating little loophole."

Damian nodded in approval. "That seems fair," he said. "Or as fair as a bargain with the Principal of Darkness can be."

A new song throbbed from outside the Psychomanthium.

"Far-out!" Lester Lobe yelled. "I haven't heard this song since . . . since . . . the *last* time I heard this song!"

*"The devil gets bolder,
    and blows through your mind.
 He hops on your shoulder and
    kicks your behind . . ."*

Bea "Elsa" Bubb leaned close to her vanity to get a better look at the Elvis Abduction Chamber.

"What I'd like to know is how exactly you were able to contact the underworld with this . . . this—"

"Psychomanthium," Damian answered. "I don't know, exactly. It's weird. The weird hippie dude outside put on some music; then Algernon here said something and—"

The lawyer mumbled from beneath Damian's hand.

"Oh, right," Damian said, taking his hand away and wiping it off on his jeans.

Algernon Cole stood up and brushed smooth his slacks.

"This joke isn't funny anymore," he said. "Besides, your time is up."

Damian pulled the lawyer down by the leg. Algernon Cole landed with a muffled thud in the beanbag chair.

"I'll pay you overtime," Damian said, his offer sounding more like a threat. "Just tell the principal what Milton said—you know, the freaky hocus-pocus stuff."

Algernon Cole sighed and gulped, staring at the six

nightmarish Bubbs surrounding him. Heavy metal music shook the chamber.

> *"The devil hunts for treasure*
> *that's locked in your soul.*
> *He burns through your pleasure*
> *and leaves you with coal."*

Algernon Cole clapped his hands over his ears.

"Fine, anything to get out of here," he whined. "Milton said something about the guardians of the spirit realm hearing his cry and summoning those spirits from the other side . . ."

The mirrors trembled and shivered.

> *"I traded my sweet Lucy for,*
> *A date with heat and Lucifer . . ."*

The principal's image stretched, shimmered, and blurred before swirling away into an optical whirlpool. A patch of red slowly formed, gradually gaining clarity and definition.

> *"One night I cashed my fate in,*
> *Coming face to face with—"*

A dapper, red-skinned figure, with a neatly trimmed goatee and massive steel-tipped horns that coiled elegantly, their ends nearly touching over the creature's head, appeared in the mirrors. Algernon Cole fainted dead away. Damian's mouth dropped open like a hungry, hungry hippo at the sight of the ultimate marble. The creature in the mirror arched his thin, black eyebrows and expelled a cloud of cigar smoke as a clangorous guitar chord shook the Psychomanthium.

"*Satan!*"

20 · HiJiNKS iN LOW PLACES

MILTON AND VIRGIL crept carefully down the gently rolling floors of Blimpo's main hallway, each pushing a large metal barrel. They had stolen out of their bunks in the dead of night and hijacked two of Dr. Kellogg's overflowing Q-tip receptacles.

"Careful," Milton whispered as he cautiously trod on the billowing floor, "we're starting to get out of sync."

For added insurance, Virgil had left puddles of gooey lentil casserole outside the demon den. The casserole, as Virgil had unfortunately discovered before Milton's arrival, possessed a peculiar adhesive power and could potentially slow down the guards if Milton and Virgil were found out.

Milton and Virgil rolled the barrels down a slow bend in the hallway until they reached the inside of the drawbridge. Milton eyed the empty hook by the sealed tongue and the Turnkey-leg-shaped lock beneath it.

"Well, it would have been too easy that way," Milton said as he rotated his barrel beneath one of the observatory windows bracketing the bridge. "Just unlocking the door and tripping off the tongue."

He reached inside the barrel and unraveled the ladder he and Virgil had spent the first part of the night constructing. Stolen burlap leotards were knotted together to form two parallel ropes, while rough, woolen gym socks were tied as crosspieces every foot or so.

Next, Milton unfolded a cage constructed of hundreds of used swabs joined together with sticky—nearly cementlike—globs of rainbow navel wax mixed with lentil casserole.

"Do you think the ladder will hold you?" Virgil asked, concerned.

Milton unrolled the ladder out of the round, glassless window, wrapping one end around the heavy barrel and then securing it with several hitch knots.

"Well, not in this thing," Milton replied, taking off his Blimpo uniform. "Can you help, um . . . *unzip* me?"

Virgil grimaced with disgust as he looked nervously down the hall, not sure which would be worse: to be discovered by a demon guard or by a fellow student.

"You look like . . . like . . . a big shaved Muppet covered in cat sick," Virgil said. He sighed and pried apart the seam running down Milton's back. The Pang skin clenched Milton tightly, fighting Virgil's attempts to remove it.

"Your skin is . . . *fighting me*," he panted.

Finally, after a particularly spirited tug, Milton fell out of the skin and onto the floor, slick with Pang juice and gasping for air. The skin writhed next to him.

Virgil grinned and helped Milton to his feet. "Nice to *really* see you," Virgil said. "What does it feel like?"

Milton took off his glasses and cleaned them on his sopping wet POD clothes.

"It's like being the center of a living Twinkie," he answered sluggishly, winded and dazed from having been "birthed."

Milton shivered, feeling strangely naked even though fully dressed, and looked out the window at the Gorge. Hundreds of Pangs writhed below—fat pink zombies swarming with hunger. Milton could see Jack Kerouac's upturned shopping cart almost directly beneath.

"It's time," Milton said as he slipped the Q-tip cage over and around him so that it formed a protective barrier, like a shark cage composed of abandoned hygiene products.

"I hope that's strong enough to keep them out, or you in," Virgil said as he nervously bit his lower lip.

Milton examined his gross, white-with-vaguely-multicolored-joints cage.

"I doubt it," he replied softly. "But I'm just hoping they're so dumb they'll *think* they can't get in."

Milton's Pang skin twitched on the floor.

"No offense," he said as he climbed onto the windowsill.

Virgil nodded and pulled out several containers of Hambone Hank's Soul Food—mostly leftover hush puppies, black-eyed peas (with *real* shiners), and a whole lot of sauce—as well as several plastic desserts filched from the Lose-Your-Lunchroom. He slathered sauce all over everything until it became a nondescript yet tantalizing mound, then positioned himself at the opposite window.

"Ready," he replied. *"Ready to waste all this delicious sauce."*

Milton smiled as he mounted the dangling ladder of soiled gym clothes.

"It's for a good cause," he said sincerely. "Just be quick . . . I don't know how long all this stuff will hold together."

Virgil nodded and reluctantly hurled armloads of food and pseudo-food alike out into the Gorge below.

The Pangs were temporarily paralyzed at the sight of the plummeting feast. Then, suddenly, the creatures thrashed about in a frenzy, climbing over one another to get to the food. It was like a bizarre game of football, only, in this particular case, all the players in the huddle were obese, naked pink blobs with taste buds all over their bodies.

As the Pangs surged en masse to sate their insatiable hunger, Milton clambered down the delicate ladder, like half a spider descending a web of rank, woven laundry. The abandoned shopping cart was just beyond the bottom of the swaying ladder. The squirming pile of Pangs, only ten or so yards away, were completely oblivious to his presence.

Milton took a deep breath and hopped off the ladder. He tried his best to tune out the horrible, slobbering grunts and growls that echoed through the cavernous Gorge and focused instead on the shopping cart. He waddled toward the cart in his oversized floor-length cage, knelt down beside the cart, and, as gently as possible, tipped it over. Beneath were dozens of jars wriggling with the odd, vaporous souls of Make-Believe Play-fellows. Some were broken and empty, yet there were at least twenty intact, filled with undulating, pseudo-spiritual goop that churned like Lava Lamps filled with tufts of cloud tinted with vague, muted colors. Milton scooped up several jars and felt his mind loosen, slipping backward into the hazy, comforting gauze of a daydream. He shook his head clear and quickly stuffed the jars into a stolen pair of XXXL always-tighty-not-so-whitie undies. Dangling from the barbed lip of the cart was Jack's glittering pendant. The silver liquid encased within burbled as Milton's eyes fixed upon it. The fluid—like a melted mirror—reacted to Milton's attention, becoming somehow alert, making the necklace tremble.

Suddenly, the background noise of gurgles and slurps abruptly ceased. Milton turned his head slowly, meeting the dull gaze of a hundred vacant eyes.

"Dinner's over!" Virgil declared from above in a whispered shout. "And they want dessert!"

Milton grabbed the pendant and stuffed it in his shirt pocket, looped his arm through one of the leg holes of his underwear satchel, and heaved it over his shoulder. The Pangs spilled around him, snorting and gaping stupidly at his cage. Milton slowly backed away toward the ladder. Nine Pangs began licking the shopping cart and fighting over its contents—Jack's blankets, notebooks, and old jazz albums, mostly—with slavering growls. Other Pangs, however, were not as easily distracted. They followed Milton as he reached his arms through the cage to mount the ladder and pressed their blank pink faces close, panting hot stale breath. Milton slowly climbed the ladder, stinky rung by stinky rung.

The Pangs moaned with anguish. Their humid breath melted the hardened clots of belly button wax and lentil casserole into soft, untrustworthy lumps. Two Pangs lunged up after him, but the mildewed-gym-clothes ladder shredded under their bulk. As they bellowed, Milton's cage all but disintegrated. He looked down with terror as a mewling mound of Pangs roared at him. He was now exposed, like a piece of unwrapped candy. Milton shinnied until he was halfway up the ladder.

"Grab your hand!" Virgil yelped from the window above.

"Grab *my* hand?" Milton mumbled, perplexed, as he looked up to see Virgil hanging out the window, holding Milton's Pang skin by both wriggling feet. Milton clambered up a long, knotted tangle of leotards, his eyes watering from the fumes.

Don't they ever wash these? he thought. Just as his gym-sock foothold gave way, he seized the Pang suit by the hand. Milton shuddered as he felt the hand clutch back.

Virgil leaned backward and yanked Milton through the window. They both sprawled out on the floor.

"I hope . . . it was . . . worth it," Virgil gasped.

Panting, Milton handed the tinkling underwear tote to Virgil as he scooped up his Pang skin.

"Wow," Virgil murmured softly, transfixed as he gazed into the bag. "These are weird . . . not like the Lost Souls at all. More like steam and gas than thick globs and goop."

Milton slipped the Pang skin over his head. The creature's flesh seized him tightly, squeezing him with spasmodic contractions.

"This . . . suit . . . is . . . crushing me," Milton said with gasping breaths. "Like it's trying to swallow me."

Finally, the spasms stopped. Milton shook his head clear and began to breathe normally.

"Phew," he said with relief as he finished getting dressed. "It was like choking on a big vitamin, only *I* was the vitamin."

Virgil swayed and hummed to himself as he stared at the jars. Milton gave him a soft kick.

"C'mon," Milton said as he loaded his barrel with jars. "We're only halfway there. The night is young and there's mischief to be done."

Virgil nodded, groggily wrapped up the jars in a wad of gym clothes, and put them in his barrel.

Maybe Marlo was right, Milton reflected as they headed toward Hambone Hank's Heart Attack Shack, Virgil humming "Roll Out the Barrel." *Sometimes being a little bad* does *feel good.*

21 · OUT TO LUNCH AND OUT OF LUCK

MADAME POMPADOUR'S TOWN coach turned into a bleak-looking shopping compound right off the highway to h-e-double-hockey-sticks, Route 666. The strip mall reminded Marlo of those sad little clusters of outlet stores she'd find dotting otherwise barren landscapes on never-ending family trips.

The demon driver pulled over. "So where exactly am I supposed to go?" Marlo asked him as she stepped out of the gleaming black coach.

The stooped demon, whose poor posture made him seem like a withered question mark of meat and bone, turned his head slowly to address Marlo.

"The Persecution Complex," he croaked, glaring at her from beneath his screwed-on chauffeur's cap. "Go to the Shopping Block, just inside, and a concierge will help you with your list."

The demon chortled, adding, "As much as anyone *could*."

Marlo looked at the complex with a twinge of dread. Then she shuffled across the parking lot—a sea of SUVs with sporadic herds of Hummers—and unrolled the ridiculous menu Madame Pompadour had given her for the devil's lunch.

- *A bowl of Enmity & Enmities chocolate candies with all the blue ones removed by severed hand*
- *Single-shot Better Latte Than Never coffee drink, stirred counterclockwise ONLY*
- *A monkey*
- *American Spit cigarettes (presmoked, as the devil is trying to quit)*
- *Head of raw broccoli (which the devil detests and is to be procured only so that he can have the satisfaction of throwing it away)*
- *A basket of extra-fuzzy bunny rabbits, puppies, and kittens. Don't ask. You don't want to know.*
- *A bottle of champagne for the devil's real friends*
- *A bottle of real pain for his sham friends*
- *Three 13-oz. nonrecyclable plastic bottles of H2No, the antiwater*
- *Another monkey*

- *A vegetarian platter for Satan's iguana,*
  Dr. Lizardo
- *HostiliTea service for nine, a Honey Bear pack of*
  honey, and two air impurifiers
- *1 gallon of fresh-squeezed blood orange juice*
- *1 gallon of forbidden apple juice*
- *13-piece bucket of General Gander's Unlucky Bride*
  Chicken

All food must be inspected for hair, to ensure that
there are ample stray hairs.

By the time Marlo had reached the bottom of the list of insane lunch demands, she heard the whoosh of the automatic doors and entered the Persecution Complex.

Inside was a cramped collection of pathetic, neglected storefronts—a Pottery Bunker, Scarbucks, Home Despot, and GallMart, to name a few. Much of the complex, however, was cordoned off with bright yellow emergency tape and under-destruction signs: WE APOLOGIZE—YET ARE NOT IN ANY WAY RESPONSIBLE— FOR THE INCONVENIENCE. EXPECTED TIME OF COMPLE- TION: WHEN THE COWS COME HOME. —HELLIBURTON CONSTRUCTION

What a dump, Marlo thought as she scanned the mall, her kleptomaniac fingers barely registering the faintest "must steal something . . . *anything*" tingle.

Beyond the foyer, she noticed a small hard-but-not-impossible-to-notice booth marked VALET. Marlo stepped up to the booth, wrinkled her nose, and saw that the sign had been freshly written in red Sharpie. Marlo slapped the desk bell with her palm, but the rusty old bell was muted and barely registered a sound. A slender demon in *way*-too tights appeared from behind a plastic curtain in the back.

"May I help you . . . *miss?*" the creature said snootily as it evaluated Marlo from down its nose, a ski slope of curved cartilage with an oiled, coiled handlebar mustache beneath.

"You tell me," Marlo said as she pushed her parchment across the counter. The demon regarded it carefully, its lip curled with faint distaste, before snatching and unrolling it. His black eyes glittered with amazement.

"Is this for . . . *him?*" he gasped while his eyes danced across the list. "I knew he was the Prince of Prima Donnas, but this is below and beyond. . . ."

Marlo nodded as her compact cell phone vibrated in her pocket.

"You're so vain, you probably think this song is about you . . . ," sang the ring tone.

Marlo flipped the compact open.

The second she did, she felt her throat constrict. *Collar ID,* she surmised as Madame Pompadour's name flashed in the mirror. Marlo punched one of the compact's cheek rouge pans, and the madame's feline face filled the mirror.

"You were supposed to be back by now," she snapped.

"Hello, I'm fine, thanks for asking," Marlo replied.

"Working with girls your age for hundreds of years, I assure you that I'm completely immune to the effects of both sarcasm and eye rolls," Madame Pompadour replied.

Marlo rolled her eyes, anyway.

"That one was on the house," she muttered.

"What you don't understand," Madame Pompadour continued, "is that the devil's stomach is a precision timepiece of exotic need. If he doesn't receive *just* the right meal at *just* the right time, he goes stark craving mad."

"But I just got here, psycho kitty," Marlo said. "I couldn't have gotten here any sooner if—"

"There is no scientific instrument sensitive enough to possibly detect my interest in your excuses. I expect you back immediately, if not sooner. And everything better be perfect, if not better."

Madame Pompadour hung up. The demon valet stared at Marlo with a look bridging on sympathy as she clicked the compact closed.

"And I thought *I* had a bad boss," he commiserated.

Marlo shrugged.

"No one is the boss of me," she said. "Not even me. Who needs the responsibility? So, can you help me out here?"

The demon valet surveyed the list gravely.

"Well, some of these requests border on the physically impossible . . . but I think I can get you most of these items, or at least virtually indistinguishable substitutions. Here," he said, tearing the list in half. "Most of the beverages you can procure at the Scarbucks across the concourse there. Meanwhile, I'll do my best with the rest."

"Thanks," Marlo said, flashing her lopsided, seldom-seen smile as the demon valet dashed away.

She hurried into the underworld coffee shop, which—with its sterile interior, vacant baristas, and acrid, burnt-bean aroma—didn't seem a far cry from those she had frequented up on the Surface.

"How are you today?" the bored barista asked with all the enthusiasm of someone awaiting a tetanus shot.

"Same as I always am," Marlo retorted, "not in the mood for chitchat."

She slid the list across the counter.

"I need these things and I need them now."

The woman scratched apathetically at a scar that spread across her throat and burrowed into the strap of her kelly green apron.

"Is this, like, some kind of a joke?"

Marlo leveled a gaze at the barista's glassy eyes.

"I don't think the devil is known for his sense of humor," she said, leaning slightly across the counter so that her point would have less distance to travel. "Unless you think the Black Death, World War II, and infomercials are *funny*."

The barista gulped.

"This is for . . . *the Big Guy Downstairs*?"

"Yep, and he needs his single-shot on the double."

The barista nodded as a bead of sweat broke free of her hairline and raced for her nose.

"Name?"

"Marlo Fauster."

The barista turned toward her staff, thrust her fingers in her mouth, and let forth a piercing whistle.

"People, we have a situation," she declared urgently. "I need you to stop what you're doing and get on this most unholy of orders, stat!"

Marlo sighed with relief. She wasn't out of the woods yet, but she was so close she could practically hear the freeway. She settled down into an uncomfortably warm leather chesterfield and fidgeted with restlessness. Marlo's forearm began to prickle, as if she had somehow picked up poison oak.

Statusphere, Marlo thought for no particular reason as she, unconsciously, dug out the latest issue from her messenger bag. The moment she slipped it on, the prickling sensation went away, her frantic breathing slowed, and a sense of cool refreshment cascaded upon her like a Wigglin' Waterpillar sprinkler on a summer's day.

LYON'S DEN (CONT'D)

To see where you fit in the Statusphere, take my totally fun quiz!

What's your favorite snack?
1) Sushi and Perrier
2) Granola and yogurt
3) More and more

If you could have any pet, it would be
1) a bichon frise.
2) a fluffy kitten.
3) a taxidermic lizard that you pull along with a string.

Your dream vacation is
1) Martha's Vineyard.
2) Sedona, Arizona.
3) out of your tank at SeaWorld.

What is the average number of shampoo
and conditioner bottles you own?
1) Two dozen
2) A couple
3) None. I use Ajax once a month.

You know it's going to be a bad day if
1) the limo seat is too cold and your Short Soy No
   Water Chai Latte is too hot.
2) your hair won't bend to your will.
3) you wake up.

Your score:
   0: Totally Statusphere material. Quizzes are
      for L-O-S-E-R-S.
 1–5: Très clique!
 6–10: Average, healthy . . . boring.
11–15: Marlo Fauster!

"Marlo Fauster!" the barista called. Marlo jumped, shook the fog of humiliation from her head, and sprang toward the counter. The barista wheeled out three large boxes stacked on a dolly.

"Here you go," she said, wiping her sweaty hands on her green apron. "I think I got it all . . . well, most of it, anyway."

Marlo furrowed her brow with worry.

"*Most of it?* What do you—"

"You're so vain . . ."

Marlo's heart seized like a monkey's hand around a stolen banana. She checked the compact and—who else would it be?—it was Madame Pompadour calling yet again. Marlo stuffed the phone at the bottom of her messenger bag, where it vibrated angrily.

"Thanks," Marlo muttered to the barista as she wheeled the boxes into the concourse.

The valet booth was obscured by crates and barrels. The demon concierge patted his leathery palms together.

"Well, miss, I really outdid myself with this one, I must say," the demon commented with pride, swiveling his long, greasy head toward Marlo as she approached the booth. "Of course, I did have to make some rather liberal . . . *interpretations* . . . reading between the lines, so to speak."

Marlo surveyed the crates with worry.

"What do you mean, *interpretations?*" she asked.

"You're so vain . . ."

"Aaaah!" Marlo yelped. "Stop calling me, you smug, psycho cat!"

Marlo began to hyperventilate. She could feel Madame Pompadour's disapproval grip her by the throat.

"I got to go," Marlo panted, distracted, as she heaved her booty-burdened dollies out of the complex. She was perspiring as profusely as a sumo wrestler in a sauna, but she had done it: fulfilled an impossible task that not even that picky stuck-up kitty could shake her tail at.

Madame Pompadour examined the contents of the crate. Her faint whiskers twitched as she probed each item with her keen, serpentlike eyes. She looked up at Marlo with a languid expression of contempt.

"Miss Fauster," she snarled. "Do I look like a fool?"

Marlo knew better than to answer this question in the way that she *so* wanted to. *Ached* to, almost.

"No, of course not," Marlo settled for as a response. "Fools wear those curly little shoes with the bells on them—"

Madame Pompadour coiled her graceful arms together and leveled her lethal gaze at the girl sweating before her.

"Then explain to me why you think you can so blatantly disregard my specific, clear instructions and come back with this collection of . . . *garbage.*"

"But—"

"I'm not interested in your explanations!" Madame Pompadour shrieked. She snatched two sock monkeys from the crate.

"What are these?" she asked, trembling with rage.

Marlo swallowed.

"Well," she said nervously. "You wrote that the devil

wanted 'monkeys' for lunch, and I guess the valet couldn't find—"

"I specifically wrote *live* monkeys on your list, Miss Fauster."

Marlo's face grew hot. She knew for a *fact* that Madame Pompadour had specified no such thing. Marlo grabbed the list out of her messenger bag.

"No, you didn't!" she cried. "It says right here . . ."

Marlo looked at the list.

Live monkey.

Another live monkey.

"Principal Bubb neglected to tell me that you were legally blind," Madame Pompadour purred cruelly. "Unfortunately for the rest of us who must suffer your . . . *unique look,* we are not as lucky."

Marlo scanned the list. Nearly all of the items were somehow . . . *different.* In little ways. But, in Madame Pompadour's all-seeing cat/serpent eyes, *nothing* was little: especially if it meant an opportunity to belittle one Marlo Fauster.

"But . . . but," Marlo stammered.

"Farzana," Madame Pompadour called out as she turned toward her office. "Call the custodial crew and have someone come down and cart all . . . *this,*" she added with a disgusted wave of her paw, "away."

As the haughty headmistress reached for the tasteful knob on her tasteful office door, she lobbed one last blazing scowl over her shoulder.

"The devil will be *most* disappointed, Miss Fauster," she hissed. "Most disappointed that his basic needs were not only unmet, but also mocked. You are, without a doubt, the most worthless girl who has ever been deposited on my doorstep. And after all I've done for you . . ."

This is it, Marlo fumed. She had absolutely, positively *had* it. She wasn't sure who she hated more: Madame Pompadour, the devil and his nonsensical demands, or herself for thinking that she actually had a fair chance to succeed at something down here. One thing she did know, though, was that—somehow—she had been set up.

"Okay, Madame Pompous," Marlo spat. "We've played it your way, and your way *blows*. Now we're going to play a rousing game of Marlopoly, and I've got all the hotels, got it? I know *all about* what you're up to with VaniTV."

The downy fur on Madame Pompadour's long, elegant neck rippled. Marlo could see shiny scales beneath.

"I *knew* you were snooping on me, you ill-bred piece of fresh Surface trash!"

Madame regained her composure.

"Besides, soon *everyone* will know about VaniTV. That's rather the point of starting a new network: exposure."

Marlo crossed her arms. "But I know *why* you're

doing it . . . kind of . . . to make kids insecure so that they use something called a DREADmill—"

Madame Pompadour grabbed Marlo's arm and tugged her toward her office.

"You know nothing!" Madame Pompadour whispered, her eyes fixed on Farzana. "And even if you *did,* you wouldn't know what to do with it!"

"I wouldn't know what to do with what I *don't* know?" Marlo replied. "Have you been smoking catnip?"

Madame Pompadour hissed.

"Don't you get all up on my grill, girl!"

Marlo laughed. "I love it when old people try to sling slang. It's cute. Like when they try to make calls with their remote. Anyway, I'm done talking to you, ma'am. I answer to a lower power. And he's about to get an earful—or *horn*ful, more like."

"*You wouldn't—*"

Marlo yanked her arm away from Madame Pompadour's clutches and stormed toward Satan's office. The long hallway grew darker, smokier, and lower with every step, as if she was descending a steep slope. The hot tickle of brimstone curled Marlo's nose. A noxious smog, like pepper-spray vapor, stung her eyes. The air grew so thick that Marlo practically had to chew it to breathe. Finally, the hallway ended at the devil's door.

The stone door was engraved with what had

seemed from far away to be a grotesque gallery of hideous cadavers frozen in anguished death screams but, up close, was something far worse: a group of laughing dentists.

Madame Pompadour padded down the hallway behind her, as silent as fog creeping in on little cat feet.

"Don't you *dare,*" she seethed.

Marlo gulped and grabbed the door handle: the bronzed hand of a businessman caught in mid "shake." She pressed her palm to the burnished metal and screamed. It felt molten hot. Marlo jerked her hand back and examined it, expecting it to be nothing but a charred stump. But it was completely intact, not even flushed or especially warm. She drew in a thick, syrupy breath of humid air, squeezed her eyes shut, and grabbed the door handle again. Marlo, biting her lips so hard they bled, screamed a muffled scream as she yanked open the door.

And there, awaiting her in the sweltering brick office, behind a desk carved from old-growth rain forest wood capped with a sealskin desk blotter and ivory inlays, in an imperious chair upholstered with unicorn hide was . . . *absolutely no one.*

Marlo scanned the repugnant office. Large scorched planks sat at the bottom of a volcanic rock fireplace the size of a small garage. Marlo noticed that one of the planks had written on it PROPERTY OF NOAH.

Farzana skittered into the room behind Marlo.

"You're going to ruin *everything* for me!"

Farzana's entrance caused a swirl of dust to rise off a small pentagram-shaped coffee table set before the fireplace. It was apparent to Marlo that no one had been in this office for weeks, months . . . perhaps even years. Marlo whipped around.

"What do you mean?" she asked, the adrenaline still coursing through her body.

"You were my way out," Farzana said as she wiped away her milk mustache. "My replacement. I hate it here. I had my transfer to Dupli-City all planned, pulling every string imaginable. I was going to be Mata Hari's teacher's aide!"

"So *that's* why you kept covering for me," Marlo replied, her jaw set, her eyes fiery enough to ignite the holy kindling in the long-abandoned fireplace. "Not to be nice, not to help a fellow Infern, but as some sort of . . . *inhuman sacrifice.*"

Madame Pompadour strutted into the room, her sleek head sprouting from behind Farzana's quivering shoulders. Her ears were flattened with rage while her eyes were as simultaneously cold and hot as dry ice.

"Miss Fauster," she practically yowled before delivering the worst phrase that one could ever utter: four innocent words that, when arranged just so, have christened countless emotional shipwrecks.

"*We need to talk.*"

22 · A CASE OF DO OR DiET

MILTON AND VIRGIL rolled their barrels to a stop at the mouth of the dark, deserted hallway behind the Lose-Your-Lunchroom. They studied the silent tin shed parked at the hallway's abrupt dead end behind Chef Boyareyookrazee's kitchen.

"Seems quiet enough—" Virgil whispered.

"Shhh," Milton interrupted. "I hear something."

Milton motioned for Virgil to approach one side of the shed, while he took the other.

They kicked off their shoes and stealthily trod toward Hambone Hank's Heart Attack Shack. A faint yet lusty snore rumbled from the shed, broken up by the occasional incoherent mumble.

"Anput . . . Kebauet . . . I will . . . save . . ." the deep voice grunted.

Milton slunk down as much as he could in his disguise and slowly peered inside the wide front window of the red and yellow shed. In the corner, curled up on a round foam bed, was Hambone Hank, catching some serious Zs. His long arms and legs, wrapped beneath his black robe, were twitching as if he was having a bad dream. Near him was a black cast-iron cauldron, sealed off with a lid that had welded to it a stubby coiled pipe. The pipe was roughly the size of the soul jars piled at the cauldron's base.

That must be how he mixes in the lost souls without them running amok, Milton surmised, having experienced first-hand the unpredictable buoyancy of souls, at least the good ones, when freed. Next to the cauldron was a deep fryer, another pile of jars, and a door—which, to Milton's relief, had been left slightly open. Virgil crept alongside the shed with an armload of imaginary-friend souls.

"Switch the jars," Milton whispered as he crouched down next to Virgil by the door. "Hand me the *real* soul jars through the window, and we'll stow them in our gym lockers until we figure out what to do with them all."

Virgil nodded and, with some difficulty, squeezed through the door and into the cramped shack. He tiptoed past the deep fryer—though, Milton noticed, not without first taking in a whiff of its contents— then knelt by the cauldron.

Hambone Hank stirred. *"Hush . . . puppies . . . don't . . . whimper,"* the cook mumbled before returning to the land of Nod.

Virgil froze. The hair on his forearms stood on end. After half a minute, he moved—not completely thawed out but enough to resume "the ol' switcheroo." He handed Milton the Lost Soul jars filled with squirming, seething black globs that knocked angrily against the glass.

These were definitely *some bad, bad folks,* Milton pondered. *No wonder we all stayed so heavy even after all those DREADmill sessions.*

Virgil stopped briefly to examine one of the souls of Make-Believe Play-fellows. He touched the clouded glass. His eyes became dreamy, and a faint smile crossed his lips.

Milton stuck his head inside the take-out window. "We don't have time for you to play with them all," he whispered.

Virgil sighed and handed Milton the remaining jars.

"I don't see how this is any different," Virgil argued. "They're still souls."

"Souls of *Make-Believe Play-fellows,*" Milton countered. "They were never really alive, so they never really died. Would you rather keep eating the souls of real people? Real *bad* people, judging from how dark and angry the blobs are? After all, you are what you—"

"Fine, fine," Virgil grumbled as he deposited the last

of the imaginary-friend souls in the pile. "It just seems so . . . *mean.*"

Virgil crept out of the shed and, being a decent sort of boy, closed the door behind him. The action set a precarious pile of jars trembling. Milton held his breath as the pyramid of six hastily stacked jars wobbled. The imaginary soul on top drifted from one side of the jar to the other, counteracting the stack's listing teeter. Milton sighed with relief. Unfortunately, the soul slurped back in its sea of ectoplasmic goo, and the jars toppled with a chorus of dull thuds.

Hambone Hank rustled awake.

"Woof happened?" he yelped groggily.

Milton ducked down and swaddled the Lost Soul jars while hobbling toward his metal waste bin.

"Move!" Milton hissed to Virgil, and the two of them barreled down the corridor.

"It's official," Dr. Kellogg chirped as he gestured for Hugo to step off the scale. "You boys are a bunch of losers . . . in the best possible way!"

Milton and Virgil exchanged conspiratorial smirks.

The effect had been practically instantaneous, Milton thought. After a breakfast of Hambone Hank's new recipe and their morning session in the DREADmills, all of the boys had indeed lost a few pounds. It wasn't a lot—which was probably good in terms of not raising suspicions—but it *did* mean that the boys might avoid an eternity spent running with the devil down in h-e-double-hockey-sticks.

Nurse Rutlidge strutted out across the Gymnauseum floor. She leaned in close to Dr. Kellogg with a face crinkled with worry, whispering in his ear with her thin, dull red lips. His bushy white eyebrows rose with surprise.

"Of course," he muttered to the nurse. The doctor cleared his throat.

"Boys, I will be back in two shakes of a skinless, boiled lamb shank."

The spry man walked out of the Gymnauseum with nervous, purposeful little steps.

The boys shrugged their shoulders, drained from their time in the DREADmills, yet even more sluggish than usual. Perhaps it had something to with the sudden change in diet. Hugo in particular had complained that Hambone Hank's soul food tasted kind of weird. But it was probably like that chalky soy milk Milton's mom had bought after reading an article on bovine growth hormones: it tasted strange at first, but Milton—perhaps out of necessity—had eventually gotten used to it.

Dr. Kellogg returned, each foot tapping the floor like a tiny hammer.

"Gym dandy!" he said, his smile as genuinely warm as a video of a roaring fire. "I have some good news and some less-good news! The good news is that the vice principals are very pleased with your recent, if modest, downward trend in mass."

Milton raised his great, ugly hand.

Dr. Kellogg waved Milton's question away. "The scales are wired directly to their hovering offices above, Mr. Grumby," the teacher said testily.

Milton lowered his hand sheepishly, the doctor having perfectly anticipated his question.

"Now that you have all proved that Blimpo's patented system of dynamic, stress-induced movement really *works*," Dr. Kellogg continued with a mad gleam in his eye, "the vice principals want to take it to the next level. From now on, we will be instituting a new policy of twenty-four-hour fitness."

The boys emerged from their stupor, muttering complaints.

"What does *that* mean?" Hugo asked with a deep scowl.

The diminutive doctor swelled up with indignation.

"What it means, you impertinent young man, is that you will all be working out in the DREADmills in shifts, sixteen hours a day."

Gene looked from face to face, lost. "Was that the less-good news?" he asked.

"Yeah," Thaddeus grumbled. "The lessest good news of all!"

"*Least,*" Milton corrected out of habit.

The boys glared at Milton, as if they couldn't like him any less, though they were about to.

"Boys, boys," the doctor clucked. "Children should be seen and not heard."

He ogled Milton with dull horror.

"And some shouldn't even be *seen*."

The bell rang. The boys lumbered, heads slumped down like overburdened pack animals, into the locker rooms. They slammed their bulk down on the benches and sulked.

"This is like a vacuum cleaner with Energizer batteries," Hugo griped. "It just keeps sucking and sucking and sucking. . . ."

Thaddeus kicked his locker with frustration. In the locker next to his—Virgil's—several soul jars crashed.

"What was that?" Thaddeus asked suspiciously.

Virgil blushed *hard*. His head snapped toward Milton, who knew in that instant that all manner of beans were about to be spilled.

"We . . . it's . . . just . . . a whole lot of—"

"Nothing," Milton interjected while kicking Virgil in the shin. Unfortunately, his Pang skin fuel-injected his punt so that it not only hurt Virgil but also sent several soul jars tumbling in Milton's locker as well.

"Sure is loud for nothing," Hugo noted as he shoved his bulk alongside them on the bench.

"We just w-wanted t-to help," Virgil stammered as

Milton slunk an inch or so deeper in his Pang suit. "The s-souls, you know? The food was just t-too . . . rich and so we—ha ha"—(Milton, for the death of him, wasn't sure what made Virgil suddenly laugh)—"just, you know, switched the recipe."

"You switched the recipe?" Thaddeus said with horror. *"You switched the recipe?"*

Gene's face went white. "Why would anyone *do* that?!"

The perspiration that had only just evaporated on Virgil's black rubber tube top returned with reinforcements.

"It's just that . . ." Virgil's eyes locked on to his friend, like someone sinking in quicksand gazing desperately at a low-hanging branch. *"You* tell them, Milton."

The last bean—a colossal one—spilled to the floor and rolled accusingly between Milton's feet.

"Milton?" Hugo repeated. *"Milton?"*

"I—I—I," Virgil stuttered in rapid-fire succession, "I meant Joe . . . um . . . Noah . . . uh . . . *Jonah."*

Thaddeus looked closely at Milton.

"I knew he was unbelievably ugly," the boy murmured as he eyeballed Milton's face. "Now I know why—you can see, if you look closely. Around the eyes. Like a mask."

Hugo chuckled and leaned into Milton.

"So, the famous Milton," he said, savoring every word as he rolled them slowly on his tongue. "The boy who escaped. How's that been working out for you?"

He laughed in Milton's fraudulent face.

"Now you're here, messing with the only thing that made this place bearable and making things even *worse* for us in the process."

Milton sighed. "I came back to help Virgil," he uttered softly.

"Right," Hugo said. "Helping him to more time in the DREADmill."

Virgil cradled his head in his hands, not daring to meet Milton's eyes.

"You don't understand," Milton explained. "It's all a conspiracy to keep you here. I know it is. Making you fat so you can feed those awful machines."

"*You* don't understand," Hugo said, pressing close to Milton. "I'm hungry and I hurt all over. If I don't get my barbecue back, *you're* going to hurt all over."

Milton opened his locker. He pulled out an upturned Lost Soul jar and held it out to Hugo.

"You seriously want to eat *this*?" he said as the stormy black glob squished angrily against the glass.

The boys ogled the jar. Their mouths sneered with revulsion.

"Is that mean tar stuff *really* in that yummy food?" Gene asked dimly.

Hugo shrugged. "I don't care what the ingredients

look like," he said. "I only care how they taste. And those ugly, nasty things might not be easy on the eyes, but they sure melt in your mouth."

"Maybe if we gave the new recipe a fun name," Virgil chirped suddenly. "You know . . . a silly name with lots of misspellings. Food always seems to taste better if it's—"

Hugo wedged himself between Milton and Virgil, coiling his beefy arms around the boys.

"Here's how it's going down: you two are going to switch back the jars tonight so that we get Hambone's *original* blend of souls and spice and everything nice. . . ."

Hugo smiled at Virgil. "As a peace offering, I'll even give you a tasty Smarts Doughnut."

Virgil licked his lips. "A Smarts Doughnut?"

"Yeah," Hugo said. "Here you go."

He slugged Virgil hard on the shoulder.

"Oww!" Virgil yelped, rubbing his upper arm.

Hugo grinned wickedly. *"Smarts, don't it?"*

"But eating human souls is *wrong*," Milton said, the words sounding as sensible to his ears as *fire is bad* and *school plays are humiliating for all concerned*. "It's *exactly* what they want."

"No, *you're* wrong," Hugo hissed into Milton's ear. *"You're* exactly what they want. And that's just what they'll get—*you*—if we don't get our grub back on. Got it?"

Milton's body—his *real* body, compressed inside the

Pang—grew numb and sick with dread. Though Milton wasn't completely sure what he had hoped to accomplish by coming back to Heck, he knew it wasn't simply to be served back to Bea "Elsa" Bubb on a platter. He had no choice.

MIDDLEWORD

There are two sides to everything, even things that actually have three or more sides.

Take a coin . . . actually, give it back. I only meant that figuratively. Thank you. Now, this coin is like a regular coin, only one side is a deep-fried, Gorgonzola-stuffed Twinkie triple-dipped in dark chocolate, then rolled in coconut, almonds, hazelnuts, candy corn, and toffee bits, and the other side is half a stale rice cake with all the salt licked off.

One side of this admittedly odd coin is all about padding who you are. But, though you think you're insulating yourself from the cruel world around you, you're really trying to hide away from yourself: the nougatty center of your soul that others have convinced you isn't worth a used ketchup packet. On the other side, it's just the same, only the opposite: forcing you to twist, fold, spindle, mutilate, and slenderize your body so that it fits into the narrow little space the world has carved out for you.

Insecurity flips this coin, and only you can call it heads or tails. Better still, just swipe the coin while it's still in the air and invest it. That way, you can buy the homes of all the kids who made fun of you and evict the whole jeering, mocking lot of them! Ha! Not so funny now, are you, fending for yourselves out in the unpleasantly cold or uncomfortably warm?!

Okay, maybe it's not a coin. Perhaps it's more of a rope. A tug-of-war. On one end of the rope are those who want you to get bigger. To always want more. Filling you full of food until food is all that makes you feel full. On the other end of the rope are those who want you to get smaller. To always want less. Depriving you of fullness so that emptiness is the only thing that makes you feel full. And where are you in all of this? In the middle: stretched like taffy, jerked like chicken, until you're ultimately pulled apart like pork. But you know what also happens? The tuggers fall. They need the tension of the rope. Without it, they're just on the ground, in the mud, left holding the rope. . . .

23 · LOST AND HOUND

ONCE AGAIN, MILTON and Virgil found themselves riding the old wooden swells of Blimpo's hallways—their legs aching from multiple DREADmill sessions—on another midnight raid of Hambone Hank's Heart Attack Shack.

On this outing, the hallway was graveyard quiet: no deep snores, no garbled sleep-talking, just a thick silence.

Milton waved for Virgil to stop while he peeked into the tin shed through the take-out window. Inside was . . . a whole lot of nothing. No sleeping chef (thankfully) but (unthankfully) no soul jars—either of the lost or Make-Believe Play-fellow variety. Hambone's cooking cauldron was missing, too. Milton crinkled his drawn-on brows.

"No one's here," he whispered to Virgil. "It's like the place was cleaned out—"

The boys heard a steady *tink-tink* sound coming from the kitchen. Milton crept around the shack—barely squeezing past it, considering his inflated self—and discovered a nondescript, unmarked door. He carefully opened it and found that it led to Chef Boyareyookrazee's kitchen. The *tink-tink* was the lid on Hambone Hank's simmering cauldron. Surrounding the cast-iron pot were dozens of Lost Soul jars and several small tubs of what looked like lard.

"Virgil," Milton whispered, beckoning him over. "There are more jars in here, but I don't see any of the—"

Something grabbed Milton by the wrist and pulled him inside the kitchen.

"So *you're* the one who has been tampering with my recipe!" Hambone Hank snarled from behind his surgical mask while waving a meat cleaver with his free hand. Milton was transfixed by the cook's deep, familiar eyes: so sad and—fittingly—*soulful*.

"I don't appreciate backseat cooks throwing in new ingredients. In fact, they can easily *become* ingredients, if you get my meaning."

The butcher's knife hovered over Hambone Hank's cloaked head, trembling as if deciding which of Milton's limbs to sever. Milton only hoped that his Pang suit would protect him from the mad cook's inaugural "chop."

"Milton!" Virgil cried from the doorway. "Are you okay?"

Milton laughed despite himself. "Do I *look* okay? Get out of here! *Now!*"

Hambone Hank's eyes bore into Milton's.

"Wait!" he barked.

Still holding him snugly by the wrist, the tall, slender creature sniffed Milton up and down, especially down.

"Um . . . ," Milton said as Hambone Hank sniffed the back of Milton's pants, "*this* is awkward."

Hambone Hank let go of Milton's wrist.

"Run, Milton, run!" Virgil cried.

"It really *is* you," the cook murmured in a smooth rumble.

Milton rubbed his wrist. He noticed that the back of Hambone Hank's black robe was . . . *wagging*. The cook took off his mask, revealing a long, wet nose, and slipped off his hood.

"Annubis!" Milton cried.

The regal dog god—whom Milton had last seen ingesting his gelatinous colleague in Limbo's Assessment Chamber—smiled a mouthful of sharp white canine teeth.

"Why are you wearing this costume?" Annubis asked. "Its smell confuses me."

Milton grinned. "I could ask you the same thing," he replied, "about the costume, I mean. Virgil, it's okay . . . come on in."

Virgil hesitated in the doorway.

"Sure," he yammered. "It's just that I'm more of a . . . *cat* person."

"Aah, I see," Annubis said in his dignified baritone. "You are here in hopes of freeing your friend. You have a lot of nerve for someone who doesn't belong in Heck."

"How can you tell that I don't belong?" Milton asked.

Annubis smiled and tapped his paw-hand to his snout.

"The nose knows. Your soul smells . . . *good*. A smell something like your human Froot Loops. Not that boiled-cabbage/rotten-tooth smell most of the other boys bring with them."

The steady *tink-tink* of the simmering cauldron reminded Milton of why he was here in the first place.

"Why are you, of all creatures, here, doing . . . *this*?" Milton asked as he surveyed the soul jars littering the floor.

The tail from beneath Annubis's robe drooped. His eyes grew wet, and his snout grew dry. He sat down on a container of lard.

"It all started when you jammed Ms. Mallon's rib into my associate Ammit."

Milton gulped. *Uh-oh,* he thought guiltily, *I never thought how that would affect Annubis.*

"I didn't think that you . . . ," Milton said apologetically.

Annubis raised his paw-hand for Milton to be silent.

"Ammit had it coming, I assure you," the dog god replied. "Actually, it was your sister's terrible singing that drove me to the brink, though I still check in with Bones Anonymous every once in a while to keep my *weakness* in check."

"In any case," Milton offered, "on behalf of the Fausters, I'm sorry."

Annubis folded his lean forearms together.

"Even in Heck, eating your coworkers is frowned upon. The Powers That Be Evil removed me from my post and—unbeknownst to me at the time—took my family down to—"

Annubis shivered.

"The Kennels."

"The Kennels?" Milton repeated, twisting the words up at the end to make them a question.

"A Heck for animals, of sorts."

"There's a Heck for animals?" Virgil asked incredulously. "But . . . why? I didn't even know that, no offense, animals *had* souls."

"Or why they would be darned for all eternity, just for following their instincts," Milton added.

Annubis smiled the mysterious grin of a dog.

"The same could be said for you humans, too," he replied. "Let me just say that, like everything else down here, the Furafter is . . . *complicated*. But, yes, animals *do* have souls, I assure you. All life does. It's just a matter of degree. So my lovely wife, Anput, and my daughter, Kebauet, are . . ."

Annubis whimpered softly to himself.

"*Caged* . . . in the Kennels. I can almost smell their despair. Principal Bubb said that if I ever wanted to see them again, I would have to work for a year in the Pitch-Black Market, as a *cur*-rier."

"I *knew* Principal Bubb was behind this!" Milton spat.

Annubis gave a quick shake of his head. "Yes and no," he replied. "Principal Bubb turned me over to the underbelly of the underworld, but even *she* does not know of my ultimate role."

"Which is *what*, exactly?" Milton asked. "Why does Blimpo want you to feed souls to students? You of all people . . . *creatures* . . . should know . . ."

Annubis hung his head low in shame. "Yes, that is the problem . . . I *do* know. And it has brought me no end of misery. The vice principals want the students to gain weight—*soul* weight—so that they never lose any in the DREADmills. I suspect that they are using the machines not only to power Blimpo—an illegal exploitation of resources, even in the underworld—but also to sell off the remaining energy to other realms. But that is all I know. I'm sure the plot goes higher, or lower as the case may be."

Milton stared at the bubbling cauldron.

"Who forces you to make the batches?" Milton asked.

Annubis clutched a black collar around his throat. A metal box was fused to the neckband.

"Chef Boyareyookrazee possesses my pink slip, as it were. And, if threatening my family ever loses its grip on my every waking—and dreaming—thought, he's got me, quite literally, by the throat with this shock collar."

Virgil shook his head. "Whoa, this is a lot to swallow," he commented, turning to Milton. "How do we know he's telling the truth? Last time I saw him, he stuck his paws in my chest and yanked out my soul."

Annubis's lips curled into a faint smile.

"Actually, the base of the brain and the upper back. You are wise to be suspicious. But the proof is in the pudding."

Annubis walked toward a vat of congealed blood pudding. He plunged his paw-hand into the tub and emerged with a photograph: a beautiful Weimaraner woman with sleek, silver fur and a pup chewing blissfully on a Nylabone.

"I reasoned that the safest place to keep my

mementos was in Chef Boyareyookrazee's cuisine," Annubis continued, "especially since no one is forced to eat it now, thanks to my barbecue."

Milton scratched his borrowed head.

"But that's the problem," Milton said. "Why we switched the souls last night with those of Make-Believe Play-fellows. To save the souls. The real ones."

Annubis's normally regal posture drooped.

"I have been doing my best to use the souls sparingly," he relayed with remorse. "But it's the lost souls that give the soul food its . . . well, *soul*. I discovered your switch as I was forced to prepare my latest batch, and I assumed it was some trick to test my loyalty. As if anyone would have to test a dog god's loyalty. Anyway, I *did* cut the recipe with some of the Make-Believe Play-fellows, which managed to reduce the soul content considerably—"

"And, unfortunately, the flavor," added Virgil mournfully.

Milton rubbed his disgusting rubbery face. "You've got to know that, no matter what you do for them, they're never going to let you or your family go," Milton said soberly.

Annubis stared at his sandaled feet. "But I signed a contract that specifically fixed my indentured tenure at one year. . . ."

"Where did you sign it?"

"In Principal Bubb's office."

Milton shook his head.

"In Limbo—*where time has no meaning.*"

Annubis had what could only be referred to as a hangdog expression on his face.

"Ouch," Virgil muttered. "She just threw you to the dogs."

Milton glared at Virgil, then edged close to Annubis, patting him on the back and slowly moving down his spine until finding his scritchy spot. The dog god's left leg moved uncontrollably.

"What we need to do is shake things up down here, give the fat cats a flea dip," Milton soothed. "Then, in the confusion, we get you out of here to rescue your family."

"Please stop," Annubis implored, his leg flailing about.

"Sorry," Milton said, leaving Annubis to lick his paw-hand and smooth down his fur until he regained his sleek, dignified composure.

"You are right," the dog god growled, rising, his hackles raised. "I was a fool for thinking they could be trusted."

"But what can we do?" Virgil said with distress, his voice hitting a register that made Annubis's ears flutter.

"First, we take off that collar," Milton said.

Annubis held up his paw-hands, which—while perfect for extracting souls—lacked the facility for complex tasks such as undoing the difficult shock-collar latch behind one's own neck.

Milton stepped behind Annubis, who got down on his knees and held his head low while Milton worried the latch. After a few moments, he got it loose.

"There," Milton said as he held out the cruel device in front of him. "We'll need to find something to replace it with, though, so Chef Boyareyookrazee doesn't notice."

Annubis scanned the kitchen, settling on a hamper overflowing with soiled laundry beneath a chute.

"There should be something in there," he said, motioning toward the mound of dirty clothes.

"That is so unsanitary!" Milton said with disgust as he sifted through the collection of dirty laundry. "Why would anyone collect filthy underwear right next to where food is prepared. . . ."

Annubis smirked.

"Oh, right," Milton continued. "We're in Heck. I keep foolishly expecting a shred of logic or decency down here. My bad. Oh wait . . . here we go."

Milton exhumed what he prayed was a sock garter that looked something like Annubis's shock collar. He wadded the original collar in a pair of black bikini briefs, then stuffed it down in the hamper.

Virgil grabbed a dark gray Brillo pad from the sink. "This kind of looks like the shock box."

Milton, with a little ingenuity and a lot of lentil

casserole as fixative, was able to fashion a reasonable facsimile. He secured it around the dog god's neck.

"Okay," Milton said, eyeing his handiwork. "Next up, your new recipe—do you think using *solely* the souls of Make-Believe Play-fellows could work?"

Annubis opened a larder above the deep fryer. Inside were dozens of Make-Believe Play-fellows, quivering with dreamy curiosity inside their jars as the culinary artist formerly known as Hambone Hank inspected them.

"I think so," he said, rubbing his bristly chin thoughtfully with his paw. "They will definitely be lighter, due to their weak etheric composition. At least there should be less navel residue."

"Navel residue?" Virgil replied. "You mean that gunk in our belly buttons is because of your barbecue?"

"Yes." Annubis nodded. "The souls, specifically. The navel is an umbilical scar . . . the cord through which we initially receive our souls. The souls themselves remember and leave behind a faint, ectoplasmic residue. These Make-Believe souls, however . . ."

He sniffed the jar with his keen, wet nose.

"Amazing. Energy molded by pure imagination. The flavor is weak, rather like using imitation butter instead of real butter, but—even though it's a tall order— I've become *quite* the short-order cook."

Milton clapped his hands together. Virgil winced, half-expecting his friend to yell "gym dandy."

"Then we're in business."

Milton grinned. It was amazing how, when a puzzling problem evolved into a problematic puzzle, his mind gained clarity and confidence. He had purpose. And he had friends.

Milton put his arm around Annubis.

"Every dog has his day, my friend, and you are about to get *yours*."

24 · AS QUEASY AS PiE

AT THE FRONT of the classroom, a scraggly, ancient man stood half-submerged in a deep kiddie pool fitted with wheels, at the center of which grew a peach tree. Whenever the famished teacher reached for a piece of the juicy, swollen fruit—which was often—the branches pulled away from his grasp: just inches from his trembling fingers. And whenever his ancient, leathery voice became parched from thirst—which was also often—the water receded before he could get any.

The frustrated teacher, King Tantalus, poled himself and his mobile pool to the chalkboard like a gondolier, only substituting his crutch for an oar. By giving the handle a few quick rotations, he pushed out a piece of chalk at the crutch's tip, which he used to write: "Gastrophysics: the application of the laws and theories of physics to the interpretation of gourmet cuisine."

"Told you," Virgil whispered to Milton, who had not believed that there was any such thing as "gastrophysics."

"First, some good news: tomorrow there will be a peptic rally in the Gymnauseum," the old man relayed, his voice as dry and rough as the tongue of an old boot. "Now the bad news: tomorrow there will be a peptic rally in the Gymnauseum."

Gene raised his hand.

"What's a peptic rally?"

"Good question, Mr. Blankenship."

Gene smiled brightly, happy that—while he rarely knew the answers—he could at least pose a good question.

"A peptic rally is like a pep rally, only less so. It's an unfortunate tradition here in Blimpo: a way to boost morale while dampening self-esteem."

King Tantalus eyed a fat, succulent peach that bobbed coyly on the branch just above his head. He sighed.

"And since many of you boys will, more than likely, be forced to participate in some kind of demoralizing competition as part of tomorrow's assembly, we will, today, focus on the art of pie eating."

The group of boys were now held enrapt by their odd teacher, thanks to the pairing of—to them—the two most beautiful words in the English language: "pie" and "eating."

"Competitive pie eating is the rapid consumption of sugary, artery-clogging pastry way past the point of satisfaction," he continued.

King Tantalus made a sudden lunge for the nearest peach. The branch flicked itself inches out of reach.

"One day, my luscious friend," he muttered. "One day . . ."

He returned his attention to the class.

"First, training: as far as pie eating goes, contrary to popular opinion, abstinence does *not* make the stomach grow fonder. You must keep your stomach *expansive*."

King Tantalus squatted quickly to the bottom of the pool, flailing his cupped hands by his knees. The water withdrew until it was—as was to be expected—*tantalizingly* out of reach. The teacher cursed in Greek under his breath and surveyed the obese boys before him.

"Check, by the looks of it," he replied dryly.

A roly-poly demon, who looked exactly like an upright doodlebug, from its hard black armor to the tips of its feelers, knocked on the door with several of its many spindly arms.

"*Yes*," King Tantalus snapped. "What is it?"

"Delivery," the demon chirped. "By orders of the Burgermeister and Lady Lactose. These are being installed in all of the classrooms. Hallways, too. As some kind of a motivation tool."

The teacher eyed a peach through the corner of his eye. He tried to snatch it, but the peach yanked itself away, trembling afterward slightly, laughing at him with its little fruit body.

"Fine," King Tantalus said miserably.

The demon struggled to roll a massive plasma-screen television into the classroom. He set it against the wall where it suddenly flickered to life.

King Tantalus stroked his long white beard in contemplation while the boys stared at the screen. A logo—an irritating silhouette of a girl thumbing her nose—gave way to a neon pink title:

VANITV IS ON THE AIR!

The title spun away, and a collage filled the screen—quick-cutted to the point of near incomprehension—depicting young, attractive people with perfect bodies not only enjoying their active, vivacious lifestyles, but also fiercely *flaunting* them.

Techno music pulsed like the heartbeat of a robot with panic disorder.

"Hey, *Jonah*," Hugo muttered from the desk behind Milton's. "I hope—for *your* sake—you switched Hambone Hank's recipe to its perfect, original blend."

Milton swallowed hard. He turned to face his blackmailer, the boy with cheeks like an igloo duplex.

"Did it taste the same this morning or not?"

Hugo swirled his tongue in his mouth to summon the memory of his last meal.

"Well," he recalled. "It wasn't *exactly* the same . . . the spices were a little weird at first, but I have to admit:

it was melt-in-your-mouth wonderful—and it better stay that way, if you and your friend 'Milton' know what's good for you."

Milton got goose pimples at the mention of his name out loud; however, on the forearms of his flesh suit, they looked more like *moose* pimples.

On the television screen, the hyperactive explosion of physical perfection continued. A parade of flawless, flaunted bodies leading flawless, flaunted lives. Suddenly, though, the screen was cleaved into two. Occupying the left-hand side of the screen was Milton's class, staring dumbfounded at the television like a gruesome herd of startled bovine.

"What the . . . ?" Thaddeus muttered. His televised self, warped, contorted, and swollen to new levels of portly unsightliness, muttered as well, only it came out as a low, disagreeable bray.

"Class," interjected King Tantalus, "there will be plenty of time for you all to watch television later on. . . ."

"B-but," sputtered Gene as his broadcast counterpoint grunted, "we're on TV . . . sort of."

King Tantalus appraised the screen.

"Ah, yes," he said before pivoting backward abruptly, in hopes of surprising a nearby peach that, unsurprisingly, escaped his grasp.

"I could almost feel the fuzz on that one," he mumbled sadly. "Anyway," he continued, addressing the class, "it seems to me a simple yet effective form of contextual torment: juxtaposing impossibly exquisite ideals of human beauty against caricatures of your own selves, drawing out and exaggerating your ample flaws."

The small trickle of drool that had been dangling from Gene's open mouth connected with the top of his desk.

"So, to conclude our pie-eating primer," the teacher said, "let me sing the praises of the pregame stretch, widening your stomach to get it growling just before the big event."

He gestured to a nearby sack in the corner of the classroom.

"Now, if one of you would pass out the contents of that pouch over there, you may all practice the art of comp-*eating* against one another at your leisure, while I tell you about the upcoming holiday."

Virgil, being the closest to his teacher's soaking-pool prison, picked up the sack and pulled out a half-dozen foam-rubber pies with long strings attached to their middles. He passed them out to the boys.

"What are we supposed to do with these?" Hugo asked as he examined his simulated pastry.

"Why, eat them, of course," the teacher answered simply. "As fast as you can . . . then just pull them out when you're through and repeat. Now, next week is Hollow Wean, so you'll need to—"

Gene raised his hand, the flab of which settled in several rings around his shoulder.

"Mr. Blankenship," King Tantalus replied wearily.

"My mother won't let me celebrate Halloween," Gene said. "She says it's evil."

"I'm not talking about *Hallo*ween as in 'trick or treat, smell my feet,'" the teacher interrupted, "but *Hollow Wean,* as in 'oh, poor me, I feel all empty inside. It started when I was little and began confusing the act of eating with emotional fulfill—'"

As all teachers, living or dead, know, there is a moment when you lose your class, and King Tantalus realized that this was such a moment.

"It's basically a chance for the faculty to have a good laugh at your expense," he clarified plainly. "Getting you into embarrassing costumes in the middle of the night, forcing you to perform for disgusting food . . ."

The bell rang. A flicker of an idea was kindled in Milton's head. It danced, weakly yet purposefully, like the flame of a candle.

Costumes. Chaos. The perfect cover for escape! Milton thought as he plodded out of the room.

"And rumor has it that we'll even have a special appearance from our very own Principal Bubb," King Tantalus continued.

Milton shuddered as his brief flicker of hope snuffed out with a wet sizzle.

25 · TENDER LOVING SCARE

MADAME POMPADOUR TUGGED Marlo into her office by her wrist and shut the door behind her, sealing Marlo inside the tastefully decorated tomb. Madame Pompadour grinned, a lioness with a mouthful of veneers, and beckoned for Marlo to sit down next to her on the luxurious, sophisticated cream-colored love seat. Marlo felt as comfortable as a prisoner having tea and biscuits with her executioner on the gallows.

"I would like to apologize for my unconventional techniques in attempting to mold you into something you're clearly not," Madame Pompadour said as she scooched closer to Marlo on her dainty haunches. "I assure you, every hurdle was designed to teach you how to *soar*. The devil's office, for instance. It is true: he does indeed have a work space here, but it is only one of—"

"Let me guess," Marlo interjected. *"Six hundred and sixty-six."*

Madame Pompadour smirked.

"Yes, very astute. I find my girls are much more motivated when under the impression that the embodiment of all evil is just down the hall, take a left at the broken umbrella plant and sulfur watercooler."

Marlo trembled as violently as an old man playing Yahtzee, trying desperately to gather her wits before they were shaken apart. Madame Pompadour had set her up to fail while Farzana had simultaneously set her up to *succeed*. Marlo didn't know whom to trust less. And after Marlo had blown up at Madame Pompadour, instead of being instantly clawed apart, she was taken—albeit roughly—back to her office for a little dead-heart-to-dead-heart chat.

"Since we may have started off on the wrong foot," Madame Pompadour said genteelly, "I thought this might be an opportunity for us to set our personalities aside and develop a rapport."

Marlo's gaze darted back and forth from Madame Pompadour's green cat eyes to her tiny forked tongue as if she were watching a tennis match. They seemed as if they had different agendas, her eyes not seeing eye to eye with her words.

"You might say that I'm something of a . . . *fashist*," Madame Pompadour continued pompously. "Fashion is many things. For one, it is a visual language with its own distinctive grammar, brimming with unconscious symbolism. Most ensembles speak clearly and to the point."

She waved her gloved hand at Marlo, as if batting away an objectionable smell.

"Yours, for instance," Madame Pompadour said with disdain, "is a metaphor composed of thrift-store hand-me-downs."

Marlo looked down at her outfit: her deep burgundy vintage waistcoat, silk Victorian mourning gown, Goth-Darn-It tights (with carefully fabricated holes), and shabby granny boots. It was, in Marlo's mind, a tastefully distasteful collection that merged the essentials she had managed to save from the Surface with some choice finds nabbed in Mallvana.

"It has an 'angry baby' energy about it," Madame Pompadour continued as her eyes assessed Marlo's clothing, interpreting it like a ready-to-wear Rorschach test. "Ill-fitting, ill-matched childishness with a touch of noisy frolic, dampened by a disparate, funereal mess of hopelessness bequeathed from a time of which you have no real understanding."

Marlo fidgeted self-consciously.

"Right," she replied. "That's what I was going for."

Madame Pompadour smirked.

"While I find your costume personally repellant—a stinging slap on the *chic*, if you will—it is, I grudgingly admit, preferable to many of the fashion atrocities so prevalent on the Surface."

Marlo realized that this was probably the closest thing to a compliment that would ever slide off the scratchy cat/serpent tongue of Madame Pompadour in Marlo's general direction.

"We are all books judged by our covers," Madame Pompadour said as she padded across the floor toward a towering armoire. "See for yourself. Come."

Marlo swallowed and reluctantly joined her. Madame Pompadour opened the doors of the armoire, revealing a dazzling collection of clothing, everything from an Amber Argyle Afghan to a Zippered, Zebra-Skinned ZeBra.

"People don't wear clothes just because they *like* them," she explained. "No, there are much deeper forces shaping one's fashion persona. Pick a few combinations and I will tell you what they mean."

Marlo shrugged and pulled out a miniskirt, boots, and sheer blouse. Madame Pompadour held her fist to her chin in contemplation.

"Summer babe by day, club queen by night. Streamlined but not shy. Another, please."

Marlo picked out another ensemble, trying to be as random as possible.

"Hmm, a see-through shirt, preppy sheath skirt, and pink flats," murmured Madame Pompadour. "*Quel* mixed messages! This may be the sign of a deep schism, someone literally *skirting* their childhood issues."

Madame Pompadour closed the armoire's doors. Marlo felt a pang of disappointment. She was almost having . . . what was that word? It had been so long . . . oh yeah: *fun.*

"Secondly, fashion is manipulation," Madame Pompadour said, smoothing down the scales of her snakeskin skirt. "To choose an outfit is to choose a self-definition, a way to use our vast vocabulary of clothes to lie to our advantage. To *fashion* ourselves into anything we want, or—more accurately—anything we want others to think of us."

Marlo crossed her arms, trying hard to resist the madame's verbal catnip.

"Is that what you're doing with your big plan for *Statusphere*?" she posed with a scowl. "To fashion the underworld to suit your . . . your . . ."

Marlo stared at the mirror behind Madame Pompadour's desk.

"*Vanity?*"

A small storm cloud passed over the sky of Madame Pompadour's perfect face. She blew it away with a sharp, hollow laugh.

"You're smarter than I gave you credit for," she replied. "In fact, you remind me of myself, when I was just a kitten, err, *girl*. Before I learned that it takes sharp, expertly manicured nails for a girl to claw her way to the top."

"But what *is* your plan, anyway?" Marlo asked from beneath a muddle of conflicting thoughts and emotions.

Madame Pompadour sashayed to her desk.

"There'll be plenty of time to talk about that after our . . . *girl* time."

Oh no, Marlo thought. *Girl time.*

Madame Pompadour flicked a switch beneath her desk. To her right, the green bookshelf with the cast-iron grill opened, exposing an elegant room beyond.

"Welcome to my little slice of Heaven," Madame Pompadour purred. "Or as close as one can hope to achieve so far south. Behold . . . *Me-Wow.* My own private spa. Just for me. A place to curl up and dye, or wax, or simply unwind."

She stepped inside, with Marlo—literally—on her tail. It smelled of exotic, soothing spices, the air thick and humid, the consistency of a good nap. Marlo crossed the white tile floor, gazing up through swirls of steam at the vaulted ceiling.

Two demons with hands sporting extra fingers stood at the opposite end of the spa behind two plush massage tables.

"Me-Wow is a spa with *chutzpah,*" Madame Pompadour explained. "It features an array of ancient and cutting-edge therapeutic techniques, all meticulously designed and administered to pamper one into a state of bliss."

Marlo eyed a bubbling tub of fragrant green-black mud.

"Do you invite all the girls here?"

One of the demons handed Madame Pompadour two sumptuous white robes and matching slippers.

"I only invite the . . . *special* girls here." Madame Pompadour grinned as she threw one of the robes across a gilded, three-framed dressing screen covered by patterned velvet. "The ones who are crying out for some quality time with the madame."

Madame Pompadour glared at Marlo's outfit, scanning it up and down as if she were trying to erase it with her eyes.

"Let's get you out of . . . *that*. We'll have it destroyed, and a proper outfit will be selected for you, one that expresses not who you are but who you *could* be."

Marlo, intoxicated by clouds of heady, aromatic herbs, nodded groggily and stepped behind the screen.

"I've got our entire day planned out," Madame Pompadour said while nodding to one of her demons. "We'll enjoy seaweed body wraps, an exfoliating salt scrub, and vigorous shiatsu."

"Gesundheit," Marlo replied as she languidly undressed.

One of the demons filled a strange enclosed tank with gallons of white liquid poured from a huge carton marked MILK OF AMNESIA. Madame Pompadour quickly waved for the demon to hide the carton as Marlo shuffled from behind the screen in her robe and slippers.

"It sounds great." She yawned. "Though I may sleep through most of it. . . . I'm suddenly so tired."

Madame Pompadour grinned.

"That's your body relaxing . . . preparing to let go of tension, of worry, of . . . *everything*."

Marlo cocked her eyebrow at the odd tank.

"What's that?" she asked as a demon opened the hatch on top of the capsule.

"It's a sensory-deprivation tank," Madame Pompadour explained. "It's a surefire way of forgetting all your troubles . . . every last one. But why don't you try it out for yourself?"

Marlo scrutinized the creamy white water.

"That isn't milk, is it?" she asked. "I'm totally allergic."

"It's . . . *pistachio* nut milk," Madame Pompadour shot back. "Much more therapeutic."

Marlo shrugged as the demon slipped off her robe.

"It must take tiny hands to milk a pistachio," she said as she eyed the demon's larger-than-normal mitts. "Obviously you don't milk them here."

"Very droll, Miss Fauster," Madame Pompadour said. "Now, we mustn't dawdle. We've got a big day of doing very little ahead of us."

Marlo slid into the tank.

"Ooh, it's like sinking into a hot vanilla milk shake. So how come you're not soaking in this stuff?"

Madame Pompadour shot her demonic assistants a look, quick and quiet, as if shot with a silencer.

"Side effects."

"Side effects?!" Marlo yelped as she bolted upright in the tank.

"Yes, such as utter tranquility. As the director of Heck's premiere Infernship program, I can only afford to be *so* relaxed."

"Oh," Marlo muttered as she succumbed to the Milk of Amnesia's velvet tug.

Another demon, cradling a small jar of blue goo, began to slather the mixture onto Marlo's face as she settled into the tub.

"What's this?" she mumbled.

Madame Pompadour folded her arms smugly, a wry smile forming on her thin pink lips.

"My own, personal mixture," she said. "A moisturizing, deep-penetrating mask, a blend of chloroform, ether, bergamot, and mud dredged from the bottom of the Bermuda Triangle."

Marlo slid into the milky bath. Her expression was as blank as a new chalkboard.

"I can feel it . . . working . . . already," Marlo mumbled, every thought, every memory slowly loosening its grip on her mind. "It's like taking a vacation . . . from myself. It's . . . nice."

Madame Pompadour nodded to the demon, who secured the tank's hatch with three swift, powerful turns of its wheel.

"Oh, forget about it, Miss Fauster," Madame Pompadour murmured as she played with the newest charm dangling from her wrist, one marked MARLO.

"Forget . . . *everything.*"

26 · RUNNING OUT
OF ESTEEM

THE TEACHER LAY slumped across his desk. He looked like a snoring top hat. The boys lumbered to their seats and forced their considerable bulk into the undersized chairs. The maddening squeak of massive, corduroyed thighs struggling into torturous metal and wood awoke the teacher.

The man scowled down his bulbous red nose at Milton, who fidgeted inside his tightening Pang skin.

"My goodness, boy," the teacher said with a snide drawl, "you look like you've been beaten with a whole forest of ugly sticks."

The boys (except for the ever-loyal Virgil) laughed. The teacher clapped his ears.

"Apart from the yap of a new puppy on Christmas

morning, nothing offends my delicate ears more than the cackling of children!"

The teacher pushed himself away from his desk with a grunt and wobbled over to the chalkboard. VaniTV screens crowded with perfect, tan boys and girls playing volleyball on a beach were bolted to the wall on either side of the chalkboard. The teacher scowled at the screens. Scowling back at him was a hideous, warped parody of himself—lumpy, wrinkled, and swollen, like a piñata of the Elephant Man that had been bludgeoned beyond recognition.

"Egads! If beauty is in the eye of the beholder, someone must have stolen my eyes," he grumbled as he wrote on the chalkboard: "W. C. Fields, Self-Esteem."

Wheezing, the teetering grouch returned to his chair.

"It's my unfortunate job to teach you bloated, use-less wind-breakers about self-esteem," Mr. Fields droned. "But let me tell you this: as much as I can't stand the sight of you, I will treat each one of you the same way that I would treat anybody else. And that's *terribly*."

Milton squished inside his Pang suit to get comfort-able. But it was no use: in the Pang, the most he could hope for was something just outside of tolerable.

"Stop fidgeting . . . *Jonah Grumby*," Mr. Fields scolded while consulting his seating chart. "You're mak-ing me queasy. It's like watching a Jell-O mold that wants to eat *you*."

Gene raised his hand enthusiastically, causing the back of his neck to jiggle like a pack of excited hot dogs.

"Are you married to Mrs. Fields, the cookie lady?" he asked hopefully.

The teacher massaged his tired, splotched-red face between his hands. "No, but I worked with Amos and Andy on the vaudeville circuit, before Amos became famous."

Thaddeus, wedged tightly in his seat near the front of the classroom, chose that moment to break wind. The boys giggled, some releasing their own wind in response.

"Unfortunately, that's the most intelligent thing I've heard all day," Mr. Fields replied dryly. "Anyway, I like to start off each class with a story and a smile. A story because I love the sound of my own voice and a smile to get it over with."

Mr. Fields gave what he thought was a smile. It wasn't. It was more like a grimace on its day off. The teacher folded his pink, piggish hands together.

"Once upon a time, there were two ponds," Mr. Fields began. "One was filled with runoff from a toxic-waste dump, and the other sparkled with fresh water from a clear stream. One day, one of the filthy, disgusting, contaminated fish poked his head out of the muck and saw a flawless, beautiful fish stick her sleek head out of the clean pond. He thought about her for days. Finally he decided to jump into the other pond and profess his love for the pure, perfect fish. And one day, he did just that. And, surprisingly enough, the beautiful fish was so touched by the revolting fish with the big red nose that she agreed to marry him. And they did. Got married. And all the while, the toxic fish tried to live in the sparkling, pure water, but he had mutated so much in his poisoned pond of filth that the clear water only made him sicker. So he lay down on the bottom, where the sediment settled, which made him feel a little better, but not much, and he spent most of his days complaining. Slowly, over time, the beautiful fish's love and respect for the dirty, no-good fish turned to loathing and disgust. And ever since, I can't stand water because of the things fish do in it."

Mr. Fields took off his top hat and wiped his forehead with a filthy handkerchief.

"The end," he grumbled.

Milton looked around the class and observed the same baffled expression that he himself was trying to express through his lumpy Pang skin.

"And the moral?" Milton asked.

Mr. Fields bolted up. Then, after swaying unsteadily for a bit, he succumbed to gravity and sat back down in his chair.

"The moral is that there *isn't* any moral!" the teacher barked indignantly. "Why should stories have nice, tidy endings when life doesn't?"

Mr. Fields's nose was so red that had there been any

cars in the classroom, they would have waited for it to change to green.

"If I was forced to dredge up some sorry excuse for a moral from my—*that*—sobering tale," he said, grinding out each word slowly with his nasal voice, "then it would be that, in this and all worlds, there are the haves and the have-nots."

He scanned the overweight boys with his dull, yellow eyes.

"Or, in your cases, the haves and have-*way*-too-muches. Look at those boys and girls on the screens. . . ."

The class watched the beach volleyball game on VaniTV. The players effortlessly leaped, swooped, and bounded like Greek gods and goddesses on spring break.

"It's like they're an entirely different species. There's simply no comparison. The fickle finger of Fate endowed them with perfection, popularity, and health. The only thing healthy about *you-all* is your appetites."

Milton heard Virgil sniffing back a tear next to him. Indignation welled up inside Milton.

"You will never be them . . . not as liked, not as respected, not as happy," Mr. Fields taunted. *"Not even close."*

Milton stood up, shaking.

"Doesn't what's inside account for anything?!" he spat. "Isn't that what this place is all about—the possibility of

becoming better people? One last chance before we turn eighteen?"

Mr. Fields sneered.

"Sit down, boy. You're embarrassing yourself."

"No, I won't!" Milton replied. "Every boy here has the chance to make himself perfect inside . . . at least better. To make smarter, healthier choices and live a happier afterlife. We all have wings inside of us. It's just a matter of learning how to use them."

Mr. Fields snorted.

"The only wings inside of you, boy, are *buffalo* wings. Lots of 'em, by the looks of it."

Milton seethed inside his Pang suit. "You don't know who I am. Who I am *really*."

"Oh, I think I know exactly who you are, Mr. Grumby . . . *inside,*" Mr. Fields hissed, grabbing a yardstick off the blotter on his desk.

"You do, do you?" Milton fumed. "You have *no* idea. In fact—"

Virgil grabbed Milton's leg.

"Don't blow your cool . . . *and* your cover, *Jonah,*" Virgil whispered.

Milton sighed and slowly settled back into his unsteady chair.

Mr. Fields snickered as he slapped the yardstick in his palm. "A smart, healthy choice, Mr. Grumby," he said.

Mr. Fields stooped over, grumbling, and pulled out

a heap of Bibles from the lower drawer of his desk. He laid them in a tall, perilous stack before glancing down at his seating chart.

"Um . . . you . . . *Mr. Farrow.*"

"Yes, Mr. Fields," Virgil replied, straightening in his seat, his kind eyes sparkling with attention.

The teacher stared at Virgil, affronted by his eagerness.

"Tone it down a notch, son," Mr. Fields replied. "You're not going to win any brownie points here."

A wave of stomach rumblings shook the classroom.

"Mmmm . . . *brownies,*" Gene muttered with groggy yearning, as if slowly waking from a wonderful dream.

"Mr. Farrow, come up here and pass out these Bibles," the teacher said wearily.

Virgil uprooted his husky-sized frame out of his petite-sized desk and lumbered to the teacher's desk. As Virgil passed the books out to the seven boys, Mr. Fields put his shabby shoes up on the desk and leaned back in his chair.

"Now scooch your desks together with a partner."

The boys heaved and grunted into pairs. Milton flipped through the dog-eared Bible and raised his hand.

"Yes, Buffalo Wings?"

"What are we supposed to be doing?" Milton asked. "How is anything in this class supposed to build self-esteem?"

Mr. Fields held up a Bible.

"First of all, you great, galumphing eyesore, no one ever said this class was intended to *build* self-esteem. It's just *about* self-esteem. And how there isn't any point in *having* any if you have no reason to *have* it. Otherwise it's just a lot of hot air in a lead balloon. But that isn't to say you big-boned buffoons can't be of some use to me. I want you all, as I have been attempting to do for so many years here, to scour this good book you hold in your hands and search for loopholes."

Milton gulped. Looking for loopholes in his contract had once been his overriding obsession. He had recently lost sight of it, what with dying again, roaming the after realms with dispossessed phantoms, and rescuing his best friend and all.

"After all, a thing worth having is worth cheating for," Mr. Fields continued as he tipped his top hat over his eyes. "And just think how good you'll feel about yourselves if you help me out of this dreary dimple in a baboon's bottom. So, young men, get cracking while I get napping."

Milton and Virgil sidled close together and studied the Book of Books.

"Hmmm," murmured Virgil. "Here's something: 'Do not join those who gorge themselves, for they shall become poor, and drowsiness clothes them in rags.' "

"Yeah," Milton replied, his mind churning as it always did when confronted by a good puzzle. "But aren't the poor blessed or something? Guaranteed a place in the kingdom of God?"

"I think so."

"Wait, here's something else," said Milton. "'The Son of Man came eating and drinking, and they say, Behold a man gluttonous.' It sounds like even Jesus was accused of having, you know . . . a big appetite."

"I'm Jewish, so that 'Son of Man' stuff is not really my specialty," said Virgil with a shrug of his shoulders. "Here's another one: 'Behold joy and gladness . . . let us eat and drink, for tomorrow we shall die.'"

"A little grim, but encouraging. This one is a bit nicer: 'Take thine ease, eat, drink, and be merry.'"

"Amen," Virgil murmured.

"Yeah, it almost sounds like an order. Get a load of this: 'Whose God is their belly, and whose glory is in their shame, who mind earthly things.'"

Virgil crinkled his freckled nose.

"I don't like the sound of that one."

"But wait," Milton continued feverishly, "it makes overeating seem like a weakness, an addiction, almost. A *venial* sin more than an absolute one that hurts other people."

Virgil stared at his friend with eyes devoid of comprehension.

"A veal sin? Like eating baby cows?"

"No, *venial*," Milton explained. "It means forgivable. Something not worthy of, in our case, eternal darnation."

Virgil mulled over this theological nugget.

"So being fat maybe isn't so bad after all?" he said, his chest puffing out slightly, giving his belly a run for its money. "I'm not . . . evil. Just a little weak-willed?"

Milton smiled at his friend, so wide that Virgil could actually see Milton's teeth through his grinning meat mask.

"Why would I rescue someone evil? I only rescue the best!"

Virgil leaned in close to Milton, his eyes darting about guiltily.

"So," he whispered, "have you and Annubis thought of a way out of here?"

Milton, through his borrowed Pang eyes, stared at the snoring teacher.

"No," he murmured. "Not yet. But he's got some ideas cooking."

Virgil stared off into space. His eyes glittered as if he were wearing diamond contact lenses.

"Maybe it isn't *just* about escaping," Virgil said in a voice deeper and surer than Milton was accustomed to. "Maybe it's about something *more.*"

27 · SOME ASSEMBLY REQUIRED

LYON, HER POM-POMS shaking softly in neutral, sneered at the crowd of overweight boys, girls, and teachers perched upon the Gymnauseum's bowed bleachers.

"Hey, Dijon!" she shouted in her silver satin, two-piece cheerless-leading outfit. "Do you know why Blimpo is like a candy store?"

Dijon smiled, her teeth sparkling like pearls chemically whitened at great expense.

"No, Lyon. Why *is* Blimpo like a candy store?"

Lyon jutted out her hip in sassy defiance.

"Because it's full of so many big, fat *suckers!*"

The five girls laughed wickedly, then assembled in a V-for-vain formation.

"Hey, Bordeaux!" Lyon called out, twirling like a top. "Do you know what time it is?"

Bordeaux furrowed her eyebrows at her watch.

"I, like, so don't know!" she replied with a dopey curl of her lip.

"It's time for a Nyah Nyah cheer!" Lyon screeched.

Milton and Virgil wriggled uncomfortably at the very top of the bleachers.

"Wow, and I thought these things were bad when I was alive!" Virgil said.

Milton stared at one of the many banners strewn across the Gymnauseum: CHAMPIONS ONLY BELIEVE IN THEMSELVES IF EVERYONE ELSE DOES, AND TRUST US: YOU'RE NO CHAMPION.

"Yeah," he replied softly. "This bites . . . mega bites."

"*Giga* bites!" Virgil added as the cheerlessleaders hopped atop one another to form a pyramid.

Milton thought he recognized two of the girls, Lyon and Bordeaux, from the time that he was led—bound and gagged—to Mallvana, right after his second death (not that he was counting). He couldn't be completely sure, though, what with the sack he had been forced to wear over his head and the fact that he had always found it difficult to distinguish one cheerleader from another. Across the auditorium, he saw an immaculate woman watching the cheerlessleaders' every move. The woman's bearing was both fussy and sinister, sleek and scaly. For some reason, Milton visualized a python full of Persian pussycats.

> *"We're the Nyah Nyah Narcissisters,*
> *and we're here to say,*
> *We're like an all-you-can-watch beauty buffet!*
> *We've got the moves and grooves*
> *You've been aching to see!*
> *You so wish you were us. . . .*
> *Don't make us laugh! We might pee!"*

Milton gazed at the other boys sitting several bleachers below. Even though they had had only a few servings of Hambone Hank's new recipe, they seemed . . . *different*. Lighter. More carefree and childlike. Thankfully for Milton and his not-so-secret identity, Hugo seemed to be satisfied with his altered soul food. Heck, the boys were even smiling at the squad of conceited girls brought here to Blimpo for the expressed purpose of berating and humiliating them.

> *"S-P-I-R-I-T,*
> *We've got that spirit,*
> *Can't you see it?*
> *It could raise the dead.*
> *From the tips of our toes to our perfect heads!"*

"So, you think Hollow Wean is the night?" Virgil whispered, though no one besides Milton could possibly hear him over the din of debutants debu-*taunting*. "You know, for escaping?"

Milton nodded. "Yep. I think even if the principal rears her ugly, ugly head, it's our best, maybe our only, chance to slip away. Annubis and I have been trading some ideas back and forth on napkins."

The self-centered pyramid crumbled, girl by girl, with the Nyah Nyah Narcissisters falling into a fiercely perky line. Marseille took the lead—pried it away, more like—from Lyon.

> *"And you fatties can just shake your chins,*
> *We're sleek as sharks, but we ain't got fins!*
> *Gonna psych you out:*
> *P-S-Y and C and K*
> *So let's yell and shout,*
> *And put it on display!"*

Out of the corner of his eye, Milton noticed something crawling on the back of Thaddeus's head. He stared at the boy and realized that there wasn't anything crawling *on* his head but that the crawling *was* his head: for a split second, his thick, dark hair rippled—becoming a hazy light purple and nappy, like a child's worn toy. Thaddeus tipped back his head and giggled at nothing in particular, his eyes gleaming like black buttons, and—with that—he was his same old self.

It must be the Make-Believe Play-fellow souls, Milton speculated. *The souls affect the boys like the Lost Souls did—mixing with their energy as they're "digested"—only they seem to cycle through fainter, faster, and more . . . fantastical.*

"Do you have any idea where we'd go?" Virgil asked. "After the escape?"

Good question, Milton thought. But he didn't want to discourage his sensitive friend.

"Annubis said he had some friends who could help us," Milton fibbed, rationalizing to himself that the dog god more than likely had friends and that some of them, statistically speaking, could probably help them. "He didn't go into specifics," he added, which *was* true, as Annubis had not gotten into specifics whatsoever. "He wants to keep it on the down low, just in case."

And with Bea "Elsa" Bubb dropping by, Milton continued to himself, *anywhere is bound to be better than here.*

Across the Gymnauseum, Madame Pompadour scrutinized her Nyah Nyah Narcissisters with the deep green liquid pools of judgment that were her eyes. Suddenly, her clutch bag began to hiss and purr. She pulled out her compact and flipped it open.

Text message from HubbaBubb13 to Pr3ttyKat9.

HubbaBubb13: RU there? This is Bubb.

Of course I know who it is, Madame Pompadour
thought. *Who else would have a profile pic so ugly that even
a bowl of Rice Krispies wouldn't talk to it?*
She sighed and reluctantly texted a response.

Pr3ttyKat9: Of course. 2 what do I owe this honor?

HubbaBubb13: Is your new Infern Marlo Fauster acting
odd?

Pr3ttyKat9: Odder than usual?

HubbaBubb13: Anything about conspiring with
her brother, Milton? I had him tracked, but lost him
just outside Blimpo. Lady Lactose informed me of
some unusual readings in something called a
DREADmill.

Madame Pompadour was so mad she could spit im-
ported venom.
I don't want Bubb scratching in my kitty litter, she
seethed to herself. *Not now. Not ever.*

Pr3ttyKat9: I M in Blimpo now. Everything is fine—

HubbaBubb13: I will be there tomorrow to see 4 myself.

HubbaBubb13 has left the chat.

Madame Pompadour's pads worked furiously on her compact's keypad, as if she were tenderizing a freshly seized mouse.

Initiate chat with Mi1kSh4k3

Mi1kSh4k3: Hello, Madame. 2 what do I owe this—

Pr3ttyKat9: Y did you tell Bubb about the DREADmills?!?!

Mi1kSh4k3: Calm down! Dr. Kellogg noticed some odd activity in one of the DREADmills, so I told Bubb myself, rather than have her find out on her own. This way, she'll only see what we want her to see. And if she finds the boy, all the better. We'll be in her good graces (if she has any) and she'll leave us alone. Don't worry. Next stop: Fat City! :-D

Madame Pompadour sighed. Even on the best of days, she hated emoticons.

Pr3ttyKat9: Fine. I will see you tomorrow to hash out the details of our dastardly plan. Au revoir . . .

She clenched her pearly white teeth together.

;-)

Madame Pompadour shut her compact and resumed her critical appraisal of her Nyah Nyah Narcissisters. The formation of sleek, snobby girls parted, creating a row down the middle. Strasbourg sprinted down the aisle, tumbled, and then executed three back-to-back handsprings. Lyon regained possession of the microphone from Marseille and skipped around the gym floor in a wide circle, goading the front row.

"Piggies in the front, let me hear you grunt."

The girls turned up their noses with their index fingers behind her, oinking.

"Fatties in the middle, let me hear you sizzle."

The squad swiveled their hips while pretending to fry bacon in a pan.

"Porkers in the rear, let out a cheer."

Lyon rejoined the other girls, who were now parading in a tight circle in the middle of the floor.

"You suck! We rule! We sisters soar,
    you Blimpos drool!"

Like a fireworks finale, the Nyah Nyah Narcissisters leaped in the air, their hands touching their toes, and ended their abusive routine by performing a series of cartwheels, aerials, and round-offs. The girls beamed contemptuously, their NNN jerseys heaving with each breath, and eyed the crowd under the mistaken impression that they were about to bask in waves of wild adulation. Bordeaux—thinking that the crowd needed one last stunt before detonating in a riot of noise and acclamation—jogged to the edge of the mats, turned on the pad of her foot, then made a mad dash for her "sisters" before soaring in the air. Unfortunately, as Bordeaux had failed to inform the rest of the squad of their need to catch her, she landed face-first upon the mat. Finally, the audience applauded and whooped in delight.

Two demons wheeled King Tantalus and his woeful wading pool to the center of the gym floor.

"Charming!" he commented into a microphone strapped to a peach branch. "And what a punch line! Okay, boys, girls, faculty, demons, and everything in between, it's the time you've been waiting for: our pie-eating contest!"

One of the demons, a walking eggplant overlaid with a mesh of muscle, walked over to a table covered with a white cloth and surrounded by four chairs. He yanked away the cloth, revealing a mound of pies. The small crowd roared.

"Now all I need are four volunteers," King Tantalus announced. "Please look under your seats. If you find a wad of chewed gum, then come on down!"

The crowd looked under the bleachers. Two students from Girls' Blimpo—an enormous Asian girl and a sturdy German girl with blond braids piled on top of her head like a hunk of hair strudel—squealed, gum in their fists, and waddled down to the stage.

"Gum!" yelped Gene as he popped an uncovered nugget into his mouth and tumbled off the bleachers.

Milton felt beneath his seat and plucked off a hunk of gum.

"Wow," Virgil said with awe. *"Lucky."*

Lucky, Milton reflected sadly.

When Milton had escaped from Limbo, he had done so at the expense of his etheric energy—the spiritual glue that kept his body and soul fused together. After his pet ferret, Lucky, had inadvertently interfered with Milton's attempt to harness the life force from a swarm of bugs, the two had shared a peculiar energetic bond. *I haven't felt his energy in weeks,* Milton recalled. *I still feel somehow connected to him, but it's so dull, so sluggish, so . . . un-Lucky.*

Milton noticed the longing in Virgil's eyes as his

friend stared down at the festivities brewing on the Gymnauseum floor.

At least I can pass a little luck on to Virgil, Milton thought.

"Here," he said, tossing his friend the disgusting, still-sort-of-squishy wad of gum. "Eat your heart out."

Virgil grinned from ear to ear.

"Thanks!" he called out behind him as he made his way down to the table.

The boys and girls grabbed their seats and eyed the pies with unreserved gusto.

"Now, before you we have a selection of fine pies," King Tantalus announced. "Humble Pie, Mince-Mystery-Meat Pie, and Dingleberry Pie—courtesy of our very own Chef Boyareyookrazee."

The flush-faced chef tipped his towering toque and grinned wickedly.

King Tantalus whispered to the children. "I would avoid the Dingleberry at all cost," he cautioned.

The boys and girls nodded gravely as demons tied bibs around their stocky necks.

"On your mark, get set . . . *go!*" the teacher called as the contestants shoved pastry into their mouths.

"Great form!" King Tantalus commented. "Crust first, ask questions later . . . a winning strategy!"

Virgil stood up as he rolled a pie into a flaky, oozing burrito.

"Look at Mr. Farrow go! It's like he's bagging groceries in his gut!"

The German girl eyed Virgil with worry and stood up next to him, seeing his pie and raising him another.

"Whoa, ante upped!" said King Tantalus.

The girl, however, began to turn a sickly hue reminiscent of the Jolly Green Giant in the throes of envy.

"I must remind everyone that what goes *in* must stay *down*!"

The girl charged out of the Gymnauseum, her hand to her mouth.

"I warned you about the Dingleberry," King Tantalus said, shaking his head.

A buzzer blared.

"We have a winner!" King Tantalus announced after a quick study of the empty pie plates. "Mr. Farrow, who can swallow, it seems, just about everything—including his pride!"

A sloppy, pie-eating grin spread across Virgil's face.

Mr. Presley, seated with Mr. Waller on the sidelines, hooted and hollered.

"Nicely done, son!" the rhinestone-studded man yelped. "Your pie eatin' takes the cake!"

Virgil blushed modestly underneath gooey patches of Humble Pie.

King Tantalus waved for Virgil to come closer.

"So, Mr. Farrow, would you like to know what

you've won?" the scraggly, partially submerged teacher asked.

Virgil nodded.

"Well, in honor of our principal Bubb's impending visit," King Tantalus explained with a smirk, "you'll have the esteemed privilege of . . . *giving her a hoof massage on behalf of Blimpo!*"

The crowd groaned. Gene, who was on the verge of hurling anyway, ran out of the Gymnauseum, retching.

"That's *sariously* nasty," Mr. Presley mumbled with a sneer.

Virgil's grin faded gradually, like an old picture left in the sun. Tears welled in his eyes.

Mr. Presley rose out of his seat with a grunt, shaking his head as he joined Virgil at the center of the floor. He wrapped his arm around the mortified boy.

"Now, now, son," he soothed, "Principal Bubb's nasty feet aren't worth your tears, which reminds me . . . I just wrote a song 'bout tears. Do ya wanna hear it?"

Virgil looked up at Mr. Presley and nodded faintly.

"Okay, then," the teacher replied as he caught the guitar Mr. Waller threw him. "A-one, a-two, a-three . . ."

He strutted out across the mats, hips swaying.

"I cried so many tears on the day you left me,
  That those bitter poison tears made a
    strychnine sea.

Chlorides, sulfates, sodium, and pain . . .
    A magnesium, calcium, and potassium rain."

The girls started screaming. Mr. Presley, looking years younger, as if the energy of the crowd was turning back his spiritual odometer, beckoned for Virgil to join him. Virgil trotted over beside the sequined singing sensation.

"I got the words written on the inside of my sleeve," Mr. Presley whispered, adding with a wink, "Now, that's a trade secret, son. Be sure to keep it to yourself. Now, I got them all warmed up for you. I'll lay down a low, slinky baritone and you come in with that crazy opera thing you do, just like in class. Okay?"

Virgil nodded and shared the mic with the King of Rock and Roll.

"These elements dissolved,
    make the ocean taste salty,
Like tears when the wiring of love proves faulty.
The ocean's salinity is thirty-five parts per
    thousand,
Your love was divinity,
    now my heart's stuck in quicksand."

The blend of their voices was peanut-butter-and-chocolate perfect. Mr. Presley's surly, smoky rumble and Virgil's clear, piercing soprano braided together snugly, weaving an achingly beautiful tapestry of tone that completely enveloped the audience.

> *"Thoughts of your lovin' won't let me be,*
> *And I feel like I'm drownin' in your*
> *strychnine sea."*

Mr. Presley shimmied the crowd into a frenzy while Virgil's voice soared. Its richness embraced the crowd like a warm, musical hug. Milton watched as his friend became transformed. Virgil wasn't the big-boned, freckle-faced boy whose innate sweetness made him the target of many a mean spirit. No, with his chest puffed out and his tone pitch-perfect and assured, Virgil was pure confidence with a side of aplomb.

Milton noticed a burly girl with wavy black hair sitting several bleachers below him. Wedged onto one of her arms was a weird magazine. The shimmering pages fanned out around her forearm, as if her arm were wearing a dress made of electric fashion ads. But one of the pages captured Milton's attention. A picture of a girl who seemed strangely familiar and strangely *unfamiliar* at the same time. A girl with black eyes, bluish hair, spooky, sun-challenged skin, a turned-up nose . . .

"Marlo!" Milton exclaimed as he hopped down the bleachers. He grabbed the girl's arm.

"Sorry, but she's my sister," Milton explained to the girl. She stared back at him with flat, fishlike eyes. It was as if she were drugged or had been forced to watch public television during a pledge drive.

"I'll, uh, give you your arm back in just a sec," he said as he scanned the brief article.

Madame Makes Over
Miscreant Miss!

Marlo Fauster, the lucky recipient of a much-coveted scholarship with the Girl Friday the Thirteenth Finishing School, has just graduated with dishonors. Her first real underworld job? We hope you're sitting down (because she certainly will be) . . . the devil's very own, personal deceptionist!

Madame Pompadour, Infernship program head-mistress and *Statusphere*'s very own publisher/editor/columnist/sales manager/circulation director, had this to say about her latest low-flying, get-up-and-go-getting protégé.

"Miss Fauster came to me, quite frankly, a crazy mess," Madame Pompadour elegantly states through her girlish, cherry-red lips framing refined, pearly white fangs that glisten like captured moonlight. "But I always appreciate a challenge. Through my expert tutelage, effortless grace, infinite well of patience, and unrivaled humility, I took what was basically a feral, ill-mannered, uncouth blob of insalubrious clay and—like a modern-day

Pygmalion—transformed this No Flair Lady into the epitome of élan. I expect great things from her. And there will be you-know-what to pay if she doesn't deliver."

Miss Fauster, immaculate in her crisp new Donna Skaran French Navy Cotton Viscose Constructed Trouser Suit . . ."

Milton was mesmerized by Marlo's photograph. It was as if—yes, he was almost sure of it—she had allowed *someone else to put makeup on her face.* Marlo's hair also seemed as if it had actually been *brushed* and perhaps even *styled.* With product. She looked like a model. Not like a skinny, hot-shot Brazilian fashion model with a name like Vendetta or anything like that, but like one of those models who still had to work part-time at a coffee shop in between photo shoots for the local outlet store.

Though Marlo looked good, she didn't look like *Marlo.* It freaked Milton out. Her crooked grin, like a regular smile that had been broken and glued back together poorly, was now smooth, perfect, and somehow joyless in its perfection. How an alien would smile after observing humans through a high-powered Double Hubble telescope. And the fire behind her eyes had been snuffed out. That scared Milton most of all.

Milton's thoughts drifted to the last time he'd seen

his sister, back in Rapacia. He had told her that he'd come back for her. He had promised.

His Pang skin contracted. The tightness came in spasms that were now arriving with greater frequency, each one pushing him slightly farther down into the creature. He had no idea how long it would be before he was either compressed into oblivion by his trash compactor of a disguise or digested whole.

Both Milton and Marlo were in way over their heads. But at least Milton *knew* he was in way over his head, while Marlo's head seemed to have no idea how over it she was in. Her head, that is. He had also made a promise. And in a dark, despairing place like Heck, a promise—even one made between a brother and sister who never truly got along—was all you really had. Milton had made good on his vow to at least *try* and rescue Virgil. Now he would make good on another. Maybe making good on promises was the first step in unmaking all the bad.

"Can I have my arm back?" the hefty brunette girl asked Milton, causing him to jump with a start.

"Yeah," he mumbled, releasing the girl's arm. "Sorry."

A banner fluttered on the other side of the Gymnauseum.

JUST BECAUSE YOU ARE UNIQUE DOES NOT MEAN THAT YOU ARE SPECIAL

Milton didn't know if he was right or wrong, good or bad, sane or completely, utterly mental, but he *did* know that he was unique . . . special . . . *different*. And being different can make a difference. He would start by going *down there*—to the fiery pit of h-e-double-hockey-sticks itself—to save his sister. *To make a difference.*

28 · HOLLOW, GOODBYE

PRINCIPAL BUBB PEERED into the creature's stable. Her left eyebrow crept upward, like a fat, fuzzy caterpillar emerging from its cocoon just to be gobbled down by a crow.

"What is it?" she asked.

The bull demon scratched the itchy rim of its growing horn nub.

"Heckifino," he replied.

The principal scowled.

"I find it most distressing that you don't even know the names of the creatures you supposedly care for—"

"It's a *Heckifino*," the demon clarified. *"That's what it's called.* It also goes by 'Alfonse,' or 'Hey' if you shout loudly enough."

Bea "Elsa" Bubb stiffened. She drew in a deep breath

that was, unfortunately, sharp with the tang of exotic waste matter.

"Just another test," she replied as she tugged smooth her leather vest. "Want to keep you on the tip of your hooves."

The bulky creature in the stall stared back at the demons with its mismatched eyes—one round and violet, the other an orange, almond-shaped sliver—located on either side of its coiling, corkscrew tusk. The Heckifino's disjointed features made it seem as if it had been hastily assembled from a variety of unrelated animal kits by a team of color-blind builders, puzzling over Sanskrit instructions by strobe light.

"So, if memory serves me correctly," the principal said cautiously, "then the Heckifino is a . . . a . . . a . . ."

The principal dangled the letter "a" in the air between her and the stable keeper, hoping that he would bite.

"A mystery, mostly," the bull demon replied after a longer-than-comfortable silence. "It's probably the product of genetic mutation, selective breeding, or a particularly wild holiday party at a very liberal zoo. It's a true riddle of animal husbandry, and animal wifery as well. It sure is . . . *big*. Beautiful plumage."

Bea "Elsa" Bubb considered the row of multicolored, yard-long feathers sprouting around the creature's knotted rope of a tail.

"Yes," she said dryly. "Does it have any unique and exploitable traits?"

"Not especially," the bull demon snorted, scratching himself beneath his filthy overalls.

The Heckifino chose that moment to produce a freakish gobble, like a frightened tofurkey suddenly endowed with life.

"But, as I said before," the bull demon continued, "it's big, garishly unsettling, and—perhaps most importantly of all—*available*. The perfect match for you . . . and hopefully more trustworthy than a cluster of nervous flicks!"

The bull demon smiled just as the principal frowned. In fact, her sagging look of disapproval formed the exact *opposite* of a smile.

"For your sake, I hope so," Bea "Elsa" Bubb growled. "Or the next beast I'll be saddling up will be *you*. And I've got spurs that jingle, jangle, mangle in ways you wouldn't *believe*."

The bull demon gulped as a variety of unpleasant scenarios played out in his head. Bea "Elsa" Bubb clacked down the concrete floors to the swinging double doors of the Unstables. She stopped, turned, and tugged on the drawstring of her cowgirl hat (and never had a hat been so confused as to whether it was perched atop the head of a *cow* or a *girl*).

"Have the creature ready for me within the hour,"

she ordered as she cinched the strap tightly between two of her chins. "I want to be in Blimpo by midnight. It seems that one of those rotund ragamuffins has the *exact* same fears as that wretched Milton Fauster. And, considering that the only friend the dweeby milksop *has* is in Blimpo as well, it seems that I'll be spending Hollow Wean among the rich and *flabulous.*"

Virgil strained as he sat atop the bulging suitcase, overstuffed with laundry pilfered from Chef Boyareyookrazee's abundant hamper.

"Almost," he puffed as the suitcase finally closed with a grudging *click.*

Milton smiled.

"Well, that's the last of them," he said, eyeing the other three suitcases vibrating with high-pressure laundry in the corner beside their sleeping bunks. "If we get some resistance in the Gorge, these should help blast our way through."

Milton looked over at Virgil, who was staring at his feet with an intensity he usually reserved for Sloppy Joes.

"What's up?" Milton asked. "Are you nervous about—"

He looked furtively around at the other boys who were settling, oblivious, in their bunks.

"The escape?" he continued in a whisper.

"No," Virgil murmured. "Not especially, since . . . since . . ."

Virgil stopped contemplating his tootsies, though his eyes still couldn't quite seem to meet Milton's.

"I'm not. Escaping, that is."

Milton gaped at Virgil.

"What do you mean? Annubis will be there, if you're scared that—"

"It's not that I'm scared; it's just that . . ."

Virgil took a deep breath, puffing out his chest, which gave him an uncharacteristically unslouchy demeanor.

"I was talking to Elvis, Mr. Presley, and he thinks that I could be a really good singer."

"You already *are* a really good singer," Milton added warmly.

Virgil grinned self-consciously. "Thanks," he replied softly. "But he thinks I could be even better. And I believe him. . . . It's hard to explain. When I sing, I just sort of leave my body."

He shook his head.

"That's not quite right. I'm still in my body, but—for the first time in my life—my inside becomes bigger than my outside, which is saying something. Plus, there's something else . . ."

Virgil reached underneath his bare, stained mattress and pulled out a flyer. He handed it to Milton.

*** JOIN THE *** BLIMPO: OVERWEIGHT WITH ERRONEOUS LAWS (BOWEL) MOVEMENT!

What's the big fat deal about being full-figured? Answer: nothing! We accept that some people are tall and some people are short, yet how come we think that everybody should be thin? The skin-and-bones brigade thinks we "fatties" just need to exercise more and eat less. Sure, being as healthy as possible makes you feel good, but what's wrong with a little padding here and there? Being plump doesn't make us bad—it's not a moral failing or a character flaw; mostly it's genetic or because we've been made to feel so bad about being big that we eat more to make ourselves feel better. Okay, sometimes when confronted with a piece (or five) of cheesecake, we get a little weak, but is that a sin? Is that any reason to be sent to Blimpo for all eternity or until we turn eighteen, whichever comes first?

So let's raise a big stink as only we can! We're fat as Heck, and we're not going to take it anymore!

"I snuck a flyer under everyone's pillow," Virgil explained. "It's like we figured out in Mr. Fields's class—

overeating is a problem, sure, but not a sin, which makes this place *wrong. I get it now.* Before I was just too scared to really consider the injustice of it all. But . . . I don't know . . . maybe you're helping me to see that we can really do something. We don't have to take it. After all, what do we have to lose, really? I mean, we're dead, if you think about it. Even if you *don't* think about it, we're still dead. . . ."

Milton smiled, a quiet, sad smile but a smile nonetheless. Virgil seemed so different. It was as if he was finally seeing who he really was, the person Milton could see all along, inside. He seemed so excited and confident that Milton didn't have the heart to tell him what a terrible, terrible name BOWEL was for anything, much less a movement. Why not the Oval Teens? Or Stout and About? *Anything* but the BOWEL movement. Milton sighed.

"But I need your help," he said softly. "You're the only person I can trust, who isn't either doglike or godlike, that is."

Virgil leaned close. His eyes were like round, glittering, root-beer-flavored Jolly Ranchers.

"Exactly!" he replied. "You can't do it all. You need help. Seriously."

"Well, I did see a therapist for a while, back on the Surface, but I just spent most of the time coloring my feelings with crayons and hitting pillows with a badminton racket—"

"No, not *that* kind of help," Virgil clarified. *"Help shutting this place down.* Not just Blimpo, but the whole shebang. You need to create like a, uh, like when you have a whole bunch of the same restaurant—"

"A franchise?"

"Yeah! You need a Milton Fauster franchise! Secret agents everywhere, helping you to help all of us!"

The fluorescent lights winked on and off.

"Lights out, you filthy manatees!" the demon guard bellowed by the light switch of Blimpo's Totally Bunks. "And no talking! Talking only leads to camaraderie, which leads to self-validation, which leads to trouble, which leads to the vice principals' office, understand?"

The boys mumbled their comprehension as they prepared for another long night of sleep apnea.

"Oh," the demon said as it switched off the lights. "Happy Hollow Wean! Get plenty of rest because the festivities start at midnight, whether you like it or not!"

The demon snickered away like a helium-filled hyena. In the darkness, Milton slid and squeaked into his smothering rubber sheets.

"Good night," whispered Virgil. "And good luck."

Milton fought hard to stay awake. He needed to be sharp and ready for his impending escape. He shivered, despite how insufferably hot it was under the sticky sheets. Marlo's face on the cover of that weird magazine. It was so . . . *creepy.* Her eyes were so vacant, completely devoid of that mischievous sparkle that had launched a thousand misdemeanors. She also looked almost pretty, or as pretty as a sister can. Marlo had never seemed particularly interested in using her appearance to draw people closer to her. Mainly her makeup and wardrobe selections were the equivalent of a KEEP OUT: DANGER! sign trussed with yards of bright yellow caution tape. Something was wrong with Marlo, Milton mused as his breathing became slower and deeper. *Her face so . . . blank . . . her eyes so . . . hollow . . .*

"Happy Hollow Wean!!" the trio of demons shrieked, splashing a bucket of blue paint on Milton and Virgil. Virgil screamed as the shocking cold dye oozed down his hair, onto his face, and across his chest.

"What are you doing?!" Milton gurgled before spitting out a mouthful of disgusting paint.

The three demons—one with a face that looked like a half-eaten cantaloupe, another who seemed like a mummy wrapped with rotten bacon, and another that resembled an overbaked potato with glowing eyes and a shock of scraggly white hair—exchanged the same wicked laugh among each other.

"Your costume!" said the cantaloupe demon as it heaved Milton out of his bunk and onto the floor. "You're a Smurf! This year's theme is mass-marketed cartoon-and-toy properties from the 1980s!"

The baked-potato demon shoved a white, oversized knit cap on the freshly painted Virgil.

"It's a great idea!" the bacon mummy said while ripping off Milton's pajama top and forcing him into a pair of itchy white pants with huge padded footies. "Turning yesterday's cheerful memories into today's waking nightmares!"

"But we're too young to even remember that stupid—"

"You're never too young to be the butt of our jokes!" the cantaloupe demon screeched as it strapped a canvas sack over Virgil's head. "And we wouldn't want to forget your trick-or-feed bag!"

As the demons shoved Milton, Virgil, and the other boys toward the door, Hugo—his cheeks tinted and swollen like eggplants—turned to face their tormentors.

"How come *you* guys aren't wearing costumes?"

The cantaloupe demon shot its allies in anguish a knowing look.

"Oh, but we *are*," it hissed. "See, a demon is always wearing a mask."

The three demons simultaneously reached behind their ears and pulled off their faces. Inside their skulls, swaddled in chunks of putrid meat, were tiny chubby-cheeked baby heads, grinning wickedly like porcelain dolls. The boys screamed.

"Back on!! Back on!!"

The boys were pitched out into the hall, leaving behind them splotches and smears of blue paint. Each of the three demons took a pair of boys and prodded them with pitchsporks in a different direction. The bacon mummy jabbed Milton and Virgil down the dark hallway leading to the classrooms. Milton was supposed to rendezvous with Annubis at a quarter after midnight in the Lose-Your-Lunchroom, which—from what Milton could make out through his crusty blue eyelashes—he was getting farther away from with each step.

"Where are we going?" Milton asked.

"Why, trick-or-treating, of course." The demon smirked as it poked the boys to one of the classrooms.

He tapped his pitchspork on the door. The door creaked open. Mr. Fields—his face red, puffy, and creased like an overripe tomato—peeked out through the crack in the door. He sighed and expelled breath so redolent of alcohol that no one under twenty-one should have been allowed to inhale it.

"Oh, goody gumdrops," Mr. Fields said tartly. "If it isn't Violet Beauregard and her twin sister."

"We're *Smurfs*," Virgil explained. "They're like gnomes or something."

The demon elbowed Virgil hard and handed him a scrap of paper.

"Read it," he ordered.

Virgil squinted at the sheet of paper.

> *"'Trick or treat, snack on deceit*
> *Stranger give me something sweet'?"*

The demon looked over at Mr. Fields, glaring at him through its gray oily eye slits. The teacher grumbled.

> *"'Don't make me laugh, here's something sour,*
> *To keep you sick this midnight hour.'"*

Mr. Fields then took two fistfuls of stinky meat and dropped it into the boys' trick-or-feed bags. Milton gagged from the reek.

"What is this?" he gasped. "It smells like old fish and cat pee."

"It's a delicacy, boy," Mr. Fields replied. "In Greenland, that is. It's called *hákarl*—fermented shark. You bury a chunk of shark meat in the sand, dig it up after four months, and then hang it on a hook to let it develop a little character."

The bacon demon kicked Milton in the shin. "Thank the man . . . you've got a long, disgusting night ahead of you."

Milton and Virgil mumbled their thanks as Mr. Fields slammed the door.

Walking down the hall, Virgil began to munch on his slab of hákarl. Both Milton and the demon guard gazed at him with slack-mouthed revulsion.

"It's not bad, really," Virgil commented.

The bacon demon shook its head.

"Way to spoil my holiday, you fat little freak."

Virgil began to gag and cough silently.

"Are you okay?" Milton asked with concern.

Virgil, his eyes bulging, motioned to his throat.

"Hey!" Milton said to the guard. "I think he's choking!"

The bacon guard scrutinized Virgil for signs of fakery.

"How can you tell?" he considered as he scratched beneath a rotten meat bandage. "I mean, how can you tell if a Smurf is choking? Do they just get . . . really, *really* blue?"

"Take him to the infirmary!" Milton cried out.

The demon groaned and took Virgil by the arm.

"Okay, maybe he *is* choking," the demon grumbled as it strained to drag Virgil away. "Besides, I hear that all the nurses are dressed as Intensive Care Bears tonight. You stay put. Don't go anywhere, or else I'll take my face off again."

Milton swallowed. "Um, sure. I won't move an inch."

Just as the demon hauled Virgil around the bend, Virgil gave Milton a quick wink and a thumbs-up. Milton's paint-caked face creased into a grin.

Maybe Virgil's BOWEL movement has a chance after all, Milton thought as he raced back toward the Totally Bunks for his explosive suitcases. *And I'm not really lying. I'm not moving an inch, per se . . . I'm moving—hopefully— much, much farther than that. . . .*

29 · MIDNIGHT SHACK ATTACK

MILTON CREPT DOWN the dark hallway toward the Lose-Your-Lunchroom, lugging two trembling suitcase bombs. The sounds of forced trick-or-treating at spork-point echoed in the distance.

"Stinky maggot cheese with cricket heads!" Milton heard Gene shriek before dissolving into spasms of inconsolable blubbering.

Milton arrived at the end of the hallway, where Hambone Hank's Heart Attack Shack lay shrouded in ominous shadows. Milton heard a faint rustling.

"Hello?" he whispered.

A loud, metallic smack clanged from beneath the tin cart, followed by a low growl and what sounded like an exclamation of *"Cat gone it!"* Suddenly, Annubis slid out from beneath the mobile hut on a padded board with wheels. The dog god, his refined features smeared with grease, considered Milton comically. He removed a chewed-up bone from his mouth.

"I didn't expect you, out of the blue like that," he said.

Milton set the suitcases down against the shed.

"Looks like you've been gnawing on my funny bone, because I ain't laughing," Milton chided.

Annubis put the bone he had been chewing on in one pocket, while pulling out the Turnkey drumstick from the other.

"This key should work . . . but I trust that demon guard about as far as I could throw him—which was about twenty-seven feet."

Annubis sniffed the air with his wet snout.

"Where's Virgil?"

Milton stared at his puffy white Smurf feet with sadness.

"He decided to stay and work the system from the inside," he explained. "If it weren't for him, I probably wouldn't have made it here in time."

Annubis picked up some stray tools that lay strewn about the shack and set them inside the structure.

"I wouldn't have left without you," Annubis said as he closed the door to the shed. "Besides, it gave me time to tinker, in case we need an alternate means of escape."

Milton poked his head into the shack. At the front, beneath the main awning window, was a small steering wheel and a gas pedal.

"I didn't know this thing was a car," he said.

Annubis grinned, his mouth a museum of molars, a cathedral of canines.

"It used to be an ice-cream truck," he explained. "An Ill-Humor Wagon."

Milton eyed the bright red and yellow corrugated tin cart dubiously.

"Isn't it a little, well . . . *conspicuous*?"

Annubis grabbed two of the suitcases with his usual effortless grace.

"As I said, it's only in case we encounter any—"

"Complications?" boomed Chef Boyareyookrazee from behind.

Annubis and Milton jumped as Chef Boyare-yookrazee slapped the hefty leg bone of some butchered creature into his palm.

"And, like my infamous Lamb Shank Redemption, my flavors of pain are *quite* complex."

Milton hyperventilated inside the constricting confines of his bright blue Pang suit. Annubis stepped in front of the petrified boy.

"Chef, please," the dignified dog said calmly. "This whole distasteful operation has run its course."

"We had an agreement!" Chef Boyareyookrazee shouted as he raised the lamb shank above his head.

Trembling, Milton stepped from behind Annubis.

"An agreement as worthless as the parchment it was printed on!" Milton shouted, pulling up the itchy white footy pants that kept threatening to dip past the point of no return.

The chef rubbed one of his jiggling chins.

"Hmm . . . maybe I'll put a little Smurf 'n' Turf on the menu for tonight."

Annubis, hackles raised, stalked forward. "The best thing to do, before our less-than-legal enterprise is officially sniffed out, is for us to just part ways and—"

"I thought dogs were supposed to be loyal!" the chef seethed.

Chef Boyareyookrazee's furious scowl melted into a wicked grin. He lowered his leg of lamb and pulled a black remote control from his apron pocket.

"There's been a change of menu," he snickered. "The chef's special is *shockolate mousse* . . . and lots of it!"

The chef pressed the red button. Reflexively, Annubis whimpered and reached for his throat. The chef's sneering face collapsed in on itself like a fallen quiche as he doubled over in agony.

"Looks like the chef wore fresh undies today," Annubis quipped as Chef Boyareyookrazee writhed on the ground, howling.

Milton gazed anxiously past the cart, nested in the dark cul-de-sac. The sound of lumbering footsteps grew louder in the main hallway.

"His howling is going to give us away," Milton whispered.

Suddenly, Mr. Presley turned the corner.

"Too late," Annubis growled.

The teacher rubbed his eyes as he stared at Annubis, his mouth gaping open like a freshly caught catfish.

"Good *night*!" he murmured in his smooth, rumbling tone. "You ain't nothin' but a hound dog!!"

Milton stepped forward.

"Look, Mr. Presley, it's a long story, but please . . . he and I don't belong here. I've got to go and save my sister down in h-e-double-hockey-sticks, and Annubis here, he's got to rescue his family from the Kennels. If you could just find it in your heart to let us go . . ."

Mr. Presley's lips curled into amused disbelief.

"Serves me right for getting the mad midnight munchies," he said, shaking his head.

Demon hooves clacked down the hallway.

"Well, I've always had a soft spot for his hush puppies," Mr. Presley replied with a laugh. He flipped his cape over his shoulder and swaggered into the hallway. "Looks like it's time for an encore . . . and you two better make like an old dog with worms and scoot . . . no offense."

"None taken," Annubis replied as he yanked open the door to his cart.

"What are you doing?" Milton asked.

Annubis slid behind the steering wheel.

"Our departure is already, unfortunately, conspicuous," he said. Annubis twisted the key in the ignition and brought the cart to chugging life. "So hop on and strap yourself in. I have a feeling we're in for a bumpy ride."

Milton heaved his suitcases into the cart just as Annubis wedged the stick shift into gear. The cart lurched forward, and Milton fell back into several tubs of pilfered lard.

The cart jerked around the corner. Mr. Presley slapped the side of the shuddering vehicle and turned to face the oncoming demon horde. He waved, his hand festooned with glittering rings.

"Thank you very much."

The tin shed squealed down the hallway toward the main gate. Milton looked behind him to see Mr. Presley swaying his hips, warming himself up for his surprise performance.

The demon guards skidded to a halt, mesmerized by the hypnotic metronome of Mr. Presley's gyrations. Then, inexplicably, the whole gruesome mob dropped their pitchsporks to the ground and began to dance.

The cart lurched down the hallway like a doddering old man with a walker. A jaunty little ragtime tune— "The Entertainer," Milton was fairly certain—squawked from several tinny speakers on the side of the traveling shed. Annubis pulled out his bone and gnawed it nervously.

"It's like a portable torture device," he said as the bone dangled from his slavering lip like a cigarette stuffed with marrow. "It's always the same three songs. Maybe our trip will be short enough so we don't have to hear 'Turkey in the Straw' or . . ."

Annubis shuddered.

"'*Pop Goes the Weasel.*'"

Annubis clutched the steering wheel so hard that his paw pads, even the weird one near the elbow, turned white. He chewed the bone to disgusting, slobbery bits, then choked down the shards.

"Are you okay?" Milton asked.

Annubis gave his head a quick nod.

"Driving just makes me nervous," he replied. "I keep wanting to hang my head out the window."

After a sharp, albeit painfully slow, turn around the corner, the Heart Attack Shack rolled toward the main gate, leading to the drawbridge.

Annubis brought the cart to a stop. Milton opened the door but was suddenly caught in another full-body Pang contraction, this one squeezing like a vice grip of muscle. He fought the spasm that tried to drag him down to the depths of his borrowed skin. After a few seconds, the contractions stopped and Milton forced himself back up behind the Pang's face.

Annubis bounded out of the cart and pulled the Turnkey drumstick from his overalls. He thrust the poultry-shaped key into the hole, turned, and . . .

nothing. The ten-foot tongue that served as the inner door for Blimpo was motionless yet taunting, as if it were sticking itself out at the two would-be escapees. Annubis gave the now meatless bone a sniff.

"Uh-oh," he murmured as he patted his stomach. *"Wrong bone."*

A riot of hoof clacks echoed down the hall.

"Looks like Mr. Presley's little shindig has been broken up," Annubis growled as he sprang into the cart. He rummaged through a collection of cutlery and emerged, arms laden with soul jars and spatulas.

Annubis quickly formed a pyramid of jars in front of the large window to the left of the tongued drawbridge. He tugged on the pair of spatulas until they, oddly, became as long as skis.

"What's with the spatulas?" Milton asked.

"Telescoping," Annubis said as he slid back into the driver's seat. "Chef Boyareyookrazee may be a sauciopathic maniac, but he has the good sense to stay as far away from his recipes as possible. We're going to use the spatulas to make a little ski ramp. Come on!"

The dog god twisted the ignition as Milton dashed back into the shuddering shack. The bouncy strains of "The Entertainer" took on a creepy, slurpy quality, playing backward as the cart reared back down the hallway. After about fifty feet, Annubis stopped the cart.

"Hang on," he panted, grinding the stick shift into first gear. "We're flying coach."

The music gained in tempo and manic ragtime exuberance.

Milton looked behind him. A squad of demon guards trotted down the hallway almost as slowly as the Heart Attack Shack.

"Can't this thing go any faster?" he asked nervously.

"It's an ice-cream truck, not a race car," Annubis said as his foot pressed against the gas pedal.

"But why the window?!" Milton said as he gripped the sides of his seat.

Annubis's panting grew more frenetic as the truck edged forward, faster and faster. "There's no way to . . . *pierce that tongue,*" he replied. "Brace yourself . . . *here we go!*"

The cart bumped up onto the incline of spatulas and soul jars, lurched onward and upward, and slammed into the wide but not-quite-wide-enough window. The shack squeezed through the portal with a grinding squeal of collapsing metal and pulverized stone. Milton shut his eyes and clutched his seat. The cart groaned through the window and into the moat beyond, accompanied by a scream, a howl, and the warped sound of "The Entertainer" winding down, down, down. . . .

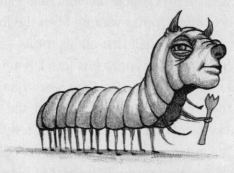

30 · LUCKY RUNS OUT

LUCKY LICKED THE foam from his thin, pink ferret lips and stirred awake. The white, musky animal was used to sleeping eighteen out of the twenty-four available hours in a day. Yet, ever since he had been abducted by the bony, spooky girl with the dark hair and candy perfume smell, he'd been sleeping almost constantly, only coming to for a few bites of food before succumbing to the undertow of slumber.

He twitched and sniffed the air around him, which smelled vaguely of matzo balls. The girl and her friends—the old people in the robes, the ones who smelled sour and sad—weren't in the room outside the cage.

Lucky's stomach rumbled. His food dish was overflowing with glistening, succulent cubes and crunchy Weasel Chow. He instinctively lurched toward the dish, yet, just before his first gobble, he hesitated. Hidden beneath the delicious aromas wafting from the food was that sharp medicine smell that all his meals—even his water—seemed to have lately. His ferret brain turned and clicked like a small gray Rubik's Cube. If he wanted to escape the creepy clutches of this girl and find his master, Lucky would have to summon the few drops of willpower he possessed and refrain from eating.

He stuck his snout through the bars of his cage and pressed as hard as he could. Unfortunately, while his snout savored freedom, the rest of his body was still imprisoned. The luckless Lucky wedged himself in the small slit surrounding the door. He squeezed until his pink eyes bulged but to no avail. Dust tickled his nose, and Lucky sneezed, his head lurching spasmodically and knocking into the metal latch, secured by a combination lock.

"I'll only be a second, Mom," the girl's voice squeaked from outside the curtains. "Just look around . . . No, I didn't know that pigs had knuckles either. Ask Mrs. Smilovitz . . . she won't bite. I just need my algebra book."

Thinking like a ferret always does—quickly—Lucky rolled over onto his back and let his tongue loll out to the side as Necia entered the room.

"Hmm," she muttered, dressed in a black wool overcoat with white stockings and white leather flats.

"Maybe I left it on the altar, by the sacrificial dagger and bronze blood collection bowl. . . ."

Something caught Necia's eye. She turned to see Lucky convulsing in his cage.

"Lucky!" she squealed, running to his cage. Necia knelt and worked the combination lock with her spindly fingers.

"I must have given him too much sleepy juice," she fretted as she reached into the cage. Suddenly, the ferret sprang. He leaped out of the cage onto Necia's shoulder. He dug his claws into her as he coiled up for another vault. The girl rose and frantically batted at Lucky as he bounded onto a stack of boxes laden with ceramic Seder plates.

Necia turned, her dark eyes glittering with betrayal.

"You little ingrate!" she spat. "Damian wanted you stuffed! But *no*, I thought you'd make a cool pet. I spent nearly all of my allowance on your stupid tranquilizers to keep you behaved!"

Lucky reared up on the teetering pile of boxes and hissed.

Necia crept nearer, waving her outstretched arms in slow circles, a motion that Lucky found unbearably distracting.

"Plus, you reminded me of Milton," she said calmly as she stepped closer. "I cared about him . . . maybe even had a little crush on him, despite the fact that my religion strictly forbids crushes and meaningful eye contact. That's why I wanted to be sacrificed with him, to cross that bridge into the next world, away from all these . . . rules. So I could just be myself. With Milton."

Lucky shivered sadly at the sound of his master's name. He ached for his smell, his careful touch, his knowledge of prime scritchy spots—all the little things that Lucky had spent so many years scrupulously training Milton to do. He felt the gentle boy's presence, not from without, but from somewhere deep—miles and miles away—within.

Milton lay panting, slick with spit and slime, behind the sagging blob that had been his Pang disguise. He shuddered as he considered the route of his unfortunate "eviction" from the blue-tinted Pang body, forced from the premises by unbelievably powerful contractions until, next thing Milton knew, he had been thrown out its, um, *back door* in a fit of intestinal labor.

He looked back at the remains of the Heart Attack Shack and saw Annubis emerge, dazed, from the wreckage. The chirpy strains of "Pop Goes the Weasel" leaked through the damaged speakers of the cart. Even though the shack was a complete shambles, somehow—like the mysterious black box recorder that always seems to survive a plane crash—the cart's music box was all too intact and functional.

Annubis sniffed the air, growled deeply, and gave himself an invigorating, full-body shake. He trotted over to Milton and hoisted him up as the mob of Pangs assessed the situation, looks of dim realization dawning on their crude, indistinct faces.

"Milton," the dog god said calmly, "I think it's time to feed the Pangs before they chow down on us."

Milton swallowed and nodded. He reached for the suitcases still in the clutched hands of his former Pang skin. Milton carefully unfolded its trembling fingers from the suitcases' handles and grabbed the luggage. He joined Annubis as the horde of Pangs stirred, sniffing the air with their gouged-hole nostrils. The mass of insatiable appetites moved forward as one. Milton held out one of the suitcases, labeled YUMMY SNACKS in bright red barbecue sauce.

Growls pealed from Pang stomachs. Fresh streams of slobber dribbled down the accordion folds of their chins.

"On the count of three," Annubis murmured as he backed away from Milton and began to slowly spin in circles. Milton watched as the proud dog god held the suitcases out at his sides, gaining momentum, like the casket cars on the Grave Spinner ride back home at Six Flags Topeka.

Milton clenched the handles of his heavy suitcases and began to twirl.

"How can we be sure . . . we'll hit them?" he puffed.

"*One* . . . we don't really have a choice," Annubis said as he reeled ever faster.

Milton spun. His arms ached with every gyration, as if they were in danger of freeing themselves from his arm sockets.

"Where should I . . . fling these things?"

"*Two* . . . Just aim for the center, as deep as possible for maximum impact."

Suddenly, Milton became profoundly dizzy. Sure, he was spinning around at the bottom of a gorge, attempting to hurl luggage at starving zombie blobs, but it was more than that. His nose twitched. The air smelled . . . more complicated. Sounds untangled themselves from one another to become more distinct. The images that streaked and swirled about him gained clarity and vibrancy.

"*Lucky,*" Milton whispered, his senses fully alive as he felt the energetic connection with his pet ferret switch on. "He must be awake!"

"*Three!*" Annubis shouted. He flung his suitcases toward the advancing mass.

In an instant, Milton knew just when to release his high-pressure projectiles. The suitcases hurtled through the air toward the heart of the mob. Annubis's load hit a clot of Pangs, who then almost immediately recovered and began fighting over the greasy baggage. Milton's suitcases struck dead center of the writhing throng. The Pangs—each resembling an oversized glazed ham—pushed, pulled, shoved, scratched, punched, and mewled with rage until, suddenly, the suitcases exploded. The creatures were thrown end over end as an explosion of dirty underwear, socks, shirts, slacks, and belts flew out of the luggage with deadly velocity. The Pangs lay in scattered heaps, bruised and bludgeoned by the stinking shrapnel.

The drawbridge above slowly creaked open. Annubis rolled his sad dog eyes upward with grave concern.

"Looks like we've got company," he growled.

The great lolling tongue of the bridge slapped against the outer lip of the Gorge. The wooden walkway trembled under the oddly dainty feet of some massive, galumphing creature as it passed through the gates and onto the drawbridge. A gruesome, blobbish, and unfortunately familiar figure, perched atop a saddle mounted upon the beast, leaned forward over the edge.

"Peek-a-boo," Bea "Elsa" Bubb snarled from above. "I see you."

Milton gulped.

"Nice costume," he replied, doing his best to keep from trembling.

The drawbridge creaked as the creature beneath the principal shifted its considerable weight. A spray of splinters rained down from beneath the wooden walkway.

The principal smirked.

"This is indeed a treat for me, and a nasty trick for you," she said with fiendish delight. "Now the only question is, should I force you to smell my feet, or give my Heckifino something good to eat?"

Principal Bubb pulled a delicious Reuben sandwich, dripping with Thousand Island dressing and sauerkraut, from the inside of her leather cowgirl vest. The twisted pile of Pangs stirred as their gruesome yet finely tuned snouts detected the presence of food, like a drop of blood hitting shark-infested waters.

Milton stared at the mountain of wriggling Pangs. The mound shifted like a game of Tetris played with fatty blobs for blocks, and in an instant of sparkling clarity, Milton saw a path.

Four KOOKs swished into the stockroom in their blue robes.

"What is going on, Junior Knight Necia?" the Guiding Knight demanded as he spied Lucky atop the pile of boxes. "I thought we had expressly forbidden the exercising of that, that . . . *rodent* you insist on keeping."

In that moment, Lucky saw with his keen pink eyes a human bridge spanning from his box to the open curtain. The ferret coiled backward, compressing his haunches with intent to spring.

"Oh no, you don't," Necia muttered as she lunged forward.

Lucky leaped through her arms as she went to grab him, landing on the Guiding Knight's shoulder.

"*Eeeeeee!*" the tall man squealed shrilly. "Not my face! Not my face!"

Lucky leapfrogged to the next frantic knight's shoulder, then to the next, and then finally he landed atop a small Filipino man just emerging from the curtained doorway.

"Ack, you filthy animal!" he yelled as he swatted at the ferret grinding its back claws into the side of his neck.

And, with a faint parting spray of musk, Lucky sprang through the curtains into the store beyond.

Milton darted across the bottom of the Gorge toward the shifting, writhing mass of Pangs.

"Oh no, you don't," Bea "Elsa" Bubb hissed as she yanked the reins of her Heckifino. The creature stumbled back. Its spindly back leg snapped through a rotten plank as two demon guards in tofu suits watched from the open maw leading into Blimpo.

Milton scampered up the mountain of slowly awakening Pangs, stepping on each with an athletic grace he exhibited only when linked to Lucky. He bolted up to the top of the quivering mound and turned back to Annubis.

"C'mon!" Milton yelled. "There isn't much time!"

Annubis stared fixedly at the drawbridge. Bea "Elsa" Bubb locked eyes with the dog god's, their glares clashing like swords.

"What up, *dawg*?" the principal seethed, tightly drawing in the reins to her Heckifino. The creature gobbled in protest as it teetered backward on gangly red-and-gray-striped legs.

Annubis winked at the principal and gave her a conspiratorial thumbs-up, as much as a half-dog can.

As the principal puzzled over Annubis, the dog god drew in a deep breath, then bounded toward Milton on all fours, doing his best to follow the boy's path precisely.

"What's that cur got cooking?" Bea "Elsa" Bubb pondered aloud as Annubis scampered away.

Meanwhile, Milton nimbly sprang from the plump pile of Pangs and grabbed the lip of the Gorge. He swung himself up almost effortlessly. Annubis trotted behind him as the Pangs untangled themselves from one another.

"Hurry!" Milton called as his former path—slowly filling in by sluggish, stupefied Pangs—disappeared behind the panting dog god. With all the strength he could muster, Annubis leaped from the collapsing mound and landed next to Milton on the salty, dusty rim of the Waistlands.

"Where to?" Milton asked.

Annubis scanned the bleak terrain, sniffed the brackish air, and cocked his head to one side.

"That way," the dog god said soberly, pointing to a murky, mountainous mass in the distance. "The last place anyone would think we'd go without being bound, gagged, and dragged there."

"That is *hardly* what I'd consider kosher!" screamed the only customer to enter Mazel Top-to-Bottom in the last two weeks as Lucky skittered across the gleaming floor.

Mrs. Smilovitz gasped at the ferret currently undulating through her store.

"*A klog iz mir!*" she moaned, clamping her hands to her cheeks.

Necia raced after Lucky as he made his way to the door.

"Come back!" she called with tears streaming down her face. "I promise I'll hardly ever drug you if you just come back!"

Lucky passed through the automatic sliding door and bounded into the mall. Necia and the other KOOKs followed close behind.

"*Oy gevalt!*" cried Mrs. Smilovitz as the robed zealots rushed past her. "Let this incident serve as your eviction notice, you meshuggeners!"

Lucky darted through the shocked crowd of Generica mall. His wet pink nose twitched, sucking in knots of aroma that he untied with his mind. The faint smell of burnt marshmallow tickled the back of his memory, a sharp sweetness that was half-fear and half-sadness, yet was entirely his only means of escape.

Milton ran so hard he felt like he had pins in his lungs. Annubis—lean, lithe, and limber—struggled to keep up.

"How are you . . . doing this?" he asked with his tongue hanging out the side of his mouth. "I never took you to be an . . . athlete."

Milton smiled and wiped away a trickle of sweat that dripped into his eye.

"It's my link with . . . Lucky," Milton panted. "My pet ferret. He must be running on his wheel . . . or something. It's like he's been asleep for a week and . . . only now . . . woke up."

Bea "Elsa" Bubb roared from behind them.

"Not again!" she said as she snapped her whip on the Heckifino's leathery flank. "After them!"

The animal cautiously trod across the rickety draw-bridge.

"Faster!" she bellowed, shooting bits of corned beef out of her mouth. She took another big bite of her succulent sandwich.

"Just being near Blimpo makes me ravenous," she grumbled as rye crumbs tumbled into the Gorge.

Beneath her, the Pangs became agitated. The smell of food—a marvelous specimen straight from the underworld's infamous Psycho Delicatessen—roused the creatures awake like strong smelling salts. With their insatiable stomachs roaring and their chins slick with slobber, the Pangs piled on top of one another to get at the irresistible Reuben.

"Faster, you lumbering, incompetent—"

The Heckifino paused briefly to relieve itself.

"—and shamelessly incontinent beast!" Bea "Elsa" Bubb bellowed.

The drawbridge groaned and splintered.

"Careful!" the stout demon guard yelled from the doorway.

Pangs gripped the sides of the drawbridge as they clambered onto the straining span.

"Don't you 'careful' me!" the principal shouted. "I'm not going to let these fatheaded, overgrown, walking *snack attacks* let that little creep make a break for it—"

The Heckifino stumbled as the drawbridge listed violently to one side. A dozen Pangs spilled onto the bridge at the beast's pointed feet. The tonnage finally proved too great, and with a gnashing groan of shattering wood, the principal, her beastly steed, and the hungry Pangs tumbled end over end into the Gorge.

The knights tumbled into a heap at the bottom of the up escalator.

"Quick!" Necia yelled as she rose to her feet,

frantically scanning the crowded atrium. "He's making a break for it!"

Warder Chango retrieved a missing Van before it ascended back up the escalator.

"What's, like, the big deal?" he asked Necia, wobbling as he slipped on his errant shoe. "Just let the thing, you know, *go*."

Necia stood on her tiptoes and stared out over the crowd toward the exit.

"No! He's my only connection to . . . *him*."

She noticed a commotion up ahead, the crowd suddenly breaking like waves, leaving a faint musky scent in its wake. It was like Moses parting the Red Sea, only instead of a Hebrew prophet and lawgiver, the cause of the disruption was a speeding white ferret.

"There he is!" Necia yelped as she ran through the crowd.

Bobbing and weaving like an eel in a fur stole, Lucky skillfully dodged the footfalls of shocked Genericans. Faux marble tiles whizzed beneath his sprightly feet with geometric regularity. His bright pink eyes winced at the gush of light pouring from the exit. Lucky stopped briefly to pant his little weasel pants.

Necia's patent-leather shoes slapped the mall floor, tapping a steadily quickening rhythm.

Startled shoppers pitched out of Lucky's way as he made his final push toward the parking lot. Necia dashed through the door, hot on his furious ferret heels.

"Stop!" she shrieked. "You're going to get your-self—"

Wheels screeched across the asphalt of the parking lot. A Ford FrankenFuel hybrid slammed into the side of a Solar Lexus with a metallic crunch. The drivers rushed out of their vehicles and stared at the lifeless white lump lying prone between their hot, ticking cars.

Fresh tears streamed out of Necia's dark, quivering eyes.

"Killed."

Milton and Annubis sprinted across the Waistlands. Milton looked over his shoulder with amused relief at the tumult in the Gorge. Suddenly, some invisible force slammed painfully into Milton's side.

"Milton?" Annubis exclaimed as the boy keeled over onto the ground. Milton tumbled and rolled in the dust, energy draining from him like water through a sieve.

One moment he had been filled with the sure-footed confidence of a superhero dodging raindrops. Now Milton's temporarily ferret-heightened senses dulled and receded until all was black, and Milton was, for all appearances, dead to the underworld.

31 · DIVINE INTERVENTION

MOTES OF TWINKLING dust flitted playfully in the artificial sunbeams streaming through the stained-glass windows. The heady, honey-sweet scent of ambrosia filled the spacious cathedral.

A luminous white marble table stood in the middle of the meeting chamber, standing atop ornately carved legs some twenty feet tall. Surrounding the table were seven sleek chairs of equal height. Here, perched atop their towering thrones, the seven archangels held their quarterly meeting.

"Let us tarry not and partake in this most holy of meetings," Michael said imperiously, flexing his majestic wings just a little farther than any other creature could. "As you all know, the Big Guy Upstairs has been, shall we say, *distracted* as of late, and the bulk of His duties has fallen on our wings. . . ."

"I'm up to my halo with governing paradise as it is," Zadkiel interjected, sipping from his Heaven's Best Angel, MDCXII mug.

Raguel scratched beneath the white Nehru collar of his immaculate vestments.

"What I wouldn't *give* to govern paradise," he grumbled while rubbing his molting wings on the back of his chair. "Try being the archangel to the infirm and woebegone. I just came back from consoling a pediatric head lice ward. You've got paradise, Zadkiel, and I've got *parasites*."

"Oh, wherever did I leave my tiny violin?" Zadkiel mocked as he and the other archangels subtly scooted their chairs farther away from Raguel.

Rafael raised his hand.

Michael smiled. "Yes, brother Rafael?"

"Firstly, while the Big Guy Upstairs has his existential crisis or whatever," Rafael said, "what are *we* supposed to be doing?"

"Doing?" repeated Michael as he swatted away a playful cloud of motes. "What we always do, only more so: show humanity that our gates are always open. Metaphorically speaking, of course."

"Metaphorically?" Sariel asked, removing one of his earbuds. Harp-driven dance music squawked from the dangling earpiece.

"Yes," Gabriel answered sarcastically in his crisp British accent. "It's a big word that means *not really*."

"Technically the gates are locked," Michael explained. "We sure as heck can't just let *anyone* in, or it would cease to be exclusive. Speaking of Heck . . ."

Gabriel and Uriel stiffened as Michael reviewed the bottom of his parchment. Uriel's forehead beaded with holy perspiration.

"Apparently," Michael continued, "there has been a series of disturbances that have caught the Galactic Order Department by surprise. And, as an organization that strictly adheres to a Divine Plan, we do not tolerate 'surprises.'"

Uriel began to twitch. Gabriel glared at him, silently entreating the nervous angel to keep it together.

"A boy named . . . *Milton Fauster*," Michael went on, "was darned for all eternity despite a lack of compelling transgressions to justify such a judgment. Shortly thereafter, said boy *escaped* from Limbo."

The archangels surrounding the table gasped, save for Gabriel and Uriel, who gaped in feigned surprise.

"But that's impossible," Rafael remarked.

"And that's not all," Michael went on. "The Fauster boy used lost souls to make good his escape. The Prime Defective is very clear about the reintroduction of unprocessed souls to the Surface. To say that it is frowned upon is to say that the Great Flood was a bit of a drizzle. Then the boy had the audacity to *return,* aiding and abetting his sister in the disruption of a ceremony in Mallvana. . . ."

"Ooh," Sariel cooed. "Mallvana. *There's* a place I'd like to warm my Sacredit Card!"

"The girl is now undergoing an Infernship down under," Michael continued, "while the boy is still at large."

Gabriel straightened his white silk tie.

"A fascinating story, Michael, but what does this have to do with us? Surely this is a matter for the Powers That Be Evil. . . ."

"This has *everything* to do with us," countered Michael.

The archangel polished his gold Galactic Order Department (GOD) badge—a pair of wings sprouting from a glowing pyramid with a little eye perched at the tip—unconsciously with his thumb.

"I've got a feeling that this goes deeper than *down there*," Michael continued. "It upsets the whole scheme of things. On its own, this Heck business is inconsequential. But if it set some kind of precedent, it could unravel the very fabric of creation!"

"The Academy Award for Best Actor goes to . . . ," Sariel scoffed.

"Listen here, you *cupid* fool . . ."

As the two archangels argued, Gabriel scribbled a quick note on the torn corner of his parchment, plucked out one of his feathers, attached the note with a dab of saliva, then put it in his palm and blew it surreptitiously over to Uriel.

The feather floated gently into Uriel's coffee mug. The angel fished the small note out with his fingers.

CALL ME. *NOW*. THEN HANG UP.

Uriel shot Gabriel a sideways glance before scratching behind his ear, causing the gleaming gold band crowning his head to hum ever so slightly. Immediately, Gabriel's halo began to ring and hover. The other archangels frowned at him.

"Whoops," Gabriel apologized. "I must have accidentally left it on."

He tilted the rim of his halo down to his ear.

"Hello, this is . . . oh . . . *sir* . . . yes, of course!"

Gabriel mouthed "It's Him" to his fellow seraphs. The angels' eyes widened. Michael's perfect features soured with jealousy.

"Immediately, sir. We're just wrapping up . . . Uriel, too? Yes, we'll tend to it. Godspeed."

Gabriel fingered his headpiece, causing it to settle back onto his salt-and-pepper hair.

"Well, apparently *He* is planning an act of Himself and wants me and Uriel to chip in on some of the details. . . ."

Gabriel nodded to Uriel and the two scooted back their chairs.

"Michael, I'd like to say it's been lovely," Gabriel said with a smile. "But I, in good conscience, can't. So, until next quarter, fare thee well . . . Come on, Uriel."

The two angels fluttered down to the white marble

floor. Gabriel led Uriel across the basilica to the relative privacy of an ornately carved marble column.

Uriel nervously chewed his nails, which, with each nibble, grew back to their original length.

"I can't take much more of this," Uriel whined.

"It's not up to us," Gabriel asserted. "It's what the Big Guy Upstairs wants. He *believes* in us. That's why he picked you and me *specifically* to head His most righteous covert operation."

Uriel leaned against the column and sighed.

"I don't know . . ."

"We can't just clasp our hands together and pray that this will all go away," Gabriel replied.

Uriel looked up with a hopeful smile.

"Well, if you think about it, we *could*—"

Gabriel shook his head.

"He's testing our faith. And, by the looks of it, this isn't some open-book pop quiz. He's getting ready for the final exam."

Uriel stared back at the imposing table of bickering angels.

"Everything is moving so *fast*," he said nervously. "Why start with Heck?"

Gabriel shrugged his wings.

"GOD works in mysterious, patent-pending ways," he replied. "Until He contacts us, we simply need to shut our angel-food-cake holes and take everything on faith value."

Up above, Michael eyed Gabriel and Uriel with suspicion. He leaned close to his remaining archangels.

"I'd like to propose an emergency measure," Michael whispered.

Raguel scratched his feather-bare wing.

"But we need all seven present to—"

"Drastic times call for drastic measures," Michael muttered spookily. "And this is one drastic measure."

Zadkiel wrinkled his perfect nose.

"Does this come from upstairs?" he asked.

Michael smiled. His brilliant white teeth were so blinding that they obscured both his face and his motives.

"We are His instruments, tasked with acting on His behalf, which is what I intend to do," Michael replied coolly. "Act upon His implied meaning, the Good Word unuttered. See, sometimes you have to engineer something really, really bad for the greater good. Something so bad it could—and will, if all goes according to plan—give even the devil nightmares."

32 · WAKiNG THE DEAD

"HEY, POPSICLE," JACK Kerouac murmured through Milton's mental fog. "You done catching cups?"

Milton stirred awake. Jack, Annubis, and Moondog were looking down at him like understudies from the *Wizard of Odd*.

"Welcome back to the land of the once living!" Moondog exclaimed, staring at him with sightless eyes.

Milton leaned up on his elbows and blinked awake. "What . . . happened?" he asked.

Annubis patted Milton on the top of the head. "You were unconscious for seven hours."

"*Seven hours!*" Milton yelped, bolting up to his full, upright position.

The dog god shook his head until his velvety, chocolate-brown ears flapped.

"Sorry," Annubis apologized. "For me it was seven hours . . . for *you* it was only one. I always forget that."

Milton looked beyond his small group of friends. Judging from the bleak, desolate tundra of salt dunes and barbed-wire brambles, they were still in the Wastelands. Yet just beyond, in the distance, the smooth, barren landscape slammed abruptly into a steep, rocky crag. At the bottom of the rugged cliff was the mouth of a large dark cave that stared back at Milton like a dead crow's eye. He looked up into Annubis's soulful, hangdog face.

"But we were running really fast and then suddenly—"

Milton gasped.

"Lucky!"

Milton's friends shared the same look of sympathetic knowing.

Finally, Moondog spoke up. "Your energetic connection with your pet . . . your ferret," he said, scratching the thick white hair that billowed out from beneath his horned helmet. "For it to cause this kind of reaction must mean that it was abruptly . . . *severed*. The connection."

Milton gazed back and forth between the three faces.

"What do you mean by *severed*?"

Moondog prodded Jack with eyes that, while

incapable of sight, were more than effective at passing the proverbial buck. Jack sighed and ran his fingers through his slicked-back hair.

"Your pet has, like, blown the Stage, dig?" Jack explained.

Milton had known, in his heart, that this was true. Lucky was dead. But actually *hearing* it made the whole thing feel cruelly real. Sadness churned inside Milton until it became a thick, salty sorrow that gushed out of his eyes. He cried until he felt hollow, numb, and—ultimately—somewhat less than completely awful inside.

Milton gazed up at Jack and Moondog, as if they had suddenly just materialized out of thin air, which to him, in a way, they had.

"What are you two doing here?" he asked as he wiped his red-rimmed eyes. "I mean, I'm glad to see you, but I just didn't expect it to be so soon."

Jack reached instinctively for the pendant in Milton's pocket. He patted it reverently, as if it held a baby's first smile.

"We lost people had gotten even *loster*, like," Jack explained in his cryptic way. "So Divining Rod was doing his divine thing to help us get back in the groove. And, when his crazy dowsing stick wobbled beyond Blimpo, we knew you must have either escaped or been kicked out."

"So we hotfooted it back to Blimpo and found you

two here," Moondog interjected, "in between there and . . ." He casually leveled his long, yellowed finger at the cave beyond.

"*There.*"

A stale wind, like the belch of a thousand-year-old giant after downing a water tower full of rancid Clamato juice, rustled through Milton's hair.

"Is that the entrance to . . . you know?" Milton asked.

Jack nodded.

"One of many," he replied with a nervous edge to his voice.

Moondog frowned, an expression only readable through the downward slopes of snowy white beard.

"Annubis told us about your plan to rescue your sister from . . . *there.* While that's a noble cause and all, I'm not sure if you know what you're getting yourself into. That place makes Heck seem like an ice-cream social in Candyland."

Milton stood up, straightened his glasses, and squinted at the cave. It was still, slumbering, yet thick with potential danger, as if it were filled with hibernating bears.

"I made a promise," he said. "And I've lost everything—my sister, my pet . . . my life. So that promise is all that I have. The only thing that seems real to me after all this."

Annubis sniffed the air. The fur on the back of his neck rose into stiff prickles.

"Whatever we do, we should do it now, and on the move. Even a creature as graceless and crude as Principal Bubb will find her way out of the Gorge and onto our trail, snapping at our heels with her dentures."

Milton furrowed his brow.

"Those are dentures?"

"Yes . . . perhaps the first."

"We should make tracks, like a jazz combo in the recording studio," Jack said with a nod, his cowlick shaking like an upside-down question mark.

Milton, the two phantoms, and Annubis plodded across the Wastelands to its abrupt edge at the mouth of the tunnel. Hot, humid wind coiled and hissed out of the burrow's mouth.

The passageway was shaped like a seemingly never-ending row of dismal, concrete croquet hoops. The floor was slick and sticky, like a second-run movie theater after a matinee—only instead of smelling like stale popcorn and dried soda, the place reeked of stale Limburger cheese and dried skunk puke. The ceaseless, hypnotizing burble of crowd noise lapped against the walls.

"What's on the other side?" Milton quavered.

"Many things," Annubis commented as he stepped across the threshold of volcanic rock and concrete. Harsh white lights embedded in the ceiling flickered on, casting streaks of horseshoe-shaped light on the rough-hewn walls. "None of which will allow a boy to pass through."

Milton hurried behind him, ironically, like a small dog keeping up with its master's long, steady stride.

"Then how—?"

"I've been thinking about that," Moondog said as he wheeled his cart across the uneven stone floor. The travelers stopped.

"First," Moondog continued as he rummaged through his shopping cart, "I saved a couple of these weird jars."

He pulled out one of the Make-Believe Play-fellows jars. The soul was nothing more than a dull, swirling clot of beige fog. Milton glanced up from the jar to Moondog.

"*That's* an imaginary friend?"

The wizened phantom shrugged.

"Not all imaginary friends are so . . . *imaginative,*" he surmised. "But you don't want to be coming out of this tunnel with a rainbow unicorn mane and fairy wings."

He handed the jar, the soul inside jiggling listlessly, to Milton.

"Just drink it down. Pretend it's like a health shake."

Milton grimaced as he slogged down the Make-Believe Play-fellow soul, gagging all the way.

"It even *tastes* beige," Milton choked out. "Like drinking a trip to a furniture store with your parents."

Moondog uncovered his Polaroid camera from the bottom of his shopping cart.

"Beige is good," he said as he felt around for his scissors, blank forms, glue stick, and other essential elements key to forging a convincing assumed identity. "Beige won't get you noticed. Although . . . we don't want it to look like you're *trying* not to be noticed. Hmmm . . . I know. Here."

Moondog doffed his horned Viking helmet and placed it atop Milton's head as if casually re-creating some ancient Nordic ceremony. Milton's eyes, which were now shifting from their greenish blue to a dull, nondescript brown, looked up at the savage, towering headgear that loomed above his crown.

"Great. I'm sure I'll just blend in like a booger under a kindergartner's desk."

"Actually," Jack said, "the horns might help, considering where you're going."

"Plus they add a few feet to you," Moondog offered. "Heightwise, I mean. Just to be on the safe side, though, I think I'll write you down as a midget—"

"Little person," Milton interjected as his features became less distinct.

"*Little person,*" Moondog continued. "Hopefully that will not only explain your youthful appearance, but also make customs a little uncomfortable so they'll just hurry you on through. Little people have a way of doing that to nonlittle people."

Jack slipped off his worn tweed jacket and gave it to

Milton, who now was of average build, with an average nose and average mouth arranged averagely at the front of his average-shaped head.

Annubis whined uneasily.

"We can dress Milton up as the devil himself, and he *still* won't be able to find his way. He needs a guide."

Moondog smirked until his snowy white beard tilted upward like a mischievous ski slope.

"He needs a guide *dog*."

Annubis cocked his head to the side.

"Guide dog? But I can't just walk in and—"

"Sure you can," Moondog interrupted as he pulled out a pair of dark sunglasses from the toolbox in his shopping cart. He took off Milton's glasses and replaced them with the heavy black spectacles.

"I can't see anything," Milton commented.

"Join the club," Moondog replied.

"So how does pretending I'm blind help me get to h-e-double-hockey-sticks?" Milton asked.

"It would help to explain the hat," Jack offered.

"And it would also help to explain a guide dog," Moondog continued, gesturing toward Annubis. "It would mean, of course, an entrance unbecoming a pseudo-god—on all fours—but a mission of dignity isn't always dignified. Smile."

Moondog snapped Milton's picture. The yet-to-be-developed picture came spitting out of the camera. After waving the photo in the fetid air, Moondog gave it a few artful slices with his scissors, pasted it to a document, stamped it with a rubber stamp, and handed it to Milton.

"Martin Foulest?" Milton said, squinting over the frames of his dark sunglasses.

"Cool, huh?" Moondog replied. "It's an anagram of your name . . . Milton Fauster . . ."

"He, like, knows what his name is," Jack chided.

"Exactly," Moondog countered. "It sounds enough like your name so that you'll answer to it. This is a major sticking point in acts of espionage. Not responding to your cover."

Moondog pulled a red kerchief from his cart and tied it around Annubis's slender neck.

"Your name is Dakota," Moondog said as he cinched the knot. "That's a good name for a dog."

Annubis sniffed the air.

"We're closer than I thought," he said as he hunkered down on all fours beside Milton.

Milton slid the sunglasses down the bridge of his unremarkable nose.

"Down there," Milton said. "It looks like the floor is moving."

"Moving sidewalk," Moondog said matter-of-factly. "What else would you expect just before entering an Errport?"

33 · A LOT OF HOT ERR

"AN AIRPORT?" MILTON asked as they reached the end of the conveyor belt that deposited them at the other end of the passageway.

"*Err*port," Moondog corrected, drawing out the subtle difference of inflection. "Where those that have erred congregate before they are, um . . . *ported*."

Milton stood tentatively at the mouth of the sticky, stinky tunnel that had seemed so bleak and despairing only a moment ago but now, considering the infamy of his final destination, felt as inviting as his cozy *Star Wars* comforter on a cold winter's morning.

He surveyed the gray congested terminal where thousands of put-upon, unpleasant-looking individuals boarded a steep escalator headed straight down. From Milton's vantage point, it seemed as if he were looking down upon the Niagara Falls of humanity.

Milton sighed.

"Do we have a plan B?" he asked.

Jack laughed. "If plan Bs were any good, they'd be plan As, right?" He hit Milton on the shoulder.

"We gotta run like a pair of cheap nylons and leave you to your destiny," Jack said. Milton stared as the lanky man walked the wrong way down the moving sidewalk, which made his exit far more gradual and far less dramatic.

"I'll be fine," Milton said sarcastically. "Don't worry about me."

Moondog patted Milton on the shoulder.

"Don't mind him," Moondog explained. "He isn't much for goodbyes. After all, to him, this is just the end of one moment and the beginning of another. He's either incredibly enlightened or is going senile. Until we meet again, Little Unborn."

The old blind man in Viking clothes trotted down the conveyer belt to join Jack. Tears leaked from beneath Milton's sunglasses.

"I hope you find the Margins . . . where those who don't belong belong."

Annubis nudged Milton's leg with his snout.

"We must go," the dog god said as he crawled toward the noisy human traffic jam outside the one-way escalators. "Maybe Heaven can wait, but the place we're going can't."

Milton and Annubis reached the end of the escalator,

which—after about a half hour of continuous descent—seemed like an esca-*much*-later. Demons—and not the pitchspork-wielding flunkies in Heck but nightmarish monsters brandishing deadly pitchforks—corralled the people into one big line, only to split them up again into three separate, backtracking lines that coiled around and around until coming back together one foot ahead of where they had been to begin with.

"NEXT!"

A skeleton in a navy blue uniform wearing a light pink crocheted shawl around "her" shoulders (how anyone, much less a skeleton, could get "chilly" in this sweltering heat was beyond Milton) greeted the arrivals as they entered the swelling lines.

"Transgression?" the creature, named Helen, judging from her badge, asked with a peculiar hollow quality unique to talking skeletons.

"What are my options?" Milton asked as the woman impatiently waved the twenty-seven bones that made up her hand, presumably to see Milton's freshly fabricated passport. He handed it to her.

"Don't be funny," Helen replied as she scanned Milton's fake ID. "Funny takes time." She glanced at Milton through hollow sockets rimmed with blue eye shadow.

"Though that hat is a riot," she deadpanned. "Transgression?"

Annubis tugged Milton's pant leg with his teeth.

"Say 'greed,'" he whispered through a mouth of beige khakis. "It's a safe, not-immediately-evident sin."

Milton nodded, straightened up, and addressed Helen.

"Greed."

"Greed?"

"Yes, I was . . . blinded by it."

"It says here you're nineteen," Helen said, glaring at Milton suspiciously "You look younger."

"I . . . um," he stammered. "*Thank you*. I'll take your word for it since, you know, I can't see myself or anything. Just a late bloomer, I guess."

"It's a pity," Helen intoned through lipstick-stained teeth. "If you only died younger, you'd be going to Heck instead. That place is an ice-cream social in Candyland compared to where you're headed."

"I've, um, heard that . . . in line."

Helen looked down at Annubis.

"It's been a long time since I've seen a dog," she chattered. "Loyalty, and all. Except for pit bulls. Those rap stars take them everywhere. Does he—"

"Dakota."

"*Dakota* do any tricks?"

Milton smirked. "Sure, he can—"

Annubis bit Milton on the calf.

"No, actually," Milton faltered. "No tricks . . . just . . . guiding me."

The crush of people behind Milton grew from testy to supremely ticked off.

"Get a move on!" shouted a balding man with a face as flushed as an old red toilet.

"Keep your pants on!" Helen shrieked at the man. "At least until we ask you to remove them."

Helen shook her head and snickered.

"I love how impatient these bozos get. If they had any *clue* that centuries from now they'll be looking back at this moment like it was a big party with live music and a no-host bar . . ."

She handed Milton back his passport. He pretended to flail at it somewhat, which was pretty easy to do considering the thick black glasses.

"You'll be passing through seven Insecurity Gates," Helen said as she finally just tucked Milton's passport into his pocket. "So if you'll just walk through . . ."

Annubis led Milton through the first gate, basically an electronic doorway. It beeped.

"Hmmm," Helen said, scanning the boy, who—thanks to his bland Make-Believe Play-fellow soul—was still, save for his outfit, physically nondescript. "Must be the hat. Take it off and pass through again."

Milton obliged, handing the Viking helmet to Helen, then passing through the gate again, this time silently.

"Okay, the greed line is to your right," Helen said as she cradled the helmet in her bony arms. "Just follow the green arrows. NEXT!"

Milton and Annubis followed the barely perceptible green arrows on a filthy, salmon-and-teal-colored shag carpet. Milton looked over his shoulder as Helen donned the helmet. Nervous, Milton scooped out the pendant Jack had given him from his front pocket and clutched it in his hand.

"I don't want them taking this away from me," he mumbled.

Milton impulsively plopped the necklace in his mouth and swallowed it. It went down like a charm, literally: painfully slow, leaving a metallic flavor trail in its wake.

"NEXT!"

Milton and Annubis passed through five more gates, each manned by a snippy skeleton—Helena, Helga, Helia, Helki, and Heloise—wearing a progressively redder shawl. At each gate, Milton was asked ("shrieked at" is probably more accurate) to remove a piece of clothing until finally he and his guide dog in disguise arrived at the final gate.

"NEXT!" screeched Helsa, who—despite not having any lungs—was the loudest gatekeeper of them all. Her shawl, cinched tightly to her neck with a brass pitchfork pin, was bloodred.

"Can't you see we're busy?"

"Actually," Milton said, pointing to his glasses, "I can't see anything."

"Regardless," Helsa replied, "your future's so dark you won't be needing shades."

She yanked the glasses from Milton's face. He winced at the sudden gush of harsh fluorescent light.

"Why did you do that?" Helsa asked suspiciously.

"Do what?"

"Scrunch your eyes up when I took off your glasses, even though you are blind . . . unless you're *faking*."

A throng of muscular demon guards looked over at Milton hopefully, hungry for a tense situation in which to overreact to.

"No, I . . . I'm not faking," Milton managed through heart palpitations. "I—"

Annubis bit Milton's leg.

"Ow!" Milton yelped, his face creased with pain. "Why the—? Oh, I see . . . I mean, I don't. It's just that my dog, *Dakota,* gets nervous and sometimes he . . . he calms himself by *biting me on the leg.*"

Milton stooped over and patted Annubis on the head. Hard. *"Good boy,"* he said between clenched teeth.

Helsa frowned as much as a smiling skull can.

"Fine, then," Helsa sighed. "Do you have anything to declare?"

"Yes," Milton said as he shivered despite the sweltering heat, naked save for his *Clone Wars* underwear. "I sure am glad there isn't an *eighth* gate!"

Annubis nudged Milton through the swelling masses surrounding a dirty luggage carousel. A variety of seedy, anxious-looking people gazed longingly at the motionless beltway leading from a dark, cobwebbed opening in the wall.

"Sad," Annubis said as he scratched the back of his neck with his leg. "They've been told all of their miserable, immoral lives that they can't take it with them, but still they wait, regardless. . . ."

An electronic billboard hung from between the rusty girders ribbing the peeling asbestos ceiling.

NOT-SO-DEARLY DEPARTING: 00:15
00:30
00:45...

Milton eyed the maddening crowd pressed against one another. For some reason, the swarm of do-badders made Milton feel desperately lonely. These accursed individuals seemed entirely caught up in their own sad, sinful worlds, either wailing and tearing at their hair or staring blankly into thin air, never once looking to one another for comfort or sympathy.

"Where do we go now?" Milton asked forlornly.

Annubis stretched, then pulled Milton forward.

"To the Interminable Terminal," he replied as he led Milton through the crowd. "The tarmac on the edge of the River Styx. Where we await the ferry leading us to our—and every bad person's—final destination."

34 · CRY ME A RIVER

"SO, WHERE ARE you folks from?" the skinny ferryman asked as he slapped down the lever of his taximeter. Milton did his best not to stare at the stooped man with the crooked nose, filthy matted beard, and poor posture, as he was still—for purposes of his mission—Martin Foulest: a greedy, blind nineteen-year-old with a seeing-eye dog. The ferryman, whose name was Charon—judging from the ID badge pinned to the rather pointless sunshade (this being the underworld) at the bow of his flat-bottomed skiff—pushed off the tarmac with his oar.

"We're from the Surface," Milton replied. Annubis, curled up on the bottom of the craft by Milton's feet, snickered quietly.

Charon scratched a filthy tangle of hair sprouting from beneath his conical hat.

"Most of you shades are," Charon replied as he rowed the boat to the center of the River Styx. "Do they still have Fiddle Faddle up there? What about *Cheers* . . . is that still on? It sounds like a great show."

"I'm pretty sure they still make Fiddle Faddle," Milton replied. "But *Cheers* went off the air years ago. Even the spin-off isn't on anymore."

Charon shook his head sadly. "That's too bad. Nothing lasts forever, I suppose."

Charon looked back at Milton. The hot, sewage-savaged wind rippled his red tunic.

"I don't suppose you have any Fiddle Faddle on you, do you?" he asked in a hushed tone of anticipation.

Milton held out his hands in a gesture of turning out his pockets—pockets he didn't have, as he was clad only in his *Clone Wars* skivvies.

"Sorry. Even if I did, I would have had to smuggle it in my underwear, and I don't think you'd want any."

Charon sighed. His eyes stared out at the dreary coast like hollow furnaces on fire.

"I suppose. Still, what I wouldn't give for that mouthwatering blend of creamy caramel and toffee."

With one hand rowing and the other steadying himself on the stern, Charon looked down upon Annubis.

"I don't like dogs on my skiff," he explained. "They shed like crazy and sniff . . . *everything*."

Annubis growled softly.

"He's my seeing-eye dog. I'm blind, so I have to have

him with me. I think it's a law. Something about him, Dakota, being allowed on all common carriers."

Charon rubbed the length of his dirty, gray, unkempt beard.

"This is hardly what I'd call a *common* carrier," he replied haughtily. "I've been crossing this stinking river and back every fifteen minutes for time immemorial...."

He stared down into the disgusting river, mesmerized by a whirlpool boiling with poop.

"Anyway, as long as you clean up after your dog, I'm fine. Don't get a lot of 'em here. Last dog I saw was one of those hyper Jack Russell terriers. Cute but crazy. The guy said that he—the guy, not the terrier—was born without a sense of smell, and so the dog was his 'smelling-nose dog.' He may have been pulling my leg."

Charon rowed the rust-colored wherry around a particularly bleak bend. The edge of the River Styx—which Milton knew from personal experience in Limbo was where all the, um, *fecal matter* in the world flowed down to, just to make things *beyond* nasty—was a sickly marsh of slimy, foaming sand sprouting black, putrid reeds that swayed in the sour-milk wind. Everything beyond was shrouded in a thick, soupy pall. It was as if the entire scene was a painting that some miserable artist simply couldn't bring himself to finish.

Milton noted the ferryman's deep-sunken cheeks and the dirty cloak knotted about his shoulders and began to feel sorry for the broken man. To think, he's had to row every sinner *ever* down this officially god-forsaken river of filth.

"So, Charon," Milton said, trying to lighten the man's heart with a little idle chatter, "that's an interesting name. Where does it come from?"

The appallingly grimy man shot Milton a suspicious look, glancing quickly at his ID badge as he poled the boat onward.

"How do you know my name?" he asked. "I thought you were blind? If you're playing some kind of trick on me, I'll throw the two of you out right now and let the River Styx deal with you."

Milton gulped. The thought of bobbing in human waste was too unthinkable to think. It was a thought he refused to entertain, even if it begged and handed him a banjo. Annubis turned in a few quick circles at Milton's feet before resuming his nap.

"No, no . . . I'm as blind as, as . . . a baseball bat. In the off-season. It's just that everybody knows about you. About the great . . . *Charon*."

The ferryman straightened somewhat, his posture becoming a new punctuation mark somewhere between "question" and "exclamation."

"It's actually pronounced with a hard 'k,' not a 'sh.' "

Milton nodded. A gargantuan wave of slimy dung slammed into the side of the craft as fresh sewage was flushed into the river. Milton gripped the side of the boat.

"Must be midnight," Charon said as he rowed the craft toward a fire-scorched bank on a barren shore. "The big flush from above."

On the shore, twenty feet from the river, was a rusty iron gate crawling with sculpted figures. The hull of the boat groaned as it made its approach.

"We have now reached the end of our journey. Please check your seats for valuables . . . and if you find any, hand them over! I kid—all of your possessions have obviously been confiscated and are being enjoyed, mocked, or desecrated by members of our staff."

With one mighty stroke, Charon brought the wherry up onto the bank.

"Watch your step now as you deskiff," he said before blocking Milton and Annubis, "after you pay, that is."

Milton patted the sides of his underwear. He swallowed and leaned close to Annubis.

"Do you have any money?"

Annubis shook himself, his whole body responding in the negative.

"No," he murmured. "But you do."

"I don't," Milton whispered. "Really."

"You *all* do," Annubis continued. "All humans. Under your tongue. For when you die."

"That's crazy," Milton mumbled as he checked beneath his tongue and, to his surprise, pulled out an ancient Persian coin.

Milton stared at the roughly minted coin, which depicted an owl among a background of exotic symbols.

Charon snatched it from his hands.

"This will do nicely," he said as he deposited the coin in his beard, where it joined what sounded like dozens of others with a satisfying clink and jingle.

Annubis led Milton onto the shore as Charon poled the craft back into the river.

"Be seeing you," he said as he twisted the craft back around. Charon slapped his forehead. "Silly me. I always say that. It's like when someone says 'Happy birthday' and you reply, *'You too.'* Anyway, enjoy your everlasting stay."

As Milton and Annubis approached the gate—a gargantuan, nineteen-foot, deep-tarnished-bronze entryway embedded in steaming volcanic rock—they noticed a small naked pink creature with a shock of rainbow-colored hair seated on a stool, reading a paper. Milton stopped and leaned close to Annubis.

"So, this is . . . *it?*" he asked in a quavering voice.

Annubis nodded. "Yes . . . the Surly Gates."

"The *Surly* Gates?"

"The exact opposite of the Pearly Gates . . . which are gleaming, bright, infinitely cheerful, and open to the *inside.* The Surly Gates, however, as you can see, are dark, depressing, frightening, and open to the *outside,* which is incredibly irritating, because you have to back up before you can enter, stepping in the revolting cesspool that is the River Styx—"

"Well, well, what do we have here?" the little troll-creature screeched in a thoroughly irritating voice, as if its insides were made of chalkboard and it had been stuffed full of tiny, frightened, scrabbling kittens who had never had their claws trimmed. "What are you, the *dog* whisperer?"

Milton straightened up. His face was hot with aggravation. There was something about this creature that made the normally peaceful Milton want to punch it in the face.

"We'd like to . . . to come in."

"We'd like to come in," the creature mocked, seeming to have grown several inches in the last few seconds. It folded up its newspaper and hopped off its stool. It leered at Milton like a living, taunting troll doll, with a smug, self-satisfied grin etched on its annoying face.

"Ugh, look at you," the creature jeered in its nasal, helium twang. "Was anyone else hurt in the accident?"

Milton fumed.

"Why, you little—"

The creature began to swell in size. When they had arrived, it had been maybe ten inches high. Now it was at least three feet tall . . . and rising.

"Why you little *what*?" the creature said, its pudgy arms pressed against its hips. "I have a name—it's Yukkah. And you'd better mind your manners if you want inside. By the way, can I borrow your face for a few days? My butt is really tired from sitting and wants a little vacation."

Milton clenched his teeth and fists, vibrating with rage. Yukkah puffed up, taller and wider, with a triumphant sneer smeared across its face.

Annubis tapped Milton's lower leg with his nose.

"Don't give him the satisfaction of your anger," he whispered. "He feeds on it."

Yukkah stepped closer, leaning toward the new arrivals in a condescending manner, as if he were addressing a pair of mismatched sock monkeys stuffed with shredded "dumb."

"Your doggie has a face like a saint," he grated. "A Saint *Bernard*."

Annubis growled as Yukkah grew.

"Hey, I'm just kidding, you two. Your dog is actually dark and handsome: when it's dark, he's handsome! Do you need a dog license to be that doggone ugly?"

The hair on the back of Annubis's neck rose. Teeth bared, the irritating troll gatekeeper was starting to look more and more like a talking chew toy to the dog god.

Milton patted Annubis.

"Now, now . . . remember, *don't give him the satisfaction of your anger.*"

Annubis grumbled as he set his haunches down on the scorched ground.

Yukkah was now roughly half the size of the gate itself. With every inch and pound he gained, there seemed only more of him to detest.

"I don't get it," Milton said. "Why would the Powers That Be Evil block the way to . . . *you know where* . . . with that awful, grating little . . . *you know what?*"

Annubis, his lip caught in midsneer on his canine tooth, shivered despite the heat.

"This place must take its *troll* on all who pass," he snarled. "Yukkah gets you so worked up that, pretty soon, you are *begging* to get in. It makes what's beyond the gates even worse, because you *willingly* went inside. The last part of you that perhaps could be saved is left at the door. You know how a vampire needs to be formally invited before it can enter a house?"

Milton shrugged. "Yeah, I think Marlo mentioned that once."

"Well, it's sort of like that, only in reverse."

The grinning troll ran its pink, pudgy fingers through it multicolored mane.

"You wanna play, you sorry-looking, bowlegged, pigeon-toed, crusty Underoos-wearin' waste of time?" the troll said, glowering down upon Milton.

Milton was so suddenly angry that, before he knew it, he had stalked right up to the ever-expanding troll, his fists trembling at his side. Yukkah now totally obscured the gate.

Milton looked down at his shaking hands. His chewed nails and the weird Rhode Island–shaped birthmark on the back of his hand were slowly coming back. His imaginary-friend soul was wearing off. Milton didn't have much time.

"What's wrong? Cat got your tongue?" Yukkah mocked. "From your nasty fish breath, it smells like you got his in trade."

Milton drew in a long, deep breath.

"It must get lonely here," he said compassionately. "Sitting outside this depressing gate, each and every day."

Yukkah's eyes bulged out, as if something were squeezing his midsection (something Milton and Annubis very much wanted to do). He wilted like leftover salad.

"What? Yes, sort of . . . I mean. NO! I love my job. I . . . I've seen people like you before, but . . . but . . . I had to pay admission!"

Milton forced his grimace into a tender smile.

"Does someone need a hug?" Milton cooed as he stepped closer to the deflating troll.

Milton wrapped his arms around Yukkah's bulbous, prickly pink belly. The troll recoiled with full-body disgust.

"Stop!!" Yukkah screamed as he shrunk down to the size of an NFL linebacker, albeit nude, pink, and with hair like a box of crayons after a few seconds in the microwave. "How did you get here? Did someone leave your cage open? Here's a dime . . . call all your friends and bring me back the change!"

Milton motioned for Annubis to come closer.

"Do we need some puppy lovin'?" Milton murmured with so much artificial sweetness that he nearly threw up a little bit. Annubis jumped up on Yukkah and began licking his face until it looked like a glazed troll donut. Yukkah howled as he got smaller and smaller.

"No, no . . . anything but puppies!" the gatekeeper whined, his voice a sonic trickle from a punctured water balloon. "I'm melting!"

Yukkah was now about as large and threatening as something dangling from a preteen, homeschooled girl's key chain.

Annubis gazed up at Milton with wide, wild eyes.

"Can I eat him?"

Milton shook his head, which was now virtually back to its usual Milton-like state.

"I don't think that would be such a hot idea. He'd only give you indigestion, which would make you mad, and then he'd just become more and more of a problem."

Milton eyed the dismal metal gate. It was cast with hundreds of suffering, all-too-detailed figures depicting every shade of agony and woe. A distraught woman hovering over a corpse. Two inconsolable lovers pried apart by laughing demons. A writhing crowd of anguished souls trapped in a pit, crawling and clawing over one another in hopes of escape. A man beginning his first day as a school guidance counselor. It was nearly too much for Milton to bear. He had a feeling that the door served as a teaser trailer for the awful movie within, like *Dances with Wolves, Shakespeare in Love, Evita,* and *The English Patient* all spliced together. He collected himself carefully as if every fear were a rare Pokémon card. He turned to Annubis.

"Can you help me with this?" Milton asked, gesturing toward the gate.

"Can you help me with this?" Yukkah teased, desperately hoping to achieve an at-least-somewhat-imposing size. Annubis kicked the creature, now the approximate shape and stature of a finger puppet, off to the side with his back leg.

Together they pulled the massive gate open, inch by inch, until they were both ankle-deep in the disgusting tributary of turds otherwise known as the River Styx. Milton's eyes were scrunched tight, like a toddler's fist around a tube of Go-GURT. Slowly, Milton wrested his eyes open and peered beyond the Surly Gates and into h-e-double-hockey-sticks.

He had expected fire, brimstone, and burning images of eternal misery and despair. And he got that—

in spades—only in the form of a painting in the lobby. Little did Milton know, the "painting" was really a framed window, looking out upon a throng of persecuted souls forced to spend their eternity in a never-ending game of freeze tag.

The lobby was surprisingly unexceptional. The walls were lined with a deep greenish brown marble bordered with bronze girders. The floors were laid with the same slabs of marble as the walls and ceiling, creating the claustrophobic sense that one was trapped in a box, despite the foyer's grand size. The lobby was virtually empty save for a massive, burnished-bronze desk with the words DECEPTION AREA spelled out in blood diamonds. Hanging behind the desk was an immense, garish corporate-style logo: two gilded hockey sticks, crossed, a real flame spouting from the point of their intersection, with a bronzed goat head skull on top. Beneath the logo was a leather banderole with the slogan COME FOR THE HEAT . . . STAY FOR ETERNITY elegantly lettered in crimson.

Milton and Annubis crept closer to the desk.

"Ow!" Milton yelped. Beneath his bare feet were shards of broken glass and cigarette butts. Milton hopped toward the massive desk on one foot. A small head leaned down toward the desk, nodding subtly. Milton saw the flash of a gleaming headset and a shock of lustrous blue-black hair, the color of the perfect bruise.

Milton and Annubis stepped nearer until they could hear the soft babble of conversation.

"How may I disrespect your call? Can I tell him what this is disregarding?"

The deceptionist held up a finger, somehow noticing Milton and Annubis despite not having looked up once since their arrival. The voice . . . so familiar yet so different. Like when you ride your bike past a home you used to live in, and the new owners have repainted, re-landscaped, and renovated everything, but your memories still manage to peek through regardless.

"Is he expecting your call? Not exactly? I'll take that as a *no*. Hold, please, and enjoy our selection of off-Broadway musical numbers as sung by lisping, two-carton-a-day smokers and hyperactive children taking hits from a helium tank."

The deceptionist looked up.

"Welcome to—"

The immaculately groomed young woman was . . .

"Marlo!" Milton cried.

Marlo, her face a made-up mask of high-fashion indifference, regarded Milton blankly.

"It's *Milton*," he added, baffled by his sister's expressionless expression.

"And I would know that name because . . ."

"Because I'm your brother!" he yelped, hobbling deeper into the Deception Area, his foot bleeding, his

body shivering, and his mind at a loss as to what to do next.

Marlo raised a perfectly plucked eyebrow at Annubis.

"I'm sorry, but there are no dogs allowed, as they're man's best friend and all. She—"

"He," Milton whimpered.

"*He* will have to wait outside . . . *forever.*"

Milton put his hands on the smooth, uncomfortably warm desk.

Marlo considered Milton's grimy fingers with disgust.

"Hands off the desk."

"Don't you even *recognize* me?" Milton pleaded, staring into his sister's dark, blank eyes, which, with their fuzzy yet steely stare, answered his question loud and clear.

"Should I?" Marlo replied, bored, doing something that Milton had never, ever seen her do before: buffing her nails. After a few curt sweeps with her emery board, Marlo gazed back at Milton, taking him in with slits that were half suspicious and half awake.

"Wait . . . ," she replied dimly, leaning forward slightly. "I think I *do* recognize you."

Milton allowed himself a smile.

"You're the boy who escaped!" she shouted.

"Milton," murmured Annubis as he nodded his head toward a bank of insecurity cameras embedded in the ceiling behind the desk. Like thirteen glowing red eyes, they glared at Milton and Annubis with a penetrating disdain.

Marlo bolted up in her perfect black turtleneck dress.

"Guards!" she shrieked as the lobby echoed with a cacophonous chorus of sirens.

35 · PRESSED TO CHANGE-O

MILTON AND ANNUBIS rushed back to the still-open Surly Gates.

"What do we do?" Milton shouted desperately against the din of alarms and his sister's shrieks. "Do we swim back?"

Milton's entire nervous system dry-heaved as he considered plunging into the pungent waterway of human waste. Annubis scanned the dreary horizon.

"I suppose—"

The dog god cut his sentence short as he saw, chugging along the River Styx in the distance, a gray metal barge. Aboard the carrier were dozens of demon guards and, at the center of it all, Principal Bubb atop her freakish, curly tusked beast.

"—not," he continued as he stood, positioning one

of his bright, checkered bandanas strategically around his waist, then tugged free his collar.

"As the jig appears to be up, I can at least elude the law with some modicum of dignity."

Milton looked down at his *Clone Wars* underwear.

"That makes one of us," he said. "So if we can't escape outside—"

"We escape *inside*," Annubis interjected.

"Are you crazy?!" Milton replied with disbelief.

Annubis eyed the approaching carrier grimly.

"Crazy like something bred to hunt foxes," he mumbled.

"When they capture you, you can tell them everything you know," Yukkah screeched from outside the gate. "That should take about ten seconds."

Annubis growled at Yukkah, baring his teeth, but then, in an instant, he began to grin.

"I have an idea," he said. Annubis stalked over to the naked, pink, rainbow-maned troll and then snatched him up quickly with his paws.

"Put me down!" Yukkah shrieked. "Have you had all of your shots?!"

Annubis set the creature at the lip of the River Styx. Milton trotted to the dog god's side.

"Mr. Fauster," a voice bellowed from the river of pungent sludge. Milton could see Principal Bubb in the distance, raising a bullhorn (from a real bull) to her lipstick-smeared gash of a mouth.

"I hope you got to stretch your legs a bit—if not, I'll be happy to do it for you later," the principal barked. "I'm beginning to take all of this running away personally, so be warned. After all, this place hath no fury like a woman scorned."

Milton trembled as the carrier ship cut closer through the stew of putrid sewage. Yukkah sloshed out a few paces into the River Styx, cupping his pink, pudgy hands around his mouth.

"Keep talking!" Yukkah shouted. "Maybe you'll stumble onto something intelligent!"

Principal Bubb's prickly chin dropped.

"You little creep, I ought to—"

Yukkah swelled to the size of a large cactus. Milton smiled, his guide dog's plan only now fully dawning on him.

"If your brain were chocolate, it wouldn't fill an M&M!" Yukkah roared.

Foam began to bubble on Principal Bubb's lips. "I'll stick you on the end of my pencil!"

The troll grew to the size of an especially creepy parade float. Annubis grabbed one of the Surly Gates and backed away, closing it. Milton took the other side of the gate, slowly shutting it while stepping backward as the gargantuan troll feasted upon Principal Bubb's bountiful rage.

Inside the Deception Area, Milton and Annubis sealed the gates with a reverberating clunk.

"That should hold them off for a while," Annubis said as he scanned the area for options.

Milton rushed toward Marlo.

"Where can we hide?" he asked her. "Is there a bathroom or something?"

Marlo snorted.

"Are you kidding? There aren't any bathrooms for *miles*. Why do you think everyone is so uptight? Besides," she said coldly, waving her manicured hand at the cameras above them. "You are *so* identified and *so* going to be caught."

Milton was beside himself. Actually, he was beside his sister, who had no idea that she even *was* his sister.

"What did they do to you?" Milton asked, on the verge of tears. "I came all this way to rescue you . . . to take you away. To make good on my promise."

Marlo snorted, then wiped the edge of her perfectly lip-lined mouth.

"Take me away? Why would I want to leave? I've got full medical; I've got stock options; I've got a closet full of the coolest haute couture imaginable. I've got it all. A *real* future."

Milton now knew, deep in his bones, the true meaning of the word "flummoxed" (perplexed greatly; bewildered). Marlo had even used French in a totally nonironic way. Who *was* this girl? More importantly, where was his sister? And could he ever get her back?

"You also had—*have*—a brother, only you just don't know it."

"Lucky me," Marlo sneered as she folded her arms together elegantly, as if shuffling a deck of cards in slow motion.

Annubis sniffed down the lone hallway.

"We've got to find somewhere to hide," he said. "That troll won't stay ticked off forever. Quick, down here."

"I'm not leaving my sister," Milton said.

Marlo cackled.

"I'm sure she'd be *really* touched . . . wherever and *whoever* she is, loser."

The heated sounds of an argument drifted through the Surly Gates.

"Out of my way, you irritating, overinflated lawn gnome!" Bea "Elsa" Bubb barked through her megaphone.

Annubis sighed.

"So be it," he said as he grabbed Marlo by the arm.

"Bad doggie!" she shrieked.

Milton and Annubis hauled Marlo down the hallway and stopped in front of a bank of three elevators.

"Where do these go?" Annubis barked at Marlo.

"Where do you *think* they go, Fido?" she said, squirming. "They all go straight to—"

"Uh-oh," Milton interrupted. "*Look.*"

All three elevators were suddenly in service. Each of the three arrows that had been hovering at six were now all headed down.

"Finally," Marlo crowed triumphantly. "The guards."

Annubis eyed a doorway just down the hall.

"This way," he said as he dragged Marlo away, with Milton—nearly—on his tail.

They ran into the room and skidded to a stop. Milton looked at the door. The room's fractured name plate, split down the middle, dangled by two screws: half the plate read BREAK DOWN while the other read ROOM.

The small oppressive room looked as if it had been quickly scooped out of volcanic rock, like a hot ladle through lukewarm ice cream. It was piled high with beaten-up copy and fax machines, massive, obsolete computers, rows of busted metal chairs, and several huge Vend-for-Yourself vending machines, loaded with what—to Milton's eye and Annubis's nose—appeared to be a selection of mouth-drying and lip-unsmacking snacks with expiration dates so past due that they were written in Roman numerals.

Bunched together in the corner like three boys at an all-girl party were several desks—doors on cinder blocks, actually—where two haggard businessmen and one woman wailed, tearing their hair out. Their mad, bulging eyes quivered curiously at the sight of Milton,

Annubis, and Marlo, though—like troubled turtles—they soon retreated back into the protective shell of their own personal turmoil.

"Didn't you hear?" Annubis said, addressing them. "The whole place just froze over. Head out and take a look."

The businesspeople stopped their who-knows-how-long ritual of moaning and mortification and slowly shambled out of the Break Down Room like distraught workaholic zombies on Free Brains Friday.

"Quick," Annubis ordered as he slammed the door with his powerful back leg, "drag those copiers and computers behind the door. We'll create a blockade. That should buy us some time."

"Yeah," Milton said, turning to Marlo, "and *you* should have bought that stupid oar!"

Milton stared at Marlo expectantly, hoping that the memory of how they got to Heck in the first place—a mad scramble to their sticky, marshmallow ends after Marlo had shoplifted an oar at Grizzly Mall: The Mall of Generica—would unlock the memory of who she really was. He could see it in her eyes: fleeting flickers of . . . *something*. Like she was lost inside the wilderness of her mind, hoping for rescue by flashing signals with a pocket mirror.

But for now, Marlo just shook her head.

"We are about as related as Kit Kats and hot dogs," she said with a sulky pout.

Milton sighed and began heaving outdated office equipment to the door. Annubis let go of Marlo's arm.

"You too," he said.

Marlo rubbed her arms. "Why should I help you two?"

"Because," Annubis growled, "we came a long way to see you. And if that's not enough, I assure you that my bite is worse than my bark."

Marlo gulped as Annubis bared his aptly named canine teeth.

"Point taken. Down, boy."

Marlo joined the boy she didn't know was her brother and scooted dilapidated office equipment in front of the door until it was completely barricaded. The two Fausters leaned against the pile, panting. Outside the Break Down Room, an explosion of noise ricocheted down the hallway.

"Sounds like Principal Bubb made it past the phantom troll booth," Annubis said morosely.

After a few more minutes of clattering, chaotic noise came a long moment of unnerving silence.

Marlo looked at Annubis askance before suddenly turning to the door and shouting. "They're in here!" she shrieked before Annubis clamped his paw over her mouth.

A few seconds of whispering passed; then someone—or some*thing,* you never want to assume in this place—rattled the doorknob.

"Locked," a demon grunted from the other side.

Suddenly, a peal of feedback squealed from the hallway, causing Milton, Marlo, and Annubis to jump as one.

"Mr. Fauster," Bea "Elsa" Bubb blared from outside the door. "I don't know how I can make this any clearer, but it's over. You're *toast*. The farm is bought and paid for. Come out, come out, wherever you are—which is right behind this door—before I send the demons in to play boccie ball with your head."

Milton rubbed his throbbing temples. He opened his unspectacled eyes and scrutinized the room. His prospects of escape seemed as hopelessly fuzzy and indistinct as his vision.

"And nice try with Yukkah, by the way," Principal Bubb added. "Poor creature. Killed with kindness, I'm afraid. Now it's time you come with me. It's up to you as to *how*."

Milton turned to Annubis suddenly.

"She's right," he said in a flat, spooky tone. "There's no other way out. She's got us. But it's up to us *how* she gets us."

Annubis stared at Milton. His wet dog nostrils flared, as if he were trying to smell what Milton was up to.

"What do you mean?"

Milton glanced at his sister thoughtfully. Her eyes bulged out furiously over Annubis's paw.

"Let her go."

Annubis shrugged. "As you wish."

He removed his paw from her mouth. Marlo backed away and spat.

"Ugh. Your paws taste like socks full of popcorn."

Milton leaned into Annubis.

"Switch our souls," he whispered.

The dog god blinked, not quite comprehending.

"It *sounded* like you said—"

"Yes, *switch our souls*," Milton repeated softly. He gazed deeply into Annubis's eyes, radiating conviction like a radioactive felon. "Take them out like you did in the Assessment Chamber, but just put them back in different people. Bubb will think she's getting what she wants, only she'll be getting it in a way that will leave her wanting, only she won't *know* she's wanting—"

"Stop," Annubis replied. "I think I've got it, but the more you keep talking, the less sure I am."

The barricade lurched as demons heaved their bulk against the door. Milton frantically scanned the sad little room. Something caught his eye in the Vend-for-Yourself machine.

"One sec," Milton said as he trotted across the room. He snaked his arm up through the vending machine drop slot and grabbed a moldy, low-hanging cheese sandwich. He walked back over to Marlo.

"Hey, is that a box of old Victorian dresses?" he said, pointing to a pile of junk in the corner.

"What?" Marlo said, spinning around, her overriding thrifting instincts still very much intact.

Milton quickly unwrapped the ancient sandwich and, from behind, pressed it to Marlo's face. After a few moments of struggling, Marlo's body went slack. Milton dragged her to the wall and set her there, like a perfectly made-up doll. Annubis joined them, kneeling beside Milton, puzzled.

"She's severely lactose and gluten intolerant," Milton explained. "Not to mention incredibly allergic to mold and various fungal hyphae. I thought the combo might be enough to knock her out."

Milton looked at his sister's unconscious face, smeared with spoiled mayonnaise and what he prayed was relish. "And, apparently it worked. She'll be fine in a few minutes, though. A little gassy maybe."

The hulking demon guards on the other side of the Break Down Room door were attempting to do just that—break down the door—with a fiercely persistent jackhammer rhythm.

Milton regarded the shuddering barricade with alarm. He drew in a deep breath.

"I'm ready," he said, trembling, his mind yanked back to the time when, in Limbo's Assessment Chamber, Annubis had removed his soul for—though only a few moments—what felt like an eternity of cold, numb despair and unbearable emptiness. Annubis nodded compassionately and rubbed his paws together in slow, deliberate circles.

"We'll start with your sister, before she wakes," he said in the cool measured tone of a doctor. Annubis placed one paw on Marlo's head and the other on her upper back. His paws, now warm with eerie energy, pressed into her body. Marlo stirred as the dog god rummaged through her with a surgeon's skill.

"Hmm, it seems to be hiding," he murmured. But after a moment, he pulled out a wriggling, gelatinous blob. *"Got it."*

Milton stared at the shifting goo. It looked like a baby jellyfish that had overdosed on Oreos and a teaspoonful of rainbow sprinkles.

Annubis set Marlo's quivering soul delicately in his lap as the mound of dirty beige office equipment trembled. An old fax machine tumbled off the summit and smashed onto the floor, as if it had just lost a game of King of the Hill as played by outmoded office equipment. Marlo began to shiver.

"So cold . . . so empty . . . so *what*," she murmured.

A squeal of megaphone feedback pierced the door and elbowed its deafening way into the room.

"Little pig, little pig, let me in . . . ," Bea "Elsa" Bubb taunted.

Annubis rubbed his paws together.

"Relax. Concentrate on . . . *nothing.*"

Milton snickered as he noted the crumbling tower of computers and copiers.

"Yeah, *right*. I've never been more peaceful or contented. Just pull it out . . . like you're yanking a tooth."

Annubis nodded as he slid his warm, tingling paws into Milton's head and back.

"Oh, you're no fun," Principal Bubb continued as the demons slammed their bulk against the door. "You're supposed to say, 'Not by the hair of my chinny chin chin.' . . . Fine, I will, then . . ."

Annubis delicately grasped the knot of emotions and memories that formed the core of Milton's spiritual essence. It tickled maddeningly inside. Then, with a tug, Annubis removed a long, wriggling, rainbow-hued glob. Milton yelped.

"Not by the hair of my chinny chin chin . . ."

Milton stared at the shimmering gunk in Annubis's outstretched paws with a dull, throbbing detachment. It was as if his identity, his entire sense of what it meant to be *Milton,* had been put through a food processor, then poured onto the floor, each battered lump jabbed with a cold hypodermic needle full of Novocain. It was agony as smothered by a pillow.

"So I'll huff . . ."

Annubis took the struggling blob that was Milton's soul and gently set it into Marlo's body. Marlo moaned, her eyes fluttering like butterflies caught on flypaper. A faint warmth radiated through Milton, though distant—

a faraway sun whose heat and light has traveled count-less, weary miles. He felt as if a part of him were some-where else, having a unique experience that he would never truly know. Milton looked down on Marlo as she slowly began to awaken. He could see a strange prickly dance of familiar colors radiating from around her edges, a scribbled outlined of Lite-Brite hues. It was like seeing someone at school wearing one of your favorite shirts, one you thought that only *you* had.

". . . and I'll puff . . ."

Annubis delicately juggled Marlo's soul between his two paws.

"This will feel incredibly odd," the dog god cau-tioned. "You may black out, like restarting a computer."

Milton nodded dully, though he had no idea what Annubis was talking about. The dog god's voice—everything, actually—was muffled, flat, distant, and hollow.

Annubis reached toward Milton, holding Marlo's gelatinous Slinky of a soul. Its fluttering gunk was filled with many more dark clots than Milton's soul, but it still shimmered with a faint, cheerful rainbow sheen. Annubis placed Marlo's soul inside of Milton, connect-ing it, in a way, like snapping a nine-volt battery into a remote control.

An odd surge of unfamiliar lights, sounds, images, and feelings gushed through Milton until his head and heart were overloaded. His consciousness fell backward into a warm, black murk before winking off, short-circuiting like an overtaxed fuse box, submerging all awareness in complete darkness.

"... and I'll blow your house in!" bellowed Principal Bubb as the demons smashed through the barricade and stormed into the Break Down Room.

36 · POOP D'ÉTAT

VIRGIL SMILED WITH pride as Gene, Hugo, Thaddeus, and a hefty handful of new arrivals slathered barbecue sauce all over the insides of the DREADmills. Virgil's BOWEL movement was unstoppable! He knew it couldn't last forever, even here in eternity. Yet he and the other boys had accomplished a great deal in the few hours since Milton's escape, which had sent Blimpo into a chaotic tizzy. Virgil's impassioned speeches and handouts—which bemoaned the injustice of being sentenced to Heck strictly for lacking willpower in the face of probable metabolic or glandular disorders exacerbated by a society obsessed with second helpings—had struck a surprising chord with the other boys. The infectious energy of mass confusion and civil unrest didn't hurt either.

"That's the last of it," Gene said sadly as he wiped

clean the bottom of his purloined tub of barbecue sauce before licking his pudgy fingers. "Now what?"

Virgil tugged an old electric fan across the checkered Gymnauseum floor. Mounted on the wall was a trio of giant, newly installed plasma screens. Towering images of perfect, privileged young bodies playing extreme Frisbee on the sun-drenched lawn of a New England prep school flickered behind Virgil. The young boys and girls took a break to stretch and mock the distorted images of Virgil, Thaddeus, Gene, and Hugo displayed next to them.

"You guys hide . . . and wait," Virgil said as he flicked the fan on. It blew savory waves of scent out through the Gymnauseum's open double doors. "There are only a few guards left. Bubb took most of them to help her catch Milton and Annubis. Once those hungry guards get a whiff of the last luscious globs of Hambone's—I mean, *Annubis's*—sauce, we got 'em."

Thaddeus rose and wiped his sticky hands on his corduroy Capri pants.

"And what'll *you* be doing?" he asked.

Virgil looked up at Dr. Kellogg's office, tucked away at the back of the Gymnauseum's second floor. He fought a brief wave of queasiness caused by the pink-and-green-checkered walls.

"Pulling the plug on this place," he said as he climbed the stairs.

Up on the catwalk, Virgil edged stealthily toward Dr. Kellogg's office. He tried the door, but it was locked. Virgil rummaged through his pockets and pulled out a stolen Chickey leg (a smaller version than the Turnkeys used to open the gate). He wedged it in the keyhole and gave it a twist. The door creaked open.

The room was dimly lit, yet filled with a thick humming drone. Virgil creeped purposefully inside. At the back of Dr. Kellogg's office was a rectangular box made of gray steel with brightly colored tentacles of wire coiling from it and disappearing into the wall. The hair on Virgil's forearms, finer than frog fur, rose in the presence of the coursing electricity.

This was, if not the heart of Blimpo, then maybe its pacemaker: the humming hub of the circle's electrical circulatory system.

Virgil hesitated. Doubt scribbled discouraging messages in his mind: *Big fat loser. You'll just screw it up like you do everything else.*

He shook his head clear and studied the red warning sign above the buzzing box.

HIGH VOLTAGE JUICE BOX. KEEP OUT! DANGER! EXTREMELY HAZARDOUS! DON'T TOUCH! IF YOU CAN READ THIS, YOU ARE TOO CLOSE! IF YOU CAN'T READ THIS, YOU'RE ILLITERATE! SO NEVER MIND!

Virgil drew in a deep lungful of air and stepped toward the circuit breaker.

"What do you think you're doing?!"

Virgil spun around in shock. Hanging upside down on the wall beside him was Dr. Kellogg.

"How did you get in here?" Dr. Kellogg croaked, secured to the ceiling by his ankles and resembling a big blanched bat. "I haven't gotten my seven and a half hours of restorative sleep!"

Virgil eyed the humming electrical box. Dr. Kellogg's flushed, blood-drunk face crinkled with understanding.

"Oh no, you don't," he warned. "Don't even *think* about it!"

The doctor struggled to unclasp his ankle clamps.

Virgil's eyes darted desperately across the spartan, antiseptically furnished room. On a clean white desk was a plate of Off the Eaten Path Dusted Double Lentil Trail Mix Biscuits. Virgil lunged for the plate, grabbed a handful of the unbelievably hard, dry, and flavorless biscuits, and ran to Dr. Kellogg.

"Nurses!" Dr. Kellogg yelled with his one free leg waving about wildly. "Come quick! I have a—"

Virgil shoved a wad of biscuits into the doctor's mouth, where the lentil dust quickly created a cement-like seal.

"Mouthful of biscuits?" Virgil finished.

As Dr. Kellogg gagged on his mouth-unwatering creation, Virgil ran to the electrical box and flipped open the door. What he expected to encounter was a simple on and off switch. Instead, amid the rat's nest of tangled cords was a puzzling collection of POWER UP, POWER DOWN, POWER FORWARD, POWER BACKWARD, and TOTAL POWER TRIP switches.

"Dr. Kellogg?" Nurse Rutlidge said with a gasp as she skidded to a stop in the doorway in her white orthopedic shoes. "Is there a problem?"

Two other nurses joined Nurse Rutlidge. With their nose-pinching spectacles (which made them look as if they were continuously enduring a terrible odor) and white hair tightly wound in buns, they were virtually indistinguishable from one another. Dr. Kellogg's eyes bulged as he flailed to communicate that, yes, there was indeed a problem, a big one, and it was about to drain Blimpo's juice box.

The nurses shifted their gazes toward Virgil. Their thin lips snapped like red crayons into cruel, broken smiles.

"Young man," Nurse Rutlidge said as she pulled a roll of gauze from her pocket and unraveled a taut strand between her clawlike hands, "I'm going to have to dress your wounds."

"W-wounds?" Virgil stammered. "I don't have any wounds."

Nurse Rutlidge grinned.

"Not yet."

The three nurses walked in formation toward Virgil, wielding gauze, tongue depressors, and stethoscopes like ninja scaregivers. Virgil backed away toward the sputtering juice box.

> *"Lunch meat, tender*
> *Lunch meat, sweet*
> *Order it to go."*

The nurses stopped and swiveled toward the doorway. Just outside, Elvis Presley stood strumming his acoustic guitar and crooning.

> *"You have made my lunch complete,*
> *Li'l sloppy Joe."*

The nurses swayed in bandy-legged swoons. Nurse Rutlidge's eyes rolled back into her sockets. Mr. Presley peered over the nurse's trembling shoulder.

"I suggest you do what you need to do, boy," Mr. Presley said to Virgil. "Just remember: you got a gift rarer than a chicken's tooth. Show your gratitude by using it. I got the fillies here covered, I reckon."

Virgil nodded and studied the switches while Mr. Presley resumed singing.

> *"Lunch meat tender,*
> *Lunch meat good,*
> *Heaps of sauerkraut . . ."*

Virgil's upper lip birthed beads of sweat.

Does "Power Up" mean the power that goes up to the vice principals? he contemplated. *Or does "Power Down" mean to turn everything off?*

Mr. Presley strummed his guitar with languid sweeps.

"Slow cooked over mesquite wood . . ."

Virgil gripped the TOTAL POWER TRIP switch.

"Here goes nothing," he mumbled under his breath as he slammed the switch down.

". . . till the fire's gone out."

Blimpo was plunged into darkness. Virgil ran out of the office, knocking into Dr. Kellogg, making him swing back and forth like a scrawny, mewling punching bag. Virgil peered over the railing into the Gymnauseum. He could see the vague silhouettes of three DREADmills snapping shut.

"We got 'em!" the boys cheered from below.

Gene danced around like the Michelin Man spinning out of control on a patch of black ice. "The guards totally fell for it!" he shouted, beaming, his eyes twinkling with mischief.

Virgil turned to Mr. Presley, who had set down his

guitar, herded the stupefied nurses next to Dr. Kellogg, and was wrapping them tight with gauze.

"Thanks," Virgil said. "What about the other teachers?"

Mr. Presley nudged his mirrored aviator glasses up the bridge of his nose.

"Bein' severely underpaid and underappreciated, as most teachers are, my peers seemed less than motivated by the task of maintainin' order."

Mr. Presley bit off one last piece of gauze.

"And that crazy King Tantalus," he continued, "well, he can only make tiny little waves from his splish-splash of a bathtub."

"And what will you do?" Virgil asked.

Mr. Presley shrugged his square shoulders, causing his white satin cape to shimmy and shake.

"Don't worry 'bout the horse, son," he replied. "Just load the cart."

Virgil nodded and descended the stairs down to the Gymnauseum floor. Gene rushed to meet him.

"It worked just like you said!" Gene said, grinning, his teeth stained with barbecue sauce. "The guards followed the delicious smell, and once they were inside, we sprang out and shut the doors on them!"

The boys could hear the unintelligible bellowing of Major Bummer from inside the DREADmills.

"I wonder what demon guards are scared of?" Gene asked dimly.

Hugo joined them as they contemplated the rumbling DREADmills.

"They're probably getting baths," Hugo surmised. "With scented soap."

Gene shifted his weight from one foot to the other, a transaction that took about five seconds to complete.

"How come the DREADmills are still running?" he asked, scratching just beneath the rim of his red bowl cut.

Virgil shrugged.

"They're off the grid, I suppose," Virgil replied. "Powered by panic. But whatever's going on in there isn't important. What *is* important is that this facility is officially closed by the BOWEL movement! We're dead, well fed, and on these DREADmills we won't tread!"

The boys cheered. Just then, the Gymnauseum's double doors burst open.

Lyon and her fellow Narcissisters strode into the darkened Fatness to Fitness center. Their gleaming silver sneakers squeaked on the floor.

"Whoa," Lyon sneered as she and her squad halted in a perfect V formation. "I guess asking you *blimpos* 'What's the skinny?' wouldn't be appropriate. So just tell us what you're doing so we can tattle on you and get a big bounty for your big butts!"

Dijon shook and clapped.

"Hopefully we'll get paid by the pound!" she squealed.

Virgil stepped forward, his status as new leader fitting him like a tailored suit.

"First, why are *you* here?" he countered, putting his hands on his hips.

Bordeaux gave a sharp laugh.

"Like we'd tell *you* we're waiting for Madame Pompadour to finish up her meeting in the vice principals' blimp kingdom before we make our next stop on the Nyah Nyah Narcissister *In Your Face* tour, part of Madame Pompadour's *Statusphere* plan to make loser kids feel even *worse* about themselves so that she and the Blimpo vice principals can use the harvested insecurity to make and sell *energy!*"

Bordeaux glanced back and forth between Lyon's and Marseille's scowling faces. Bordeaux's smile faded like a clown's face in the rain.

Virgil grinned.

"Thanks for that . . . *all that*. All *we* were going to do is check out these awesome new personal spa systems Dr. Kellogg set up for us to help us relax so we could better be taken advantage of."

"*Personal spas?!*" chirped Dijon.

"Yeah," Virgil continued. "They're supposed to be great for weight issues, split ends, and skin problems— you know, pimples and large pores—"

"Out of my way, Zitzilla," Lyon said as she ran for the nearest DREADmill.

"Oh no, you don't, Swiss Cheese Face," Marseille countered as the two girls engaged in a walking catfight before plopping into the machine.

"Us too!" whined Strasbourg, Bordeaux, and Dijon as they wedged themselves into the DREADmill.

Virgil and Thaddeus stepped up to the machine.

"Enjoy!" Virgil said as the two boys sealed the grumbling Narcissisters inside.

Hugo and Gene trotted toward them, looking—while still grossly overweight—apple-cheeked and exhilarated.

"I think we're ready for the main event," Hugo panted as he skidded to a stop.

Virgil nodded. *This is it,* he reflected. *Where the BOWEL movement brings it or gets off the pot.*

Madame Pompadour gazed wearily out the window of Blimpo's floating throne room. She ached to leave this buoyant bag of fast-food führers, assemble her Narcissisters, and take the next stagecoach out of Blimpo. It had been a long night of bickering, posturing, and nervous binge eating that at times ventured near cannibalism. But despite her fatigue, Madame Pompadour's keen eyes made out the group of boisterous boys assembled below, engulfed in the shadow of the sagging blimp kingdom.

"Your student body is revolting," she said.

"You're telling *me*," Lady Lactose sneered as she applied another layer of milk-white foundation to her face, using the Burgermeister's greasy forehead as a mirror.

"No," Madame Pompadour clarified. "*The boys*—they're staging a revolt. They've turned off the power and are gathering by the tethers."

The throne room shuddered.

"And it seems that the loss of power has affected the stabilizers."

The Burgermeister shifted anxiously on his sesame-seed bun of a throne.

"Zere iz nutting zey can do to us . . . right?"

"There, there," Lady Lactose replied, patting the vanilla hair scooped high atop her head. "Principal Bubb will be back shortly, I'm sure, with our guards—and more. In the meantime, try my latest creation. It will cheer you up."

She handed the Burgermeister a frosted dish. He tilted the luridly pink contents back into his mouth.

"Mmm," he said as he wiped his mouth with the back of his hand. "Vat's in it?"

"Oh, just a few things I threw together." Lady Lactose grinned. "Amyl butyrate, benzyl acetate, dipropyl

ketone, ethyl methylphenylglycidate, isobutyl anthrani-
late, and methyl benzoate."

"Eets delicious," the Burgermeister said while casting aside the dish into a pile of wrappers by his throne.
"Vat do you call it?"

"Strawberry," she replied.

A speaker box shaped like a grinning clown
squawked by the arched entryway of the throne room.

"Hiya, m'lard, m'lady, and m'eow!" the squeaky
teenage voice crackled. "How are you today?"

The Burgermeister sizzled with anger.

"Vat eez eet?!" he shouted.

"That's great!" the squeaky voice chirped. "Just
wanted you good folks to know that I've examined the
students' attack and there *is* a danger. Should we evacuate?"

"Evacuate?" Madame Pompadour replied haughtily.
"In our moment of triumph? I think you overestimate
their chances!"

"Wonderful! Announcing a message from the angry
mob down in Blimpo. Thank you and have a nice day."

The throne room was as still as the surface of a
swimming pool before a belly flop.

"Hello?" Virgil's voice crackled through the
speaker's leering metal-grill mouth. "Vice principals?
This is Virgil Farrow, head of the BOWEL movement."

The throne room erupted with riotous laughter.

Virgil sighed through the clown box, where it translated into a sad wheeze of static.

"You may laugh at our cause, but I assure you that no one down here—as big as we all are—is the least bit jolly. Now, I contacted you to read our list of demands—"

"Demands?" shouted Lady Lactose, her breath like a blast of sour cream. "We will not entertain the ridiculous whims of a herd of tubby troublemakers!"

"Maybe vee zhould leesten to zer demands," the Burgermeister muttered. "Perhaps all zhee vant eez a leetle more pudding. . . ."

Lady Lactose's complexion became as pink as a glass of Strawberry Quik.

"Show some guts!" she snapped as she swatted the Burgermeister hard in the stomach. She stormed over to the grinning speaker box.

"Let them eat rice cakes!" Lady Lactose shrieked as she punched the throne room speaker in its fiberglass nose.

"HaVVVVe a-a-a n-NICE-ICE-ICE d-d-DAYYYY," the speaker squawked before dying a sputtering death.

Lady Lactose clapped her hands together with satisfaction. "That should send a message to those roly-poly rebels!"

The throne room tilted suddenly. Madame Pompadour, her paws gripping the sides of the polished brass porthole, peered out below.

"It did," she said as she stared down at the boys. "And now they're sending one of their own."

The vice principals joined Madame Pompadour by the window. They gazed below as Virgil and the boys did unspeakably violent things to the clown suggestion box below. Chests heaving, the boys stomped toward the five tethers that moored the floating castle to Blimpo. A gloved hand tapped the Burgermeister on the shoulder.

"Vhat?" he asked, pivoting to see the French Fried Fool behind him. He pointed to his eye.

"*I,*" ventured Madame Pompadour. "That was easy."

The French Fried Fool smiled and nodded, before pretending he was dead and writing something in the air.

"Signed execution?" Lady Lactose guessed hopefully.

The French Fried Fool frowned, then repeated his gestures again only with more exaggeration.

"A vill?" the Burgermeister speculated.

"A *vill?*" Madame Pompadour repeated.

"No, a *vill.* As in *last vill and testament.*"

The French Fried Fool clapped, then pretended he was a teapot, short and stout, pouring tea, then pointing to the rounded arm at his side with the arm formerly known as "spout."

"Handle!" shouted Madame Pompadour. "*I will handle . . .*"

The French Fried Fool nodded, holding his thumb and forefinger an inch apart.

"Small word," Lady Lactose said. *"The?"*

The French Fried Fool clapped. At that moment, his five fellow mimes entered the throne room, dressed as he was, in black-and-white striped shirts, berets, and gloves, with white greasepaint applied across their angular faces. The French Fried Fool grinned and pointed out the window. The five mimes crawled out the window and onto the ledge.

"I will handle the situation?" Madame Pompadour surmised. "Or *I will handle the five suicidal mimes.* I'm not sure which."

"Either way, we win," Lady Lactose interjected with a smirk. "Fine, Fool. Send down the clowns."

The five mimes shimmied down the five tethers, which swayed tremulously as they restrained the sagging, inflatable castle that hovered listlessly above Blimpo. The boys eyed the nimble jesters warily as they hopped off the thin cables and glared back at the boys, arms akimbo. The chalky white makeup spread across their mute faces was like war paint, making them both unnerving and defiant. The French Fried Fool leaned out the window above, shoved two gloved fingers in his mouth, and let loose a piercing pretend whistle.

The mimes sprung to attention, then, just as urgently, curled up into tiny balls on the ground.

The boys looked at one another, baffled.

"What do you think they're up to?" Thaddeus asked.

"It's like they're popcorn shrimp," Gene said, licking his lips.

Virgil glared suspiciously at the five balled-up performance artists. He spied a small rock by his foot. He stooped down, scooped it up, and then lobbed it at the closest mime.

The spry man, once hit, burst to his feet, waving his arms in the air like flames before lying down on the ground, motionless.

"Just what I thought," Virgil mumbled. "A *mime* field."

He dusted his hands on his pants and fixed his gaze on the blimp kingdom above. Since the boys had cut its power, the castle was drooping, unstable, and closer to the ground. Virgil smirked. The BOWEL movement wasn't going to last forever, but Virgil was determined to make it end with a bang, leaving its mark far and wide.

"C'mon, boys," Virgil said as he marched toward the mime field surrounding the tethers. "We have nothing to fear but the silent mimicking of fear itself."

The boys approached the tethers, setting off mimes right and left. Each boy gripped a cable and proceeded to yank in time.

"We're mad as Heck," they chanted in unison before giving a great tug. "And we're not going to take it anymore!"

Lady Lactose turned and shot the French Fried Fool a searing scowl. He countered with a breezy, Gallic shrug before backing away like a threatened crawfish. The throne room lurched violently from the relentless tugs of the boys below.

Lady Lactose stalked across the room to a metal box mounted on the wall.

"I propose that we cut our losses and take our chances in the Waistlands. Madame Pompadour, you can run *Statusphere* remotely until the rabble has been unroused."

Madame Pompadour shrugged her slinky shoulders.

"Fashion knows no zip code," she replied. "And when the cat's away, the kids shall *pay*."

Lady Lactose popped open the door on the metal box, revealing a bright red lever.

"That's the spirit," she said as she slammed down the lever. The tethers uncoupled from the floating kingdom with five explosive pops.

"We're mad as Heck and—" the boys chanted before tumbling backward to the ground.

"Watch out!" Virgil yelled as the cables fell to the ground like writhing tentacles. The boys, sweaty from exertion, stared up at the inflated castle as it gently drifted toward the Waistlands.

"Nuh-uh," Virgil grunted between gritted teeth. *"No way."*

Virgil sprinted across the mooring grounds until he was directly beneath the jostling, airborne castle. He took in a deep breath, his chest puffing out like a bull-frog about ready to croak like it had never croaked before. As Mr. Presley had taught him, Virgil visualized the note he was about to sing lifting from his head. Only this time, he pictured it an octave higher. Virgil warmed up with a low C until he could feel its soothing rumble relaxing his vocal cords. He scrunched his eyes closed and visualized the note ascending the ladder leading toward an enormous diving board. It climbed, faster and faster, until Virgil was warbling a clear, perfect high C. The pitch rattled the hull of the floating castle until it caused a sympathetic vibration.

The vice principals and Madame Pompadour clapped their hands over their ears.

"What is that awful noise?" Madame Pompadour whined.

Lady Lactose craned her delicate neck out the window, peering down at Virgil.

"Who knows? *Who cares?* As they say, it ain't over until the fat—"

The walls of the throne room quaked with fury as

Virgil's pure, devastating wave of acoustic energy streamed out of his powerful throat.

"—*boy*? . . . sings."

Down below, the bedraggled Nyah Nyah Narcissisters stumbled out of the Gymnauseum and into the open commons beneath the wobbling, floating castle.

"Worst . . . spa . . . day . . . *ever*," moaned Strasbourg as she tried vainly to pat down her hair, which was now as spiky as a porcupine with streaked highlights.

"You ditz, that wasn't a spa," grumbled Marseille as she straightened her cheerlessleader uniform. "It was some awful machine that feeds off fear."

Dijon hopped up and down on one leg, lacing her silver sneaker.

"Which one of us is afraid of running on a treadmill?" she asked.

Bordeaux, her face pale and fear-stricken, trembled. "M-me," she quavered. "When I was little, my mom used to stick me on one of those before my Li'l Miss Hottie Tot pageants to help get rid of the baby fat."

"Well, lucky for us," Marseille said. "It must have created some freaky feedback loop that short-circuited the machine."

"Yeah," Bordeaux whispered. "L-lucky us."

Meanwhile, Virgil puffed out his chest and pictured the note jumping up and down on the diving board until it leaped off. Yet, instead of plummeting downward, the note soared higher.

"What's he doing?" Lyon asked as she squinted at Virgil through tear-smudged mascara.

Bordeaux smiled weakly.

"Singing," she murmured, gazing at Virgil with far-away eyes. "Like a big, sweet bird."

The canvas walls of the blimp kingdom fluttered wildly. Splits formed along its coarse fabric. Gas hissed like a gaggle of angry geese.

"Oh, the humanity," Thaddeus muttered as the castle's frame wrenched apart, lurching savagely from side to side. Then, with a great explosive gasp, the kingdom expelled its dying breath and plunged to the ground in a twisted, crumpled heap.

Lady Lactose spilled out of the debris with the Burgermeister shambling close behind.

"Off with his bun!" Hugo yelled as he and Gene charged toward the royal couple.

Lady Lactose fumed, accustomed to getting her milky way. She tried to make a break for it, running toward the Gymnauseum, but Gene grabbed her by the arm.

"Got milk?" Hugo asked as he tied the Burgermeister's meat hooks behind his back with a frayed strand of shredded tether. Gene nodded.

The French Fried Fool sprang as if to flee, but he could only run in place, suddenly hampered by an imaginary wind.

"We'll need fries with that shake," Thaddeus said as

he grabbed the mime and tied his bony yellow wrists together.

Virgil, stunned and weakened by his killer C note, shook the fog from his head as he watched his movement devolve into an ugly mob.

"Guys, guys . . . *wait!*" he pleaded. "This isn't how all this was supposed to go down. Well, sort of, I mean—the castle was supposed to go down, that is, but not . . . *this.*"

The boys stared back at Virgil with hollow eyes, their appetites for revenge nowhere near being sated.

"But they *deserve* it," Hugo replied as a rotten-egg wind blew from the Waistlands, ruffling his short dark hair. "I thought you wanted us to bite back."

"Yeah, but I just wanted to force these power-hungry tyrants to eat some crow," Virgil said. "Not for us to eat *them.*"

As the boys chewed over Virgil's food for thought, Madame Pompadour crept cautiously out of a split atop the crumpled mound of smoldering canvas.

"What is *that?*" Gene asked, pointing at the slinky feline felon on the wreckage.

"Looks like a cat on a hot-air roof," Thaddeus replied.

"It's Madame Pompadour!" shrieked Lyon.

Marseille's coffee-and-cream complexion percolated with anger.

"You were going to leave us here!" she shouted. "At the mercy of these psychotic losers!"

Virgil turned to Marseille. "I know we don't run with the popular crowd, but if we're losers, what does that make you: the girls we tricked?"

Bordeaux stepped up to the front of her squad.

"Leave him alone, Marseille."

Marseille's jaw dropped. As she lunged toward Bordeaux, Virgil stepped in between the two girls. Marseille bounced off Virgil's belly and landed on her butt.

"Oww!" she squealed.

"Serves you right," Virgil muttered. Bordeaux smiled up at him with gratitude. Virgil's cheeks prickled and burned as if they had been rubbed with poison oak.

Madame Pompadour struggled to stand upright upon the leaking blimp as it quaked and smoked in death spasms. The fact that she was also teetering atop a pair of seven-inch spiked heels made Madame's balancing act all the more impressive.

"This is more important than even the Nyah Nyah Narcissisterhood!" she mewled, straightening her form-fitting frock.

The girls below gasped.

"*No!*" Lyon moaned pathetically as she sucked on her balled-up fist.

"This was the first step in making *Statusphere* more

than just a magazine, but its own elite realm strictly for the beautiful people so they can inspire the lowly with their sheer unadulterated fabulousness!" she roared while struggling to maintain her balance. "And by inspire, I mean humble and frustrate to the point of neurosis!"

Flames lapped the remaining balloon behind her. The canvas blackened and crinkled like an over-roasted marshmallow.

"It was perfect, the last link in the fast-food chain," she cried out, her green eyes blazing as she watched her scheme projected inside the theater of her head. "The Statusphere realm sets unattainable ideals of beauty, which gets these chunky children crash-dieting and overexercising, with us making out like bandits, selling off the energy . . ."

The blimp carcass shuddered violently as the smoldering balloon sagged.

". . . but they *never lose weight,* which fills them with shame—in addition to our fattening soul food and soon-to-be-mass-marketed Beauty Cream. So they seek out the Statusphere for comfort and meaning, and the whole beautiful cycle begins anew."

Madame Pompadour's serpent eyes pierced the haze that hung low on the horizon. Her pink lips stretched into a smile wide enough to expose every one of her white needlelike teeth.

"And I, Madame Pompadour, the most charming,

refined creature ever to strut her stuff, rise to the top like cream."

The balloon burst into a savage ball of hissing flame. Madame Pompadour careened into the air, howling and spitting before plummeting to the ground. She landed in an inelegant heap at the feet of the shocked children, her meticulously coiffed hair undone and her expensive jewelry sent scattering upon impact.

Hugo looked down at her.

"I thought cats were supposed to land on their feet," he snorted, stretching his neon-green suspenders with his thumbs.

Lyon's magpie eyes were snagged by something shiny. Strewn about Madame Pompadour was a semicircle of glittering bling.

"What are these?" she murmured with awe as she knelt down before a bauble that she found particularly beguiling. Lyon scooped it up and stared at the charm in her palm.

"*Lyon,*" she said, reading the engraved trinket that pulsed with an odd warmth in her hand. The charm—a small heart-shaped pillow of gleaming platinum with Lyon's picture in the middle—softened until it became a pool of tingling, electric liquid. It quickly absorbed into Lyon's palm. She shivered.

"My face," she mumbled as she felt her cheeks. "It's so tight."

Bordeaux leaned down next to Lyon and stared at her face with large pale blue eyes.

"Oh my gawd!" she gasped. "Your pores are like, totally gone!"

Lyon beamed radiantly and rose to her feet. Her fellow Narcissisters dove for their respective charms, innately knowing which of the sparkling baubles was their own. Within seconds, Marseille's pimples faded, Strasbourg's split ends smoothed, Dijon's extra chin melted away, and the slight fuzz on Bordeaux's upper lip vanished.

Madame Pompadour's tail twitched. She groaned and lifted her head.

"Ugh!" yelped Gene and Hugo in unison, clutching one another as they recoiled in horror.

Madame Pompadour's face sagged in folds like a feline shar-pei. Bristly patches of fur and scales sprouted in between the wrinkles. Her red-rimmed eyes, extinguished of their inner flame, drooped down into her sallow cheeks.

"The charms," Lyon said through the fog of shock. "They were . . . *our charm*! And . . . and—"

"Now that we have them back," Marseille interrupted, looking Madame Pompadour up and down, "we look blazin' hot and you look blazin' *not*."

"Yeah," Virgil said, his lip curling in disgust, "you look like the cat *and* what it dragged in."

Madame Pompadour staggered to her feet. She

unwrapped the cream silk scarf around her neck and tied it over her head into a concealing bonnet.

"Youth is wasted on the young," she rasped through a tangle of yellow teeth. "And I'm through wasting my time with you tasteless wretches. You wouldn't know style if it crawled up your ill-bred noses and yodeled!"

Just then, two vans sporting satellite dishes drove onto the mooring grounds.

"Uh-oh," Thaddeus observed as the vans skidded to a stop just beyond the fluttering wreckage. "Looks like someone is crashing our happy meal."

On the side of the van was written: THE URN (THE UNDERWORLD RETRIBUTION NETWORK) SHORT ATTENTION NEWS VAN.

"I can't let anyone see me like this!" howled Madame Pompadour as she ran into the Gymnauseum. After a moment, the boys and girls heard the doors of a DREADmill snap shut.

Virgil snorted.

"I have a feeling Madame Pompadour is about to be flea dipped," he said.

Bordeaux smiled at Virgil for longer than he was comfortable. In fact, the last girl who had smiled at him was—

Virgil noticed one last charm glittering on the ground. He kneeled down with a grunt and picked it up. The eerie, tingling pendant bore one word etched upon its perfect, platinum face: MARLO.

I'll give this to you myself, Marlo . . . someday, Virgil thought with a dopey grin as he tucked the charm into his pants pocket. He watched as a cameraman and tanned anchorwoman (*How can someone get a tan in the underworld?* Virgil puzzled) leaped out of one of the vans.

While the BOWEL movement may have pooped out, Virgil reflected, *the media feeding frenzy is just beginning.*

37 · A NECESSARY UPHEAVAL

"HE'S LYING!" SHRIEKED Milton—actually Marlo—as he/she was shoved into the lobby of h-e-double-hockey-sticks by a gruesome, eight-foot-tall demon with a face like a steaming iron. Milton/Marlo struggled against the serpent restraints coiled tightly around his/her wrists. "I'm me, not *him*. I don't know how, but . . . but . . ."

Marlo, really Milton, and Annubis were likewise pushed into the foyer by nasty demons that looked like they supplemented their respective incomes by posing for heavy-metal album covers.

"*He's* the liar, obviously," Marlo/Milton said to Principal Bubb, who marched smugly by her/his side. "I was just minding my own business, doing my . . .

awesome new job. Answering phones and handling the various duties befitting of a . . . um . . . *deceptionist.* The last thing I'd want to do is cause any trouble. I've . . ."

Milton struggled to remember what his sister had said upon their disappointing reunion.

"I've got full medical; I've got stock options; I've got a closet full of the coolest haute couture imaginable. I've got it all. *A real future.*"

Principal Bubb harrumphed.

"We'll just have to see about *that,*" she grunted. "Once a Fauster, always a Fauster, I always say. Or will make a *point* of saying, from now on."

Despite her loathing for Milton's grasping, guttersnipe of a sister, Principal Bubb found it hard to be grumpy. She had captured the quarry that had eluded her for so long. Milton Fauster was now, finally, in her clutches. And so he would stay.

"And I'm sure you've got *quite* the tale to wag," she said to Annubis. "Don't you, dog?"

Annubis looked longingly at the potted oleander bush, not having relieved himself since the Waistlands; however, he knew that once they were out of the woods, he could find a proper tree.

"Indeed I do, Principal Bubb," he said, carefully unfurling the story that he and Milton—now Marlo—had quickly hobbled together. "As you know, I was working undercover in Blimpo as part of our . . . *agreement.* I soon sniffed out a scheme that Milt—the *Fauster* boy—

was formulating and decided that it would be in the best interest of Heck—nay, *the entire Netherworld*—to pretend to aid him in his escape with intent to follow, thus simultaneously uncovering and thwarting his nefarious stratagem."

"So you gave Chef Boyareyookrazee a hundred-volt wedgie as part of your covert operation?" the principal posed suspiciously.

Annubis scratched his snout contemplatively, though he was really trying to conceal his curl of a smile.

"Collateral damage," he replied. "So I tailed Milton after his escape. If you remember correctly, I gave you a little signal to that effect in the Gorge—to find out where he was going and what his plans were once he got there. As you can see, he was trying to contact his sister with the hopes that she could help him get closer to the Big Guy Downstairs. Actually, I suppose that since we are already downstairs, he would simply be the Big Guy *Here.*"

Principal Bubb nibbled her foreclaw nervously.

"Fortunately for all of us, the devil took a holiday," she murmured. "Continue."

Annubis shrugged.

"There isn't much more to say, really," he replied. "Miss Fauster refused to cooperate, Madame Pompadour obviously having done her job exceptionally well."

Milton/Marlo wriggled free from the demon guard holding him/her.

"The dog is lying!" he/she shrieked. "I mean, he might be telling the truth about how—"

Milton/Marlo struggled for words as he/she glared at Marlo/Milton.

"I . . . she . . . *whatever* . . . got here . . . and . . . and that I didn't cooperate . . . but . . . but the rest is . . . is—"

"Utter nonsense!!" roared Principal Bubb. She clacked over to Milton/Marlo and slapped him/her hard across the face. "You are finally back where I want you, right by my side, which is to say, on your way to Sadia!"

"*Sadia?!*" Milton/Marlo yelped. "B-but . . . but that's for the worst, most violent, most despicable, most vicious—"

"Yes, you're quite right," Principal Bubb cackled. "It will be like dropping a fuzzy bunny in a pit of vipers. For you, it is unspeakably cruel. For them, feeding time. See? It's all a matter of perspective."

"But I'm not Milton! I'm me! I'm Marlo!"

Annubis strode toward the principal.

"May I have a word with you?" he asked as he gently led her in front of the bronze deception desk.

"What is it?" she hissed.

"Principal Bubb," Annubis said in a clear, louder-than-necessary voice as he positioned her subtly in front of the bank of cameras. "Mr. Fauster is clearly lying."

"I am not!" Milton/Marlo protested. "I'm a girl! I'm my own sister!"

Principal Bubb expelled a rancid, impatient breath.

"Clearly. But what does that—"

"Milton has *always* been a liar," Marlo/Milton broke in. "Just ask anybody. How else could a goody-goody like him even *be* in Heck unless he lied his way down here?"

"So, Principal Bubb," Annubis went on, "as it is your job, and has been for time immemorial to—quite expertly, I may add—assign awful, grubby children to the circles most suited for them, wouldn't you think that Fibble—the circle reserved for liars—would be the best choice for Mr. Fauster?"

The horde of demon guards grumbled and nodded in assent.

"Fibble?" the principal exclaimed. "But that's—"

Annubis rolled his eyes toward the bank of cameras. Principal Bubb froze in the burning stare of thirteen scrutinizing lenses recording every word, every gesture, every decision. She sighed. The principal may have nabbed Milton, but she still had to play things safe, considering the even-more-volatile-than-usual state of Heck. A rash decision now could erupt into a scaly, stubborn rash she'd have to sit on for quite some time, bureaucratically speaking. Sadia would have to wait.

"—*exactly where I was thinking of sending him,*" the

principal said, switching her verbal horses midstream. "At first, that is. That little creep can work his way down to Sadia. Once we confront his . . . *lying.*"

She clapped her claws together.

"Guards, strap this lying liar to the back of my Heckifino. And he's extra farty today, Mr. Fauster."

The demons clicked their hooves together and goose-stepped out of the Deception Area, dragging Milton / Marlo kicking and screaming behind them.

"I'm Marlo!" he / she screamed as he / she was hauled through the Surly Gates. *"And this isn't over!"*

Principal Bubb turned quickly to Annubis.

"This isn't over!" she yelled in a whisper as she grabbed Marlo / Milton by the arm. "As for you . . ."

Bea "Elsa" Bubb's pus-yellow eyes burned. Though, after an indecisive moment, her scalding scowl cooled to a simmering stare.

"You may return to your post . . . but I assure you, Big Sister is watching you!"

The principal's No-Fee Hi-Fi Faux phone rang. As Principal Bubb read the caller ID on her thumb thimble, Annubis leaned into Marlo / Milton's ear.

"I will track down your pet, Lucky, in the Furafter," he whispered. "He's either down in the Kennels or up in the Really Big Farm. In any case, as I search for my family, I will try to reunite you with a member of *yours.*"

Marlo / Milton's eyes welled up with appreciation.

He/she wiped away a tear and, with surprise, noted a smudge of mascara on the back of his/her hand.

"Thanks," Marlo/Milton murmured. "You're a boy's . . . *or whatever's* . . . best friend."

Meanwhile, Principal Bubb gulped as she stared at the number scrolling in a slow, foreboding orbit around her thumb thimble: 1-666-666-DEVL.

"Hell-hello?" she stammered into her outstretched pinkie. "This is Principal Bubb."

Lucifer crossed his gleaming black hooves on his ottoman: a mummified thirteenth-century Turkish soldier on all fours. His massive plasma wall flickered like a window into an alternate reality, one that Lucifer himself wished were far more "alternate" and far less "reality."

"I know who I called," he seethed into the near-invisible phone embedded into his bloodred manicured claws. "That's why I called you and not, say, my tailor, masseuse, or financial adviser. Are you watching what's going on?"

Reflected in his raging serpent's eyes were unruly images of Blimpo as skewed and distorted by the Underworld Retribution Network Short Attention News crew. The unnaturally tanned newswoman clutched her microphone as if she were grasping a SENSATION (Society for Entertainment News Shows

Announcing Terribly Incredible Occurrences Now) award, which, as a matter of fact, she was hoping this very story would earn her.

"This is Barbra Seville with URN News—on the scene and on the ball. We interrupt tonight's edition of *When Grandparents Attack* with this live report. As you can tell by the Golden Archway behind me, I am in Blimpo—the circle of Heck reserved for the full-figured—and, I can tell you now, the situation here is a full-blown fracas, a flabby free-for-all, the likes of which this reporter has never seen."

The pimples on Principal Bubb's forehead—which happened to form the shape of a shark fin peeking above her monobrow—grew shiny with nervous perspiration.

"I am, I mean I always watch what's going on," the principal went on. "I take great care to watch what's going on, is what I mean to say—"

"Are you watching what's going on in Blimpo . . . *on the news?*" the devil clarified with gnashed fangs. "If you could call it *news.*"

Principal Bubb glanced at the various demon guards—most of which she had "borrowed" from Blimpo—huddled beyond the Surly Gates.

"Blimpo? But I was just there. . . ."

The principal immediately and literally bit her tongue. It had slipped and was now paying for its clumsiness: in blood. Hopefully, Bea "Elsa" Bubb thought, the devil hadn't picked up on her blunder.

"You were just in Blimpo?!" Lucifer shouted, not only picking up the principal's blunder but also hurling it over his majestic horned head. "And now it's falling apart. Fancy that."

"I just caught Milton Fauster," the principal blurted out. She had wanted to present this fortuitous turn of events to Lucifer elegantly, strategically, all gift-wrapped and tied up with a bow. But she had panicked and carelessly tossed out her news as if it were her turn in a game of hot potato.

"What?" Lucifer said, distracted, as Gene and Thaddeus toppled Blimpo's Golden Archway before high-fiving one another and giving V-for-victory signs at the camera. "Milton Fauster? It's about time. Wait, something's happening."

Barbra Seville shoved her microphone into Virgil's face.

"An URN News exclusive!" the newswoman gushed. "I have with me now the instigator of this rotund rebellion, Vern Fallow—"

Virgil's face reddened.

"It's actually *Virgil Farrow*—"

"Whatever," Barbra continued. "An exclusive interview by any other name is just as exclusive. So, Mr. Farrow, what do you, a *shy* Guevara, a Gandhi for the grossly obese, have to say for you and your insurrection of ample midsections?"

Virgil stared at the camera with the open, paralyzed horror of a dwarf rabbit in a wheelchair at the sight of a swooping hawk. He swallowed.

"I . . . *we*," he managed, "are the . . . the BOWEL movement."

Barbra cocked her eyebrow at the camera before emitting a nervous twitter.

"Darned children say the *darnedest* things!" she snickered.

Virgil appeared confused. "I don't know why people think that's so funny," he said, shaking his head. "It stands for 'Blimpo: Overweight With Erroneous Laws.' And we feel this whole place is . . . is . . . illegal. And should be shut down. Having a healthy appetite, even if it makes you sick, isn't a sin. It's more like a weakness. Or a choice. Or something in between. After all, it doesn't really hurt anyone, so why should we be down here?"

Virgil's speech was like a baby bird that had been nudged out of its nest, where—after a momentary free fall—was now taking tentative wing.

"We accept the fact that we were sent down here for whatever it was the Powers That Be Evil think we did wrong. But we think that you're all *nuts* for expecting us to take it sitting down . . . especially in those awful, super-small chairs."

Behind him, Hugo was leading the bound vice principals of Blimpo in a humiliating circuit around the grounds. Lady Lactose squirmed in the restraints wrapped around her and strained toward the camera.

"Don't listen to these ungrateful, root-beer-bellied delinquents!" she shrieked. "Serves them right . . . taking extra servings. Justice will be served!"

Virgil turned to address the curdled, girdled queen.

"You only see us as you want to see us—in the simplest, most convenient terms: a bunch of selfish, food-obsessed fatties. But we're more than that . . . we're smarter than that."

Lady Lactose snorted until milk ran out her nose.

"Yeah, you boys are brilliant. *Geniuses.* So smart you should form your own club for brainy, blubbery boys and call it *Immensa!*"

Thaddeus prodded the group forward, sending Lady Lactose tumbling to the ground.

"Boo-hoo," he mocked.

"Hey," Hugo replied. "Don't cry over spilled milk!"

Virgil continued his speech to the camera.

"Inside, lots of us kids here in Heck are essentially the same. Only, those of us sent to Blimpo crave rich foods because we feel poor inside. But I have the perfect recipe to fill us all up. Take two cups of self-discovery, one cup of self-acceptance, twelve ounces of respect for others, a dash of open-mindedness, and a heaping tablespoon of collaboration. Stir the contents slowly, as our finest qualities often take a while to develop. Then cook the whole thing over the fire of conviction. Sure, the weak may have inherited the girth, but so what? If we stand together—all of us—we could all stand to inherit a whole lot more."

Lucifer clapped his hands together angrily, turning off the television. On the other end of the phone, Principal Bubb winced.

The Big Guy Downstairs flushed as red and angry as just-plucked madder root. "First, Limbo's security was brought into question after the Fauster boy's escape; then Rapacia was sent reeling after the Grabbit's attempt to suck our profitable little underworld into a self-made black hole, and now *this*."

He sighed a fallen angel's sigh: full of lost light, an eternity of bitterness, and no hope whatsoever for redemption. Lucifer looked down at the manuscript splayed out on his lap. His dashing tail swayed with a playful confidence.

"Still, not all is lost," he said with a dazzling grin that blended perfectly the predatory precision of a shark's bite with the hypnotic smile of a veteran car salesman. "I have something up my sleeve," Lucifer snickered as he patted the manuscript's cover—*Heck: Where the Bad Kids Go.* "And it sure as *heck* isn't my heart!"

"Yes, sir, of course," Principal Bubb murmured, not understanding anything other than the fact that her moment of victory had been taken away from her and that Milton Fauster was somehow to blame. She had expected Lucifer's praise at the boy's capture to flow like champagne. But instead it had gone down like a can of flat generic soda left open in the back of the refrigerator.

Her snout flared as she saw the boy, still maintaining his innocence, shoved onto the barge that bobbed atop the waste-clogged waves of the River Styx. As Milton/Marlo was lashed, squealing, to the back of the principal's Heckifino, Bea "Elsa" Bubb smirked. Above all else, she had *him*—and this scrawny boy who shouldn't be here was about to have his butt gold-plated and placed in her trophy cabinet.

Note to self, the principal reflected, *acquire trophy cabinet.*

As Principal Bubb boarded the gray barge, Marlo/Milton was now alone, shivering despite the flame spouting from between the two gilded hockey sticks on the wall. She/he watched her/his brother/sister struggling on the back of the principal's ridiculous, gobbling beast.

Now that Marlo is relatively safe as me, Marlo/Milton surmised, *I can work the system from the inside, perhaps from the root of all evil itself.* She/he glanced at the slogan behind her/him on the wall: COME FOR THE HEAT . . . STAY FOR ETERNITY.

"We'll see about that," Marlo/Milton murmured as

the phone rang. Even if it meant legally tearing down each and every circle, Milton wouldn't rest in peace until Heck rested in pieces.

"Thank you for calling," she/he said as she/he answered the phone with a knowing smile. "How may I misdirect your call?"

BACKWORD

For so much of our life and death, we pine to be some-one else, someone perfect. Inside and out (usually out). The catch is that no one is perfect, in particular those who say they are, since conceit is a flaw; there-fore, those who claim they aren't perfect are closer to being perfect, unless they are just feigning humility because they read this, and nothing screams "flaw" like feigned humility. And reading ahead. And screaming "flaw."

The point is, we should spend our time wanting to be ourselves—deliciously flawed as we are—rather than wanting to be someone else.

Let's say that you wanted to be, I don't know, let's call her Zazu Zenith. First, let's assume that you aren't Zazu Zenith: a multibillionaire pop star/ actress/perfume/clothing line with a face that launched a thousand A-list parties. Now, it's no one's fault, really, that you aren't Zazu Zenith. Not being Zazu Zenith is hardly a crime: after all, people who are not Zazu Zenith outnumber those who are by about 6.5 billion to 1. This makes "not being Zazu Zenith" the second most common moral failing on Earth—just after "taking a piece of candy from a box of chocolates, biting into it, realizing it has some weird whipped pork and jelly bean crème center (with just a hint of braised rhubarb), and putting it back."

Sometimes the only thing separating the "flawless" from the "lawless" is the letter "f."

Down in the hot, humid, and humility-free recesses of Heck (where there is no recess), the laws are changing, and many are finding themselves hip-deep in all manners of stews, jams, and pickles. Even those divine, pristine creatures upstairs may soon find themselves down in it.

But this mess of perfection and misconception, flawlessness and lawlessness isn't simply confined to Below and Above. It's about to leak into the In-Between. Gush, in fact. And a whole lot of people—namely, you and all of your friends—may be in for a rude awakening, like the unfortunate child who actually falls asleep at a sleepover, waking up to find that their so-called friends have done something terrible to them.

Sweet dreams.

ACKNOWLEDGMENTS

THE BOOK IN your hands—which you *paid* for, not just checked out from the library (I'm on to your tricks . . . besides, can you imagine how many germs call your average library book "home"? I'm just sayin' . . .)— wouldn't have been possible without the complete lack of support from the following persons:

The countless boys and girls who seemed so confident on the outside, yet, if they truly were inside—deep below their flawless complexions and ideal body-fat-to-lean-body-mass ratios—wouldn't feel the need to put others down in order to uplift themselves.

The tireless teeter-totter of capitalism that keeps us nauseous, seesawing between pictures of ninety-nine-pound supermodels and pitchers of ninety-nine-ounce Super Gulps.

The inventor of German dodgeball.

ABOUT THE AUTHOR

DALE E. BASYE, a recovering journalist and advertising copywriter, has written his way out of many a tense situation. He was a film critic, winning several national awards, and studied neon sculpture in art school, which—puzzlingly—never resulted in a consistent income. Dale E. Basye once made a plaster cast of himself in class and passed out, awaking to find himself in class in a plaster cast.

Here's what Dale E. Basye has to say about his latest book:

"*Take a heaping helping of boys and girls, soak them in preadolescence until their bodies are unrecognizable, then blend them together until all lumps of reason have been smoothed into self-consciousness. Bake at half the appropriate temperature until half-baked. Now throw the whole mess—and everyone's expectations—out the window and onto a group of smug authority figures. Serves: them right.* Heck is like that. And, no matter what anyone tells you, Heck is real. This story is real. Or as real as anything like this can be."

Dale E. Basye lives in Portland, Oregon, inside of a giant rotating loaf of fiberglass bread. His spinning domicile provides him with an excellent vantage point from which to fight crime, though his principal foe tends to be debilitating vertigo.

TURN THE PAGE FOR A SNEAK PEEK AT THE NEXT BOOK ABOUT MILTON AND MARLO'S ADVENTURES IN HECK!

COMING IN MAY 2011!

Excerpt copyright © 2011 by Dale E. Basye.
Published by Random House Children's Books,
a division of Random House, Inc., New York.

1 · WHAT LiES AHEAD?

BEING A BOY *feels really weird*, Marlo thought as she dangled her brother's gross feet off the backseat of the stagecoach taking her to Fibble, the circle of Heck for kids who lie. Her borrowed body felt alternately simpler and more complicated—frustrating in its sheer, dull straightforwardness. *Just like boys*, she reflected. Marlo tried her best not to overanalyze the skin she *ached* to jump out of: just thinking about being her younger brother, Milton—at least on the outside—made her skin crawl. Or his. *Whatever.*

Marlo was still fuzzy on the particulars of her current situation, but flashes of what had happened, and who she *truly* was, floated to the top of her brain like the cryptic messages of a Magic 8 Ball. She remembered graduating from Madame Pompadour's Infernship program and becoming Satan's Girl Friday the Thirteenth. Then she remembered

Milton—though for some reason, at the time, she'd had no idea that the little twerp hopping around in his *Stargate Atlantis* underwear *was* her brother—storming the Surly Gates of h-e-double-hockey-sticks with Annubis, the dog god, and dragging her from her Deceptionist post to the Break Down Room with Principal Bubb and her demon guards in hot pursuit, before drugging her with a moldy cheese sandwich.

It was here that things got a little strange.

When Marlo had come to, she hadn't felt quite . . . *herself.* Annubis had once presided over Heck's Assessment Chamber, where souls were weighed on the Scales of Justice, so he had the power to pluck people's spiritual essence from their bodies with his bare paws. *He must have switched Milton's soul with mine,* Marlo presumed. To what end, Marlo could not be sure. But as she dredged the sludgy slough of her mind—still yawning and stretching from its peculiar nap—Marlo knew that her little brother was essentially a good kid, so whatever Milton's specific intent, his heart was sure to be in the right place (even if his soul *wasn't*). Marlo also knew that Milton had an ulcer, not because of any prior knowledge as his sister, but because of the waves of pain radiating from the pit of Milton's stomach.

The man sitting across from her in the musty stage-coach coughed. He leered at her with a freaky smirk: a knowing grin that was totally one-sided.

"How long are we going to play this little game?" the

old, dough-faced man said as he ran his fingers through his slicked-back hair. Marlo swallowed down the bile that kept creeping up her throat.

"I'm afraid I don't know what you mean," she replied in her brother's squeaky voice. "And I'm not afraid of anything."

The man laughed mirthlessly.

"You could have fooled me," he said, training his beady black eyes on Marlo. "You seemed plenty afraid back in Limbo."

Her stomach suddenly felt as if it housed an unchaperoned, all-ages dance club. *He must have been some teacher in Limbo,* Marlo speculated. *One of* Milton's *teachers . . . and that's who he thinks I am, naturally, because that's who I am. But I can't blow my cover, or else I'll screw up whatever Milton has planned.*

"Yeah, of course I remember you . . . *sir,*" Marlo replied. "You were my, um, teacher. Back in Limbo."

The stagecoach shuddered. The hoofbeats of the Night Mares pulling the carriage clattered uncertainly before regaining their confident rhythm.

The man squinted so hard at Marlo that it looked as if the bags beneath his eyes would burst.

"What's my name, then?" he asked, suspiciously, as he leaned in close to Marlo and stared into her borrowed hazel eyes.

"What, did you forget?" Marlo replied, using her

patent-pending "tact-evasion" technique. "Didn't your momma sew it in the lining of your jacket?"

"I can tell you're covering up something," the man spat back. "I can see it in your—"

Suddenly, the stagecoach bumped and shook so violently that the old man slammed his head into the top of the carriage.

"Oww!" he yelped as the demon driver—a swollen, bespectacled creature with goat horns and a white goatee rimmed around his orange duck bill—leaned into the carriage.

"Are you injured, Mr. Nixon?" the demon quacked. "I mean, Mr. President, sir."

Mr. Nixon rubbed the swirling slick of hair atop his head.

"Pardon me, *Mr. Nixon*?" Marlo said, making Milton's voice smugger than it had ever sounded before. "You were saying that you saw something in my *oww*?"

Mr. Nixon's ashen face flushed red.

"I pardon no one! *I'm* the one that gets pardoned!"

The stagecoach fishtailed wildly, sending Marlo and Mr. Nixon crashing to the floor. The carriage skidded to a stop. Marlo crawled up off the floor and gazed out the window.

They were on the edge of a vast, frozen mound of water that shimmered weakly beneath the filmy crust. The swollen sea of frost resembled a massive Hostess Sno Ball dipped in crystal. Studding the distended icy knoll were clumps of scraggly bushes that—when rustled by the breeze—almost seemed to . . . *talk*. What they said, Marlo couldn't make out. It just sounded like yammering nonsense.

Marlo pushed open the door and hopped onto the ice, steadying herself with the carriage. The horizon was clogged with a thick, gently seething bank of sparkling pea-soup smoke. The glimmering, billowing murk spewed from a towering structure in the distance perched atop the summit of the swollen, frozen sea.

Through a fleeting crack in the clouds Marlo could see that the structure was a cluster of grand, gaudy tents propped up on massive, swaying stilts. The wound in the cloud bank quickly healed, leaving Marlo dazzled, disoriented, and wanting to disgorge whatever her brother had last eaten all over his freaky skinny-long feet.

Mr. Nixon moaned as he rose from the floor. He crouched through the open stagecoach door, waving "V" for victory signs at the nonexistent crowd that roared in his mind, and joined Marlo. The demon driver waddled over to them, handing the ex-president a thermos.

"Thank you, doctor," Mr. Nixon replied as he twisted the top.

Marlo gently patted her stomach, as if it were a nervous stallion she was trying to calm.

"Doctor?" she repeated.

"Yes, Dr. Brinkley," Mr. Nixon continued as the demon

shuffled to his team of Night Mares. "License revoked many, many times. Which explains his current condition."

Marlo studied the ducklike doctor.

"The big bill?" she inquired. "You know, because doctors charge too much?"

Mr. Nixon tilted the thermos but nothing came out.

"No, because he was a quack," the old man replied as he spanked the bottom of the empty thermos.

The duck demon patted the ice and grit from his white-feathered hands as he tightened his horses' bridles.

"The team is ready," Dr. Brinkley said in an odd, duckish drawl. "I trust they'll find the least perilous path."

Marlo scowled as she noted the Night Mares shifting uneasily on the ice.

"Find the path?" she said. "Haven't you been to Fibble before?"

The duck demon's feathers ruffled in the wind.

"No, young man, I haven't. Snivel is my customary route. The usual driver, Baron Munchausen, called in ill today . . . something about contracting swine flu from a pork chop, which—even as a fraudulent practitioner of medicine—I don't believe is—"

"Maybe we should just walk the rest of the way," Marlo said as the wind tickled the fronds of the ragged brown shrubs, their leaves rubbing against one another in a murmuring chorus that sounded a lot like *"walk the rest of the way."*

"I'm strictly a female female, and my future I hope will be," the demon warbled from beneath a mask of cold cream into the mirror, *"in the home of a brave and free male, who'll enjoy being a guy having a girl like . . ."*

Damian leaned into the mirror as the demon, eyes closed and singing into a scare brush, came perilously close to losing the white towel cinched around its jiggling bulk.

"Principal Bubb?" he muttered with horror.

"Me?!" Bea "Elsa" Bubb croaked as she twirled around in shock. She pulled up her towel—which, in Damian's eyes, could never be big enough to properly cover what needed to be covered—and peered into the mirror.

"Mr. Ruffino!" she screeched. "Why are you in my vanity?"

Algernon Cole swooned, falling back onto his overstuffed sack of dried beans. Damian scooched his Fat Elvis bag closer to the nearest mirror.

"I'm on the Surface," he said.

Bea "Elsa" Bubb wiped away a clawful of cold cream.

"That's impossible," she declared. "This must be one of your jokes, like the time you replaced the toilet tissue in the demon washroom with sandpaper."

Damian snickered.

"That didn't sit too well with the guards," he

recollected. "But, seriously, I'm up on the Surface in some magic box in a freaky museum in Kansas. It's called a psycho-something: like a phone booth where you can reach out and touch someone, just as long as they're dead."

Principal Bubb massaged her surly temples.

"With kids going back and forth like this, we're going to have to install a turnstile and start stamping people's hands. . . . This is terrible. However did you—"

"It's *not* terrible," Damian interrupted. "It's an opportunity. And when opportunity knocks, don't knock it. This goofy band of religious weirdos have this cult and think I'm their savior. They practically worship me."

Bea "Elsa" Bubb leveled a flat, unbelieving gaze through the mirror. "You've *got* to be pulling my leg."

Damian shuddered.

"Ugh. I don't want anything to *do* with your leg," he replied. "But, I might be able to get a *real* following up here, do thy bidding for a while—think of it as a franchise—before coming back down with a whole *lot* of souls for you to put in your underwear drawer."

"Best not to mention my unmentionables," the principal replied before the cracked vanity of her not-so-secret lair. "Though I must say that I find your plan intriguing. My financial adviser is always on me about investing."

Damian grinned.